PRAISE FOR TEA COOPER

"Delightful and intriguing, this gentle story of love, loss, and betrayal set in Australia's Hunter Valley is based on real characters and events, including a major discovery."

—Rhys Bowen, *New York Times* bestselling author of *The Venice Sketchbook*, for *The Butterfly Collector*

"An enthralling, unforgettable story of heartbreak and hope, featuring equally compelling dual timelines, dynamic heroines, and a twisty mystery spanning generations. Tea Cooper's latest historical stunner is not to be missed."

—Lee Kelly and Jennifer Thorne, authors of *The Antiquity Affair*, for *The Butterfly Collector*

"Inspired by real Victorian female fossil hunters, Cooper fills the page with strong and intriguing female characters. There's a soupçon of romance, but the real focus is on these trailblazing women. Highly recommended for all libraries."

—*Booklist* for *The Fossil Hunter*

"This elegant dual narrative historical from Cooper follows a young woman as she pieces together the fate of a 19th-century paleontologist . . . Cooper's confident prose and deep empathy for her characters will keep readers hooked as she unspools her intrigue-filled mystery. Historical fans will want to dig this one up."

—*Publishers Weekly* for *The Fossil Hunter*

"Beautiful writing makes way for a beautiful story in *The Fossil Hunter* by Tea Cooper. With the same care a paleontologist unearths a fossil, Cooper has crafted a historical mystery that reveals itself layer by layer, piece by piece, and secret by secret. Highly entertaining and much recommended!"

—Jenni L. Walsh, author of *Becoming Bonnie* and *The Call of the Wrens*

The Butterfly Collector

ALSO BY TEA COOPER

The Fossil Hunter
The Cartographer's Secret
The Girl in the Painting
The Woman in the Green Dress
The Naturalist's Daughter
The Currency Lass
The Cedar Cutter
The Horse Thief

(AVAILABLE IN EBOOK)

Matilda's Freedom
Lily's Leap
Forgotten Fragrance
The House on Boundary Street

The Butterfly Collector

TEA COOPER

HARPER MUSE

Published by Harper Muse, an imprint of HarperCollins Focus LLC.

Map by Alex Hotchin

This book is a work of fiction. The characters, incidents, and dialogue are drawn from the author's imagination and are not to be construed as real. Any resemblance to actual events or persons, living or dead, is entirely coincidental.

Scripture quotations are from the King James Version. Public domain.

Any internet addresses (websites, blogs, etc.) in this book are offered as a resource. They are not intended in any way to be or imply an endorsement by HarperCollins Focus LLC, nor does HarperCollins Focus LLC vouch for the content of these sites for the life of this book.

Library of Congress Cataloging-in-Publication Data

Names: Cooper, Tea, author.
Title: The butterfly collector / Tea Cooper.
Description: First Australian Paperback Edition. | [Nashville] : Harper Muse, [2022] | Summary: "What connects a botanical illustration of a butterfly with a missing baby and an enigma fifty years in the making? A twisty historical mystery from a bestselling Australian author"--Provided by publisher.
Identifiers: LCCN 2023009662 (print) | LCCN 2023009663 (ebook) | ISBN 9781400245178 (softcover, US) | ISBN 9781400245192 (epub) | ISBN 9781400245208
Subjects: LCGFT: Detective and mystery fiction. | Novels.
Classification: LCC PR9619.4.C659 B88 2023 (print) | LCC PR9619.4.C659 (ebook) | DDC 823/.92--dc23/eng/20230306
LC record available at https://lccn.loc.gov/2023009662
LC ebook record available at https://lccn.loc.gov/2023009663

Printed in the United States of America

23 24 25 26 27 LBC 5 4 3 2 1

THE
BUTTERFLY
COLLECTOR

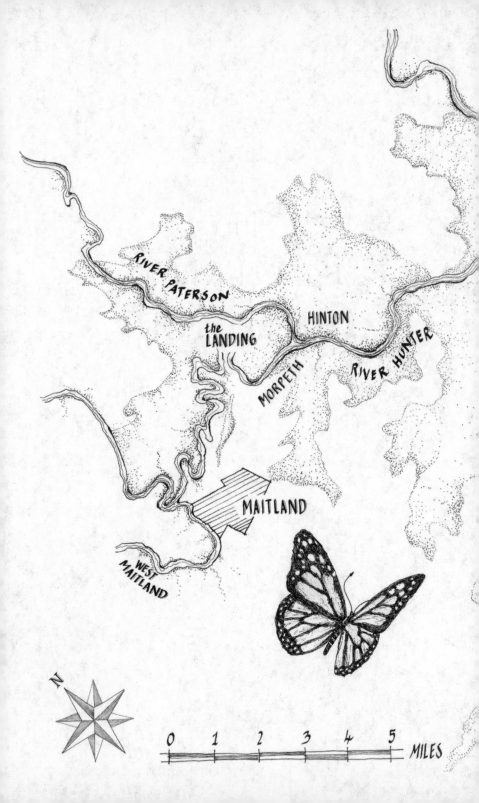

RIVER WILLIAMS

RAYMOND TERRACE

SCOTTS' HOUSE

ASH ISLAND

FROM NEWCASTLE

SOUTH PACIFIC OCEAN

CHAPTER 1

"My office, if you please, Miss Binks."

Verity flinched. Mr. Bailey sounded very serious for a Friday afternoon. Usually at this time of the day the chief editor was full of bonhomie and a hankering to get down to the Glebe Hotel before the six o'clock swill before they closed.

"Certainly, Mr. Bailey. I'll be right there." She dropped her coat and hat over the back of her chair and picked up her notebook and pencil.

"You won't be needing that. Just a moment of your time."

Verity smoothed down her skirt and crossed the floor to his office.

"Close the door behind you." Twisting his swivel chair from side to side, his face hidden by a wreath of smoke, Mr. Bailey offered a half-hearted smile. "I was most impressed with your article. I think we can find room for it in the weekend edition. Bicycles—who would have thought? An excellent angle."

A great bubble of happiness blossomed in Verity's chest and she beamed at Mr. Bailey.

"Chip off the old block, hey?"

Perhaps. It was the first full-length piece Mr. Bailey had ever accepted. Grandpa Sid would have been so very proud. "I have another idea that I would like to—"

He raised his hand. "Verity, let me speak." With a long and rather painful cough, he stubbed out his cigarette in the overflowing ashtray. "I really don't want to have to do this, but I'm afraid I have no option. The management"—he pointed to the ceiling with a yellowed finger—"has decided to implement government policy to the extreme. We have so many returned servicemen out of work. They've fought for their country and they deserve all the help they can get."

Of course they did. So many men—homeless, injured, and down-at-the-heels—begging for money on street corners or curled up in doorways. It was a disgrace. Maybe she should think about writing a piece about that. A call for government assistance, job schemes, housing . . .

"And so, unfortunately, I am going to have to let you go. Your job has to go to one of our returned soldiers." He handed her a small buff-colored envelope. "A week's pay in lieu of notice."

Her bottom hit the seat of the chair and a streak of pain shot up her spine. A week's notice? "I didn't write the bicycle piece during work hours. I wrote it at home."

"I'm happy to pay you stringers' rates, per column inch, for the bicycle article. Verity, believe me, the last thing I want to do is lose you, but I don't have any option." He knocked a cigarette out of the packet and twirled it between his fingers.

"What about Sadie?" She and Sadie were the only two stenographers employed by the paper, and they were run off their feet almost every day. Mostly with the classifieds that filled the front and back page of the daily newspaper and brought in a large chunk of revenue. Sadie had lost her husband, had a little boy, lived with her mother in rented rooms, and could hardly make ends meet as it was.

"I've already spoken to her. There's nothing I can do. You've both got a week's money. Verity, you've got a lot of promise. We could do with some more of these life interest stories for our women readers; there's only so much food, fashion, and relationship rubbish I can stomach. You bring me anything you come up with and I'll do my best for you. Least I can do for the daughter of one of our heroes, never mind the promise I made Sid." Mr. Bailey stuck out his hand.

Verity sat, dumbstruck. She hadn't expected to lose her job. At least she wasn't as badly off as Sadie. Didn't have to pay rent, thanks to Grandpa Sid. She had a bit put by, which would see her through for a month or two, but regular jobs were impossibly difficult to find. As a last resort she could let out a room, but she didn't want someone else living in Grandpa Sid's house. It wouldn't feel right.

"Might be time to think about your personal life." Mr. Bailey raised an eyebrow. "Sid wouldn't like to think of you on your own."

A wave of anger swept through her. What right did he have to comment on her personal life? At twenty-five she didn't have to answer to anyone, was entitled to make her own decisions. She wouldn't be the first not to marry. Many women were making the choice to forgo marriage these days; besides, there simply weren't enough eligible men to go around.

"Keep in touch, Verity." Mr. Bailey gestured to the door. "Don't forget to bring me anything you think might be of interest." He lit his cigarette and vanished behind a haze of smoke.

Her legs didn't want to cooperate, but Verity shuffled off, trying to keep her chin up. It was only when she buttoned her coat that she noticed Sadie's cleared desk. No teacup, no ash-tray, no pot of pencils—just the typewriter sitting in splendid isolation.

Verity scooped up the debris on her desk and dumped it in her satchel, put on her hat, stuck her nose in the air, and marched out through the sea of faces. A few muttered good-byes filtered in the air, but she couldn't bring herself to speak to anyone. Didn't dare, more like—she'd make a fool of herself and burst into tears.

A particularly gray drizzle coated the footpaths and puddles of yellow reflected from the streetlights. She slipped her satchel across her shoulder, unlocked her bicycle from the railings, and pushed off. The rhythmic motion of the pedals and the cool wind cleared her head as she meandered through the city and headed for Sussex Street.

Bicycles might have emancipated women, given them a de-gree of freedom and improved their physical condition, but what good was that if a woman couldn't work? She'd only managed to hang on as long as she had due to the sense of guilt Mr. Bailey harbored because he'd promised Sid he'd keep an eye on her.

Women had voted for the last twenty years, but it hadn't made much difference in the real world, especially since the war ended. Why couldn't a woman do as good a job as a man? It wasn't as though she needed to be stronger or brawnier to lift a pencil, answer the telephone, or hit the keys on the typewriter.

She coasted down the hill toward The Cut, possibly her least favorite place in the world; in fact, she hated it with a vengeance. The dank, dismal tunnel stank of rats, piss, puke, and the sweat of the thugs and petty gangsters who plied their trade in the half-light, but it took ten minutes off the trip home and saved lugging her bicycle up the steps that snaked their way over the road tunnel. A chill lifted the hair on the back of her neck, bringing with it the peculiar sense of being watched. A nasty shiver that had her looking over her shoulder every few seconds. The first time it had happened she'd put it down to imagination; now she wasn't sure. She slowed, listened for the sound of footsteps.

Nothing, other than her gasps and the blood pulsing in her ears.

The rough stone walls, mossy green with seepage, magnified her every breath, every sound giving life to the spirits of the convicts who'd hewn the roadway through the sandstone.

Imagination. Nothing but imagination.

She picked up her pace, forced the pedals down. There wasn't a stretch of The Rocks she didn't know—every alley, every back street, and every row of terraces. After Grandpa Sid died, she could have sold up, moved on, but she'd chosen not to. Tara Terrace, home of her heart and her history—the only remaining link she had with her family.

Without a backward glance, she flew out of the tunnel and along Argyle Street where the lights from the terraces shone a welcome. When she finally swung into the familiar labyrinth of alleys linking the terraces, her thumping heart rate settled. Bent double from the stitch in her side, she sucked in a gasp before slipping her fingers through the white-ant-ridden fence to the latch.

The gate groaned as it swung open, and she wheeled her bicycle into the yard and slumped against the shed, waiting for the blood to return to her cramped muscles. The dunny door swinging on its rusty hinges creaked its usual greeting. She cast a hurried glance around, kicked it shut, then propped her bicycle underneath the decrepit lean-to next to the copper and wringer.

Squinting into the pool of light thrown from next door's yard, she made her way under the clothesline and past the small patch of dirt that had originally been home to Grandma Clarrie's prized vegetable garden. Since she was out of a job, she'd have no excuse not to restore it to its former glory. She traipsed up to the house and retrieved the key from under the rock outside the door. It slid silently into the lock; one twist and she'd be inside, the door shut fast, bolts secured.

"You're late, love."

Verity slapped her hand to her chest to still her thumping heart. "Mrs. Carr, you made me jump."

"Not surprised, skulking around like that." Mrs. Carr squeezed through the gap in the fence. "Why don't you use the front door?"

She didn't want to confess her fear. No one who'd lived their entire life in the crazy warren of streets that made up Sydney's oldest suburb would admit to being fazed by its occupants. "I came through The Cut. It was getting late and I had my bicycle." Besides, she hated using the front door, which opened directly into the parlor. It was like inviting the world into her sanctuary.

"Wondered where you were. There's a parcel. On the kitchen table."

Ever since Grandma Clarrie and Grandpa Sid had passed, Mrs. Carr had extended her role of next-door neighbor to mother hen and general busybody, but Verity couldn't fault her—she'd provided a welcome shoulder on so many occasions. There'd been times, more than she'd like to count, when the offer of a cup of tea and a scone had saved the day. However, Mrs. Carr's habit of nipping in and out of the house rankled. Maybe the time had come to move the key to another hidey-hole. "A parcel? Who from?"

"No idea." Mrs. Carr shrugged. "No return address, no name, no nothing. Young lad brought it. I found him hammering on the front door. Personal delivery, he said. I've left it on the kitchen table."

She wasn't expecting anything. In fact, couldn't ever think of a time when she'd received a parcel other than Christmas. "Thank you."

"Right you are, love. Let me know if you need anything." Mrs. Carr eased through the gap in the fence and disappeared into her kitchen.

Verity stepped inside, shrugged out of her coat, and hung it onto the back of the chair, then pulled off her cloche, shaking her hair free. A sliver of moonlight shone through the window; it threw quite enough light to see what was what—every step, every creaking board as familiar to her as the lines on her palm. The fragile pool of light revealed a large box—three foot by two, white cardboard. She ran her hand across the smooth surface and the strangest quiver rippled down her spine.

Once she'd stirred the coals to spark some latent warmth in the stove, she reached for the box of matches, lit the lamp's wick, and took a long, slow look at the box. She hooked her fingers under the lid and wriggled it, releasing a tantalizing scent of the unknown, exotic—a mixture of rose, spices, and something woody. Beneath the lid she discovered a mound of soft, white tissue paper and in the center a thick cream envelope, her name scrawled across the front in black ink. The sort of envelope that would contain an invitation to a wedding—and just not any wedding, a society wedding. The sort of invitation that sat on a marble mantelpiece next to a carriage clock, not that she'd ever received one.

A matching card slipped out, the writing as bold and flamboyant as the event.

SYDNEY ARTISTS MASQUERADE BALL

Town Hall, August 23, 1922
Dancing 8:00 p.m. to 2:00 a.m.

ADMIT ONE
TICKET £1

One pound! Almost a week's wages. She flipped it over.

TICKET NUMBER: 768
PAID IN FULL

The invitation slipped from her hand and fluttered to the tabletop. Who'd sent it? More to the point, why? Her attention flicked to the window where the scraggy fig tree in the backyard rubbed its branches against the dirty panes. Shadowy wings flitted past—bats searching for a roosting place, more than likely—but her reflection hampered the view, and the recollection of the unease she'd felt as she'd cycled through The Cut returned. Stepping away from the window, she shook off her uncanny sense of dread.

Imagination, nothing more.

She repeated the mantra. The same overactive imagination that had plagued her for the last week or so.

The box lay innocently enough in the middle of the table, calling her bluff, willing her to investigate the cloud of tissue paper. She plucked at the corner, peered underneath.

Black material, neatly folded, rustled in approval as she lifted it from the box. A plain black round-necked, sleeveless dress. She held it by the shoulders and dangled it in front of her body. The handkerchief hemline fell just below her knees.

She swirled this way and that, admiring the simple lines and fingering the expensive material. Nothing like anything she'd ever seen, never mind worn.

As intriguing as the dress was, it didn't seem to belong to the invitation. She laid it on the back of the chair and peered into the box. Beneath the next layer of tissue, a silken haze danced: bright orange edged in black, a row of white dots accentuating the outline. She shook it free and held it high. It hung from a choker-like collar and draped down to two points like folded wings. She picked up either side of the cape. The wings spread, revealing wrist straps.

She fastened the shimmering silk around her neck and tucked her hands inside the loops, raised her arms, then lowered them. The wings fluttered like a bird preparing for flight. Her reflection stared back at her from the darkened window. No, not a bird—a butterfly.

Her curiosity drifted back to the invitation. The envelope carried her name, but the costume? Obviously intended for the ball, but who had sent it? It couldn't be a mistake; her name was emblazoned across the envelope.

The Sydney Artists Masquerade Ball. Everyone was talking about it, the first since the end of the war. Sydney's statement to the world that the dark, dreary days and the scourge of the influenza lay behind. An opportunity to celebrate and raise funds for those less fortunate. Sydney Town Hall and its basement would be transformed. All the newspapers were full of the story, more than two thousand tickets sold and every available piece of accommodation in the city booked. Dressmakers sworn to secrecy, working late into the night to produce the obligatory costumes. Once an annual event, the balls had ceased during the war but would be spectacularly relaunched with a modern makeover. And she, Verity Binks, had an invitation.

But did she dare to attend?

She dived back into the box, lifted the remains of the tissue paper, and discovered a smaller box. With fumbling fingers she prized it open.

A mask—of course, all masquerade balls relied on a mask, identities concealed until the midnight reveal—half-faced with elongated eyes and black ribbons to hold it in place, long eyelashes painted to sweep like wings across the domed fore-head. She lifted it and stared into the night at the creature she could become.

If only she had the courage.

CHAPTER 2

MORPETH, 1868

Cloudless sky of cobalt blue arched overhead, the autumn sun throwing jagged splinters of light across the river. Theodora Breckenridge picked up a dry brush and licked the fine horsehairs before adding the tiny lines needed to accentuate the depth of the flower and its stamens. Once that was completed, she could concentrate on the background. She liked to include a little of the landscape, a vignette, to show the exact location of the specimen. Today it would be the drystone wall surrounding Mama's garden with a view through the gothic window to the river. She'd always thought it strange that someone would go to the trouble of building a ruin; however, Mama had insisted—it was a replica of the old monastery in the grounds of her family home in Cornwall.

Time concertinaed into a tunnel of oblivion as her painting took shape. When she next raised her head, the shadows had lengthened and a chill breeze blew up from the river. She wrinkled her nose, the tight skin heralding a warning. Her face would be bright red and the spray of freckles across her nose would have popped—the price she paid for being a redhead, although quite why she was the only one of the

11

four sisters to suffer from the effects of the sun never made any sense. They all had the Celtic coloring of their parents but in a variety of shades. Constance, with her beautiful curtains of shimmering copper; Florence, her smooth chestnut locks drawn tightly into a bun and never a hair out of place; and Viola, with her shining cap of strawberry waves. Leaving Theodora with what her brother, Jamie, had always described as a "mop of dirty carrots." She gathered her paints and dismantled her easel before making her way to the house. The afternoon tea ritual couldn't be avoided. Before long, Florence would determine the weather to be too cold, but not yet. The autumn afternoons still carried a pleasant warmth.

Even from a distance the geometric precision of the chairs set in a semicircle to the right of the front doors filled her with apprehension. Despite the changes in their lives, Florence clung to tradition, leaving nothing to chance.

With every step, the figures came into closer focus—Florence, as always, in the center. It had taken only a matter of days for her to assume Mama's seat. On her right sat their housekeeper, Mrs. Barnett, upright, head tilted to one side, her black dress stark against the bleached stone walls, her small white lace collar the only concession to the fact mourning dress was no longer required. On Florence's left sat Viola, plump as a pigeon with skin as smooth as a ripe peach, resplendent in a gown that shimmered in the golden light, and next to her Constance, her saffron-colored dress blending with the turning leaves of the wisteria. And set apart, the empty chair awaiting her arrival. Not part of the semicircle facing the house; instead overlooking the river and the wharf, like a suspect in a witness box. The solitary nature of the chair made her heart wrench. In the past, Papa and Jamie would have flanked her, but not anymore. She sneaked around the corner and in through the kitchen.

"Oh, miss, I'm sorry I didn't see you there." A very flustered-looking Biddy stood balancing the silver tea tray with its teapot, sugar bowls, cups, and saucers. "You'd better get a move on. Miss Florence is all fired up."

Theodora sighed. The entire household tiptoed on eggshells around Florence. Since the accident she'd clung to Mrs. Barnett like a fractious toddler. "Do you think you could stall the tea tray for a moment, Biddy? I need to wash my face and hands." She ran her fingers through her unruly locks.

Biddy stepped closer and peered at her. "Look at your poor face. Why weren't you wearing a hat?"

"Bad, is it?"

"Mrs. Barnett will have you covered in one of her weird and wonderful concoctions before you can say Jack Sprat."

"Hopefully she's run out of potions. Although her chamomile cream is quite soothing." Better than the foul mixture of sour cream and nettle she'd smothered her in last summer. "I just wish she'd leave me be."

"I think you're beautiful. Freckles or no freckles. I'd give anything for eyes like yours, the exact same blue as those cornflowers in the meadow, and that lovely hair."

"Thank you, Biddy. I'd better make myself presentable. Just give me a minute, then take the tray out." She leaned over the scullery sink and splashed cold water over her face and scrubbed at her hands before capturing her hair that had, as usual, escaped from its upswept knot. "Better?"

"Much. Off you go and I'll be right behind you."

Theodora made her way down the hall, pulled open the front door, and peered out onto the veranda.

"You're late again." Florence didn't even lift her head from her contemplation of her buffed fingernails.

"I'm sorry." Theodora edged past the table and perched on

her chair. "The time passed so quickly." Her voice petered out as four pairs of eyes studied her face. She interlaced her fingers and tried for an apologetic smile.

"If you had attended to the task I set you, you might have spared yourself the heat of the afternoon sun." Mrs. Barnett studied her with narrowed eyes. The tone in her voice made Theodora want to scream, but she had promised to prepare the accounts. Mama had hated the task too, and now it fell to Theodora to organize the paperwork in date order before Mrs. Barnett entered a record of every penny spent—a list of names, wages paid, and the number of days worked in her wretched ledger.

"It's Friday." Mrs. Barnett let out a long-suffering sigh. "And I'm expected in Morpeth."

"I'm sorry. I'll organize them directly." Theodora made to stand. The perfect excuse to escape.

"Sit down." Mrs. Barnett's icy voice and glacial stare kept her riveted in her seat. "Where is the tea tray?"

A timid cough answered Mrs. Barnett's enquiry, and Biddy stood, arms outstretched, tray balanced.

"Put it down, girl. Theodora, I shall provide you with some lotion for your face when I return from Morpeth. It is better applied overnight." Mrs. Barnett rose and swept from the veranda, leaving a hollow silence, as though no one else was capable of filling the void her absence created.

Biddy balanced the tea tray on the small wicker table. "Shall I pour?"

"Leave!" Florence's strident tone echoed. "Theodora, the cake."

Theodora shot to her feet and handed out the plates and napkins, then made her way around the circle dispensing slivers of Mrs. Starling's orange cake. Since Mrs. Barnett had caught Bette pilfering leftover food from the kitchen, they'd been down to one maid, which meant the task of serving often fell to her. Quite why they couldn't employ another maid of all work she didn't know. Papa hadn't left them penniless. They were far from destitute.

Duty done, cake and tea provided, Theodora sank back into the wicker chair.

"Now is as good a time as any." Florence took a deep breath and clasped her hands together. "We have decided to visit Sydney. Mrs. Barnett and I believe it is time we reintroduced ourselves to society. There are a series of functions next month, and we will need several appointments with the seamstress to equip ourselves with new wardrobes before the season begins."

"No!" The word popped out of Theodora's mouth unbidden, producing a collective gasp of amazement from her younger sisters. No one ever questioned Florence; certainly not when she had Mrs. Barnett's support.

Sydney would mean a steamship. A river trip to Newcastle, then down the coast overnight to Sydney. Her hands grew clammy. Some days she wished she hadn't read the sole survivor's account of the wreckage of the *Cawarra* on the dreaded oyster bank, the graveyard of so many of the ships seeking to enter Port Hunter. She couldn't imagine how Mama, Papa, and Jamie must have felt to be dragged into the swirling waters before sinking, exhausted, into the churning sea and terrifying waves. The truth, when she finally read it, was far worse than the fantasy she'd spun. The vivid description of the grinding of the hull on the oyster shells, the almighty crash, and the influx of the freezing waters still haunted her dreams. Hundreds of people had gathered on the shore, launched their boats, and tried unsuccessfully to pull the bodies aboard until there was nothing left but the bobbing remains of timber and bloated corpses.

"I would rather remain here." Her voice carried a high-pitched, wavering note. "Someone needs to stay. What about Mama's garden? Autumn is the busiest of times. There's always a lot of work, pruning and harvesting, and now Hench has gone . . ."

"I'm sure Wilcox can manage." Florence brought the teacup to her pinched lips.

"I can't go to Sydney," Theodora appealed. "I have to stay and tend the garden until we find someone to replace Hench."

"The matter is not for discussion." Florence's red-faced bark took Theodora by surprise. "We will be leaving in three weeks and you will accompany us."

Viola and Constance clasped hands and squealed. They had been waiting impatiently for this moment. Viola wanted nothing more than to perform on her beloved cello, and Constance longed for the city. They'd both seen the period of mourning for Mama, Papa, and Jamie as a hardship where Theodora saw it as a blessing. A time to come to terms with their changed circumstances and be thankful for the security Papa had provided. Mama and Papa had been so happy, their love shining bright, unblemished even after over twenty years of marriage and five children. At least they had died together; a small comfort, perhaps, for if only one of them had survived, the other would have been broken beyond repair. She looked across at her sisters' glowing faces. How could their attitude to life be so different?

Florence, Viola, and Constance yearned for Sydney, the sense of anticipation in the air, the crush of people, and the constant noise, whereas she, Jamie, and Papa reveled in the natural beauty of the river and the surrounding country. The mere thought of the proposed trip sent a trickle of perspiration down her back. She hated Sydney, hated the way it made her feel, the air thick with foul smells and underfoot the mud and detritus of the ever-expanding city. Once she'd admitted her loathing, Papa had agreed she could stay with him in Morpeth while Mama and Mrs. Barnett took the girls to Sydney. A meaningless flurry of new dresses, recitals, tea parties, and calling cards, and now Florence wanted to reinstate the entire debacle—and include her.

"I would have thought, Theodora, you would embrace the opportunity to renew your acquaintance with the Scott family." Florence threw down the bait. It might have attracted her but for the fact she knew from Harriet's and Helena's regular correspondence they were away from Sydney.

"They're not there at the moment; they're working on a new set of illustrations for a book due for publication next year—*Mammals of Australia*."

How could she ever hope to emulate the sisters' achievements if she had to leave? She had a series of paintings she intended to complete over the cooler months. "I have work to do."

"Work!" Constance's derogatory tone made her hackles rise. "One is paid for work. You, like the Scott sisters, have a hobby. Ladies do not work."

She opened her mouth to contradict Constance and then snapped it closed. Harriet had requested in her last letter that Theodora not let anyone know she received money for her paintings. And then, interestingly, had gone on to lament the fact that if she were a man, it would be acceptable to earn money, as would her search for recognition. Theodora covered her mouth with her hand, trapping the snort of laughter as she remembered Harriet's concluding sentence that she might be more successful if she changed her name to Harry.

Maybe she should follow suit and become Theo. At the age of twenty-one, surely she should be permitted to make her own decisions. She couldn't hone her skills without the opportunity to pursue her passion.

The conventional feminine arts of music, polite conversation, and fluttering eyelashes held no interest. She was different; she knew she was. She'd always known. Something was out there waiting for her, and one day she would grasp it between her fingers and know her search had ended.

CHAPTER 3

Y ou're taking your time, girl." The Reverend Lodestar's voice echoed from his study.

Clarrie bit back a retort as she carried the large wooden tray to the table. The regular five o'clock Friday afternoon "At Home" was possibly the worst part of her job as maid of all work, far more effort than the mere hour scheduled every week. Nevertheless, the ladies of Morpeth held it high on their list of social necessities, a time to indulge in some serious gossip and tittle-tattle and lay claim to a contribution to the Sunday sermon. It also gave the ladies the opportunity to dangle their unmarried daughters in front of the reverend, whom, for some strange reason beyond her comprehension, they regarded as Morpeth's most eligible bachelor. He adored the adulation. The sooner he made up his mind and chose a wife, the sooner she could hand over her position behind the tea urn to whoever won the prized role as Mrs. Lodestar.

She lifted the napkins from the plates of sandwiches, savory tarts, pastries, and the Victoria sponge she'd spent the entire morning preparing, ensured the candle was still alight underneath the urn, then straightened the last of the teacups.

Standing back, she admired her handiwork. Surely there was nothing the reverend could complain about. Not a mark on the pristine white tablecloth, upon which the bowl of freshly picked garden flowers, flanked by two candelabra, set off the silver urn and floral teacups to perfection. Scattered between the plates of sandwiches, cakes, and bonbons were salted nuts and crystallized fruits. On the right stood the tea urn and opposite a large punch bowl of lemonade.

Clarrie moved behind the table, her back to the window. The reverend liked her to stand ready, hands behind her back, and allow his chosen guest to play hostess—a highly sought-after role. The reverend entered the room and the hum of conversation stuttered to a halt and a dozen expectant faces brightened. "Mrs. Patchett, would you be so kind as to act as hostess, and perhaps Prudence and Amelia could assist our guests—"

Before he could finish his sentence, Mrs. Patchett elbowed her way through the circle of chairs and took up her station next to the urn, ensuring she wouldn't be pipped at the post.

Clarrie masked a smile. Mrs. Patchett would be dining out on the privilege for the next week at least, as would Amelia and Prudence, whichever one managed to get the reverend his cup of tea—a slice of lemon, no milk—and his preferred asparagus rolls and Gentlemen's Relish sandwich, crusts removed.

The general chatting and tête-à-têtes resumed, interrupted only by full plates and equally stuffed mouths, giving Clarrie time to settle. What she wouldn't give for a chair.

Before the reverend could complain, she untied her pinafore and slipped it underneath the table. She couldn't bend down and adjust her boots, but she could tell her ankles had swollen to a ridiculous size. She tugged at the sides of her dress, then clasped her hands and took two steps to the right until she stood shielded by the flower arrangement. From the moment she'd noticed the hardening of her belly and felt the first flutter of movement, she'd nursed the secret only Sid shared.

Feeling less conspicuous, she observed the room. Largely the usual ladies, although Mrs. Babinger and Mrs. Brownish weren't in attendance. The two Whitehorn girls were also absent. She'd heard tell of a new piano teacher who visited once a week from Maitland, and they were both keen on their music. Her mouth quirked. Perhaps the piano player was more of a catch than the reverend. She'd hazard a guess he would be younger.

Sitting to one side of the fireplace was a woman she'd never noticed before at the reverend's Friday At Homes—a widow, if her severe black dress was anything to go by. A small white lace collar emphasized her thick neck and somewhat mannish features. Something struck a chord, but Clarrie couldn't place her.

As though alerted to Clarrie's scrutiny, the woman lifted her head and stared. Heat flushed Clarrie's cheeks and her hands tightened across her belly.

The reverend crossed the room. "Mrs. Barnett, it's a delight to see you here."

Mrs. Barnett, of course. She lived in the big house, The Landing. No wonder she wore black after the dreadful wreck off Newcastle. Only one man had lived to tell the tale. His account had been written up all over the local newspaper, *The Morpeth Want*. Sid had told her about it. He always had the news first. It stood to reason, since he wrote it. Not really "wrote." Lined up all the letters in their neat little trays so dozens and dozens of copies of the paper could be printed and distributed. Dear Sid. They'd been stepping out for more than three years and had intended to be married by now, but their savings hadn't grown as fast as her belly.

"Clarrie!"

She jumped, miles away and caught out badly.

"Some more water for the urn."

"Yes, Mrs. Patchett." She masked a groan. More hot water and the afternoon would go over its allocated hour. A second cup of tea was most unusual. She edged around the end of the table, Mrs. Barnett's continuous observation making her cringe. Just as her hand reached the doorknob, the reverend rose.

"Ladies, thank you. Thank you, as always, for your input. I have settled on the text for my sermon—Mark 10:14: 'Suffer the little children to come unto me'; most appropriate, I believe. I look forward to seeing you all in church on Sunday. I must leave you. Attend to the Spirit while it is upon me. Clarrie will see you out."

And with that, the Reverend Lodestar barged through the door, almost knocking her for six, and as good as galloped across the hallway into his study—most likely for a glass of long-awaited port. Not that she was one to judge. She could do with one herself. She had a good two hours cleaning up ahead of her, though the reverend only ever took a cold plate on a Friday so, if she was lucky, she might be tucked up in her attic bed before eight.

Clarrie put the finishing touches to the reverend's supper tray and sank onto the kitchen chair to unlace her boots. The knock on the back door took her by surprise, more so when it swung open a crack and a tousled head appeared, sporting a wide grin. "Hey, Clarrie. How're you doing?"

"Archer! What're you doing here?"

"Got a note for you from Sid. He says he'll meet you on the corner at quarter past eight." He stepped inside and handed her a scruffy piece of paper. *Meet you on the corner at quarter past eight. Sid.*

"Why did you bother with the note?"

"'Cause Sid told me to deliver it."

"But you read it first?"

His face rivaled damson jam. "Well, yes." He scuffed his feet.

"It might have been private."

"Wasn't, was it? And besides, what's the point in learning your letters if you don't read things?"

"There are other things to read beside private letters."

"He'll be waiting for you. Shall I tell him yes? Will his nibs let you go?"

Clarrie took a quick look around the kitchen, checked the reverend's tray, and nodded. "Tell Sid I'll be there, but I can't stay long." By eight thirty it would be well and truly dark. "Here, take this." She handed him the leftover slice of sponge cake and opened the back door. "Be good."

"And if I can't be good, be careful. I know." He threw her a cheeky grin and slipped out. "I'll tell Sid."

She hadn't expected to see Sid until Sunday, her afternoon off. Usually she packed a picnic after she'd served the reverend his lunch and they'd take it down by the river, out past the town, and spend the afternoon there. In warm weather Sid swam, and he'd taught her, though she preferred to paddle in the shallows, and they'd eat the sandwiches she'd brought

23

while they dried out, and in the winter they'd light a fire and have tea and toast. And that's where the problem started. Not the toast and dripping but what happened afterward. Once would have been bad enough, but several times . . . She knew she'd go to hell for it, knew as sure as eggs were eggs, and the Reverend Lodestar would be there holding open the fiery gates.

She pulled her pinafore off and examined the side seams. With a bit of luck she'd be able to let it out once more, and her dress too, but after that she didn't have a hope, despite the weight she'd managed to lose in a vain attempt to keep her secret. At least the reverend hadn't noticed anything untoward, though she doubted he had much experience of women's bodies, being a man of the church and all that.

She didn't regret her condition, not for one moment. She and Sid were meant to be together. She'd come to depend on him, his comfort and humor, his kind, gentle ways. He was a real gentleman, despite his lousy start to life. From the moment she'd first clapped eyes on him she'd known he was the one. She'd been hurrying to get home, and when her foot caught on a stone, she'd dropped her basket, sent all her shopping scattering across the road, and dived after it. A pair of hands had clasped her under the armpits, dragged her back. She'd struggled free, mouth full of abuse.

"Couldn't face the thought of you going the same way." He'd pointed to the shattered remains of a dozen of Mrs. Tonks's fresh brown eggs intended for the reverend's breakfast, scrambled by the great clumping hooves of the Clydesdale pulling the lucerne dray.

Her angry words had dried and she'd sunk into the gutter, head in hands.

By the time her heart had stopped pounding and she'd collected her thoughts, he'd picked up the odds and sods of her shopping, except for the eggs, and stacked them back in her basket. She'd managed to take a decent look at him then. A young man, not much older than she was, with hair the color of sunshine and skin she had an urge to touch.

"Most of your shopping has survived."

But not enough to get her out of trouble. "The reverend's not going to be happy."

"Reverend Fire and Brimstone? He's never happy. Not unless everyone's listening to him."

She'd raised her hand and he'd flinched, then they'd both burst into the most ridiculous laughter, rocking and rolling, grinning at each other like fools. He'd cupped her cheeks in his hands, looked deep into her eyes. "What a waste."

"It is."

"Not the eggs—you. What a waste it would be if you'd got scrambled." He stood up, towering over her, and held out his hand, black and stained by the ink from the printing press, though she hadn't known it then. "Up you get. I know where we'll find some more eggs."

And true to his word he'd scored a dozen eggs free of charge from someone down the road and fixed her problem, just the way she knew he'd fix this one.

Once Clarrie had taken the reverend his tray, banked the fire, doused the lights, and left the kitchen ready for the morning, the clock in the hallway had struck eight. She thumped up the stairs and closed the door to her little attic room with a bang. The reverend never disturbed her once he had his supper tray, especially not after his At Home—too busy writing down notes and ideas he'd gleaned from the ladies for his sermon.

With the hood of her cloak hiding her face and her hands buried in its folds, she slipped back downstairs and out of the door into the lane behind the parsonage. Sticking to the shadows, she made her way along Tank Street to the corner of Swan. She knew exactly where Sid would be waiting, back pressed against the wall, legs sprawled, and a mischievous grin on his face. He was Newcastleborn, and after a childhood growing up on the wrong side of town, he'd quickly learned every one of Morpeth's nooks and crannies when he'd got his apprenticeship with the newspaper. Right from the start the boss, Mr. Kendall, let him have a corner of the basement for his own. Ten years on and the reek of printers' ink had soaked into his pores and Clarrie would swear his hearing was off because of the constant thumping of the presses. Still and all that was the least of her worries. What she liked most were the plans and dreams they shared.

Her heart flew to her mouth when a hand landed on her shoulder and the smell of printing ink clouded her senses.

"What's a pretty young lass like you doing skulking around here?"

"Sid! How many times do I have to tell you"—her belly gave a lurch and her hands cupped it protectively—"you can't do that anymore." The ground swayed beneath her and she slumped against him. "You'll frighten my baby."

He slipped his arms around her and pulled her into the darkness. "My baby too," he murmured. "How is he?"

"*She's* fine, but she won't be if you carry on like that."

"How much longer, do you reckon?"

She lifted her shoulders. She had no idea. She hadn't even known she was carrying until the funny blue veins started to show on her breasts and her back kept aching, then she'd had to let her dress out, not once but several times. "Two, maybe three months." Before he could give his usual "she'll be right" reply, she added, "We're going to have to make some plans.

Soon, very soon. Once the reverend notices, I'll be out on my ear and then what?"

"Then I'll look after you. I told you I would, and I mean it."

She couldn't argue with that. They'd made long-term plans, but nothing for the right now, which seemed to be galloping closer every moment.

"As soon as we've got some more money together we'll rent one of the cottages down by the river. I'll have a word with Mr. Kendall, ask him to keep an ear to the ground."

It all sounded so lovely, but no matter what he might dream, the baby would be with them a lot sooner than their savings would allow. "But where am I going to have the baby?"

"I've been thinking about that and I've got a few ideas."

The tingling in her chest settled and she relaxed into him, resting her cheek against his broad chest.

"What say you 'fess up and tell the reverend? After all, he's a man of God. He's not going to turn you out."

For goodness' sake. "Sid! Don't be ridiculous." She pulled away from him, not wanting his hands on her. That's how she'd come to be in this mess in the first place. "That's not going to happen, and besides, I'll need help. A midwife or someone, and that costs money too."

"What about your mother?"

"My mother?" She wouldn't do anything to help. She'd chuck her out faster than the reverend. The last time she'd wasted a whole five shillings of her hard-earned savings to take the steamship down to Sydney in an attempt to make her peace with Mother and tell her about Sid, she'd returned with nothing but a flea in her ear. And that was before the baby. "Not a hope. She'd be too worried about her precious clients and her reputation."

"Just as well I've got another solution then, isn't it?" He placed his hands on the warm, round mound of her belly.

In the darkness she couldn't read his face, but his voice held a triumphant note. And for a moment she imagined the little cottage by the river and a baby tucked in a basket in the sunshine under the trees while she sat mending Sid's shirts, waiting for him to come home from work.

"I've got this."

A pale outline fluttered under her nose. A piece of paper and the smell of printers' ink. Or was that Sid? "What is it?"

"A classified. Found it in the newspaper. Someone who'll help."

"I've heard about those awful women. They take your baby and sell it, or worse. Forget it. I'm not giving up this baby." If she'd wanted to do that, she would have gone and had herself sorted long ago. Though she'd never been too sure whether it had been fear for herself or love for the wriggle growing inside her that had prevented her. "It's our baby, Sid. Surely you don't want . . ." A sob stifled her words.

"Shh. No, it's not that. I'll tell you what it says. It's too dark to read it. The woman's a midwife and she offers a lying-in service. You go there, have the baby, then she'll look after it and you can go back to work."

"And how much is that going to cost?"

"I don't know. I didn't want to find out until I'd run it past you. Says here she's a loving, caring woman." He fluttered the paper, then folded it in half and pushed it down into his jacket pocket. "What do you think?"

A bubble of lightness lifted her mood. Not the perfect solution but better than any alternative. Better than crawling on her hands and knees to Mother and having the door slammed in her face.

"And maybe, if we got married before the baby came, the reverend would keep you on. This woman could look after the baby, and we'd go visit him on our days off . . ."

"Her."

"What?"

"It might be a her, not a him. We need to think of some names."

"What about Maud?"

"Maud?" Her lips stretched wide, almost a scream. "That's a horrible name. Why Maud?" She drew the word out and couldn't help a shudder.

"That's the woman's name. The midwife, Maud. If she helps us, it would be nice."

"Does the classified give her name?"

"No. I did some asking around. She lives in one of the cottages down the far end of Swan Street."

She'd badly misjudged Sid. "You did?"

"It's my responsibility too, not just yours."

And that was why she loved him. She stretched onto her tiptoes and dropped a kiss on his bristly cheek, inhaling the sweet smell of ink and Sid.

"And I'd like to call him Charlie."

"Why Charlie?"

"'Cause he can be Charlie when he's a kid and Charles when he grows to be a fine man."

"Let's just get him born, shall we?"

"Him." He moved to give her a dig in the ribs, then stopped. "Sorry, Charlie. Best be careful. Your job, my love, is to pick the time to talk to the reverend, then tell him you're going to need a week or so off work. It ain't the normal way of things, but you never know, the reverend might have a heart underneath that stuffed shirt of his. I'll have a word with Maud and find out her charges. And don't worry too much about it. I've got a bit of a money-making idea too. Mr. Kendall reckons he'll pay me a bit for anything I write that he can use in the paper. Thruppence for every string of words. I just need to find a decent story." He grasped her hand and brought it to his lips. "Happy with that, Mrs. Binks?"

CHAPTER 4

When the first fingers of dawn illuminated the rooftops and the sky lightened, Verity finally slept. She awoke in a tangle of sheets and discarded pillows and reality dawned. She shot upright. Had she dreamed it? Dreamed the costume, the invitation? She ran down the stairs. The box sat where she had left it—the black dress, wings, and mask allaying her confusion. It was no dream.

A flamboyant flourish underscored her name on the envelope, bold as brass. It was intended for her. No one else. She had to talk to someone, ask for their opinion, but who? Mrs. Carr or Sadie, perhaps? But Mrs. Carr would throw her hands up in horror and tell her not to go, and she didn't know exactly where Sadie lived and could hardly go back to the newspaper office and ask.

Her attention drifted to the mantelpiece above the stove and she picked up the rectangular silver frame, tarnished and in need of a polish—the photograph taken just days before he'd left. *Charles Binks, War Correspondent* splashed across the bottom of the cardboard. Charlie had become a legend in newspaper circles when he'd been selected to accompany the Australian Imperial Forces to Egypt—all he had ever dreamed, all he'd waited for his entire life. It hadn't mattered that he was twenty years older than the other correspondents, Mr. Bean and Mr. Murdoch. He'd put up such a fight, said it needed an older man's wisdom, and the powers-that-be had finally caved.

"I'll be back before you know it, safe and sound. Sid and Clarrie will take care of you, just as they always do when I'm away." And she'd believed him. Had no reason to doubt him. He'd never let her down. From the moment Mother succumbed to childbed fever only ten days after she'd given birth, Charlie had been there for her.

She hadn't imagined he'd be in danger; rather, she'd thought he'd be sitting in some shoebox of an office with a view over the pyramids, hammering away on his Remington typewriter just as he'd always done in Sydney. She wiped her thumb over the glass and placed the picture back on the mantelpiece.

Charlie wouldn't be standing around procrastinating, wondering whether he'd got the courage to show up. Heaven forbid—it was a ball. Just a ball, not a war! She didn't even have to RSVP. The ticket was paid for, the costume a perfect fit. Whoever sent it intended that she should wear it. More than likely they'd introduce themselves at the ball. She wouldn't be difficult to spot, dressed like an orange and black butterfly.

Besides, it was the event of the season. If she couldn't dig up a decent story in the Town Hall full of Sydney's toffs and everyone who was anyone in the art world, where could she? She might as well chuck Grandpa Sid's Remington and her dreams of becoming a writer out of the window. Heavens above, if she tried hard enough, Mr. Bailey might even mention her name in the paper. Verity Binks, not some pseudonym like

"An Old Bachelor" or "Vernacular" that the few women who did get a column in the paper hid behind.

Verity threw back her shoulders. "Verity Binks, correspondent." The words brought a smile to her lips and sealed her fate.

The tram slowed and drew to a halt outside the Town Hall. "Enjoy your evening, sweetheart." The conductor grinned. "I'll want to hear all about it."

Read all about it, if everything went according to plan. "You will. I promise."

Verity blew him a kiss and swung down onto the footpath, her trailing wings hooked over her arm like a bride's train. She'd already spoken to Mr. Bailey and asked if she could show him her report of the ball. He'd made some comment about wanting the story from inside the Town Hall, not outside, barely breaking his stride until she'd told him she had an invitation. His bushy eyebrows had crawled up his domed forehead and he grunted. She'd taken it as a yes, and a sense of warmth had infused her body and remained for the rest of the day—although she still had no idea who'd delivered the invitation or the dress. She'd ended up grilling Mrs. Carr and they'd tracked down the delivery boy, but all he'd said was that he did odd jobs for the post office in Argyle Street and they'd asked him to deliver it. A trip there hadn't brought any further information and so she was none the wiser.

High above the roof of the Town Hall, the central clock tower struck the hour and the heavy doors swung open. The crowd surged forward, carrying her in its wake until she reached the foyer, handed over her invitation, and stepped into a blaze of color and blinding light. The area where she'd sat only four months ago listening to Dame Nellie Melba entertain a crowd of over three thousand people had been transformed into a vaudeville-like arena, with enormous friezes and grotesque stilted figures that reached from the floor to the gallery and loomed like sentinels.

She plastered a confident smile on her lips and eased her way into the shoulder-to-shoulder crowd, racing to imprint every detail of the spectacular scene in her memory. Enveloped in the swirling mass of people, she reeled from the mixture of exotic aromas.

Fantastic figures in bizarre gowns, veiled women, masked men, parsons escorting ballet dancers, stately dignitaries coupled with scantily clad mermaids, Indian chiefs, troubadours, artists, monks, dairymaids, Queen Elizabeth and Drake, nurses, and merry widows. All manner of characters thronged the cavernous space, and in front of the organ a stage had been erected, framed by two immense female figures' hands outstretched to hold back black and purple curtains.

It was as glamorous as she had imagined, but she had no idea what to do next. For want of anything better, she took a glass of champagne from the tray of a passing waiter and backed up against the wall. Surely whoever had sent the invitation and the dress would recognize her and make themselves known. Every time anyone's attention lit upon her, she searched for a flicker of recognition behind their mask but found nothing.

A fanfare heralded the arrival of the vice regal party. The crowd parted, forming a passage. Led by tripping jesters and ten dancing girls, the procession swept through the room.

A hush descended.

"I am the governor," one of the party announced. Two other figures dressed in matching, richly braided costumes of fuchsia, gold, and blue stepped forward and disputed his claim. The crowd roared its approval.

Verity couldn't hear any more, but their waggling fingers, thrusting chests, and strutting gaits made it obvious that they had no intention of stepping down.

She shouldered her way through the crowd, determined to identify the governor, Sir Walter Davidson, and his wife, Dame Margaret, and speak to them. Was he happy to be part of this charade or had he been coerced? Was he even present? Neat type-written lines filled her vision, all the words she would write. It would make a marvelous cameo, and if she could find out before midnight when the masks were removed if Sir Walter was present, she might have the scoop she dreamed of before they put the paper to bed. Mr. Bailey would love it.

Just as she reached the stage, the chief jester blocked her path. He raised his hand and silenced the crowd. "Bring me the kip." His voice boomed out across the room.

Another jester danced onto the stage, a flat wooden paddle holding two bright, shiny pennies balanced on a tasseled cushion. "Our governor for the night will be decided by a game of two-up."

Another roar filled the room and the three contenders stepped forward.

"Place your bets."

The men called their preference—two called heads and the other tails. The jester raised the kip and with a flick of his wrist sent the two pennies spinning through the air. They hit the stage with a thud and he leaned down and made the call. "Heads."

One of the "governors" stepped aside and a mixture of groans and hoots rippled through the crowd.

"Place your final bet," the jester cried.

"Heads."

"Tails."

The jester flicked the kip. The two coins twisted and twirled in the lights and landed center stage.

"Tails," the jester cried and waved aside the loser. The crowd bowed low while the jester led the unknown "governor" to his throne. The reveal would have to wait until the stroke of midnight when the masks would be removed, unless . . .

Verity edged around behind the throne, intending to lean forward and whisper in the man's ear to see if she could ascertain his name. A hand clamped down on her arm and pulled her aside, enveloping her in a cloud of incense and saffron.

"Wonderful evening, isn't it? So good to see the city shining again. It's been too long."

She shrugged free of the grip and studied the masked face, one of the many troubadours roaming the floor in their long-sleeved black shirts with lace-trimmed collars and flouncy cuffs and capes. A mandolin dangled loosely from one of his gloved hands, but it was the mask that made the hairs on her arms prickle. A white beak and black circles emphasizing the eyes, reminiscent of the plague doctors of old.

"You have me at a disadvantage. Have we met?"

He grasped her elbow with his gloved hand and escorted her from the stage.

The pounding of her heart filled her ears as she struggled to free herself. His lips moved below the half mask, but a series of squeals rang from the crowd and a glass shattered.

"I beg your pardon?"

The troubadour stepped closer. "Let me introduce you to David Treadwell, chair of the Treadwell Foundation. He knew your father."

"My father?" Her words came out as a strangled squeak.

Without answering, the troubadour approached a man on her right. "Mr. Treadwell, may I introduce Verity Binks." He knew her name. Did he also know who had sent her invitation? His mask made it impossible to read his expression; however, his voice had a shrill tone that she hadn't noticed when he first spoke.

"Miss Binks. Lovely to meet you. Your father was a fine man, brilliant correspondent. Taken far too soon."

"Miss Binks works for *The Sydney Arrow*. I thought she would be the perfect person to write the story of your charity." The troubadour's raised voice carried over the noise.

Mr. Treadwell straightened his black and gold mask and stared at her. "It is a story that should be told. I have been contemplating it for some time. A piece in *The Sydney Arrow* would be most fortuitous."

Verity opened her mouth to make mention of her new role, but before she framed the sentence, the band began to play, the crowd erupted, and the dancing began. She simply nodded and gave an ambiguous grunt.

"I'd like to offer you the opportunity." Mr. Treadwell lifted her hand, his attention roaming greedily over her body in the ridiculously short black dress. "I would like someone to write the history of our foundation. I always hoped to engage your father, but since that is not possible, who better than his daughter? As one of the recipients of tonight's proceeds, and in recognition of our excellent charitable works, I felt it would be only right and proper that we offered an insight into the wonderful work that we do."

Perhaps she'd missed the point. She'd read that the proceeds would benefit the Red Cross project to establish a pottery workshop for disabled soldiers "I'm sorry, Mr. Treadwell. I'm not sure that I am familiar with your charity."

He took a couple of steps back. "Not familiar with our work." Disbelief laced his voice and he shook his head before moving away from a pair of gyrating dancers. "My dear mother established the foundation after my father passed. Our property, Treadwell House, is dedicated to its purpose."

"Its purpose, Mr. Treadwell?"

"Why, assisting young women. I would have thought you would be aware of our mission."

No, she'd never heard of it, but it did sound as though it might be a story she'd like to tell. One that might be far more interesting than the identity of the man sitting on tonight's throne.

"I'm looking for someone with an intuitive sense of human values and public reaction."

A rush of pleasure warmed Verity. That was exactly the way she'd like to be seen. "I'd be delighted to write an account of your charity." There, she'd done it.

"Excellent, excellent. So perfectly fitting that the daughter of a local hero should pick up her pen and spread the news of our work." He puffed out his chest. "I can assure you that it will encourage further donations."

Surely he hadn't gone to all the trouble to send her an invitation and a costume to ask her to write about his charity? He simply could have called into the newspaper offices or sent her a note. "Thank you for the invitation."

"It is my pleasure. I look forward to meeting with you and telling you all about our charity. Shall we say eleven o'clock on Saturday morning at Treadwell House?" He handed her a small white card. "And now, if you'll excuse me, my presence is required. Supper is being served in the basement very soon." He spun on his heel and exchanged a few words with two men, then merged into the crowd.

How strange, how very strange. He'd clearly misunderstood her and presumed her mention of an invitation referred to his request that she write about the Treadwell Foundation. She should have just asked him outright. His flattering words about Charlie and the lure of a job, a real writing job, was far too enticing to ignore. Thank goodness he'd misunderstood her. If he hadn't sent the invitation, she would have appeared a complete fool.

Once the music stopped and the crowd dispersed, Verity made her way toward the basement. Revelers packed the stairway and a group of troubadours hovered, directing people this way and that, the deafening noise bouncing from the high ceilings and adding to the surreal nature of the evening. While she hovered at the top of the stairs, another troubadour greeted her. She couldn't tell if it was the one who'd introduced her to Mr. Treadwell—they all looked identical.

"Let me show you to a table, Miss Binks." The foppish voice and the whiff of the exotic scent pinpointed him as the same troubadour.

"How do you know my name?"

She didn't want to spend the entire evening with anyone; she wanted to make some quick notes and prepare a piece for Mr. Bailey about the ball. Apart from anything else, the troubadour's strange hook-nosed mask made her skin creep. "Thank you. I can manage."

"I mean you no harm." The troubadour leaned toward her. Eyes bright as Venetian glass, blue and green and brown with the hint of a smile, sparkled behind the mask and the strange, exotic scent swirled. "Come. We'll find somewhere a little quieter."

Batting down the curl of caution, Verity followed him to the basement. Decorated with hessian, plastered with posters for films, and packed with drunken revelers falling over each other, she backed against the wall, senses swimming. Small cubicles offered a haven from the collection of fortune tellers, sculptors, crystal gazers, and cartoonists entertaining the crowd.

The troubadour led her to a rough table spread with all kinds of food served on crockery as chipped and worn as her own, with serviettes of newspaper. "Supper a la grabbo, they are calling it."

Food didn't interest her at all. Treadwell's words still echoed, as did the way he'd appealed to her vanity. Her sycophantic acceptance made her light-headed and confused. "Really, I'm not hungry."

"The costume is a perfect fit."

Her head came up with a snap, the troubadour's horrifying mask filling her vision. "What do you know about my costume and the invitation?"

"It served its purpose. After you have visited Treadwell House we will speak again. It is a story begging to be told."

A wash of moonlight from the high windows illuminated the troubadour's mask and with a brief lift of his hand he slipped into the crowd.

Verity dashed and weaved after him through the crowded basement, up the stairs, out of the Town Hall, and down the steps two at a time. As she reached the street, the black-cloaked figure slipped around the corner.

Verity chased after him, an enticing, flickering glimpse of the white mask that he now carried in his hand acting as a beacon. She kept him in sight until she reached Market Street, then he merged into the crowd leaving the State Theatre.

Breath rasping, she darted to and fro searching for another glimpse. Finally she admitted defeat, ducked into the

Strand Arcade, and collapsed against the wall, her heart hammering and her chest heaving. She would have to wait until after she'd visited Treadwell House for the troubadour to make contact.

CHAPTER 5

MORPETH, 1868

The sun rose, burning off the lingering morning mist and encouraging Theodora out into the garden long before breakfast, her sketchbook balanced in her lap, determined to complete her illustration before the cooler weather sent the blooms to seed and destroyed the autumn color.

Mama's walled garden brimmed with an array of flowers—delphiniums and hollyhocks, their tall flower spikes nodding in the breeze; the spicy-scented bell flowers and pinks; the blue cornflowers and the roses, all hedged by rosemary interspersed by spikes of lavender—remembrance and devotion. So poignant.

All the seeds and cuttings originated from Mama's home in Cornwall, and the garden had become a place of solace and comfort. Painting kept Theodora from dwelling on all that had changed and the bouts of melancholy she'd suffered since Mama and Papa passed.

She sat back to appraise her handiwork, waiting for the paint to dry and the colors to lighten or change, Florence's sudden announcement of the trip to Sydney foremost in her mind. She still hadn't summoned the courage to revisit their conversation, and with every passing hour her dismay increased.

She didn't want to leave home; the thought of being in a crowd made her dizzy and disorientated. She'd even cut short her last trip to Morpeth when she found herself caught in the tide of people swarming Queens Wharf as the steamer pulled in. She'd run all the way back to the punt and then made a foolish excuse about a broken bootlace to explain her hurried departure.

Rocking back against the wall, she lifted her face to the sun. A black shadow moved on the edge of her vision. As surreal as a fading specter, a light graze brushed her cheeks. A butterfly hovered, wings lifting and falling in perfect harmony before it alighted on her fingertips.

The tensing of her muscles sent it darting to the garden, dancing through the flower beds, its tongue uncurling in search of nectar to fuel its flight. Arcing above the flowers, it wheeled around and landed on the corner of her page.

Barely daring to take a breath, she let her focus settle on the striking orange, black, and white markings. She'd painted a hundred or more species of butterflies since the first time Papa had taken her to Ash Island to meet Harriet and Helena Scott—a day that had cemented her passion for nature. This glorious creature, unlike any she'd seen before, epitomized her purpose. Its wings spanned at least four or five inches, their reddish-orange tints shimmering in the sunlight, fine white dots highlighting the obsidian black, as rich as Mama's velvet opera cloak. She breathed a sigh, just enough movement to send the glorious creature on its way once more.

With a cry she leaped to her feet, her paint tray falling to the ground as she snatched up her muslin butterfly net and tiptoed along the border of the garden. A flash of orange as the butterfly hovered above the pelargoniums sent her creeping forward. She lifted the net until the butterfly sat within the circumference of the hoop and with a flick of her wrist twisted the handle.

She laid the net on the ground and lifted the folds of muslin, searching for a splash of color. Surely she'd caught it. Despair lent panic to her movements as she twisted the gauze this way and that. How could she have missed?

Vision blurring, she searched the garden, but there was no sight of the beautiful creature that had alighted for such a brief moment in her world.

She slumped onto the grass and threw aside the net. Poking around among the broken stones and startled lizards, she found no evidence of her visitor, so unlike anything she'd seen before. Perhaps her imagination had conjured the iridescent colors and startling palette.

Her hand shook as she reached for her brush, stroking the fine hairs across a fresh sheet of paper, trying to recreate the orange and black pattern and the white spotted band lacing the edge of each wing.

Tugging her hair back from her face, she scrutinized her paltry effort. If only she had managed to capture the beautiful creature. On occasions when she painted she became so absorbed she no longer controlled her actions, but this time, try as she might, she'd failed to replicate the intricate patterns of the butterfly's wings.

How long she sat at her easel she had no idea, but as the sun began its downward journey, painting the river a liquid gold, she scooped up her easel and paints and headed back across the lawn as fast as she could. The strains of Viola's cello wafted in the breeze as she crept into the library where Papa's pipe still sat on the desk and the aroma of tobacco faintly lingered, overlaid by the musty scent of his collection of first-edition books.

Paint was embedded in her nails, mud sat in the valleys between her fingers, and the pages of her sketchbook bore the sweaty imprint of her hand, but none of this seemed significant save the bold splashes of color of the butterfly's wings. She dragged the library steps into the back corner and carefully climbed to the very top. Standing on tiptoe, she stretched to the shelf where Papa's most precious editions resided and ran her fingers along the spines until she found the book she was searching for.

With a deal of reverence, she carried it down to lay it on the desk and opened it to the title page: *Australian Lepidoptera and their transformations drawn from life by Harriet and Helena Scott; with descriptions, general and systematics, by A. W. Scott.* Only one hundred copies of the book Harriet and Helena had worked on alongside their father had been published in England, and this gift from Mr. Scott had been one of Papa's most treasured possessions.

Her index finger traced the sisters' names beneath the pen-and-ink drawing of their home on Ash Island, sending a thrill through her. She inhaled, counted to three, and exhaled. Theodora Julianna Breckenridge—what she wouldn't give to see her name on such a frontispiece.

But for Papa's friendship with Mr. Scott, she never would have discovered the world of Ash Island and the magical gifts the Scott sisters possessed. Those halcyon days when she would travel upriver with Papa, Jamie, and Redmond, her brother's closest friend, tacking and jibing until they reached the island near the delta of the Hunter River. Papa would spend the day in Mr. Scott's study while Theodora sat in awe and watched the sisters weave their magic, until one day they handed her one of their finest paintbrushes and encouraged her to recreate the intricate patterns of a butterfly's wing—her first measly attempt, which they had applauded and encouraged with more kindness than due.

Happily, they shared their knowledge, and so had begun her long and devoted journey into the world of Lepidoptera and hours and hours of fun exploring Ash Island.

She ran her finger down the index searching for . . . She had no idea of the name of the orange and black beauty, so instead she carefully thumbed through the book, leafing through every page, fruitlessly searching the illustrations and descriptions. The color, texture, and minutely detailed body parts were more accurate than she ever could hope to achieve, but not one of the paintings, as beautiful as they were, depicted the orange, black, and white butterfly.

Sinking into a chair, she leafed through the remaining pages, scanning the descriptions she'd read a hundred times, finding nothing that resembled the enchanting creature that had alighted on her fingertip.

A thrill of possibility whispered across her skin, goose bumps stippling as realization settled. She grabbed her sketchbook and opened it to the page where she had roughly painted her unexpected visitor. Forcing down the blossoming thrill of unscientific exhilaration, she inhaled deeply. There would be no jumping to conclusions. The book represented only a tiny portion of the sisters' work—even before they'd left Ash Island they'd been talking about a second and possibly a third volume.

How she missed them!

A little like a butterfly, she'd alighted on her passion and Harriet's and Helena's encouragement had steered her along the path.

The thoughts of Ash Island and the two sisters made the

corner of her mouth twitch into a smile. It had been such a long time since she'd truly enjoyed any company other than that of her sisters. She missed not only the island and Helena and Harriet but also the days with Jamie and Redmond and the wonderful array of people the Scotts had introduced her to. She'd watched Mrs. Gould paint the intricate details of a bird's feather; discussed shade and light with Conrad Martens; and heard tell of Ludwig Leichhardt, the explorer who'd visited Ash Island before he'd vanished in the wilderness. Mr. Scott liked to recount Leichhardt's claim that he'd found the island such a romantic place he'd be content to live and die there. But most importantly, she'd been accepted—not as a foolish young girl but as a person of intellect, capable of scientific assessment and recording, intent on discovering the truth in nature. Papa's and Jamie's unexpected passing and the Scotts' departure from Ash Island had left her more than bereft; it had clipped her wings and stilted her imagination.

Closing the book, she reached for a pen and nib, opened the desk drawer, and took out a sheet of paper. She would write, tell Harriet and Helena of her visitor, enclose her rough, somewhat conceptual painting, and ask for their opinion—and forgiveness of her lack of skill.

Maybe the butterfly brought a message. People said butterflies were the messengers of the gods, and she'd seen it in Mama's garden, her favorite place.

When Papa had proposed to Mama, he'd promised to recreate the garden of her childhood when she arrived in Australia. She said his act had secured her acceptance to his proposal, but she'd spoken with a twinkle in her eye and a look to Papa of such loving that Theodora doubted she spoke the truth. Nevertheless, he'd kept his promise and her garden had grown and flourished.

Theodora tossed her fey thoughts aside and concentrated, determined to write her letter in a scientific and systematic manner, as she had been taught. She had no room for romantic fantasies. The heavy lace curtains billowed in the breeze, bringing with it the scent of lavender from Mama's garden as she put pen to paper.

My dear Helena and Harriet,

It is with great excitement that I enclose a rough, very rough, painting of a butterfly that alighted but for a moment on my fingertips while I was at my easel in Mama's garden. I can hardly explain the beauty of the creature with its finely patterned wings, which my illustration sorely fails to convey.

The markings included bright orange wings covered with black veins and rimmed with a black border scattered with white dots. To say the creature took my breath away would be an understatement. It also sadly stole my senses, for I failed to capture it, although my net lay close at hand.

I cannot believe there is a winged creature that you haven't cataloged, but I can find no reference in volume 1 of *Lepidoptera*. I beg of you, share your knowledge with me, for I am captivated by its beauty.

> With the kindest regard and
> long-held respect,
> Yours most sincerely,
> Theodora Breckenridge

CHAPTER 6

MORPETH, 1868

Clarrie spent all of Saturday and Sunday morning pacing the floor, planning what she would say to the reverend. She couldn't even bring herself to go to morning service, which wasn't going to endear her to him, but when she'd arrived at the doors of the church, she couldn't set foot inside the cool interior that hummed with forgotten prayers.

All very well Sid having these bright ideas, but he'd left her to carry the can. She had to face the reverend alone and throw herself on his mercy. She'd chosen Sunday morning after the eleven o'clock service in the hope he might be in a kindly mood, that his sermon would have gone down well. The topic he'd settled upon had firmed her resolve: "Suffer the little children to come unto me." She murmured the words over and over, hoping they'd bring her some luck. The reverend always came back to the parsonage and took a glass of sherry before she served his Sunday lunch: roast meat, roast potatoes, and two vegetables followed by a bowl of trifle, which he liked with more, rather than less, jelly and cream. Then he'd retire to his study. She intended to approach him when he had a full belly.

Everything went according to plan, except she couldn't stomach one mouthful of her own lunch so it ended up in the pig bucket. As soon as the study door clicked shut, she went and knocked.

"Come in."

She swung open the door and hovered.

"Well? What is it?" He looked up from his copy of *The Morpeth Want* and threw her an irritated glance.

"Could you spare me a moment, Reverend Lodestar?"

"Can't it wait? I'm quite exhausted."

The temptation to back away and close the door swamped her. She clamped her jaw tight. "It's quite important." More than quite. A life in the balance. Two lives, truth be told. Suffer the little children . . .

With infinite care he folded the paper and then looked up. "Don't stand there with that cow-eyed look, prevaricating. Close the door."

A lot more than prevaricating was going on; her heart was beating so fast, echoing in her ears, she could hardly hear him, never mind breathe. Why had she taken matters into her own hands? She should have insisted that Sid come with her.

"Well?"

She licked her lips, swallowed the taste of bile. "Sid . . . Sid Binks and I have been walking out. He's asked me to marry him and we wondered if you—"

He raised his hand to halt her. "Take off your pinafore."

What? Why? A cold sweat skimmed her forehead. She'd heard stories of churchmen who did things that didn't bear thinking about rather than break their vows and marry, but the reverend wasn't Catholic. He could take a wife. Everyone expected him to. Why else would all those women bring their daughters to his Friday At Homes and parade them in front of him? Not that he ever showed a flicker of interest. "I beg your pardon." Her voice squeaked.

"You heard me. Unfasten your pinafore."

Her fingers flopped like raw sausages as she fumbled with the ties, pulled the pinafore over her head, and bunched it in her fist.

"Now turn and face the window."

She pivoted on her heels, unable to frame a coherent thought.

"It seems that for once the local gossip is accurate. When is the event?"

An embarrassing whoosh of air slipped between her lips and her hands came up to cradle her belly. No point in trying to hide now. "I don't know exactly."

"And what do you intend to do about it?"

The silence hung as heavy as her head, and then she lifted her chin. She had to do this, tell him, ask for his assistance. "Sid and I are going to get married, but we can't afford for me to stop working, so we've decided to wait. There's a midwife in town and I can have the baby there. If I could keep working until my time came, then I could be back in a few days and she'd look after the baby. It wouldn't make no difference— just a day or two off. And then . . . the Bible says suffer little children . . ."

Whatever possessed her to say that?

Two patches of red spread like spilt jam across the reverend's cheeks until his whole face resembled a squashed plum. "You come to me with a belly full of arms and legs and expect God's forgiveness?" He rose to his feet and towered over her. "My house, the house of the Lord, will not give succor to wanton whores."

Beads of sweat popped out across her forehead. "But Sid and me, we're going to—"

"Get out! And do not darken my door again. May the wrath of God visit just deserts on you and your heathen child."

Clarrie's stomach twisted and her hands reached to protect Charlie from the foul filth spewing from the reverend's mouth. Her temper snapped. "You're nothing but a nasty, dirty, evil, self-centered man. I wouldn't stay here if it was the last place on God's earth." And with that she flounced from the room, then belted up the stairs as fast as her swollen ankles would carry her.

It took only a matter of moments for her to collect her belongings, stuff them into a bundle, and toss her cloak over her shoulders. She galloped down the stairs in a flash, paused at the kitchen, shot a look at the reverend's open study door, but thought better.

Throwing back her shoulders, she stuck her nose in the air and marched across the polished floorboards, making sure her heels sounded every step, then flung open the front door and sashayed outside and through the gate without a backward glance. The Reverend Lodestar could take his pompous, highfalutin airs and graces and stuff them up his proverbial . . .

Once Clarrie reached the river she stopped to draw a breath. Her bundle of belongings slid from her fingers. A fierce stitch shot through her insides and turned her legs to jelly. She slumped against the trunk of a tree and slid slowly down, knees bent, and tried to calm herself. Her bellyful of arms and legs took on a life of its own, kicking and twisting and punching, fighting against the tight confines of her dress. "Charlie, shh! It's all right. You're safe. We're safe. We'll find your dad soon. He'll look after us."

"Too right he will." Sid dropped down on his haunches beside her and ran a roughened hand across her forehead, brushing back her sweaty hair. "Take it easy. You'll be fine."

Would she? She snatched in a gasp. "I think Charlie's coming."

"No, he's not. You've just shaken him up. It's not time yet."

And how would Sid know?

His cool hand smoothed her hair in slow, rhythmic sweeps and he dropped a kiss on her cheek. "So the reverend didn't take it too well."

She shook her head, not game to speak.

"Settle down, catch your breath, and I'll tell you our plan." His calming words wrapped around her like a warm hug and her head dropped onto his shoulder. The football match in her belly slowed and she offered Sid a half-hearted smile.

"That's better. Here, sip this." He handed her a beer bottle. "It's not ale. Just sip it slowly."

The cool water eased her rasping throat.

"That's good. Feeling a little better now?"

"Oh, Sid. He was so horrible. And I shouted back at him. He called me a whore." The word caught on a sob and she clamped her lips together. She wouldn't let the stinking man get the better of her. "He told me not to darken his door. So I grabbed my things and barged out the front door. I left it wide open."

"That's my girl. Now, do you want to hear the plan?"

She nodded again and took another sip of water.

"I spoke to Maud, the midwife. She said she needs to meet you. Find out when Charlie's likely to come because she's got others she's promised to help."

Others made her feel a little less alone. Other women who maybe had nowhere to go and no one to help them. She reached for Sid's hand and squeezed it. "When can we see her?"

"I told her I'd call in again this afternoon."

"But you didn't know the reverend would kick me out."

"No, I didn't, but either way you were going to need her help and she'd want to see you." He stood up and held out his hand. "Think you're good to stand now?"

Her head swam as Sid pulled her to her feet, but once she stood upright the world fell back into place. She'd made it down to the river to their spot without knowing.

He slung her belongings over his shoulder, then wrapped his other arm around her. "Come on. We'll take the tow path. It's not too far, nice and slow, just to the end of Swan Street. It's a pretty little cottage. We could do with a place like that." He squeezed her arm. "Charlie behaving now, is he?"

"Yes, he is."

"So we're settled on Charlie then."

"Unless he's a she . . . then she could be Charlotte, and you could still call her Charlie."

"I reckon you've got an answer for everything."

Sadly she hadn't, but Sid had come up with a few, and most importantly they were in it together. She'd known from that first time she'd met him how he'd be. She'd no idea how she'd known. Perhaps it was the way he'd looked at her: not like other people, but really looked as though he could see inside her, to her very soul.

The rest of their walk passed in a cozy silence, Sid's arm firm and strong as she leaned into him. Not because she needed to be propped up, more because he made her feel safe. As though together they could sort this through.

They found Maud's house, which was, as Sid had said, a pretty little cottage. A picket fence and a gate, not much of a garden, but the way to the door marked in stones. She must have passed it a hundred times but never paid much attention, not knowing what went on behind the front door. She'd always thought families of the workers employed on the wharves or the railway lived there, but maybe times had changed.

Sid knocked on the front door and after a few moments it swung open to reveal an apple-cheeked woman, younger than Clarrie expected, arms full of a sleeping baby who didn't stir when she propped it against her shoulder. "So you're back. And this must be Clarrie. Come inside, lovey, and take the weight off."

Clarrie followed her down the hallway, past a series of closed doors, and out into a room at the back furnished with a scrubbed table and a couple of faded stuffed chairs in front of a glowing fire. "Sit yourself down. I'll be back in a moment." She retraced her steps down the hallway and disappeared through one of the doors.

"What do you think?" Sid rested his hands on her shoulders.

Clarrie shrugged. The room looked clean and the woman seemed friendly enough, a nice little fire burned in the grate, and she couldn't hear any crying babies. Through the window a row of white cloths dangled from a washing line, blowing in the breeze. "Let's wait and see what she says. I've never done this before."

Sid spluttered a laugh. "Neither have I, but I promise you we'll do better next time."

A moment later the woman came back without the baby, a clean apron covering her well-worn skirt. "So, Clarrie, you're looking to have your baby soon."

Clarrie's hands came up to cover her belly as Maud studied her body. Charlie lay all quiet now she'd got over her mad rush. "Not for a while."

"That so. I'll take a look at you. Off you go, Mr. Sid. Take yourself out into the backyard or up the road a bit. Give us ten, maybe fifteen minutes."

Clarrie's stomach, Charlie included, took a dive and she reached for Sid's hand.

"You'll be fine. He won't be far away. This is women's business." Maud rested her hand on her shoulder. "Off you go, Sid."

With a frail smile, Sid took himself down the hallway. The door closed behind him.

"Come on, now. Take off that cloak and hop up on the table, here." Maud unrolled a blanket and laid it on top of the scrubbed table and then covered it with a large, somewhat stained white cloth, but Clarrie could tell from the scent of soap and sunshine that filled the room that it was clean.

After a series of questions and a lot of poking around under her skirts, all too embarrassing to dwell on, Maud gave Clarrie a shrewd look. "Unless I'm mistaken, and I'm rarely wrong, you've got four, maybe six weeks at most. I don't know how you've managed to hide it, but you're just a slip of a girl and carrying tight. I guess an unmarried man of the cloth doesn't have too much experience with expecting women. Someone must have tipped him off and that's why he gave you the push. Did you not have any sickness?"

"No, none at all."

For a moment the vision of the woman dressed in black at last Friday's At Home slipped into Clarrie's thoughts. The way she'd scrutinized her and the need she'd felt to shield herself and Charlie behind the flowers. But if she'd said anything to the reverend he wouldn't have waited until Sunday to have a go at her. "He didn't sack me. Least, not until I told him. Then he called me a whore and kicked me out." The now-familiar coil of anger twisted her insides, disturbing Charlie.

Maud gave a dismissive snort. "Men are bad enough. Men of the cloth even worse. Still firmly convinced women can do it all by themselves, like the Virgin Mary."

"You don't truly think Charlie will be here so soon, do you?"

"Charlie?"

Clarrie patted her stomach, then swung her legs over the side of the table. "The baby. Sid's convinced he's a boy."

"Right. Right. Have you thought about what you're going to do in the meantime now the very reverend reverend has kicked you out? Sid said you're in need of a place to stay."

Clarrie dropped her head into her hands. So much had happened so quickly. "I don't know what I'm going to do. I've got nowhere to go."

"What about Sid? Go and live with him."

"We're not married."

"You and half the people in the colony, I reckon."

"I can't live with Sid. He bunks down in the basement at the newspaper offices. I can't take a baby there, and besides, Mr. Kendall wouldn't let it happen. And we can't rent anything. We've got some savings, but not enough. I can't get another job like the one I had." For the first time since Charlie had made his presence known, she wished they'd thought a bit more about it instead of getting carried away. She let out a mournful wail. "I've been so stupid."

"No, love, not stupid. Why don't you go and call that young

man of yours and tell him Charlie's doing fine, and I'll put the kettle on and we'll have a bit of a chat about this lying-in."

Clarrie heaved herself up. A wave of dizziness swamped her, weighed down by Charlie's presence and the reality of it all. Just as well the reverend had kicked her out; she couldn't imagine running up and down the stairs at his beck and call much longer.

Clarrie found Sid leaning against the gatepost chatting to Archer. Gossiping more than like. The two of them were as thick as thieves, always sticking their noses into other people's business—following leads, she corrected herself. Following leads. If Sid truly did want to be a newspaperman, he had to know what was going on, at least that was his excuse. Maybe she shouldn't nag about it, otherwise he wouldn't have found Maud. "You can come back in now."

He gave her a broad smile. "Everything all right?"

"Yes and no."

He must have heard the tremor in her voice because he flicked his head in Archer's direction and the boy took off like Stephenson's Rocket. "What is it?"

"Seems like Charlie might be here sooner than we thought."

"How much sooner?"

"In a month or so."

His face blanched as he took a good look at her stomach, which seemed to be growing by the moment. "Right, well, no time to waste. What does Maud want?"

"To talk about lying-in. I'm worried, Sid. What if we haven't got enough money? I'm not going to get a job looking like this." She sketched a wave over her stomach and then felt a tug in her heart. She couldn't blame Charlie for the mess they'd got into. "Come on."

He followed her down the hallway and back into the

kitchen where Maud had the kettle on the boil and the makings of a pot of tea.

"Ah, there you both are. Sit yourselves down and we'll have a nice cup of tea and a chat."

Clarrie eased into the chair by the fire. She wanted to know what it would cost. She'd worry about the rest once she knew they could afford her lying-in. She'd heard stories about girls caught out, having to have their baby in some dark and dismal alleyway. Charlie deserved more than that.

Sid propped himself on the arm of the chair and his hand came down over hers and stilled the drumming of her fingers. "Clarrie tells me Charlie's going to be with us sooner than we thought."

"That's my opinion, though you never know with babies. They come when they're ready."

Clarrie's mouth dried. She couldn't just sit here, take tea, and chat. "How will I know when to come here?"

Maud pushed a cup across the table toward her. "You'll know. When the pains come. Have you not had any experience of birthing babies? Not your mother, sister, aunt, any of the like?"

"No, nothing. I'm an only child. No family other than my mother." The last person on God's earth she wanted to think about.

"And where's she, might I ask?"

"Sydney."

"And you don't want to go to her?"

"I can't. I just can't." Clarrie screwed up her face. She didn't want to have to explain the whole horrible story to Maud. It was none of her business. Maud's business was helping girls have babies, not fixing the unfixable.

Sid gave her hand another squeeze. "I've got no experience

either. So can you explain what happens, what you do, and how much it'll cost?"

Thank goodness for Sid. She rested her head back against the chair.

Maud's lips twitched into a smile. "I can promise you I won't be calling any storks for help. Clarrie will know when her pains start and you bring her here. Once the baby's born she can spend a few days recovering and then you're all set. I'm busy. Got five little ones here at the moment, but a couple of those will be going soon."

"Going? Going where?"

"To their new families."

Next thing Clarrie knew she was on her feet. "No. We don't want to give Charlie away, do we, Sid?" That wasn't what would happen to Charlie.

"Settle down, lovey. There's lots of alternatives, all of which we can talk about once the baby is born. Now, as to the charges. Twelve shillings all up for the lying-in and then nine shillings a week to look after the baby. And you can come and visit once a week on your day off. Providing, that is, you can find yourself another job. Does that suit?"

Sid reached out with the pad of his thumb and wiped away the tear trickling down Clarrie's cheek. What was the matter with her? She never cried. Not when her mother had accused her of stealing her beau; not when she'd arrived home to find her belongings bundled on the doorstep; not even when the reverend used her as a whipping post.

Sid pushed back his chair. "You've got a deal, Maud. Thank you. Come along, Clarrie. Time to get going. I'll call in tomorrow with the money. We need to find somewhere for Clarrie to spend the night; she's had it."

Clarrie placed her palms flat on the table and attempted to heave to her feet. The room tilted and a great roaring filled her ears. The world spun, black spots danced in front of her eyes, and the floor came up to meet her.

CHAPTER 7

SYDNEY, 1922

The wintery evening air dampened Verity's face and each breath formed a puff of mist as she pedaled. The promise of tomorrow hovered, keeping her warm as her thoughts churned and her blood pumped.

The past five days since the ball had crawled. After she'd lost sight of the troubadour, she'd made her way back to the Town Hall, waited until after midnight for everyone to remove their masks, then caught the last tram home. She'd written a brief piece about the Artists' Ball the next morning and dropped it off to Mr. Bailey, who'd seemed quite impressed. He'd loved the detail of the costumes and decorations, and chuckled at her recount of the two-up game and the list of Sydney's social elite revealed on the stroke of midnight.

But no matter how hard she'd tried, she couldn't concentrate on job hunting. Pages and pages of classifieds blurred into a mass of infuriation. Hundreds of job opportunities for men, many she'd gladly jump at. If she'd been happy to take a job as a dressmaker or domestic, she could pick and choose, but none of those positions entertained the possibility of a woman with a working knowledge of shorthand and typing.

It was all Grandpa Sid's fault.

He'd insisted she should attend the Metropolitan Business College and made her practice her shorthand every night by taking down the words he read from the newspaper, then making her repeat them back to him, checking she hadn't missed a single phrase.

She couldn't see the point of it all now. Why couldn't a job be allocated on merit? Not like her job at *The Arrow*, which she had because she was Charlie Binks's poor daughter who'd lost her father to the war and her grandparents to the influenza.

In her darkest moments after Grandpa Sid's death, she'd railed against fate, left all alone in the world without another person she could claim as a relation. Grandma Clarrie had told her Charlie had wished for a boy to follow in his footsteps. Quite what poor Ma had thought she'd never know, although Grandma Clarrie insisted everyone loved her enough to make up for her loss.

Now they had all gone.

She shook away her maudlin thoughts. Thanks to Grandpa Sid she had a roof over her head and the ability to earn a living, maybe even make a name for herself. The unexpected invitation to the Artists' Ball had given her the opportunity to write another article for Mr. Bailey, and when she'd told him about the Treadwell story, he'd asked to look at that too. If the stars aligned she might well have it ready before too long.

Head buzzing with the few facts she'd managed to acquire about the Treadwell Foundation, Verity swerved to avoid a Tooth's dray and narrowly missed becoming sandwiched between it and a tram. She swung into Broadway. The Foundation was longstanding, held in high regard, offering a service to young girls who found themselves in a precarious position. They claimed to help them reestablish their lives, providing homes for the poor unfortunate babies and thus making childless couples complete. Nothing that smacked of anything but a short, sharp article praising the altruistic efforts of Mr. Treadwell, member of numerous boards and highly respected citizen of Sydney who'd opened his house to the needy.

Mr. Treadwell had stipulated eleven o'clock on Saturday morning—tomorrow—for their meeting and said he would answer any questions she might have. Unfortunately, she couldn't think of many to ask other than the one thing that she couldn't put aside: Was he responsible for the invitation and her costume?

She'd gone over every aspect of the evening. The troubadour's strange introduction to Treadwell, his knowledge of her name and his comment about her costume fitting, and Treadwell's mention of Charlie were all most peculiar. Perhaps the troubadour was acting for Treadwell. How she wished she hadn't lost sight of him in the crowds outside the Town Hall. He'd said they'd speak again after she'd visited Treadwell House. But why?

She stood on the pedals, forcing her bicycle to gather speed as she entered The Cut, her vision fixed firmly on the lights marking the end of the tunnel, and sped through with her heart in her mouth.

She coasted down the incline and along Argyle Street. She'd lived all her life in The Rocks and never suffered a moment's concern about her well-being. Everyone knew her, from the tram drivers to the shopkeepers and publicans; called her Old Sid's girl. They all kept an eye out for her. Perhaps the peculiar sense she'd had of being watched over the last weeks had been the troubadour following her home. Is that how he'd known where to have the parcel delivered?

None of it made any sense. She had to ask Treadwell, and

then, if the troubadour contacted her, she might be able to ferret out the rest of the story. Grandpa Sid always said she should trust her instincts. If she wanted to be a journalist, she must get both sides of the story and uncover the truth. And remember the five questions: Who? What? When? Where? And most importantly, why?

On the dot of eleven the next morning, Verity raised her hand to the brass lion-head knocker adorning the shiny black door of Treadwell House. A slight breeze from the harbor tugged at her hair and brought the clang of the halyards and the tang of brine with an underlying taint of coal smoke. She twisted around to admire the view stretching out toward the Heads, an uninterrupted route to the rest of the world, populated by craft of every size and shape imaginable. She shook out her cloche and rammed it back on her head.

"Good morning."

Verity spun around and smiled at the girl in her black uniform and lace-edged apron. Not exactly what she had imagined. For some reason the description of the foundation she'd unearthed had led her to envisage a hospital-like scenario with a starched, large-nosed matron and an aroma of disinfectant, not this palatial Greek temple.

"Good morning. I'm here to see Mr. Treadwell."

"He's not available." A wash of color tinted the girl's face, filling Verity with an enormous, and somewhat strange, sense of anticipation. "We're not taking clients at the moment."

Verity smothered a snort and smoothed down her skirt, hoping to make it obvious that she didn't need the services the foundation provided. "Mr. Treadwell asked me to call when I met him last week at the Artists' Ball."

Why in heaven's name was she explaining herself? She lifted her chin and peered down her nose.

"Please inform Mr. Treadwell that Verity Binks is here, as arranged." She took a step forward but the door closed, leaving her standing on the step, face plastered against the paint.

Jumped-up little miss. Verity rearranged her cloche again and looked down at her dusty shoes with a grimace. She lifted her foot and buffed her toe on the back of her stocking. Thank heavens she'd had the foresight to leave her bicycle at home.

A few moments later the door reopened. "Mr. Treadwell says he'll be with you in a moment. You are to wait in the library." The maid swung the oversize door wide. "Follow me."

The girl's heels tip-tapped across the chessboard tiles as she led the way through the domed hallway, past a wide, sweeping staircase to a closed door. She stopped on the left of the hallway and stood back to allow Verity to step inside.

The door closed behind her with a clunk.

A small desk with carved legs and a mass of drawers and cubbyholes stood between two huge floor-to-ceiling sash windows overlooking the rose garden and, beyond, the view of the sparkling harbor. An array of shelves holding row after row of identical leather-bound books in a variety of reds, greens, blacks, and tans, as straight as soldiers on parade, covered the other three walls.

Verity wandered around the room, running her finger over the books' ridged spines and down the embossed writing and came to rest on a set of Charles Dickens novels. She hooked her finger over her favorite, *Great Expectations*, and tilted it, releasing a hint of leather and beeswax polish. Six books slanted toward her, all perfectly bound but empty. Faux. Not a single sheet of paper. Simply a row of conjoined leather-covered spines. Nothing but an illusion. Her imagination took flight.

Somewhere there had to be a secret door. She ran her hand down the edges of the shelves and pressed various corners, but her wishful fantasy proved futile.

With her hands behind her back, she strolled over to the marble fireplace where a watercolor sat, not hung but propped against the chimney breast. Not at all what she would have imagined. No pastoral scene or windswept seascape, this was a botanical drawing. A butterfly hovering above a plant with masses of tiny red and pink flowers and, in the background, a beautiful stone house sitting on a small rise overlooking a sweeping expanse of water, the sparkling sunlight imbuing the entire painting with a magical golden glow. Below the illustration a title, the ink somewhat faded:

Wanderer Butterfly, *Danaus plexippus*
The Landing, Hunter River, Morpeth

Morpeth! Grandpa Sid had lived in Morpeth. That's where he'd met Grandma Clarrie, but she doubted it would have been in a house as fine as the one depicted in the painting. She lifted the picture and tilted it toward the light. Only then did the colors of the butterfly register. Orange and black with a band of white dots rimming the wings—the same colors as the cape she'd worn to the ball. She reached one hand to her chest to still her heart as she pulled the painting closer, studying the details.

It couldn't be a coincidence; Treadwell must be responsible for the invitation and the costume. She would ask him as soon as he made his presence known. She'd had enough of this shilly-shallying and skullduggery.

A shadow fell across the painting. She lifted her head.

"I apologize for keeping you waiting. I see you have made yourself at home."

Heat flew to her cheeks and her mouth dried. "Mr. Treadwell. I . . . Yes . . . What a wonderful painting."

"Shall we sit down?" He took the painting from her hand, waved her to one of the two winged chairs fronting the fireplace, and put the picture on the oval occasional table before sitting opposite her. "It is delightful, isn't it? My mother found it in a little gallery in the Strand Arcade. It's unsigned, but she believes it might have been painted by either Harriet or Helena Scott, the botanical artists. Are you familiar with their work?"

"They paint Christmas cards, don't they?" There'd been a couple propped up on the mantelpiece at home for years. She'd put them away only a few weeks ago in some vain attempt to sort out Grandpa Sid's belongings. She hadn't got very far.

"A little more than Christmas cards. They were renowned artists and professional illustrators. Unusual for two women to distinguish themselves in the scientific world. Due largely, of course, to their father's support."

Her mind seesawed again. Perhaps the very strange coincidence of the dress she'd worn to the ball matching the butterfly in the painting was nothing more than that—a twist of fate— but the house in the background sparked a visceral memory. Grandpa Sid and Grandma Clarrie rarely spoke of their early life in Morpeth, but the connection wasn't lost on her.

"It's very kind of you to see me." She licked her lips, trying to find the words to ask if the painting held any particular significance, but the moment slipped away.

"Let us get down to business." Treadwell rubbed his hands together. "As I mentioned at the ball, I require a history written of the foundation. After all, it is only right and proper that people should be aware of the work we do and the sacrifices we make. I would also like to use the history in our new prospectus. The fact you work for *The Sydney Arrow* is an added bonus."

Verity opened her mouth to explain the arrangement she had with Mr. Bailey, then snapped it shut. It would be madness to jeopardize this opportunity.

"We rely heavily on donations and any publicity is greatly to our advantage." He rubbed his hands together again, his lizardy skin making an unpleasant scratchy sound. "Where shall we start?"

Ask a question, an open-ended question. Let the person speak, and with any luck nervousness, or in the case of Mr. Treadwell, pomposity, would take over. People felt the need to fill silences. *Who. What. When. Why* . . . Grandpa Sid's voice echoed.

"Who started the Treadwell Foundation?" Verity tipped her head and folded her hands neatly in her lap.

"My mother founded the charity after my father died. She felt she would like to help the women of Sydney—from various echelons of society, you understand. And more recently women left destitute by the loss of a loved one to the war. We are still losing so many of our returned soldiers." He laced his fingers together and rested them on his chest. "Would you like to take some notes?"

What was the matter with her? Her attention kept straying to the painting of the black and orange butterfly. His mother had founded the charity. Had she sent the invitation and the costume? It seemed far more likely a woman would be responsible for such an elaborate dress. She dived into her satchel and brought out a pencil and notepad purchased specifically for the meeting, and waited with rapt attention.

"We offer a haven for young women who have fallen by the

wayside. A sanctuary. A place where they can rest and recuperate before resuming their life."

All very well and good, but then what? "And once they leave?" Presumably they must find somewhere to live and sufficient funds to bring up their child, or did the foundation continue to support them?

"Many of our clients simply want to start their life anew. In that situation, we find placements for the children in private homes. Childless couples who wish to make their family whole. It's a situation that benefits both parties. Since my mother started the foundation over thirty years ago, many girls have passed through our doors and have gone on to lead far better lives, their indiscretions forgotten."

Verity offered silent thanks to Grandpa Sid as her pencil flew across the paper, the curls, dots, and dashes of her much-practiced Pitman shorthand coming into its own. The Treadwell Foundation was no different from those places she'd heard of in the country. Once the child was born it would be adopted out and the mother would return to her life as though nothing had changed, some story put about that she'd been visiting relatives or traveling. She looked up and raised her eyebrows, hoping her silence would encourage Mr. Treadwell to continue.

"Of course, we make no charge for facilitating the arrangements."

Verity tapped her pencil against her teeth while she picked the most suitable words. "It sounds most admirable." But hardly enough to make a story. She flipped the page in her notebook and took a quick look at Grandpa Sid's list: *What?* She ticked that off and circled *Who?* "Would it be possible to have a look around? Perhaps meet some of the women under your care?"

"I can certainly show you the grounds and our vacant

rooms at some stage. You must understand that our guests would not wish their stay to be publicized. It's a question of confidentiality."

Verity mentally kicked herself. How foolish of her to imagine that anyone would be happy to discuss an illicit pregnancy. "I can provide a guarantee names would not be included in the article." Grandpa Sid said a good journalist never revealed his sources. Neither would she. A curl of excitement coiled in her insides. Such a wonderful opportunity. "And your aim is to raise awareness and encourage further donations?"

"Indeed, it is. I will, of course, need to see your piece before it goes to publication."

Her attention strayed to the painting on the table again.

"I presume you have sufficient information."

No. Nowhere near enough. Her pencil hovered over the *Why?* A very good question. What made a wealthy widow dedicate her life to helping others? Something must have prompted his mother to start the foundation. "Would it be possible to speak with Mrs. Treadwell?"

"Unfortunately she is indisposed and not receiving visitors. And . . ." He leaned forward, enveloping her in a cloud of pomade and tobacco. "I would like to do this for her. A gesture of recognition for her admirable work."

One more question, not one on her list. Not related at all. "You said your mother bought this picture." She gestured to the table between them. "Did your family come from the Hunter?"

"The Hunter? No, not at all. I'm directly descended from Oliver Treadwell, one of the early free settlers in the colony. He received a grant of land and built this house. I was born beneath this very roof, as were the last three generations of the Treadwell family."

"But your mother's family?"

Treadwell paused for a moment, fiddling with his pocket watch. "That is in no way relevant." He scratched at his neck. "As I said, when my father passed, my mother felt the need to involve herself in charitable works. It's such a large house. What better use than to share our bounty?" He ran his finger around the inside of his collar.

Her muscles tensed. Why would the man encourage her to write about his mother's work if he wasn't prepared to tell the full story? "Do you have any papers relating to the history of this house and the Treadwell family?"

His face brightened and he moved to the desk and opened the center drawer. He scooped out a few odds and ends: a magnifying glass, a beautiful Waterman fountain pen, a bottle of ink, some envelopes, a skein of embroidery silk, and a packet of needles. "My mother is responsible for the day-to-day running of the foundation, and this is her domain. I believe there may be something here." He dumped a pile of papers and a large red notebook on the desk, rummaged a little deeper, and removed a thick manila folder bound by a blue ribbon. "The history of the Treadwell Foundation. You'll find everything you need here."

Verity tucked her notes into her satchel and slipped the pencil into the front pocket before reaching for the folder and the book. "May I take these with me?"

"The folder, yes." He picked up the red notebook and fanned the pages. "Ah! Just the record of accounts." He pinned her with a steely stare, and a hair-prickling draft grazed her skin as though someone silently watched her. She glanced over her shoulder and caught the click of the door closing. "Miss Binks, may I speak in confidence?"

Almost expecting him to drop his voice to a whisper, she slipped the folder into her satchel and leaned forward.

"As you rightly surmised, my mother does have a connection with the Hunter. She spent time in Morpeth as a child and has fond memories of the house in the painting. The property sold many years ago, and she's never had the opportunity to return. Any overtures she made were stonewalled." He picked up the painting, glanced at it, then placed it facedown. "My point, when I let it be known that I required a history written, was to concentrate on the foundation and the work it has done for nigh on thirty years in Sydney, as a tribute to my mother and her philanthropic venture. I see no reason to bring her past into the equation. In fact, I would rather the Treadwell name was not connected with Morpeth."

"I understand." She didn't, but he'd aroused her interest. "I would, however, like to speak to Mrs. Treadwell. It would be very helpful. I needn't mention the article."

"I shall see what I can organize."

"Thank you. And perhaps I could follow up with some of the families who have adopted children."

He didn't reply, simply delved into his pocket and brought out a card, a replica of the one he'd given her at the ball. "My telephone number is here. Contact me in a week when you have had time to study the paperwork. We'll discuss your progress." He headed toward the door—a definite sign of her dismissal.

She slipped the card into her pocket, picked up her satchel, and followed him into the hallway. She couldn't leave it. She had to ask. "Mr. Treadwell?"

He spun on the heel of his immaculately polished shoe and raised an eyebrow.

"When we were introduced at the Artists' Ball, you seemed to know a lot about me. Did you send me the invitation?"

"I beg your pardon?"

"An invitation and costume for the ball were delivered to my house. I thought perhaps . . ."

Treadwell took a step closer to her, scrutinizing her from the top of her head down to the tips of her still-dusty shoes. "One of the organizers suggested I speak with you. As I said, I knew of your father's service. Please see Miss Binks out, Mary."

"Thank you, Mr. Treadwell. I'll be in touch."

Mary's smirk, and the sound of the front door closing behind her, removed the last traces of skin-crawling the episode caused and brought Verity up sharp. Treadwell didn't seem to have any knowledge of the invitation. The troubadour must have acted for Mrs. Treadwell, but if that were the case, why had he disappeared into the night?

CHAPTER 8

MORPETH, 1868

Theodora lay motionless while the clouds of swirling orange, black, and white dissipated. She leaned out of the bed and picked up her sketchbook from the floor. The letter she had written to Harriet and Helena and tucked inside the pages fell onto the counterpane. Clenching her fist against the temptation to screw up her paltry illustration, she wrinkled her nose. What would the sisters think? Most likely that every tiny piece of her talent they had nurtured had evaporated since they'd left Ash Island. If only she had managed to net the butterfly, but the sheer magic of it had stunned her.

She bounded out of bed, threw on her clothes, stuffed the letter into her paint box, and hurried downstairs. What had attracted the butterfly to the garden? Some plant or flower? She knew well enough that each species had their favorite. Flowers for nectar to nurture them, plants where they laid their eggs, the leaves food for the larvae once they hatched and a haven for the pupae. Why hadn't she looked more carefully yesterday? Perhaps somewhere in the garden the butterfly had laid her eggs. She'd make one more attempt to find some further evidence before she went into Morpeth to post the letter.

A low mist hung over the river, bringing the promise of a fine, warm autumn day as she ran through the grass. The brightness of the flowers gave her hope. She worked her way around the lush beds, the strong scent of the herbs teasing her senses.

But not a butterfly or any eggs in sight.

Toward the back wall, the woody stems of the cotton bush drew her; their seedpods had been a source of constant amusement when she was a child. As the seeds swelled and darkened, they exploded with the slightest encouragement, leaving a fluffy ball of cotton. The birds stole it for their nests and strangely, Hench, Papa's man of all work, liked to collect it, but Mama had grown it for its petite, star-shaped flowers in a range of intense and glorious pinks, reds, and oranges. As yet, only a few seedpods had formed. She snapped off the spent flowers, hoping there might be more before the days shortened.

Lost in her musing, she started when a shadow fell across her feet.

"Redmond. You made me jump!" Her heart lifted. Redmond and Jamie had been inseparable when they were growing up, but even before the accident, old Mr. Kendall's illness had meant Redmond had to take over the newspaper and he hadn't time to spend at The Landing anymore.

"I'm on my way back from Hinton; Father took another turn. I haven't seen any of you in such a long time. How are you?" He held out a hand to help her up.

"I'm well, thank you. Has your father recovered?"

"The same. Grumpy, bad-tempered, unable to come to terms with his lot. What are you up to?"

"Just tidying up a little." She wiped her hands on her skirt, the sticky residue from the cotton bush coating her skin. "Now Hench is caretaking for Mr. Scott, the jobs are mounting. We can't survive without any help. I'd hate to see Mama's garden go to wrack and ruin. What are you doing here today?"

"Checking the pipes. Bit of a problem with the reticulation." He bent to the small pond in the center of the garden and ran his fingers across the surface. "No problems here." He pulled some rogue weeds from between the surrounding flagstones. "I could give you a hand if you like."

"You?" She couldn't see Redmond as a gardener. His skills lay in other areas. He'd completed his apprenticeship with Papa's steamship company as an engineer, and he and Jamie had designed the waterworks, Papa's pride and joy. A system of pipes beneath the ground that took the water from the river and supplied the house and kept the gardens green even in the hottest of summers.

Everyone knew Redmond had stepped into his father's shoes because he had no option. *The Morpeth Want* was the lifeblood of the river community but about as far away from engineering, Redmond's first love, as a man could get.

"I'm good with a shovel. I could spare an hour or two."

"I couldn't ask you."

"I'd like to help, and I might know just the person to come on a regular basis. He does a bit of running around for me at the newspaper." Redmond lifted his hand to his forehead against the sun. "There's a bit to do. Archer's a young lad, full of energy, and could do with a few extra shillings. Wouldn't set you back as much as Hench."

"It's more having to organize it." Theodora sighed. So many changes in such a short time. "I'll speak to Mrs. Barnett.

She's got a far better understanding of the household finances than I have." She bent down and reached for the pile of offcuts lying on the grass. "I saw an unusual butterfly down here yesterday. Orange and black with tiny white dots all around the edges of its wings. Have you ever seen one like that?"

"Not that I've noticed." His lips curled into a faint, rueful smile. "I haven't got a lot of time to spend admiring butterflies. Shame the Scott sisters have gone. They were the ones for butterflies."

"I've written a letter to them, but I'm searching for eggs. I haven't found any. I tried to catch the butterfly when it was hovering over the cotton bushes." She scratched at her hands. Burning, itchy red welts covered her fingers. "I think I've been bitten."

He took her hands in his and rolled them over. "That doesn't look good. Go and wash them." He picked up one of the stems she'd broken off. "See the sap? White and sticky. It's probably that. Better ask the Hedge Witch for one of her potions."

"Redmond! She's not a witch. Her mother passed on her herbal knowledge and she has merely followed a family tradition."

His deep, rumbling laugh welled and he slapped his thigh. "I miss Jamie."

When Jamie had come up with the title Hedge Witch, he'd incurred Mama's wrath, and on one occasion Papa's belt, but he'd refused to give up, said anyone who knew as much about herbs, tinctures, and tonics had to be a witch. Mrs. Barnett had established a business for herself selling her lotions and salves to shops in Morpeth, Maitland, and even as far afield as Newcastle.

Redmond took off his jacket and pulled down the sleeves

of his shirt to cover his hands before scooping up the pile of offcuts. "You know the seedpods on these are great insulators. Hench reckons everyone used to pad out their jackets with the stuff in the Californian goldfields." He blew on one balanced on top of the pile and watched the boll drift away in the wind. "I expect that's how they come to be growing here. Amazing thing, nature. It won't take long to get the garden up to scratch. Can't have all your mother's hard work going to waste."

A sudden wave of misery swept over her. "It's not only the garden. Sometimes I feel as though nothing will ever be the same again, no one will ever be truly happy." Her voice caught. It wasn't as though she'd forgotten about Mama and Papa, but after Florence's announcement of a trip to Sydney they'd dominated her thoughts. "I miss Mama and Papa so much, and Jamie, and the lovely trips we used to make to Ash Island." She opened her paint box and brought out the letter she'd written last night. "Could you do something for me?"

He deposited the offcuts onto the burn pile on the other side of the low stone wall. "For you, anything."

Ignoring his glib remark, she held out the letter. "Could you post this for me when you go into Morpeth? It's for Helena and Harriet. I want to ask them if they can identify the butterfly I saw."

He glanced at the address before slipping it into his pocket. "I'll get it on the evening steamer. You're mightily taken with that butterfly, aren't you?"

"I am." She offered a smile but couldn't make it genuine. For some ridiculous reason tears welled behind her eyelids.

Redmond reached out toward her, his expression mirroring her distress. "I tell you what, why don't we take the boat out for a run?"

"Will you be able to manage it?" The words tumbled out of her mouth and she smiled to remove their sting.

He smirked at her. "Have you forgotten I installed the engine in the *Petrel*? I thought the arrangement was that I'd take care of it."

"I beg your pardon. I always think of it as Papa's boat."

He stuck his hands in his pockets, his scrutiny making the color rise to her cheeks. "When would you like to go?"

Tomorrow. She trapped the word before it could fly free. Florence and Mrs. Barnett would have an apoplexy if she took off in the boat with Redmond, unchaperoned. "Perhaps Viola could come too, if she's not too busy with her music." Not Florence or Constance. They would spoil the day with their fussing and feminine wiles. "Soon. I'll ask Viola. I miss the river so much, especially Ash Island. Even the mosquitoes and stinky mangroves."

"Sounds like that's a yes. Just let me know when. Go on, off you go. I'll speak to Archer about the garden. I'm sure he'll jump at it. I found him mumbling about money and poring over the classifieds with Sid only yesterday."

Theodora glanced up at Redmond. Sweat glistened on his face, and his shoulders heaved with the effort of moving a fallen boulder on the edge of the garden bed. He swiped back the unruly lock of hair covering his forehead and dusted his hands against his trousers.

"Take yourself up to the house and find the Hedge Witch before you scratch all the skin off your hands." He threw her a flippant smile and held out her sketchbook and paint box and she tucked them under her arm. "I'll send Archer up in the next few days or else I'll be back to give you a hand as soon as I can."

Theodora popped on her straw hat. "Thank you. I'll see

you soon." Lifting the hem of her skirt, she sprinted through the wildflower meadow and slipped through the kitchen straight into Mrs. Barnett.

"Slow down, slow down."

"Have you got a salve or lotion for my hands? I was working in the garden and I've got a rash." She held out her hands.

Mrs. Barnett examined them with an impatient sigh. "Cotton bush. Nasty. You know it's poisonous. Why didn't you have gloves on?"

Theodora shrugged. She couldn't remember anyone mentioning it was poisonous, but experience told her there was little point in making excuses. She scratched at her burning hands again.

"I'll get you some chamomile ointment." Mrs. Barnett reached for her chatelaine, the collection of keys, scissors, and other bits and pieces she wore attached to her belt, and opened a small cupboard behind the scullery door. "There'll be no more gardening until the rash has cleared up, and you'll have to wear a pair of cotton gloves. The sun will make it worse. You know perfectly well there are medicinal plants in the garden."

Why would a butterfly be attracted to a poisonous plant? "What about the birds and insects? Doesn't the cotton bush kill them? I saw a beautiful butterfly hovering near the spent flowers."

"Insects and birds know what's what. For us it's a question of how it's used—care must be taken. The sap removes warts, and the roots are good for dysentery. I use an infusion for Viola's asthma. It suppresses the cough."

Theodora scratched at the red blisters erupting on her hands. It seemed as though the top layer of her skin would burn off.

"Wash your hands with soap and water, and once they're dry apply the cream." Mrs. Barnett thumped a small brown jar onto the table. "It's time for lunch. I'll make your apologies."

The rash on Theodora's hands didn't improve over the next few days, and she spent most of her time at the small table that served as a desk in her bedroom. Littered across the floor were piles of fruitless attempts to recreate the butterfly. Much to her surprise, Mrs. Barnett had encouraged her to remain inside, bringing frequent trays and a continuous supply of salve for her hands.

She studied her latest effort and wrinkled her nose. She couldn't get the pattern on the wings right. With a sigh, she collected the drawings and put them into the drawer, then peered out of the window.

A boy ambled up the path, his nose in the air as he gazed up at the roof and then behind him to the river. He looked young, not more than thirteen or fourteen, with a shock of tow-colored hair. She couldn't see his face, but his exuberant walk and general air of purpose made her think of Redmond and his offer to send someone to help her in the garden. He carried a large white letter in his hand. The mail never arrived this early; usually Wilcox took the rowboat across to collect it from the courthouse after lunch.

She belted down the stairs and out the door, coming to a slithering halt at the bottom of the steps as the boy rounded the curve in the driveway and reached the front of the house.

He doffed a nonexistent hat and grinned at her. "Miss Theodora?"

"Yes. Good morning."

"I'm Archer. Mr. Kendall told me you might be looking for

some help in the garden and I'm to deliver this. It came on this morning's steamer—a letter for you. He thought you might want it straightaway."

She took the thick folded paper, seeing at once the Scotts' trademark butterfly imprint on the seal. Her fingers itched to tear it open. "Thank you. Why don't we go to the stables and get the wheelbarrow and the tools, and I'll show you what needs doing." Mrs. Barnett and Florence would be less than impressed if she employed Archer without mentioning it, but today could be a trial run, and if he did a good afternoon's work she'd speak to them, and if he didn't—well, she'd pay him out of her pin money and that would be the end of that.

Archer barely came up to her shoulder, but he had no trouble pushing the barrow laden with a shovel and rake, Mama's prized secateurs, and a pair of long, thick gloves.

"This was my mama's garden." She gestured to the sandstone wall surrounding the profusion of flowers and herbs. "There's a lot of deadheading to prepare for winter and a layer of straw needs to be laid around the plants. You must take care with some of them. Some are poisonous and others can irritate your skin. Make sure you have gloves on and don't eat anything."

He threw her a wink. "No worries about that. Had a decent breakfast." He pulled on the gloves, which reached his elbow and gave him the look of one of the green frogs that frequented the bushes around the water tanks. "Where do you want me to start?"

"Over here would be best." She took him to the remains of the cotton bush. "It all needs to be cut down to ground level and then straw laid. But you must keep those gloves on. It'll give you a nasty rash." She flapped her white cotton–encased hands at him. "Stack it in the wheelbarrow, and if you go through the break in the wall and toward the clearing beyond the trees, you'll see the burn pile."

"Right you are." He set to work in a flurry of enthusiasm.

"I'll be over there." She pointed to the small circular pavilion overlooking the river, beyond the garden—Mama's most favored spot. She'd sit in the folly and wait for the first sighting of Papa when he returned from a trip. "Come and get me if you don't know what to do."

With the letter burning through her gloves, she turned away from Archer, peeled open the seal, and unfolded it. A smaller piece of paper fell to the ground and she trapped it beneath her boot, intent on reading the letter first.

Sydney
September 2nd, 1868

Dear Theodora,

I must apologize for my hurried reply to your most interesting letter and illustration, but I am due to return to the Illawarra today. At first, I thought perhaps your description might fit *Danaus petilia*, but there were several characteristics that did not align with our observations. Somewhat perplexed, we asked Father to take your illustration to the meeting of the Entomological Society and I have some information which I believe will both thrill and excite you.

Theodora sank onto the stone bench inside the folly and peeled off her gloves before continuing.

As in all these matters, luck plays an important part, and one of the entomologists from the Australian Museum seems firmly convinced that your illustration closely resembles *Danaus plexippus*, known as the Monarch butterfly.

And this is where the mystery deepens. These creatures frequent the Americas but have never been seen on our shores; however, they are capable of wide migration and sightings in the New Hebrides have recently been recorded. I have included his notes for your perusal.

Theodora bent and picked up the somewhat scrappy piece of paper from beneath her boot, unfolded it, and stared at the almost indecipherable scrawl. A series of rapid descriptions and random words, almost as though the author could barely spare the time.

6 to 8 mths life span. Wingspan 3 and one half to 4 inches. Native North and South America. Wide, seasonal migration. Easily identified—orange wings laced with black lines bordered with white dots.

Theodora's toes curled at the lines underscoring the words *Easily identified*, without doubt a reprimand.

Male small black spot surface of hind wings. Marginally thinner wing veins . . .

She hadn't imagined the sisters would pass her paltry sketch on to their father, certainly not an entomologist from the Australian Museum. Chastised, she pocketed the scrap of paper and returned to Harriet's letter.

Their seasonal migration and life cycle is most interesting. The details are not included in the notes, but Father gleaned the following information while at the meeting. They are strong fliers and can cover long distances during their adult life. Over winter their lifespan can be extended as they enter a period similar to hibernation. The climate and the surrounds are most important. Nearby trees, water, underbrush, and mist form the necessary environment. They cluster together, covering whole tree trunks and branches. Tall trees and bushes provide a thick canopy, soften the wind, and shield the butterflies.

Father doubted very strongly they would winter inland in the Hunter, as despite the proximity to the river the area is well known for its savage frosts and icy winds, and on occasion even snow; however, perhaps closer to the coast in a sheltered position they might find a haven. Pine trees or paperbarks would seem to be their preferred habitat. Which made us of course think of home—the two pine trees flanking the house and the paperbark grove.

It still grieves us deeply to have left Ash Island; however, we are well and very much absorbed in the preparation of Mr. Krefft's book of Australian mammals. There is to be an Intercolonial exhibition in Sydney at Prince Alfred Park to mark the centenary of Captain Cook's landing and our paintings will be exhibited there.

In other news, Helena and I were pleased to discover we are to be made honorary members of the Entomological Society, a rare distinction for mere females!

Please keep us informed of your search, and we wait with bated breath for a more accurate representation of your little wanderer.

With kindest regards,
Harriet Scott

Theodora stared at the winding ribbon of water, a flurry of questions and half-answered queries crowding her mind. And then a tingle began to work its way outward from her chest and spread down to the very tips of her fingers and toes.

She'd done it. She'd discovered something unusual, something special. *A native of the Americas . . . never before seen on our shores.*

She sprang to her feet and swirled around the tiny folly, arms outstretched. At last, at long last, she might contribute. A wave of dizziness swamped her and she sank down. Until she had examples of not only the butterfly but also the larvae and pupae, she could offer no further information or claim any credit.

CHAPTER 9

MORPETH, 1868

Clarrie woke to a darkened room, the leaves rattling in the wind, bashing against the window and bringing her to her senses. She lay still, cradling her belly as Charlie's elbows and feet rearranged themselves, then she pushed back the rough blanket and swung her legs over the side of the bed.

The reverend would want his morning tea, the fires needed cleaning, and the mound of washing in the scullery couldn't wait another day, let alone the ironing. Her feet scuffed against the rough floor—rough floor? She couldn't feel the rag mat. She peered across to the curtained window and the sound of the scratching branch. Then shot to her feet.

Everything came rushing back. Maud, the kitchen table, the horrid poking and prodding, and Sid—what had happened to Sid? And her belongings? She let out a mournful wail. She'd never been particularly attached to her mother's parting gift, a woven woolen blanket that had sat at the bottom of her bed for longer than she could remember, but now it contained everything she owned: her few personal items; her nightgown, handkerchiefs, hairpins; her one spare dress; her Sunday best; and her undergarments. Most importantly, her savings, wrapped carefully in her clean chemise, tucked right into the middle so she wouldn't lose it.

She blinked the room into focus, unable to tell whether morning had come or if it was evening. She stumbled across the room and made her way to the door. Pain shot through her foot and screeched up her leg. The culprit—a chair—stood in front of her. Sinking down, she tried in vain to reach her throbbing toe.

The door opened, throwing a shaft of light into the room. Maud stood silhouetted in the light from the hallway. "Awake, are you? Feeling a bit better?"

"Where's Sid?" she spluttered, ignoring her throbbing toe and reaching for her aching head.

Maud crossed to the window and threw open the curtains. Much to Clarrie's surprise the day hadn't passed, although the sun had slipped behind the hills across the river.

"He's gone. He'll be back later. I expect you're hungry. Feeding two."

Her stomach made a mournful rumble and her head throbbed in response. "More thirsty," she lied, not wanting to seem rude.

"And hungry, I reckon. Sort yourself out and come to the kitchen. There's some soup and bread. That'll see you right. That, and a nice cup of tea." Maud retreated down the hall-way, her heels clacking.

Clarrie bent as best she could and tried to reach her smarting toe and there, beside the chair, sat her bundle of belongings. She sank onto her knees and with shaking hands untied the blanket. Her fingers fumbled until they closed on her chemise.

It took only a quick glance to make sure nothing had gone astray. What little strength she had leached out of her body and she slumped forward. She'd misjudged Maud and Sid. She should know better than to think he'd leave her if she wasn't safe.

The room held two single beds separated by a trunk with a jug and bowl on the top, a chair, and not much else except for a pile of old clothes on the other bed. With a lot of huffing and puffing she managed to discover her boots under the bed amid a musty collection of damp clothing and a sweet smell she couldn't place. She sat on the bed and wriggled her feet into her boots. Tightening and tying the laces was another matter, and after a few moments she tucked them inside, wrangled her hair into some sort of a knot, and made her way down the hallway, one hand flat against the wall, taking great care not to trip.

"I'm not sure why I'm still here," she said to Maud when she reached the kitchen.

Maud angled the lamp on the table. "Sit yourself down. You passed out, dead faint. Sid and I got you onto the bed and I sent him on his way. He explained the full story. Best if you stay here for a day or two."

She couldn't do that. They couldn't afford to pay board and lodging. There'd be no money left for Charlie's birthing. "I can't. Thank you, but I really can't." She struggled to her feet, but her ankle twisted and with a squeal she flopped back into the chair, head in hands, as weak as a kitten.

Maud gave a snort and slid a cup of tea across the table. "Yes, you can. Sid and I came to an arrangement. You'll stay here until young Charlie makes his appearance. Give me some help. Once you've eaten and had a drink, you'll feel better. I've got plenty of work for another pair of hands."

Clarrie lifted her head, her mouth gaping. "I can work here for you until Charlie's born? Even if I'm—" She sketched her hand in front of her stomach, which in fact was the least of her worries. She couldn't even think straight.

"Seen enough girls in your condition and the work I need doing ain't hard. It'll give you a bit of practice. Told you I had five babies here. Always lots to do with a house full of babies. You'll learn the ropes and be ready when Charlie arrives."

What had she done to deserve such kindness? Kicked out by a man of God but taken in by a woman who owed her nothing. "That's very kind."

"You won't get paid. Work for your board and lodging, but I dare say it'll be easier than running up and down those stairs at the parsonage. Now, let's get some food inside you and then I'll show you around."

By the time Clarrie had cleared her plate and drunk her tea the light had faded and her headache had vanished. Maud picked up the lamp and led her to the first closed door opposite the room where she'd rested. She pushed it open to reveal four cots against one wall and two drawers on top of the dresser.

"All sleeping like little lambs." Maud clucked and ran her finger over the brow of one of the babies.

Clarrie tiptoed around the room, peering at each of the babies swaddled in blankets, only the top of their heads showing. Her heartstrings tugged. "How old are they?"

"Bit of a range. The youngest ones sleep here." She gestured to the two drawers repurposed as cradles. "And once they grow a bit, into the cots they go."

Five babies. Five babies belonging to girls who, like her, couldn't look after their own. "What happens to them when they get older?"

"Depends on the mother." Maud held open the door and they tiptoed out. "Not all of them stay here. Some mothers make good and take their baby, bit like you and Sid plan to do. Or they get a position where the child can be with them. Others, we find homes for."

"Find homes?"

"The ones the mothers don't want. There's plenty a family who'd like more children than the good Lord allows."

A shudder traced her skin. "That won't happen to Charlie."

"Never can tell what fate will decide. But Sid's a good lad. He'll do his best." Maud led the way back into the room where she'd slept and held up the lamp, revealing a pile of baby clothes and blankets folded on the second bed. She reached down and picked up a fine lawn nightgown and shook it out.

"I haven't got anything ready for Charlie." Clarrie's voice caught; she hadn't had time to even think of clothing.

"Don't you worry about that." Maud moved the jug and bowl and threw open the lid of the trunk between the beds, full to the brim of baby clothes, shawls and blankets, tiny white nightgowns, and knitted singlets. "Plenty here for the little lad when he arrives. And last of all, my room." Maud motioned across the hallway with a jerk of her chin but made no effort to open the door.

Before Clarrie could reply, a knock sounded and Maud reached for the doorknob. "That'll be Sid. I'll take myself to the kitchen so you can have a word. Come back and tell me, once you've decided what you want to do. There's just one rule."

Clarrie braced herself, waiting for the axe to fall. "One rule?"

"While I'm out and about, you don't let anyone in the house, not even Sid." Maud handed her the lamp and, with a swish of her skirts, drifted into the darkness.

Clarrie opened the door a fraction and peered out. Sid stood with his hands behind his back staring down the street. "Sid."

He spun around and took two steps toward her, then

caught her in his arms. He nuzzled her neck. "How're you feeling?" he murmured, his breath warm against her skin.

"Fine. Perfectly fine. I slept until not long ago." She leaned away from him. "I can't believe this has happened. Maud says I can stay here. Help her around the house."

"Are you happy with that?"

"I think it's perfect, and then, when Charlie's born, I can find another position and she'll look after him. She's got five babies here in her care. She's so good with them. They are all fast asleep. Not a murmur when we looked in on them."

"I can't stay. Work to catch up on. If you're sure you're happy being here, I'll get back."

"Sid, I don't know what I'd do without you." She stretched up and planted a smacking kiss on his bristly cheek.

"You don't have to worry about that. I told you we're in this together." He unpeeled her arms and returned her kiss. "I'll drop by tomorrow when I have a moment."

She stood at the door watching his jaunty stride as he merged into the shadows and thanked her lucky stars.

Clarrie's days took on a regular pattern. Thankfully her senses cleared and apart from a bit of clumsiness she managed all the tasks Maud set her. Up early before the babies awoke. Bottles cleaned and washed, arrowroot and sago mix heated on the stove. Five clamoring mouths to feed, diapers to change, cots to make up, clean clothes all around, then everything into the copper to wash and hang out to dry. Hungry mouths to feed again . . . and if she was lucky a visit from Sid, usually in the afternoon before the witching hour when every one of the babies would wake at the same time demanding a feed, a cuddle, and some love.

In between times, Maud would serve up meals she conjured after she'd come from town, shopping bag full of vegetables, bread, and the occasional piece of meat or fish—not as fine as Clarrie had cooked for the reverend but nothing to complain about, wholesome and belly-filling.

Maud's jaunts happened more days than not. She said she had customers to see, those due to have their babies and others who'd already given birth. Not just in Morpeth but farther afield—Maitland and sometimes the farms outside the town. She'd made some arrangement with one of the drivers from the wharf and he'd take her in his wagon. Rounds, she called them.

"Why don't you let me help with the cooking?"

Maud tossed Clarrie a smile. "And when do you think you'd have time for that?"

"You made time for it before I was here." She had no idea how Maud had managed on her own.

"You're doing a grand job, and right now I couldn't do without you. I have a . . ." She paused for a moment and a shadow crossed her face. "I have someone who comes and helps me out, looks after the babes while I do my rounds, but she's caught up at the moment with other matters."

Clarrie threw some wood into the stove and stirred the soup. "I could make some dumplings to go in the soup, if you like, if there's some spare flour, and there's parsley in the garden."

"Why don't you sit yourself down and put your feet up?"

"I feel fine, better than I did early on, and the babes are used to me now. I've sorted out the chest full of clothes and mended anything that needed it."

"Nesting." Maud laughed and reached for Clarrie's wrist, held her still, then ran her other hand over her stomach. "Not long now."

"How can you tell?" Heat rose to Clarrie's cheeks. She'd had a feeling—nothing she could put a finger on, but she did feel different. Sid said she was blossoming; she felt more as though she might burst.

"Been having back pains, haven't you? And can't stay away from the privy?"

Clarrie placed the flat of her hand on her chest, trying to still the mass of butterflies taking flight at Maud's words, and nodded.

"Right then, you'd better make those dumplings tonight. Might not get another opportunity."

CHAPTER 10

SYDNEY, 1922

As the tram rattled and clanked its way from Old South Head Road and along William Street, Verity regretted her instinct to leave her bicycle at home. The pumping of the pedals and the wind in her hair tended to free her thoughts and allow her to make sense of anything that bothered her.

Every few minutes the tram stopped to allow passengers on and off, the conductor swung up and down, his cry of "Fares 'ease," ringing above the clanging and clattering. His fancy sideways footsteps, one hand always grasping the vertical handrails, were worthy of a ballroom dancing class.

She peered through the grime-smeared window, trying to catch a glimpse of the harbor, and her thoughts returned to the painting. She could understand why Treadwell might be keen to promote the foundation and encourage donations, but it was the picture of the butterfly and the house on the banks of the Hunter River that fascinated her.

She was no authority on botanical paintings, but anyone could see the quality of the work, and the pattern on the butterfly was an exact match for her costume. It couldn't simply be because Mrs. Treadwell had visited Morpeth. There had to be a connection, something more than a reminder of a childhood visit.

In the Binks family, personal treasures were few and far between. Her father's early notebooks, the one and only photograph of him before he left for Egypt, and his press card. Little else, and of Grandpa Sid and Grandma Clarrie nothing but the house, its furnishings, and Sid's Remington typewriter.

Sid had relied on charity growing up, been lucky enough to land himself a job as a copy boy and then go on to an apprenticeship and, finally, his life's dream: writing for *The Sydney Arrow*. That was why she loved the house and was so thankful he had left it to her—it was a way of honoring his haven. He'd spread his arms wide as if trying to gather the house close, as though he couldn't believe his luck. A man who, for so long, hadn't even had a kettle to his name. For years, he and Grandma Clarrie had rented the small two-up, two-down terrace with its poky little attic that had been her room from the moment she'd left her cot. They'd saved every penny until they were able to buy. Sid loved to tell the story—the way he'd stumbled inadvertently upon it in the classifieds. *Suitable for small capitalists*. A very small capitalist, he claimed. The phrase would make him puff out his chest and hoot with laughter. He and Clarrie became one of only two owners of a house in Tara Terrace; the others were rented to a mariner, a carpenter, and a shipwright.

Her lips twisted in a grimace as she caught sight of her reflection in the tram window. She could understand if Mrs. Treadwell had bought the painting because it was a link to her past, but what about the coincidence of Verity's costume matching the butterfly in the painting? That's where the story lay.

"All change for Circular Quay." The conductor's voice

rang out, dragging her back to the moment. She slipped off the bench and swung down onto the footpath, the winter sun and expanse of grass a pleasant relief from the cramped confines of the tram.

There was no doubt about Treadwell's self-importance. Truth be told, the man made her hackles rise. In any other situation she'd just walk away, but a job was a job—a paying job—and if she was going to make ends meet, she'd have to face people and situations that made her uncomfortable.

What would Grandpa Sid have done? Long before he was her age, he'd taken his courage in both hands and brought his family to Sydney to try his luck as a stringer, paid for the number of words he could string together. Nothing safe about that. Trouble was, she'd had it too easy.

She brushed down her skirt as she set off back home. There had to be more to Mrs. Treadwell's story. What made a wealthy widow dedicate her life to others? Why had she set up the foundation? And what was the significance of the painting? *"The property sold many years ago . . ."* Treadwell's words popped into her head and exploded in a shower of color that culminated in the painting of the house at Morpeth and the beautiful butterfly.

Grandpa Sid's voice echoed. *"Follow your nose, my girl. Follow your nose; you never know where it might lead."*

Less than twelve hours later, Verity sat in the corner of the guard's van on the Newcastle train, her bicycle propped between three bags of mail and a welcome mug of tea cradled in both hands. She'd hoped that the troubadour would make contact as he'd promised, but after waiting twenty-four hours she'd acted on impulse, something she rarely did. It wasn't part of her character—responsibility had landed heavily on her shoulders once Clarrie became ill with the influenza. She'd taken on the running of the house, and when Clarrie died, Grandpa Sid had sickened and withdrawn. Without Clarrie he'd become nothing more than a shell, which was strange, because Clarrie had always said Sid was her rock.

The stationmaster's whistle cut through Verity's thoughts and the train took off with a bellow and a hiss, juddering over the intersecting rails as it threaded its way through the outskirts of the city and picked up speed.

The troubadour would simply have to wait for a day or two. She sipped the remainder of the scalding tea, then let out a long sigh.

"You all right there, love? Your bicycle won't come to any harm. I'll keep an eye on it if you want to go and find yourself a seat. Just leave the mug in the corner there."

"I'd rather stay here. I won't get in your way."

"Got family in Newcastle, have you?"

"Morpeth." Not the complete truth, but that was far too hard to explain.

"Ah, upriver. It's a bit of a hike. A good twenty-five miles. Shame the old steamers don't run anymore. River's silted and any decent-sized ship can't get under the new bridge. Still, you can get the train to Maitland. That'll save your legs. Best to hop off there since you've got the bicycle."

And that's what she intended to do. She'd had a good look at the station map before she'd boarded the train. "It's only about six miles to Morpeth from there, isn't it?"

He grunted. "Nice little town, Morpeth."

Verity delved into her satchel and pulled out her notebook. Anything she could glean about the place might be useful. "My grandfather came from the area."

"I'll bet he'll be pleased to see you, then."

"He's in Sydney now." No need to go into the details of which cemetery. "I'm looking for a place called The Landing on the banks of the Hunter River. Do you know it?"

The guard's jowls wobbled as he shook his head. "Newcastle born and bred, I am. Been to Morpeth a few times. Place isn't what it used to be. Before the rail came it was the gateway to the Hunter. You boarded the steamer in Sydney in the evening, arrived in Newcastle in time for a breakfast of flathead and fresh damper, and be in Morpeth for morning tea. Bit faster these days. We've got a quick stop here, then we'll be across the Hawkesbury. Should get to Newcastle by eleven. Trains run to Maitland regularly. Now, if you'll excuse me, I've got some mail here to sort. Tuck yourself in the corner there."

Verity hunkered down on an upturned crate and opened the folder Treadwell had given her and flipped through the contents. Didn't appear to be anything she hadn't already discovered. The train picked up speed again, and the repeated sound of the wheels on the track replaced the wheeze of steam.

The next time she raised her head, the steep track was dropping down, and in front of her stretched a huge expanse of water edged by towering cliffs with eucalypts clinging to every available space. "It's beautiful."

"Can't beat the Hawkesbury. Reckon it's the way Sydney would have looked when the First Fleet dropped anchor."

The train shuddered to a halt and a pair of hands reached in and captured her bicycle.

She snatched at the back wheel. "I'm not getting off here."

"Don't you worry about a thing. This is Brooklyn. Just got to unload the mailbags. Why don't you hop off and stretch your legs? Won't go without you."

Verity stepped down onto the platform. Below her sat a neat village and wharves, rows of timber boats bobbing in the sunshine. She'd lived all her life within cooee of Sydney Harbour but had never taken more than a ferry ride to Manly, never explored beyond the sprawling city.

"Right you are, love. Give us a hand with your bicycle. Gotta keep to the timetable."

With a final glance at the lovely little village, she heaved the front wheel of her bicycle onto the steps and it disappeared into the bowels of the guard's van.

"We'll be in Newcastle in a couple of hours."

"There's a rail line from Maitland to Morpeth, isn't there?"

"Tram. The bicycle might be a problem. Like I said, best bet is to take the branch line as far as Maitland and cycle from there. Got somewhere to stay, have you?"

"I'll sort that out when I get there." She'd raided her savings before she'd left and had enough to stay for a few days in a cheap hotel. When she returned to Sydney, she'd try to track down the troubadour, write the article, and see Mr. Bailey about publication and hopefully earn some more money.

The train pulled into Maitland station as the courthouse clock struck the hour. A group of men dressed in prison uniforms were working on a vegetable garden and in the distance she could see sentries on the top of the prison walls. The guard lifted her bicycle down. "Know where you're going?"

"Just follow my nose until I see the river."

"That'll do you. You'll know you're on the right track once you go past the blue barn. There's a sign advertising Dr Morse's Indian Root Pills painted on the side."

"Indian Root Pills?"

101

"Yep! Magic stuff, cures just about everything—headaches, indigestion, rheumatism, pimples, boils, you name it. Plenty of women swear by them. Just the thing to have for an emergency."

Verity strapped her carpetbag onto the back of her bicycle and slung her satchel over her shoulder, then made her way down the platform and onto the road.

Fresh air redolent with the fragrance of cut lucerne filled her lungs. No matter what she discovered about Mrs. Treadwell, the trip was a wonderful idea. The wide-open spaces and sparkling blue sky filled her with a sense of anticipation and, strangely, well-being.

As promised, she passed the blue barn advertising Indian Root Pills and before long the river appeared on her left and then spread into a lagoon lined by willow trees and full of a bewildering array of waterbirds. No other vehicles shared the road, and soon she found herself coasting down a small incline. Spires marked several churches, mills, and warehouses, and white cottages stood out against the backdrop of green fields. On her right an impressive sandstone house stood on a rise and then ahead of her the main street meandered into the town.

Swan Street, the sign proclaimed. A broad street, it ran parallel with the river and was lined with hotels and stores and a few workers' cottages, although the majority of the houses were on the streets leading up from the river. As the sun sank behind the hills, she stopped at a two-story hotel with lacy white fretwork not unlike the terraces in the city. A woman with flyaway hair and a wide smile greeted her at the door to the Ladies Lounge like a long-lost friend and introduced herself as Mrs. Peers, owner of the Commercial Hotel. She showed Verity the back shed where she could leave her bicycle, then took her upstairs to a delightful room overlooking the main street.

Several hours later, Verity had a full stomach and a longing for the plump pillows and eiderdown on the cozy bed, yet she couldn't bring herself to go to sleep. Instead, she slipped through the French doors, her bare feet silent on the worn timber boards of the veranda. Cloaked by the velvet darkness, she squinted up at the pinpricked sky. So many more stars away from the city. In some strange way she felt as though she'd come home. The surface of the river shimmered, a pulsing artery leading from the coast to the inland regions of the vast Hunter Valley.

It made her a little nostalgic, overlooking the very streets Grandpa Sid and Grandma Clarrie once walked. She had no idea why they'd never returned to Morpeth for even a visit; they'd rarely spoken of their life before Sydney. It was only after they'd received the telegram telling them of Charlie's death that Grandpa Sid had pulled out an old Arnott's biscuit tin and placed the telegram inside with a degree of reverence that piqued her curiosity.

She snooped. No other word for it.

Beneath the telegram, she'd discovered the registration of her father's birth, but the date had been months after the day Grandpa Sid and Grandma Clarrie celebrated his birthday. When she came across their certificate of marriage, dated only days before Charlie's birth, she'd put two and two together and kept mum. She hadn't wanted to pry any further.

Tomorrow she intended to see if she could find The Landing, see if anyone remembered the family who'd once lived there, and—if luck was on her side—pay a visit. The hairs on her arms bristled. Time would tell.

After an undisturbed night, Verity bounded out of bed and threw back the curtains. The street below was alive with people, and she must have slept late because the sun carried a touch of warmth. She washed and dressed and made her way downstairs to the dining room, wondering whether she'd missed breakfast.

Clattering and crashing echoed from the back of the hotel, so she went through to the dining room where she'd eaten last night. The place was empty and all the tables cleared except for one, next to the window. Unsure whether to announce her arrival or simply sit down, she strolled around the room studying the pictures on the wall, which she'd missed last night. Hardly surprising since she'd barely been able to keep her eyes open.

Scenes of the early days in the town, the river crammed with ships of every shape and size, the overcrowded wharves teeming with workers. Underneath each one was a title and the date. The earliest, the SS *Sophia Jane* in 1831, long before Grandpa Sid's time, and a hotel called the Rose and Crown, carriages and horses clustered in the courtyard and a backdrop of sailing ships with their rigging reefed leaving no doubt of the history of the town.

Mrs. Peers offered a cheerful smile. "Morning, dear. Did you sleep well?"

"I did. Thank you. I hope I'm not too late for breakfast."

"Got it waiting in the kitchen, keeping warm, and a nice pot of tea. Be back in a twitch of a lamb's tail." She bustled out of the room and came back not two moments later with a tray bearing a plate with a metal warming cover, a pot of tea, and a rack of toast. "Sit yourself down."

Verity's mouth watered when Mrs. Peers lifted the lid to reveal a mound of scrambled eggs, two sausages, a lamb chop, and a pile of tomatoes. "I wasn't sure what you'd want so I saved a bit of everything. Shall I pour the tea?"

"Yes, please."

"Tuck in." She poured out two cups of tea and sat opposite Verity. "Can't have you eating all by yourself; besides, I'm spitting feathers. I've been up since sparrow's. A nice cup of tea will do me good."

Despite the ample dinner she'd eaten the night before, Verity made short work of her breakfast, and when she put down her knife and fork, she became aware of Mrs. Peers's intense scrutiny. She offered a tentative smile and raised an eyebrow in question.

"Don't mind me. Nosy as all get out, I am. We don't see a lot of visitors in Morpeth, although I've just taken a booking for tonight—maybe things are on the up-and-up. Back in the time of the steamships, when Newcastle was little more than a coal terminal, Morpeth was a hive of activity. Gateway to the Hunter." She gave a wistful sigh. "Still, we get by."

"I'm"—Verity licked her lips—"a writer." There, the first time she'd said it aloud and it sounded so good. Best start the way she meant to go on.

"An author! My, my." Mrs. Peers leaned forward across the table with a dreamy look on her face. "I do love a good novel, especially some of those romances. They're making a talking picture of that story about a sheik, you know . . ."

"Not an author. I write factual stories, not fiction. I'm trying to find out about a property called The Landing for a piece I've been asked to write."

"Like in the newspaper or one of those ladies' magazines?" Mrs. Peers looked over her shoulder. "I think there's a copy or two over there of *The Home* and *The Australian Women's Magazine*. Not really my cup of tea. Most people around here know the story of The Landing—now that's a romance if you want one."

The last thing she expected. "A romance?"

"Yes, of course. Could have been one of those Brontë sisters that came up with it. Dashing young Scottish adventurer almost loses his life when his ship runs aground on the rugged Cornish coast. Meets the love of his life and lures her to Australia."

Verity leaned closer, her chin resting on her interlaced fingers, itching for more, but the impatient ringing of a bell out the back rocketed Mrs. Peers to her feet. "Haven't got time to hang around."

"Is there a library in town? Somewhere I can find out information about the past?"

"You could try the School of Arts. They've got a stack of books and old records down there. You can't miss the building—looks like one of them mausoleums you find in the big cemeteries. Hop on your bicycle and you'll be there in no time. Turn right at Northumberland Street, then right, back into High Street. Almost immediately to the right, number one hundred and ten is the School of Arts building."

Verity drank the remainder of her tea and darted upstairs. She picked up her satchel and, in a matter of minutes, was pedaling up the hill, paying more attention to the buildings and the layout of the town than the comings and goings of the people of Morpeth. The town had a quiet, satisfied air—nothing like the clatter and bustle of Sydney. She rather liked it.

Mrs. Peers's directions were perfect. The School of Arts was easy to spot with its massive pillars supporting the architrave and pediment, tucked incongruously between two weatherboard cottages complete with trailing roses and lavender hedges.

She leaned her bicycle against a convenient tree and made her way to the door. A cacophony of laughter greeted her arrival. She paused, contemplated leaving, but a voice stalled her.

"Have you come for the Ladies Reading Circle? We're just about to begin. Follow me." The girl's heels tapped on the wooden floor and the hem of her very modern dress swung from side to side, highlighting a pair of shapely calves. Verity pulled at her blouse, straightened her tie, and smoothed her boring navy skirt.

A Ladies Reading Circle. Not anything she wanted to get caught up in. An excuse for women to get together and eat cakes, drink tea, and chitchat, but she might discover something important. They entered a room to the side of the building—obviously the library, judging by the number of books packed on the shelves lining the walls and the expansive card catalogue cabinet.

"We've got a new member," the fashionable young girl announced. "I found her lurking outside."

A dozen women of all shapes, sizes, and ages sat around a large table in the middle of the room. Their heads came up in unison.

"Mrs. Peers at the Commercial suggested I come down. I'm visiting Morpeth and wanted some information about the town. I don't want to disturb your meeting."

"Everyone's welcome. Sit yourself down. My name's Primrose and this is—" She gestured to the woman on her right, who mumbled an indecipherable name, followed by everyone around the table.

Verity hadn't a hope of keeping up, so she smiled and nodded, then said, "My name is Verity, Verity Binks," before giving up and sitting in the only empty chair at the table.

"Binks?" An older white-haired woman on her right looked sharply at her, opened her mouth to speak, then snapped it shut as another woman at the end of the table, Jane someone, hammered her fist on the table.

"We're here to discuss Laura Palmer-Archer's story, *A Bush Honeymoon*."

A bit of rustling ensued and each woman produced a thin, red-covered book. The woman next to Verity leaned closer. "Not the best. Nineteen-year-old miss who marries at dawn and by dusk is regretting what she's done. Story we all know. Are you married, love?" She peered down at Verity's left hand and tutted. "Waiting for the right man. Sensible girl. Do we have any comments?"

A collection of throwaway lines stretched on interminably and slipped past as Verity pondered the sense in remaining. There was so much more she could be doing, finding The Landing being the most significant. Quite why she'd been swayed by Mrs. Peers's suggestion, she had no idea. She did not have time for this. She'd be seriously out of pocket if she stayed in Morpeth too long. The thump of a dozen books being piled in the center of the table pulled her back.

"*My Brilliant Career* next week. I'm sure you're all familiar with the story, but far more in keeping with modern times than the honeymoon nonsense." The older woman on her right gave a derogatory humph, pushed back her chair, and wandered off.

"I like reading romances." A young, mousy girl peered across the table. "I do so love Jane Austen stories."

"Why don't we ask our guest? Maybe she has some suggestions."

Verity snapped to attention. She didn't want to offend anyone, particularly as she might have some questions later. "I've read *Wuthering Heights*." Not that she'd enjoyed it overmuch.

"Far too depressing and totally unrealistic," another voice interjected.

"I don't think *Wuthering Heights* is unrealistic," a girl

with a mass of unrestrained curls announced. "Tragedies happen, time and time again. Look at the Breckenridge story. And that took place right on our doorstep."

"You have no idea of the full story. And those that might are long gone."

"I think it's a romance, certainly at the beginning, but with a tragic ending."

"Do tell." Verity offered the girl a smile, her curiosity aroused. The girl didn't need any further encouragement. "Captain Breckenridge built that beautiful house at The Landing for his bride, brought her across the ocean."

Verity sat a little straighter in her seat, the image of the painting of the house she'd seen at Treadwell's clear.

"The perfect existence, the perfect family, until it all went to wrack and ruin."

"God has a way of making you pay. Can't have too much happiness." The older woman slid copies of Miss Franklin's book across the table.

Verity had to physically restrain herself from pulling out her notebook. "What happened? Mrs. Peers started to tell me but she didn't finish."

"The most devastating story. Captain Alexander Breckenridge, tall, dashing, and handsome, the son of a wealthy Scottish shipbuilder, came to Australia to explore the possibilities in the industry. On his way home, his ship was blown off course, and instead of making land at Plymouth as intended, he washed ashore in the mouth of the Fowey River in Cornwall."

The girl with the bobbed hair leaped to her feet, hands clasped to her breast. "And there he met the beautiful redheaded daughter of a local landowner, Julianna Chegwin. It was love at first sight. No other words for it." She dabbed at her eyes with the corner of her handkerchief. "So sad. So romantic."

"Nothing sad at that stage." The woman next to her took up the story. "She accepted his proposal. So much in love she left her family to be with the man of her dreams, but not so happy to leave her garden. She loved her garden."

Regardless of her aversion to romance, Verity's heart beat a little faster as the story ensnared her.

"So he returned to Australia to build her a replica of her home and garden, then sailed across the ocean once more to marry her and bring her home. By the time they reached Australian shores . . ."

Verity stilled.

"She was with child. A beautiful son and heir."

Her shoulders sank and she let out a long, relief-filled breath. "He brought her to Morpeth, to the house and garden he'd built on the banks of the Hunter River, and there they grew and prospered. A son and four redheaded daughters in as many years, all with their mother's coloring. So very, very tragic."

Verity frowned. "I'm sorry, I don't understand. Why tragic?"

"The SS *Cawarra* foundered on the oyster banks outside Newcastle. Only one survivor lived to tell the tale. Would someone go and get the picture please?"

Two minutes later an oil painting lay on the table in front of her. Verity peered at the mass of bodies floundering in the rough waves and, underneath, the caption: *The sinking of the SS Cawarra, 1866.* Goose bumps stippled her skin—she couldn't think of a worse way to die. "The whole family was lost?"

"Not the whole family. But Alexander, his lovely wife,

Julianna, and, tragically, their only son, Jamie. The end of the dynasty before it could prosper." The Primrose woman gave a loud sniff and picked up the picture, gave it a wipe with her crumpled handkerchief, and replaced it reverently on the wall.

It couldn't have been the end of the dynasty. "What happened to the rest of the family? The daughters?"

"They struggled along for a time. Then one by one they left, journeyed to far-flung places to marry, leaving only one sister rattling around in that great big house with hardly a penny to her name. That's when Mr. Kendall stepped in and bought the place."

Verity shuffled forward on her chair. "The Kendalls?"

"Everyone knows the Kendalls. They own the newspaper, have done since—" She lifted her hands, fingers splayed. "The Breckenridge family was cursed, if you ask me."

Verity shot to her feet. "Where are the newspaper offices?"

"Down the road a piece. Arlo Kendall keeps to himself, spends as much time as he can on the river in that boat of his; more interested in the birdlife than people. Not like the old days. His father and his grandfather were in the office every waking hour. Paper's not what it used to be. Time we settled on our book for next week. No more chattering. It will be *My Brilliant Career*. Will you be joining us, Miss Binks?"

"I'm sorry?"

"Are you staying in town?"

"Yes. Yes, I am. At the Commercial but . . ." She was about to add that she had other business to attend to; however, there might be more she wanted to know and these women were certainly happy to share the history of the town. Perhaps gossip was the lifeblood of a writer.

"Why don't you take a copy? Not much to do in Morpeth.

When you leave, drop the book off, or alternatively give it to Mrs. Peers. I'm sure she'll return it."

"Thank you." She took the proffered book and slipped it into her satchel. "I'm not familiar with the layout of the town. Can you give me directions to the newspaper offices?"

"Right out of here and follow the High Street. You'll see the church and parsonage at the end of the street. Turn into Tank Street. Campbell's Warehouse is down a bit on the corner with Swan. The newspaper's just across the road from there, a double fronted, two-story terrace. You can't miss it. You'll need to take the bridge across the river if you want The Landing."

Verity retrieved her bicycle and scooted down the street until she reached the church. She couldn't see anything that looked much like warehouses, certainly not like the three brick buildings that dominated the quay in Sydney, so she crossed the road and pedaled down to the corner.

Not that she needed to. She discovered a few moments later when she reached the end of the road and a large, symmetrical gabled sandstone-and-brick building proclaiming itself to be Campbell's Warehouse. Across the road a terrace carried a somewhat faded sign swinging in the breeze—*The Morpeth Want.* A smile tugged the corner of her mouth at the incongruous name. Grandpa Sid's words came back to her. *"Everyone wants something—and old Mr. Kendall reckoned his paper provided everything anyone could want."*

Tears pricked the back of her eyelids and her chest tightened. Why hadn't she run roughshod over Sid's objections and brought him back to Morpeth? The stories he might have told.

CHAPTER 11

MORPETH, 1868

Theodora waited in vain for another visit from her butterfly, or even another letter from the Scott sisters, while time disappeared in a flurry of trunks, clothes, and much excitement on behalf of both Constance and Viola. It seemed they couldn't wait to break free and take up a position in society that had been denied them by their extended period of mourning.

Quite how Florence and Mrs. Barnett kept their patience was beyond Theodora's understanding; however, the tantalizing possibility of seeing the butterfly again and Archer's hard work in the garden cheered her. All she had to do was convince Florence that she should stay.

Two days before their departure, Florence summoned her to her bedroom—a cause for concern because it was the spot Florence always chose to impart "matters of importance." She waved Theodora to one of the two chairs drawn up at the window, taking in the view of the bend in the river and the surrounding hills.

"I still harbor immense concerns about you remaining here alone."

Theodora studied a spot of peeling paint above Florence's head. In the last three weeks they'd gone over and over her reasons—her fear of traveling in open waters; the need to tend Mama's garden, although she'd made no mention of the butterfly—and still Florence kept harping on and on.

In a very unusual gesture, Florence reached for her hand. "Is there nothing I can do to encourage you to come to Sydney with us?"

Theodora drew in some air through her nose, keeping her lips tightly closed to trap the "nothing!" that wanted to explode from her very being. Summoning every ounce of diplomacy and a great deal of patience, she shook her head.

"We will be staying at the Berkeley in Bent Street; leave a message with Mr. Sladdin if there are any problems. We expect to be away for several weeks. It is such a shame you will miss out on the fittings for new dresses."

"I have no need of new dresses, but I'd greatly appreciate it if you could purchase some more watercolors and cartridge paper and perhaps deliver a letter to the Scotts' dwelling in Sydney."

"Theodora, why not come with us and you can call yourself? It's time for you to spread your wings. Papa and Mama wouldn't want you to mourn them forever."

And that was the trouble. Florence was quite correct, but she wouldn't understand about her compulsion to track down the elusive butterfly, nor her fear of leaving The Landing. "Next time, I promise. I'm sure after Viola's musical debut, she will be in great demand and there will be plenty more opportunities. I have to be here."

"Why? Nothing you have argued thus far makes any sense to me."

Theodora chewed her lips and stared down at her hands, now fully healed thanks to Mrs. Barnett's salve. She'd procrastinated for ages, alternating between a huge desire to share her news about the butterfly and an equal compulsion to hold her secret close, at least until she secured a specimen. Apart from a collection of worthless illustrations, she had nothing to prove she'd even seen the butterfly. The only person she'd told, other than the Scott sisters, was Redmond, but he hadn't mentioned it again. Not even when he'd called in to check up on Archer. "But there is still a lot of work to be done before spring."

"I have to agree, but Redmond can oversee Archer. And that reminds me. I am going to have to ask Mrs. Barnett to see to employing another maid as soon as we come back. In fact, I might ask her to put out some feelers. She has business in Maitland and Newcastle before she joins us in Sydney. A local girl with a little more experience wouldn't come amiss, and I am anticipating that both Viola and Constance will have suitors, so they will need to look their best. I don't understand why you refuse to come with us. There will be picnics and the theater and the pleasure gardens; they have a zoo now, with exotic animals, and what about the Botanic Gardens? Mama's favorite place."

Theodora could think of nothing worse: interminable tea parties, dress fittings, and tittle-tattle, although a visit to the Botanic Gardens or the Australian Museum might be to her liking. With the exception of art supplies, she could get everything she needed in Morpeth or Maitland.

"No, I simply do not wish to go. I have far too much to do, and I really cannot bring myself to travel to Sydney on the steamship. Not after the accident." It wasn't a lie, but she was perhaps slightly exaggerating. "Not only that, I have a commission from the Scott sisters that I have every intention of fulfilling." It was a trump card she hadn't wanted to use, but she threw it down and crossed her fingers.

Florence's expression lightened and she reached for her hand. "My dear, why didn't you tell me? How very, very exciting. And all the more reason why you should come with us to Sydney and see them face-to-face."

Still the conversation wasn't going the way she intended. "They are not in Sydney at present; I'm certain I told you. They are working on new illustrations for Mr. Krefft's book of Australian mammals and are visiting the South Coast." And now she had to share the full truth, which she hadn't wanted to do in case she'd been mistaken. "I spotted a striking butterfly a few weeks ago in the garden and there is a possibility it might be unusual."

"Surely the Scott sisters have documented every butterfly in the area. Don't they know what this one is?"

"It seems that it may somehow have wandered here from the Americas."

"How could that possibly be the case? Everyone knows that butterflies only live for a matter of days."

"That is the intriguing question, and the reason I have to be here. Don't you see it is my opportunity?"

"Your opportunity for what?"

"To record a new species."

Florence peered out of the window, Theodora suspected to the heavens for an explanation, though what help that would be she had no idea, unless she'd spotted a flight of butterflies. She glanced out of the window, just in case.

"I will be perfectly fine. Mrs. Starling will be here, and Wilcox. If there are any other problems I can ask Redmond for his advice and assistance. I have no intention of going anywhere in case I miss the little Wanderer. Not only that, these butterflies spend the winter clustered together in a safe place. It's important that I am here to see if I can find the spot where they winter and then, when spring comes, I will be able to track their movements and life cycle."

With a long, drawn-out groan and another eye roll, Florence pushed out of the chair. "You are going to have to promise me that you will write weekly and let me know how you are faring. And if you go into Morpeth, make sure you are accompanied by Wilcox or Mrs. Starling. You can't trust some of the riff-raff who arrive on the steamers. And stay away from Queens Wharf."

Theodora offered a radiant smile. "You see, everything will work out perfectly. And it will leave me plenty of time to study the books in Papa's library and, at the same time, make sure nothing untoward happens here. And if you would be kind enough to remember my supplies: two more sketch-books and cartridge paper, 2B or 3B pencils, bottles of white paint, cakes of gold and silver paint, and French chalk pencils in light and dark shades. And perhaps a new set of Winsor and Newton paints; their colors stay vibrant far longer." She edged toward the door and left before Florence fabricated some other insurmountable hurdle.

Two days later, Theodora stood dutifully waving her handker-chief as the *Anna Maria* pulled away from Queens Wharf at eleven o'clock sharp. A bitter wind whipped across from the west and she pulled her jacket tight. If Papa were still alive, he would have arranged for the steamer to stop at The Landing to pick them up, but those times were long gone, as were the trips with Papa, Jamie, and Redmond to Ash Island.

As if conjured from her imagination, a small clinker drifted into midstream.

"Oi! Theodora."

She stalled, her face breaking into a wide smile. Redmond stood with his legs braced against the current, hands waving above his head, as the *Petrel* bobbed around in the wake of the steamer.

She cupped her hands around her mouth. "Ahoy there, Kendall!" she shouted into the wind.

"I thought you might like a ride back to The Landing."

"I'd love it, but I've got to meet Wilcox at the bakery. We'll take the punt across. I promised Florence I wouldn't be seen out and about without a chaperone." She pulled a face, which she doubted he could see.

"Fair enough. I wanted to make sure Archer isn't making a nuisance of himself."

"He's making excellent progress and has even endeared himself to Florence, but I haven't seen him today. He was supposed to show up before everyone left for Sydney."

The wind snatched her hat. She failed to grasp it, blinded by her windswept hair.

"I can't hear you. Stay there."

Theodora waited while Redmond fiddled around in the middle of the boat. She'd no idea what he was doing; surely he ought to be hoisting the sail. She smothered a laugh. For an engineer he could, at times, be more than a little ham-fisted.

A large bang and a plume of smoke brought her heart to a standstill. "Jump!" she cried. All the bad feelings she had about the steamship trip to Sydney and here in front of her, Papa's boat was about to explode. "Jump!" She peeled off her jacket, threw it down on the wharf, then struggled with the laces on her boots.

Through the cloud of smoke, the bow nosed toward the wharf. Then Redmond emerged standing at the stern, a broad grin on his face, the tiller in his large, capable hands.

She'd like to wrap her own hands around his throat and throttle him. "What are you doing? I thought the boat had exploded."

He nudged the clinker up to the wharf and threw her the rope. She caught it and wrapped it around the bollard, years of experience overriding her thundering heart. She could kill him.

He leaned over the side and hauled her sopping hat out of the water. "Bit cold for a swim."

"I thought the engine was going to blow up. I thought . . ." What did she think? That he'd die the same way as all the passengers on the *Cawarra*?

"Just a backfire. She needs a decent run. That's why I offered you a ride back to The Landing—beats the punt."

A trip on the river sounded like heaven, and then Florence's words resounded. "I promised Florence."

"What Florence doesn't know won't hurt her."

"I know, but I promised. It was one of the conditions I accepted, otherwise she would have insisted I went to Sydney."

"And why didn't you?"

"Because of the butterfly. I had a letter from Harriet Scott. They think the butterfly I saw might be a new species. One that's somehow managed to arrive here from the Americas."

"A stowaway?" He gave a bark of laughter. "A nice idea. And you're hoping it might come back?"

"It's unlikely to do that until the weather warms, but there's a possibility there could be more than one wintering somewhere close. They cluster together, hundreds of them, and then when spring comes, they take off and lay their eggs. I'm determined to find the spot." She gave a self-conscious smile. "It's an opportunity for me to prove my worth, and with Harriet's and Helena's backing, people will take notice. I know it's a long shot but . . . We're looking for somewhere closer to the sea, somewhere warmer than the Hunter Valley."

"That could be anywhere. Queensland even, if they travel as far as you say."

"It could be, but it could be around here as well. There have been no sightings reported in Australia, ever. Somewhere like Ash Island perhaps . . ." She gave voice to the thought that had kept her awake for the last few nights.

"Why Ash Island?"

"It's full of paperbarks and pine trees, all sorts of trees and a dense canopy, which is the environment they like for winter, protected from the weather; at least, that's what the notes said. It's unlikely, but I'd like to go."

Redmond's face became stern. "More than unlikely. Ash Island's been divided up into smaller holdings. They're selling fast. The land's being cleared and drained for dairy farms. It's a disgrace."

"How dreadful." Helena and Harriet loved the place so very much.

"The house and a few surrounding acres are still intact. That's why Hench is there caretaking, but I doubt the family will ever live on Ash Island again."

She gave a shudder. She'd never taken to Hench. Papa had employed him years ago when Mama had first come to Australia. He had been short of crew and found Hench on the wharf in Sydney, looking for a berth to anywhere that wasn't England or America.

"I'm sure he'd show us around. If that's where you want to start your search."

It was as good a place as any. She nodded.

"I'd be happy to take you."

"Would you? That would be . . . just wonderful. If I can find a chaperone."

"A chaperone?" He let out a guffaw. "Since when have you needed a chaperone?"

"I told you I promised Florence. And Mrs. Starling's almost worse. Sometimes I think she moonlights at the jail, but she won't set foot on a boat, Papa's or anyone's. She walked all the way into Maitland the last time she went rather than take the steamer. And besides, she's going to have so much work to do now Mrs. Barnett and Biddy have gone with the girls. It wouldn't be fair."

"Leave it with me. We could take a picnic, make a day of it. When do you want to go?"

"As soon as possible." Now she'd given voice to her thoughts, she couldn't wait. She'd like to jump aboard right now.

An incoming barge sounded its horn. Redmond lifted his head. "That's a warning. I'm going to have to cast off. Let me know if you need anything."

She untied the rope and threw it down to him. He pulled away from the wharf amid a series of shouts and jeers as the laden barge took his place.

CHAPTER 12

"Thanks, Archer." Redmond handed over the corrected proofs. "Get them downstairs and ask Sid if he can come up. I want a word."

"He ain't here."

"What do you mean? He doesn't knock off until we've put the paper to bed."

"It's Clarrie." Archer looked down and shuffled his feet. "She's . . . um . . . she's . . . Her time's come," he blurted over his shoulder as he shot through the door.

"Oi! Come back here. So where's Sid?" Poor boy shouldn't be on his own at a time like this. Not that he had any idea what a time like this was. No brothers and sisters, no experience. Redmond lived in a man's world.

"Last I knew he was pacing up and down outside Maud's in Swan Street, waiting to find out. Sent me here to cover for him. Want me to get him back?"

"No, I'll sort it out. Off you go."

Redmond stuffed his arms into his jacket sleeves and took the stairs two at a time. Least he could do was keep Sid company. He still hadn't got over his sense of guilt when he'd told

Sid he couldn't have Clarrie staying down in the bunk room. No place for a woman, all those snorting, farting, belching men, but he hadn't known she'd nowhere else to go. Not until Sid had told him about Maud's offer. Just as well, if the baby had come already. Christ, he hoped everything went all right. Still, she had Maud and Sid; plenty of girls in her situation would have to do it on their own.

He swung around the corner into Swan Street. No light showing from any of the windows in the first three little workers cottages, but a glimmer illuminated the fourth. He pushed open the gate. A small, hunched figure sat on the doorstep, head down, hands covering his ears.

"Hey." He let his hand hover over Sid's shoulder, unsure whether to offer comfort or wait and see.

Sid lifted his head, uncovered his ears. "I can't stand the screaming. Maud won't let me in. It's not like Clarrie to make such a hullabaloo."

Redmond dropped down next to Sid. Screaming didn't sound good, but he couldn't hear anything at the moment. Surely Maud would have come to talk to Sid if anything was wrong, sent for the doctor even. "I expect you know more about babies than I do, Sid, but a bit of screaming wouldn't be out of place, I shouldn't think."

"Maud didn't say nothing about screaming. Told Clarrie it was like shelling peas." His lips quirked. "I used to shell the peas in the kitchens at the Benevolent Society when I was a nipper. It didn't involve screaming. I would have had me ears boxed."

He needed to take Sid's mind off Clarrie and there wasn't a sound coming from the house. "Want to go down to the Commercial and grab an ale?"

"I'm not leaving, not until I know Clarrie's all right." He

scrubbed his hands over his face. "And the baby," he added, almost as an afterthought. "It's gone real quiet."

It had, almost eerily quiet, and then a beam of light spilt onto the steps. They both scrambled to their feet.

Maud stood illuminated in the doorway, a bundle of blankets in her arms. No sign of any blood, still no noise. Redmond's stomach performed an ungainly somersault. What if . . .

Maud held out her arms. "Say hello to Charlie." She pushed the bundle toward Sid. Hands shaking, he reached out, touched the baby's cheek, then tucked him into the crook of his arm as though he'd been doing it forever.

"Hello, Charlie." Sid's voice trembled and he looked up at Maud. "How's Clarrie? Can I see her?"

"Not yet. She's tired and needs cleaning up. Just wanted you to know Charlie'd arrived. Why don't you take yourself off to the Commercial? A bit of a celebration. Come back in the morning." Maud reached out and took the baby from Sid.

"I want to see Clarrie."

"Not right now. I'll tell her you've met Charlie. Come back tomorrow morning."

Sid's mouth turned down at the corners as the door shut. He looked as though he'd burst into tears.

And so would he in Sid's place, but it didn't sound to Redmond as though anything had gone wrong. "Women's business, lad. Come on. I'll buy you a drink."

Sid made no effort to move, so Redmond slung his arm around his shoulder and guided him down toward the Commercial.

They'd still be open, and from the stunned look on Sid's face he could do with more than an ale. A night for a whiskey, a bottle even.

When Sid downed his second drink, the color came back to his face. "I didn't believe it was real. Not till I held him in my arms. Charlie. Good, strong name that, and then when he's famous, he can be Charles Binks."

"Here's to Charlie. Congratulations, Pa." Redmond tossed back his drink. His thoughts drifted to his father, always one for a whiskey, incapable of doing much more than grumbling since the apoplexy that had sent Redmond to fill his seat in the main office of *The Morpeth Want*. Not a place he'd ever imagined he'd be. He shook away the thought. Not his time. Not now. Sid needed him.

Sid sucked in a mouthful of air and pushed back his chair. "And now comes the hard part."

Surely Clarrie had taken care of that. It wasn't as though she and Sid didn't want the child. "Why the hard part?"

"What we're going to do next. Clarrie won't have anywhere to stay, and without her wages we can't pay Maud. These last weeks, well, they were just out of the kindness of Maud's heart. Can't expect her to keep Clarrie on."

"I'm sorry, Sid. I can't have her staying with you and the other men in the bunk room, and besides, you wouldn't want to take Charlie there."

"Got Charlie sorted. Maud said she'll look after him and we can go and see him whenever we want."

There had to be something he could do. "Let me help." He foraged in his pocket.

A steely look settled on Sid's face. "That's real kind of you, Mr. Kendall, but it ain't going to solve the problem long-term. And Clarrie and Charlie are my responsibility." He squared his shoulders and pushed away his glass. "If you'd like to come good on that promise you made about taking a look at any story I come across, that'd help."

"Of course. I'll pay you stringer's rates, thruppence a line, on top of your wages. I told you that." He wouldn't get away with it if Father got back behind the desk, but for the time being he could honor his promise, and besides, he liked Sid, liked his attitude, his sense of responsibility. "What have you got in mind?"

Sid's cheeks reddened and he sat chewing his lips. "Not too sure about the full story yet, but there's talk about some racket—preying on young girls who've got themselves in . . ." He waved his hand around, as though incapable of finding the word he wanted. "Difficulties," he finally spat out.

Redmond narrowed his eyes. "Like Clarrie, you mean?"

As expected, Sid jumped to the offensive. "Clarrie ain't in difficulties. I'm not going to leave her in the lurch."

"No, Sid. I'm sorry. That's not what I meant."

"It sure sounded like it." He tossed back the remains of his whiskey, stuck on his cloth cap, and stood to leave. "Don't worry about it. Thanks for the drink."

Prickly as an echidna. "Wait up. Tell me about this racket."

Sid stalled, huffed out a sigh, and sat back down. "It's not a pretty story, but people need to know. Need to be warned. Thought the paper would be a good way of going about it."

"Go on." Redmond topped up the glasses and pushed one across to Sid.

He ran his finger around the rim of the glass, then leaned forward. "I've been keeping an eye on the classifieds; last thing I wanted was for Clarrie or Charlie to end up in strife, and no son of mine was going anywhere near the Benevolent Society." He lowered his voice. "There's women advertising all over the show, not just Morpeth—Maitland and Newcastle too. Offering a good home for unwanted babies—for a price—and the other side of the coin, mothers looking for someone to care for their child so they can earn a decent wage. I started asking around. Seems most of these babies don't survive. Just wither away. I thought maybe because they had no one to love them." His face colored again. "It's hard when you ain't got no one. But it's not like that."

"Babies die, Sid; die all the time. Mothers too." Christ, if they didn't he'd have two brothers and a mother, not just a row of stones up on the hill at Hinton.

"Nope. This is different. These women take children in and take the money, as much as ten quid for each baby. They don't feed them proper and the poor little mites die, not even given a proper burial. They know what they're doing."

"Don't the mothers worry about their baby?"

"They think they're placing the child with a caring nurse who's doing the best by them. The girls are told they can visit, and if their circumstances change, have their baby back. Everyone always hopes for the best, don't they?"

No lie in that. Redmond nodded. "And you're worried that might happen to Charlie?" Poor sod, no wonder he looked like he'd gone through a mangle.

"It ain't going to happen to Charlie; Maud's not like that. That's how I found out about this—" He waved his hand as though he couldn't find the words. "I checked her out and a couple of other women. Maud's a midwife. Good and proper. Learned the trade from her mother and took over the business when she passed. Got clients all over Morpeth and Maitland. She doesn't usually take babies in, but she's behind on the rent. That's why Clarrie got to stay with her before Charlie came—she needed a hand. Trouble is, once Clarrie's up and about, she's going to need a proper job. She's good at what she does, maid of all work, and then maybe we can get a bit put by and find somewhere of our own and have Charlie with us."

"Keep your eye on the classifieds. There's often jobs there."

"Most of the jobs are in Maitland. I don't want Clarrie there. She needs to be here in Morpeth, near Charlie and me. Needs to be live-in too. There isn't anything going up at the Breckenridge place, is there? Archer says he's been doing some work in the garden for Miss Theodora."

Nothing he knew of, especially with Theodora's sisters in Sydney. "I can have a word next time I see her." A great excuse. Bring up the trip to Ash Island if he could talk someone into acting as chaperone. Bloody stupid to suggest she needed a chaperone. No one had ever complained when Jamie was around. Now she'd turned twenty-one it was as though she had to be wrapped in cotton wool. No, not since then. Since the wreck. It had changed everyone's life. He tossed back his drink. Now he was getting maudlin. Not that he'd admit it to anyone, but he missed Jamie like an amputated limb. He lifted the bottle and made to fill Sid's glass. Sid covered it with his hand and shook his head. Sensible lad.

"How soon before Clarrie will be up and about?"

"I don't know. Maud reckoned if everything went well, a week; that's when the arrangement comes to an end. It made me cross to begin with, but I can see Maud's point. She's not running a poor house."

"I'll have a word with Theodora. Maybe, when Clarrie's ready, she could go up to the house and talk to her. Though I don't imagine anything will come of it because her sisters are down in Sydney for a while."

"And Miss Theodora's on her own?"

"Not on her own. Wilcox and Mrs. Starling are there, but she might relish a visit; she's promised she won't go out and about alone. She's got some bee in her bonnet about a butterfly. She wants to go to Ash Island. I said I'd take her, but she needs someone with her . . ." And perhaps the gods were smiling on him. "When did you say Clarrie would be up and about?"

"A week, maybe less."

"Is she a good sailor?"

Sid shrugged. "She can swim and she took the steamship down to Sydney to see her mother. Not that that ended well. Why?"

"Wouldn't be a permanent job, a day's pay at most." He'd see to that, and he'd get to spend time with Theodora. Bit conniving, but why not? Everybody would be happy. Theodora would get her butterfly hunt. Clarrie would earn some money. Sid wouldn't feel like he was taking charity. "Leave it with me. And you chase up these women. I want facts and figures, and I want to know what happens to their babies. It sounds like a story that needs telling."

Theodora closed the stable door with a thump. There'd been no sign of Archer for the last couple of days and she had no idea why. She'd sent Wilcox into Morpeth with a note for Redmond, but she'd heard nothing and now Wilcox had gone off somewhere else.

She stomped into the kitchen in search of Mrs. Starling. Thankfully she hadn't vanished; she was standing at the table, up to her armpits in blackberries.

"Have you seen Wilcox?"

"Take your boots off; they'll make my floor dirty."

Theodora sat and reached for her laces and then peered at Mrs. Starling through her curtain of hair. She sounded distinctly out of sorts. "Is everything all right?"

A grunt and a grump were the reply, so she toed off her boots and carried them to the back door.

"I haven't got time to clean your boots any more than I've got time to clean the floor. Wilcox and I are run off our feet keeping on top of everything. It's bad enough when Biddy's here; without her, it's pure torture."

A wave of guilt washed through Theodora. She knew Mrs. Starling had a lot on her plate with Biddy and Mrs. Barnett away. Not that she did much in the way of hard work, but most of the organization fell to her as housekeeper. "I'm sorry." Theodora walked over to the stove. "Is there anything I can do? Stir the jam? Get the jars?" She'd often helped in the kitchen in the past, but lately all her time had been taken with the garden and searching for the butterfly.

"Get some slippers on, then an apron, and stir the jam for me. I'll sort out the jars and then I'll make a cuppa once it's come to the boil."

Calm restored, Theodora stood at the stove, the repetitive movement of the spoon and the sweet smell soothing her. "I haven't seen Archer for a while. I'm worried he might have lost interest in the garden."

"I doubt it. He seems to like my scones." A smile tipped the corner of Mrs. Starling's mouth. "Quickest way to a man's heart . . ."

Which reminded Theodora. "I haven't seen Redmond either. I sent him a note, but he seems to be ignoring me."

"We've all got work to do. And his work is cut out with his father sick again. Has that sugar dissolved yet?"

"Nearly. Shall I make the tea?"

"You keep stirring. I'll sort the tea and leave it to draw while the jam comes to the boil. What do you want with Redmond?"

Theodora clamped her lips together. She'd written to Redmond to ask again if he'd take her to Ash Island, but she didn't want to get into the chaperone argument with Mrs. Starling. "I think there's a blockage in the water pipes." She crossed her fingers against the lie.

"No problems in the house, as far as I know." She pointed to the window. "Why don't you ask the man yourself?"

Redmond was striding toward the kitchen. Theodora put down the spoon and made for the door. The last thing she wanted was to have to explain her trumped-up excuse about water pipes.

"You can't rush off like that. What about the jam?"

Wiping her hands on her apron, Theodora bolted.

"That's a lovely reception." Redmond grinned as she slewed to a halt in front of him. "Pleased to see me, I hope."

"Yes. Yes, I am. Did you get my note?"

"No, I didn't. Is there a problem?"

"Can I talk to you? Let's go and sit down on the veranda." Redmond sniffed the air. "I can smell something good. Cake?"

"Jam, but it's nowhere near ready yet." She untied her apron, bundled it up, and tossed it onto the bench outside the kitchen door. "Come on."

Redmond settled into one of the wicker chairs outside Papa's library with a long-suffering sigh. Theodora snatched a quick look at him. Dark stubble shadowed his jaw and his shirt looked as though he'd slept in it. An air of exhaustion hung over him, and he didn't smell too good either, a bit sweaty with overtones of some sort of alcohol. "Are you well?"

"Just tired. It was a long night, a long day, and then another long night."

The memory of him delivering the news of the *Cawarra*

surfaced. "Why? What's happened?" Concern made her voice sharp.

"Nothing bad. I'm sorry." He reached for her hand. "Good news, in fact." He didn't look like a man delivering good news. "Sid Binks, works at the paper, just had a baby. That's why I didn't get your note. Haven't been in the office."

"A baby! How lovely."

"A boy. Charlie. Truth is, I'm feeling a bit guilty."

Theodora whipped around and stared into his face. "Guilty? Why?" Surely Redmond . . .

Redmond let out a bark of laughter. "Not what you're thinking. Like I said, Sid works at the newspaper. He bunks down in the printing room with some of the other men."

"What about his wife?"

"Clarrie—she's with Maud, the midwife. She used to be the maid of all work at the rectory, but the Reverend Lodestar gave her the sack when he discovered her situation."

"That's terrible. He can't do a thing like that."

"Sadly, he can, and he has."

"But why doesn't she live with her husband . . ." A flood of heat surged through her, no doubt staining her face the color of Mrs. Starling's jam. "I see." She didn't really see, or understand; for that matter, if it hadn't been for Biddy and some of the stories she'd told her, she wouldn't have a clue. "What's going to happen to the baby?"

"Clarrie and Sid are determined to keep Charlie. In fact, they've got it all worked out. Clarrie can stay with Maud until she gets over the birth, and then Maud will look after Charlie when Clarrie gets another job. Problem solved."

That sounded much more like Morpeth, where everyone looked out for their neighbors. "Then why were you up all night?"

"Someone had to keep Sid company. Archer came and got me. Sid was pacing up and down outside Maud's, waiting. The screaming got to him. Once he held his son in his arms he calmed down."

"And what about the mother?"

"Clarrie's fine. Maud shooed us off, so I took him down to the Commercial Hotel to wet the baby's head." He rubbed at his forehead. "It went on for a bit longer than I expected. I bought a bottle of whiskey . . ."

"Oh dear."

"It's what happens next that's the hard part. That's why I'm here. Clarrie won't have anywhere to stay; she'd hoped the reverend would take her back, but that's not going to happen. Without her wages, they can't pay Maud to look after Charlie. These last weeks were just out of the kindness of Maud's heart. No one can expect her to keep Clarrie on. I can't have Clarrie staying with the other men in the bunk room, and besides, it's no place for a baby. I offered to lend Sid some money, but he wouldn't hear of it. He takes his responsibilities very seriously. He did ask, though, if I'd take any stories he wrote. We'd talked about it before."

"And you said yes."

"Of course I did. I'll pay him on top of his regular wages. I won't get away with it if Father's back at the helm, but for the time being I can."

"So the problem is finding Clarrie a job and somewhere to live?"

Redmond nodded. "Sid says she's good at what she does, maid of all work. He's keeping an eye on the classifieds. Needs to be live-in. I don't suppose . . ."

". . . That she could come here?" Theodora's heart sank. She'd love to help, but she couldn't get away with it in the long term. However, with them in Sydney for at least another month, maybe there was something she could do. Get Sid and Clarrie on their feet and find her a job in Morpeth. Maybe she could convince the Reverend Lodestar to see the errors of his ways. But she hadn't even met Clarrie, or Sid, for that matter, and although she trusted Redmond's judgment, this was a big step. "Can you organize for me to meet Clarrie without getting her hopes up? We might be able to find some work for her until Florence and the girls get back. When will she be up and about?"

"She has to leave Maud's in a week, so a day or two before that, I guess. I don't know much about these things."

"Neither do I." Although she did have a vague memory of Mama being up very soon after Viola was born. Perhaps it depended on the birth. "I've got a better idea. I want to go to Ash Island. Could Clarrie come with us? Then no one can complain that I'm alone with you. Suppose you ask Sid if Clarrie would like to come along for the day. That way I can get to know her, and if everything works out, I'll have a word with Mrs. Starling and see what she thinks. She's been run off her feet with Biddy gone."

Redmond jumped up, a big smile on his face. "My thoughts exactly. I'll go and have a word with Sid." He reached out and grasped both her hands, squeezed—squeezed really hard—and stared into her eyes, then leaned closer.

For a moment she thought he might kiss her. She drew back, cheeks afire. Whatever had made her think that?

Redmond cleared his throat and dropped her hands. "It's the perfect solution."

CHAPTER 13

MORPETH, 1922

Dodging a pile of steaming horse manure and several over-loaded drays, Verity wheeled her bicycle across the road and propped it against the picket fence.

The front door of the terrace stood open. She knocked and received no response, so after a moment she went in. The familiar odor of printing ink lingered in the air and the staccato sound of a typewriter—*tap, tap, tappity-tap, ping*—drifted down the hallway.

"Hello!"

The pecking continued and no answer was forthcoming, so she continued past two closed doors until she reached the room at the back of the building where a man sat, back to the door, hammering away on a Remington about the same vintage as Grandpa Sid's. Below her feet she could sense the vibrations of a printing press—the dull *thud, thud, thud* as the steam-driven press spewed out the printed pages.

"Just put the copy on the table. I'll have a look later."

"I'm looking for a Mr. Kendall."

A final thump on a couple of keys and the chair scraped back. The man unwound his long, lanky frame and squinted at her before removing a pair of wire-rimmed spectacles with lenses as thick as the bottom of a lemonade bottle. "I don't think we've met." He dragged his fingers through his already disheveled hair, river-green eyes fixed her with a penetrating stare.

"My name's Verity Binks. I'd like to speak to Mr. Kendall."

He thrust out his hand, paused, examined the smudged ink on his palm, and shoved it into his pocket. "That's me. Arlo Kendall. Sorry about the state. Deadline looming and we're miles behind."

"Perhaps I should come back later?"

"Depends how long you're going to take. Binks, you said. Have we met?"

"I don't believe so. My grandfather worked on *The Morpeth Want* when he was a boy."

"Got it! Sid Binks." His smile widened and the faint lines fanning the corners of his eyes deepened. "Compositor extraordinaire. His name's still spoken down there"—he gestured to a steep flight of stairs that led down into a patch of dungeon darkness—"with reverence. We call it Binks's Basement."

A surge of warmth stippled Verity's skin. No matter what happened about Treadwell's story, her trip had been worth it just for this.

"How is the old man?"

"He died a couple of years ago, never recovered from the influenza. I lost my grandmother too." The words snagged in her throat. She'd offered a hundred times to bring Sid and Clarrie up to Morpeth on the train, but they'd always refused. Said the past was best left where it belonged.

"I'm sorry to hear that." His expression reflected a wealth of sympathy. "There're a few people in town who'd like to pay their respects to Sid Binks. Perhaps . . . I'm sorry, but I really must finish this." He slumped down at the typewriter. "We've cut back to one edition a week and I still don't seem to get through everything in time." With a grimace, he hooked his spectacles over his ears, turned to the typewriter, and began pecking at the keys.

"I was hoping to visit The Landing."

His head came up with a snap and he swiveled around. "The Landing?"

"I believe your family owns the property."

"Well, yes, I do, but why?"

And now she'd landed herself in a bit of a pickle. Mr. Treadwell had specifically said he didn't want his name connected with Morpeth, but she couldn't ignore the uncanny coincidence of the butterfly in the painting.

"I came across a painting of Morpeth and it reminded me of my grandfather." She stared into his eyes, determined not to fall into the age-old liar's trap by looking away.

"So this visit to Morpeth is some kind of a pilgrimage?"

A pilgrimage. One she should have made and now she had the perfect excuse. "Yes." She gave a gentle smile, hoping to mask her contrivance. "Exactly that. I know nothing of his early life. I hope to write an article about him."

"I'd be happy to show you around the place, but . . ." He pointed to the table, covered in an alarming array of screwed-up bits of this and that. "I must get the classifieds sorted. So many people rely on them, and I can't let them down. And the boys downstairs can't make a start until I finish."

Verity felt the heat rise to her face. He was so friendly. And she wasn't even telling him the truth. "Perhaps I could help out. I used to work for *The Sydney Arrow*." She waved her hand over the pile of papers. "This was my job."

His face broke into the most amazing smile sparking deep

dimples in his cheeks, and he leaped to his feet. "You are without doubt a gift from the gods, Miss Binks."

An embarrassing rush of heat made her cheeks flush again. "Most people call me Verity." Trying to appear businesslike, she took off her jacket and hat, hung them on the back of the chair, then took his place at the typewriter.

"Verity it is, then." He dived into the middle of the big pile of mixed papers and pulled one out. Shook his head, crumpled up the page, and tossed it aside. "Done that one." He swept back his hair in exasperation and reached into the pile again. "Ah! This one. Wanted to rent. Storage space close to Queens Wharf."

Verity wound the paper onto the roller and began typing. "Would you like them all on one page or individually?"

He perched on the side of the table, long legs stretched out, his hair increasingly unkempt and his square jaw showing signs of the need for a razor. "Arlo, call me Arlo. One page will do, double-spaced. Just leave a decent gap between each one; makes it easier for the boys downstairs. Hang on while I find another." He shuffled through the mess on the table.

There had to be a quicker way. Verity pulled a handful of papers toward her, but it was impossible to know which he'd completed and which he hadn't. He had no system whatsoever. "Is there anything else you need typed? I could do that while you're sorting the classifieds."

"Only a couple of letters to the editor, but they're in here." He tapped his temple. "Sometimes have to stir up the odd bit of interest in local matters."

"Just a moment." She rummaged in her satchel and brought out her notebook and pencil. "If you dictate the letters, I'll take them down, and while I'm typing them up, you can sort out these bits of paper."

It took an hour to clear the tabletop and type up the letters to the editor and the classifieds. Arlo had spent most of the time scratching his head, praising her shorthand skills, and lobbing wadded up pieces of paper into a repurposed Valvoline motor oil can with well-practiced skill.

He flopped down into the chair. "You must be starving. Let me buy you lunch."

"I could certainly do with a drink." And a sandwich wouldn't go amiss, despite her huge breakfast, but she could hardly take lunch from the man for an hour's work.

"I'll just take these downstairs while you put on your hat and we'll go next door and see what's what. The baker's wife runs a nice little tea shop. Does that suit you?"

He clattered down the stairs without waiting for an answer and not two seconds later, as she pulled on her cloche, he returned.

"I've got a better idea. Why don't I take you out to The Landing and we can find some refreshments there? I've got the boat tied up at the wharf."

"The boat?"

"Yes, a clinker; it's been in the family for years. Much more pleasant than walking."

"I have my bicycle outside."

"We can bring it in here, just to be on the safe side, though I can guarantee it won't go missing. Nothing goes astray in Morpeth. That's the trouble. No news to report."

He threw her a grin and took off down the hallway, wheeled in her bicycle, and leaned it against the wall. "Right, off we go."

He offered his arm and together they walked—no, not walked, galloped—out into the street. Arlo seemed to do everything at fifty miles an hour, except perhaps typing.

"Coming from Sydney you'd have had experience with boats?"

A ferry once in a while, but nothing else. "A little."

"Boats, ships, have been part of my life for longer than I can remember—part of everyone's life in Morpeth. You could say the town was built on the funnel of a steamer. Grandfather started *The Morpeth Want* back in the 1830s when the town first came into its own. He reckoned he'd print a paper that covered—"

"—everything anyone might want." The words popped out of her mouth.

Arlo's eyebrows shot up.

"Grandpa Sid."

"Ah! The renowned Mr. Binks."

Biting her lip, Verity nodded, her attention drawn to a large bird as it swooped down to the shallows.

"A white-necked heron. See the double line of spots running down its chest?" Arlo took the steep track down to the wharf in an energetic bound. "We don't usually see them this close to the wharf. It has plum-colored nuptial plumes during the breeding season." He turned back with a sheepish smile. "Waterbirds, the river, really, is a bit of a passion of mine. Here we are."

A small boat bobbed against the wharf, the shiny timber and brass fittings gleaming in the sunlight. "Father's first love was engineering, but he was forced to step into my grandfather's shoes and manage the newspaper. The clinker was his relaxation; same as some men ride, he liked to be out on the river. She's still going strong."

He stood, hands thrust deep in his pockets, the wind tugging his overlong hair. "This is where passengers and goods boarded the steamers heading for Maitland, Newcastle, and

Sydney. The steamers used to come right up to Morpeth, some-times beyond, but with the growth of Newcastle as a port, Morpeth has settled into a backwater. Only barges use the river beyond here nowadays. Even the old punt service has gone out of business since they built the bridge."

He unraveled a rope tied around a bollard and tugged the boat closer until it sat at the bottom of a set of steep vertical steps dangling over the side of the wharf. "The river's tidal, even this far up. Think you can handle the ladder? It's a bit daunting at low tide until you get the hang of it."

A knot tightened in Verity's stomach as she peered over the edge. She gritted her teeth and swallowed her fear. "I'll manage."

"Let me take your satchel." Without waiting for a reply, he took the strap from her shoulder and threw it diagonally across his body, then stepped over the edge.

How badly did she need to go to The Landing? Why couldn't she have ridden her bicycle across the bridge? What in God's name had possessed her?

"Untie the rope before you come down."

A quiver of trepidation made her fumble as she loosened the rope and dropped it down onto the deck. The boat bobbed and ducked alarmingly despite Arlo's efforts to hold it firm. He had his face turned aside as though he'd far better things to be doing . . . then the penny dropped. He wasn't impatient or ig-noring her. Quite the opposite, he was behaving like the perfect gentleman and looking away so he couldn't see up her skirt.

Her blood thrummed in her ears and her palms grew damp; she pulled off her cloche, tucked it in her pocket, then clung to the metal handrails and lowered herself over the edge onto the first step and struggled down, determined to get onto the boat as fast as she could.

Before she'd reached the bottom of the ladder, he grasped her around the waist and her feet went from under her as he swept her off. He spun her around, laughter dancing in his eyes, then lowered her to the deck. "There we are. Not too hard. You'll be an old hand before long."

Maybe, if she could control the ridiculous skipping of her heart. An ear-splitting blast rent the air and the boat lurched and swayed as a barge pulled up alongside the wharf. Struggling to regain her balance, she grasped for his hand; just the barest brush of skin against skin, then their fingers interlocked. His warm hand cradled hers, holding her steady.

For a moment they stood, shoulders touching, then laughing self-consciously, untangled their fingers. "We need to get out of the way." Arlo leaned over the side and pushed out into the river, then cranked the engine and, with a cough and a splutter, the boat picked up speed.

Holding her hair back from her face, Verity stood with her legs braced against the swell, reveling in the sense of freedom. Something stirred deep within her, something unfamiliar yet calming. She drew in a breath and let it slip slowly between her lips. So much closer to the water, she was at one with the birds as they skimmed the river, weightless and free.

Arlo stood, hand relaxed on the tiller, eyes scanning the river.

She stole a furtive glance at him and their eyes met. "It's my favorite way to travel."

And could well become hers. "Morpeth's a lovely little town and the river seems so peaceful now we're away from the wharf."

He let out a long and somewhat painful sigh. "It is, but sadly it's not good for business. We used to publish the paper three times a week. I'm not sure if we can keep going much longer. Trouble is, we're a bit of a tradition in the town, and I'd hate to put the boys in the print room out of a job."

In the space of a moment he looked as though he shouldered an enormous burden. So many questions she wanted to ask—the man was such a mass of contradictions, unlike anyone she'd ever met before, but the closed look on his face as he stared ahead prevented her from asking more. Instead, she changed the subject. "Arlo's an interesting name. I've never heard it before."

He gave a dry laugh. "Blame my father and his wishful thinking. He named me after Arlo Bates, the American newspaperman. He hoped I'd follow in his footsteps. I try, but to be honest I'd rather spend my time on the river—such an array of wildlife. One day I hope to publish a book. I have detailed records of all the birds, but sadly my artistic talents are somewhat lacking."

The boat nosed its way toward a sturdy wharf on the opposite bank and Arlo expertly cut the engine and drifted in. He fastened a small rope to the steps. "Welcome to The Landing."

Verity scampered up onto the wharf and caught the heavier rope he threw to her and twisted it around the bollard.

"We'll make a sailor out of you yet."

Perhaps he would. It was a tempting prospect.

As she straightened up, a tingling traced her skin. No doubt she was in the right place. Whoever had painted Mrs. Treadwell's picture knew The Landing, and knew it well.

CHAPTER 14

Clarrie scurried down Swan Street, her collar pulled up under her ears and her hands stuffed into her pockets, fighting the horrendous sense of bereavement she'd suffered as she'd peered down into Charlie's angelic face before she'd crept out of the front door and set off for the wharf.

When Sid had told her about the trip to Ash Island she couldn't refuse. Already Maud was making noises about her finding a proper job or paying board and lodging. It was only fair; that was their deal. It was just that she hadn't expected the time to go so fast or the way her heart twisted when she left Charlie.

Sid reckoned the trip might lead to a real job, but Mr. Kendall wouldn't say one way or the other. Nevertheless, if it didn't work out, today's money would still be useful. She could pay Maud off for her lying-in.

True to his word, Mr. Kendall was sitting waiting in his boat by the punt. "Down you come," he called.

The tiny boat bobbed around on the current, nothing like the Sydney steamer, which had a gangplank and a rail to hang on to. She hovered, unsure how to get onto the boat.

"That's a girl. Take it easy." Mr. Kendall's hand reached out and helped her step across onto the deck. "Not so bad, hey? Sit yourself down and we'll be off. I said I'd pick Miss Breckenridge up at The Landing. You sit back and get used to the ride. She's a nice little thing." He patted the tiller as though he were talking about a pet dog.

"Is there anything special you want me to do, Mr. Kendall?"

"Your job today is to be a chaperone." He rolled his eyes. "I can assure you Miss Breckenridge doesn't have any need for a chaperone, but if it keeps her big sister happy, then that's what we'll do. I hope the two of you get along."

So did she. "And we're going butterfly hunting?" It seemed ludicrous. Paid to go hunting for butterflies. She pushed her hands farther into her pockets and hunched down, trying to escape the wind. A trip like this might be quite nice in the summer, but winter was on the way and the air had a nasty, sharp bite.

Once they'd lost sight of the town, birds rose from the bank and flapped their way over the water, ghostly in the morning mist. Clarrie kept staring at the bank, waiting for the first glimpse of the house. She and Sid never ventured this far along the river, but she knew the barges came this way with their deliveries to Hinton and Paterson.

Mr. Kendall cut the engine and in silence they drifted toward the bank. He must have done it a hundred times because he couldn't be able to see two inches in front of his nose, what with the mist.

The front end of the boat nudged the wharf and came to a halt. Like one of those snake charmers she'd seen in pictures, he threw the rope up and it wound its way around the bollard. "Ahoy there, Breckenridge!" he called, the laughter in his voice clear as a bell.

"Ahoy there, Captain Kendall."

Clarrie buried her grin in her collar. She hadn't known Mr. Kendall and Miss Breckenridge were mates.

As the first fingers of dawn caressed the glassy surface of the river, the *Petrel* nudged up against the wharf. A swarm of poignant memories surfaced. Days with Papa, Jamie, and Redmond, drifting up and down the river, fishing; big juicy bream and flathead cooked over a fire on the bank; trips to Ash Island; visits with Harriet and Helena. Theodora shook away the thoughts and hefted the picnic hamper Mrs. Starling had insisted on providing.

"Hand it down. Good to know we won't starve."

Through the mist a dark shape moved and shifted into view. "Theodora, this is Clarrie. Your chaperone. And, Clarrie, this is Miss Breckenridge."

"Pleased to meet you, miss." Clarrie tried for some sort of a bow but a gust of wind buffeted the boat and she staggered, almost losing her balance.

"I don't think we need to stand on ceremony, Clarrie. Thank you for coming."

Once Redmond had stowed the picnic hamper, she passed down her butterfly net and satchel, unhooked the rope, and swung down the ladder, landing on the deck with a jump. Such a long time since she'd been out in the boat. It really was time she stopped moping. Jamie and Papa wouldn't want her to be miserable and they'd be pleased to know the *Petrel* was cared for and used.

"All set?"

Theodora settled down next to Clarrie. "Can't wait."

Depending on the current it would take them a while to get to Ash Island and she had every intention of enjoying herself.

As the mist lifted the river came alive, winding like a silver ribbon through the landscape. Long-legged cormorants dressed in their Sunday best sat fearlessly on the bleached-white branches of the dead trees, and Pacific gulls skimmed the water diving for fish among the black swans, sickle bills, and countless other swamp birds.

The frail warmth of the morning sun caressed her cheeks and she tilted her head up to the sky where an eagle cruised the air currents. "Look, Clarrie." She pointed up into the blue expanse.

Clarrie shaded her eyes. "It's an eagle. I've never seen one so close. It's huge."

"The Great New Holland eagle *Aquila fucosa*," said Redmond. Theodora wiggled her eyebrows, trying, and failing, to control the smile on her face.

"I didn't know you were a bird-watcher. I thought your passion lay with gadgets and machines."

"I'm a man of many talents." He bit his lip, masking his grin, as happy as she was to be out on the water.

"I can see that." With his jacket off, his shirt sleeves pushed up to the elbows, and the wind blowing his hair off his face, he looked so very different from the suited and starched man who spent his days in the newspaper office—more like the boy she remembered, always with Jamie, always getting into scrapes. "Do you remember when we came up here and camped out under the ash trees?"

Redmond's laugh echoed across the water. "The night of the Great Moth Hunt?"

"It wasn't a moth hunt; it was an ambush. You and Jamie set out to terrify me with that sheet."

Harriet and Helena had carefully hung a sheet between two trees and returned to the house for candles and a lamp, intending to lure the moths into a trap. She'd been tasked with organizing the pill boxes and nets to collect the specimens. Job done, she'd wandered down to the water's edge to watch the sunset, only to hear strange wailing sounds at the site. She'd rushed back straight into the arms of an enormous wraith who'd captured her and carried her away.

"We paid the price. We were black and blue from the struggle you put up."

"And the hiding Papa gave you both!" Laughter bubbled to her lips. "Served you right."

Clarrie's mouth gaped and she looked askance at their familiarity.

"Have you got any brothers and sisters?" Theodora asked, wanting to include Clarrie in the conversation.

"No, miss, no, I haven't. Just my mam and me."

Her mother? An only daughter and her mother had left her to face her situation alone. "Where is your mother?" Theodora clapped her hand over her mouth. Clarrie's mother must have passed. "I'm sorry. I miss my mother dreadfully too."

"She's not dead, miss. She lives in Sydney. She's a seamstress."

"And she can't help you and Charlie?" For heaven's sake, the tone of incredulity in her voice was nothing short of rude.

Redmond obviously thought the same, if his scowl was anything to go by. "Life on Ash Island was very different, Clarrie." He rescued Theodora with a change of topic. "Helena and Harriet moved there when they were fourteen, still young enough to enjoy the freedom but old enough to wander. They often camped out at night and Jamie, Theodora, and I were lucky enough to continue the tradition. We loved the place."

"We had to keep it a secret from Mama though; she would have worried. I envied the sisters the freedom they had."

Clarrie's forehead creased in a frown. "Why did they leave?"

"Mr. Scott never really got back on his feet after the depression in the 1840s. He sold off many of his other assets, but in the end there was nothing left and so he had to part with Ash Island. It bankrupted him, and the family had to leave and return to Sydney."

"Mr. Scott must have been real rich if he owned a whole island."

"Being rich doesn't save you from bad luck and foolish decisions." A wistful note laced Theodora's voice. Poor Mrs. Scott's death and then Helena's beloved husband's. She shuddered—the Breckenridge family wasn't the only one to be plagued by misfortune. "They're dividing the island up into private land holdings, but the family house is still there and a small parcel of land. A man named Hench lives there as caretaker. We'll probably bump into him."

Redmond pulled hard on the tiller and edged the *Petrel* between two small islands, so close to the bank they almost ran aground between the mudflats and mangroves. "Ash Island ahead."

"In my mind the island will always belong to the Scotts. They were the first people to call it home."

"Not the first people by any means." Redmond waved his arm around, encompassing the wide stretch of river. "The old fellas claim the area has provided food for thousands of years, long before we arrived—waterbirds, shellfish, wetland plants, mammals, and fish."

Clarrie clutched at her throat and screwed up her face. "I'm not over keen on fish. It's the bones."

"Then we'll have to catch some flathead and ask Redmond to clean and prepare it. He's a master."

Redmond quirked a smile. "Another day, perhaps. We've got Mrs. Starling's picnic and we're almost there. Keep your eyes open and see if you can pick out the house. Look for the point facing upriver."

Nothing looked as Theodora remembered until they rounded a bend in the river and two tall, straight Norfolk pines and a huge Morton Bay fig came into view, standing sentinel, marking the jetty and the cottage.

A heavy numbness invaded her limbs. An air of despondency hung over the single-story dwelling at the end of the wharf. Gone were the brightly colored lamps and the tables and chairs where she'd spent so many happy hours enjoying the breeze, the flow of the river, and the play of light across its surface. The wildly overgrown garden, once carefully tended, merged into the bush, and the rickety gate hung from one hinge, held upright by nothing more than rampant creepers. In just a few short years nature had begun to reclaim its own.

Redmond skillfully brought the clinker around, gliding between the thick green banks, and docked. "You two go and have a look. I'll be with you in a minute or two when I've secured the ropes."

Theodora wandered down the dilapidated jetty, Clarrie by her side. "It's such a pity that Harriet and Helena are no longer here."

"Maybe they'll come back. I can't imagine leaving such a beautiful spot."

Theodora shook her head. She'd harbored the same hope for some time, but she had seen the reports in the newspaper. Redmond was quite right. Mr. Scott's entire two thousand and fifty-six-acre grant had been subdivided into small farms that

were gradually being sold off, leaving just a small area surrounding the house. No sign of the orange grove that used to
provide boxes and boxes of fruit for Sydney, nor the rambling
plot that had kept the family and their multitude of visitors in
fresh vegetables.

Theodora stepped up onto the veranda and rubbed the heel
of her hand on the window of the room where Helena and
Harriet painted and compiled their notes and observations.
They called it Mr. Scott's study, but it was more than that,
so much more: the hub of the house, a meeting place for the
family and visitors alike. She stepped aside so Clarrie could
look inside. "This is the room where the sisters worked on
their illustrations. Mr. Scott's desk used to be here under the
window."

The big table still stood in the center of the room, but the
desk had vanished, and there was no sign of the trademark
paints and specimen cabinets that once lined the walls. "I miss
the sisters and the time I spent here. There was a grand piano
in the sitting room; both Harriet and Helena used to play.
Sometimes Viola would come and accompany them, but she
didn't like the trip. She said the damp air was bad for the cello,
but I rather think it was her hair she worried about."

Clarrie stifled a snort. "Miss! That's not a very nice thing
to say."

"Maybe not but it's true. I'm not missing my sisters one
wink." But Ash Island would never be the same without
Harriet and Helena. "The walls were covered in the most
amazing collection of artworks and paintings, some of them
by Conrad Martens."

"I don't think I've met him. Is he a Morpeth man?"

"He lives in Sydney, but he used to visit here." She sighed,
remembering Mr. Martens's patient tutorials. "He's the most

brilliant landscape artist. He taught me so much about light and shadow and perspective."

"Shall we go and see if we can find your butterflies? It might cheer you up a bit."

Despite the poignant memories, Clarrie's company lifted Theodora's spirits. "Yes, let's." She slipped her arm through Clarrie's.

"I don't mind helping, miss; in fact, I want to. But I don't think I could kill a butterfly. Sid said you have to stab them. It sounds a bit barbaric."

"I thought that to begin with, but they don't feel anything and I need them to stay still if I'm going to paint them." Theodora brought her index finger and thumb together. "A gentle squeeze on its thorax, the middle section of its body, is enough to stun it."

Clarrie shuddered. "You choke them? It must hurt."

"They're not like us. They have cold and sluggish juices and don't feel any pain. You'll see. I'll go and get the nets and boxes from the boat."

"I'll go. Why don't you sit down here and have a rest?"

Before Theodora could reply, Clarrie set off down the wharf. Theodora walked back to the house and tried the door. It swung open with barely a squeak. "Hello? Hench, are you here?" With any luck he'd be outside working and she'd have an opportunity to wander through the rooms and remember the past.

Receiving no response, she stepped inside. The sitting room remained as she remembered; the piano in place, though covered with a thick blanket of dust, and large dark rectangles peppering the mottled wallpaper where paintings once hung.

She returned to the hallway and made her way through the house to the kitchen at the back. As she stepped under the walkway, a swishing sound caught her attention and in the corner of her vision a black shadow slipped away into the overgrown garden. "Hench? Is that you?" She shook her head. It couldn't be Hench. The noise had sounded more like a woman's skirt. With a frown, she followed the path to the vegetable garden, but there was no sign or sound of anything or anyone other than her overactive imagination sending her heart into a pitter-patter rhythm. Was it Mrs. Scott or one of the girls she'd conjured from her memories?

"Miss Theodora, Miss Theodora! Where are you?" Clarrie's panicked cry dragged her back from the past.

"I'm here. I'm coming." Giving the house a wide berth, she tramped around the overgrown garden to the spot where Redmond and Clarrie waited. "You've got everything. Lovely."

Armed with Theodora's satchel and butterfly net, they set off into the forest behind the house, past the ploughed field that had housed the orange orchard and beyond, to the stand of paperbark trees. The rush of air whipped Theodora's hair into a tangle and she pulled it free of its pins.

"What are we looking for exactly, miss?"

Redmond reached for Clarrie's hand to attract her attention and raised his finger to his lips.

Clarrie's gasp of wonder broke the silence.

A shimmer of russet disrupted the shadows. Tiptoeing forward, Theodora pointed to a clump of paperbark trees. Huddled together to preserve warmth, hundreds of butterflies clustered on the trunks and branches—a mass of autumn leaves flickering and shimmering in the shafts of sunlight.

A weight lifted from her shoulders. It was as if she'd been holding her breath since she'd seen the first butterfly in the garden. She hadn't imagined it. Hundreds, maybe thousands clustered in the stand of paperbarks like swarms of bees, just as Harriet had suggested in her letter, waiting for spring to come.

The cluster rippled, then the first butterfly took wing and the next and the next. Starting as a stream, the cascade grew. The sound of their beating wings magnified like a waterfall and the air above became orange, blotting out the bright autumn sky.

Almost swooning, Theodora stood rooted to the spot.

"Miss Theodora, quickly."

She spun around and Clarrie held out her butterfly net. "Thank you." Grasping the net she swept it in a wide arc and with a flick of her wrist trapped several of the butterflies. She sank to the ground and reached into the net. Her fingers closed around the first butterfly. It fluttered, its wings tapping against the netting, then stilled as she gently squeezed her fingers together before it could damage itself.

"Miss . . ." Clarrie crouched next to her holding the first pill box.

She dropped the butterfly inside and Clarrie fastened the lid. Theodora tipped back her head, a sense of weightlessness, pure joy flooding her body. There was no doubt she had her specimens. She hadn't dreamed that first sighting in Mama's garden of the Monarch butterfly.

As the shadows lengthened, Clarrie and Theodora filled the specimen boxes and the swarm of butterflies began to return to the trees.

"We've disturbed them enough; we should leave." Redmond reached for the butterfly net and the specimen boxes. "I'll take these back to the boat."

"But what happens if they fly away and we can't find them again?" Clarrie sounded as though she might cry.

Theodora understood—the sight had robbed her of

coherent thought, leaving a confused sense of wonder and dis-belief. She stared at the butterflies, trying to imprint the image of the cluster in her befuddled brain. "I don't think they'll leave, at least not until the weather warms up and they go in search of a place to lay their eggs."

"Where will that be?" Clarrie whispered.

"Wherever they can find the plants they need." Taking one final glance to ensure she hadn't imagined the sight, she reached for Clarrie's hand. "Redmond's right, we don't want to disturb them any more."

When they reached the wharf, Redmond was sitting on the end, his long legs dangling over the still, dark water. Another man stood next to him, legs planted wide, cracking his knuck-les. Theodora's scalp prickled.

"Who's that?" Clarrie whispered.

"Hench. He's the caretaker I told you about. He used to work for my father."

"He looks angry."

"Come on." Theodora lifted her chin, pulse thundering, and marched down the wharf. "Hello, Hench."

He raised his head and pulled back his lips, revealing a mouth full of tobacco-stained teeth punctuated by random gaps. "Just telling Redmond, here—this is private property. Can't take a trip out here whenever you feel like it. That's trespassing."

The curl of anger Theodora had nursed since she first saw Hench standing at the end of the wharf unraveled. How dare he spoil this magical moment? "We are here by invitation."

Hench expelled a wheeze of disbelief, bringing with it the stench of stale tobacco and something worse, rotten and ran-cid. "Not likely. I'd know if Scott was in the area; he would have told me he was coming." He puffed out his chest, a look of self-importance etched on his craggy face.

"Harriet and Helena Scott invited me, and Mr. Scott is aware of my visit." Not quite the truth, but there would be little way of Hench proving otherwise. And then she remembered the figure she'd conjured as she'd walked through the house. "If our visit is a problem, why didn't you approach me when I went up to the house?"

Hench rammed his fists into the pockets of his filthy trousers. "Wasn't up at the house." He shot a look over his shoulder. "There's no one there. My camp's in the boathouse."

How strange. She must have imagined the figure at the house, some memory of time gone by. "We're leaving now." Theodora swept past him and stepped onto the deck, Redmond close on her heels. "Come along." She held out her hand to help Clarrie aboard. Hench tossed the ropes after her and, without a word, Redmond reversed out into the river.

"I can't imagine why Papa employed Hench in the first place; he's always made my flesh creep."

Redmond handed Theodora the tiller and bent to coil the ropes. "He's an experienced sailor, good with steam engines; doesn't relate to people well though. Ash Island's probably the best place for him, out of harm's way."

"You don't think he'll hurt the butterflies, do you?"

"Probably doesn't even know they're there. You heard him; he lives in the old boathouse, and I didn't mention them."

Theodora let the air whistle out between her lips, sat back, and lifted her face to the sky. "I've never seen anything so beautiful."

"All those beating wings, like a great big heart, pumping with life." Clarrie's face shone. "How long will they stay there? Can we come back again?"

"I know very little. I'll write to the Entomological Society and tell them what we've seen." A surge of excitement swept through her. "We might be the first people in Australia to witness their arrival." She reached out and grasped Clarrie's hand. "I'm so pleased you came with us." Theodora meant every word she said; her discovery was so much sweeter for having people to share it with, and Clarrie seemed to truly appreciate the beauty of the butterflies. "We should write down everything we remember about today. Will you help me?"

"I'd love to, miss."

CHAPTER 15

Verity meandered through the meadow of wildflowers; the shadows had lengthened and something new and thrilling spiked her blood. It had begun not with the arrival of the costume, or Mr. Bailey's acceptance of her piece about the ball, not even the meeting with Treadwell, but with that first sight of the painting that had drawn her into the web of curiosity and led her here, to The Landing.

Before her, cloaked in tendrils of afternoon mist, stood a two-story stone house unlike anything she had ever seen before. Surveying the river from the slight rise where it perched, the rambling manor house, with its sloping slate roof and profusion of chimneys, might have fallen from a storybook. A huge window dominated the front of the house, hundreds of tiny rectangular panes catching the afternoon sun, twinkling as though in recognition of her arrival.

"Welcome to The Landing. A sprawling ruin, I'm afraid."

Verity's voice was snatched and for a moment she couldn't answer. With the rising mist and the faded grandeur of the house as a backdrop, Arlo resembled a brooding hero from a gothic novel. "It's like a fairy tale," she breathed.

"That's probably because it was built to recapture my grand-mother's home—an Elizabethan manor house in Cornwall."

His grandmother's house? Hadn't the ladies of the reading circle said that the Kendalls had bought the house from the Breckenridge family? "Your family came from Cornwall?"

"My mother's side."

Verity studied his friendly face. And suddenly everything fell into place. His grandfather was the romantic hero who had brought his wife across the seas before they perished in the awful catastrophe of the SS *Cawarra*. "Your mother was one of the Breckenridge daughters, the one who remained in Morpeth?"

"So you're abreast of the local tittle-tattle."

Willing the embarrassed flush in her cheeks to subside, she nodded. "The Ladies Reading Circle. We were discussing romance."

His quirked eyebrow and his half smile simply increased the heat in her face. Sensing her discomfort, he reached for her hand. "Come along, we'll find a cup of tea. I'm rattling around here on my own so you'll have to excuse the mess." He led her up a set of stone steps to a flagged terrace. "The view from here over the river is said to resemble the Fowey River in Cornwall. I've never been to England. Have you?"

She shook her head and tucked a rogue strand of hair be-hind her ear. "And I've no idea of my family's origins. I've always presumed convict, nothing to be proud of." She was about to launch into the story of Sid's childhood, but she held her tongue. Large families, those with aunts and uncles and cousins, some even "twice removed," had always fascinated her, even though Grandpa Sid wore his orphan status with pride. He always said that until he met Grandma Clarrie he hadn't wanted or needed anyone. She'd proved him wrong.

"What was it you were hoping to find?"

The mere thought of having to explain herself made Verity's pulse race. The least she could do was honor Mr. Treadwell's request and not involve his family. She searched for an alternative explanation and decided she could do no better than follow Arlo's lead.

"As you said, more of a pilgrimage than anything. Grandpa Sid only talked about his early life as he got older." She licked her dry lips. She wanted to be honest. Having to conceal the truth from the man who had been so charmingly open with her made her squirm. "The painting of Morpeth I saw was unsigned—a beautiful orange and black butterfly and a house in the background. It was titled *The Landing, Hunter River, Morpeth*. I recognized the name so I wanted to come and have a look." No lie in that.

"It sounds like one of my mother's paintings, but to the best of my knowledge she never sold any. I don't have any recollection of her even gifting one. She painted the most exquisite watercolors, butterflies mostly, and she liked to set the location of the sighting by including a landmark."

Verity tried to make sense of his words; the invitation and her costume to the ball must somehow be tied to The Landing.

"Mother was very much influenced by the Scott sisters, the naturalist painters. As a child, she spent time with them upriver near Newcastle before they sold up. They went on to make quite a name for themselves, unusual at that time for women to breach the barricades of the male-dominated world of science."

Verity stood stock-still. How was she going to sort this out without telling him about the invitation and mentioning the Treadwell name? Whatever had possessed her to encourage Arlo's presumption that she was trying to find out about

Grandpa Sid's time in Morpeth? A pilgrimage? More like a nightmare.

"Come along. Let's go inside and I'll show you the house."

He saved her having to reply by wrestling with a circular handle set into one of the large double doors, then leaned his shoulder against it and pushed it open to reveal a massive room. It rivaled the Sydney Town Hall, its soaring ceiling lit by sparkling beams of sunshine from the hundreds of glass panes.

"A lot of the rooms are closed off. I mainly use the sitting room and, of course, the kitchen and a bedroom upstairs. I have a woman who comes every day and an old fellow who potters in the garden. He has trouble keeping on top of everything, but I can't bring myself to let him go."

So he wasn't married. Unable to control her wide smile, Verity glanced at him from beneath her lashes and met his attentive gaze.

"Let me show you my favorite place." He threw open a door on the right to reveal a spacious, sunlit room. Acres of leather-bound tomes lined two of the walls and a large cedar desk, the size of a small boat, sat in front of the expansive window. A peculiar cluster of museum-style cabinets lined one wall, and framed botanical watercolors adorned the remaining wall space. The air, redolent with heady notes of antiquity, paint, and a spicy, herbal scent, made her nostrils twitch.

"This is where my mother did most of her painting. Sadly, I didn't inherit her talent. I'm considering resorting to a camera to record the birdlife on the river." Arlo pulled open a drawer and took out a sketchbook, running his long fingers over the cover, almost in a caress, then laid it reverently on the table. "She loved her butterflies, particularly these—she liked to call them Wanderers, *Danaus plexippus*." He skimmed through several of the pages. "Sit down."

There was no doubt the same person had painted these pictures as the one she'd seen at Treadwell House. Every page showed a black and orange butterfly, just like her costume for the ball. The connection fizzed through her veins.

"Why don't I go and find us that cup of tea?"

"That would be lovely." With a sense of regret, she closed the book and turned to follow him.

"Stay here, have a look around. I won't be a moment; there may even be cake." He patted the back of the chair, then strode off, his boots ringing on the honey-colored floorboards.

She returned to the sketchbook and continued to admire the illustrations. The Wanderer butterfly drawn from every angle, in every position, so perfect. She could imagine them flying free from the page and the room filling with the beating of their wings. When she reached the final page, she sighed—a huge cluster of the butterflies, hanging like leaves from a group of trees, the brilliant blue of the sky behind them accentuating the intricate patterns of their wings and giving the impression that they would, at any moment, fly from the page.

Leaving the book, she strolled around the room, peering into the glass-topped display cabinet full of butterflies, their colors vibrant, their bodies impaled by long silver pins. Leaning forward, she studied them more closely, her nose tingling at the piquant, woody fragrance she'd first noticed when she came into the room.

"Here we are." Arlo bounded through the door and set down a tray.

Verity inhaled again, trying to place the smell.

Arlo sniffed in sympathy. "It's camphor. It's used to preserve the butterflies once they've been stunned."

"Stunned?"

"They're caught with a net, then stunned or killed. It's not as gruesome as it sounds—quite painless, apparently. How do you like your tea. Milk, sugar?"

"Just black, thank you." She took one last look at the collection of butterflies, repressing her shiver of horror at the sharp pins piercing their poor bodies, then sat in one of the armchairs while Arlo busied himself pouring tea, his large hands dwarfing the floral teapot.

"I found some cake. Help yourself." He gestured to the plate of fat slices of fruitcake, then slid a matching cup and saucer toward her.

Arlo made her smile. He seemed so at home in his own skin, a far cry from the confused man she'd found in the newspaper office. "Have you always lived here?"

"Indeed. I was born here, in the bedroom upstairs." He gestured to the ceiling. "And so was Mother and her brother and three sisters."

"Do you have family in the area still?"

A frown creased his brow. "No, not anymore. When my mother's sisters married they left the Hunter. The four of them weren't close—my father maintained it was the loss of their parents that caused the family estrangement. Father sold his family property upriver at Hinton and bought The Landing when he and mother married. Mother had inherited a quarter share but hadn't the means to buy it outright from her sisters. She couldn't bear to leave. She dedicated her life to learning more about the Wanderer butterflies."

He waved his hand in the direction of the cabinets. "She believed she was the first person to see them in Australia, but she was never credited with the discovery. The first sighting was claimed some years later in Queensland."

He picked up the sketchbook and opened it to the first page. "She saw the first butterfly in the autumn of 1868." He pointed to the date, then flicked to the back of the book. "And discovered this huge swarm on Ash Island just a few days later." He gestured to the painting of the butterflies clustered in the trees. "They are common now along the whole eastern coast, down as far as South Australia and up into Queensland, where they winter."

"But they were found here first?"

"Yes, but sadly they've never returned. Mother spent her life waiting and hoping she'd be able to prove her claim, but that never eventuated. She became something of a recluse. I never met my aunts." Disappointment laced his voice. "She always said Father had saved her from a life of penury and enabled her to remain at The Landing and continue her search."

Verity peered into his face, seeking some sign that he was withholding details, but she saw nothing but openness. A frisson of excitement traced her shoulders. What had Mr. Treadwell said? Any overtures Mrs. Treadwell had made were stonewalled. There had to be more to the story.

"Enough about my family." He cut the conversation with a curt wave of his hand. "You said you wanted to find out about your grandfather." He propped himself on the corner of the desk, legs stretched out, arms folded.

No, she didn't, but she'd foolishly allowed him to believe it. She couldn't admit the truth now and she couldn't risk upsetting him, not when she might be close to unraveling the link between Mrs. Treadwell and The Landing. "Grandpa Sid said he was given the opportunity to work as a stringer in Sydney—it was what he'd always wanted to do." She'd presumed it was the piercing pleasure of writing down thoughts and findings, believing someone might read them, that they might make a difference to someone's life. "He never explained the way it came about. I've always wondered about his life in Morpeth."

"So writing's in your blood." His half smile didn't take the unexpected sting out of his words.

"I've never wanted to do anything else."

"Difficult for a woman." His eyes narrowed. "Your grandfather's contacts must have helped."

"I've had two pieces published—one about bicycles and another about . . ." She paused, not wanting to mention the strange series of events that had led her to Morpeth. Arlo's easy company had made her drop her defenses. "As I said, I thought perhaps I could write an article about Grandpa Sid's early life." Such an out-and-out lie. She stifled a groan and tamped down her guilt. "Orphaned boy makes good—something like that." The glib words rolled off her tongue. "How he got his start."

"Then we'd better see what we can find out."

"We?" He was offering to help her and she hadn't even told him the truth. "I'd like to try to fill in the blanks. There are so many people without jobs, despondent about the future, and a story like Grandpa Sid's could give them hope. I thought maybe there might be some of his earlier stories in *The Morpeth Want*." And it would be the perfect opportunity to get to know Arlo better while continuing to search for a link between Mrs. Treadwell and The Landing.

He made some sort of huffing sound and ran his fingers through his hair. "Let's start with the newspaper archives."

CHAPTER 16

MORPETH, 1868

In the evening light the river glinted and the trees cast their long-fingered shadows. Redmond secured the boat, then made his way along the wharf. He'd dropped Theodora at The Landing before ferrying Clarrie across to the punt wharf so she could walk up to Swan Street. The look on her face when he'd handed her five shillings had left him feeling good. She and Sid deserved all the help they could get.

A grin tipped the corner of his lips. He'd enjoyed the day far more than he'd anticipated. To see the smile and enthusiasm return to Theodora's face, to hear her excited chatter about the butterflies, brought back the past—of Jamie and those carefree days before adulthood had come crashing down.

He'd have to get home and spend the regulatory hour with Father. Always such an active man, Father's sudden turn had sent them both into a flat spin. He'd harbored hope that the lack of control in the right side of Father's body and his inability to form the words he wanted might improve, but after six months and this second turn, the doctor didn't seem to think it likely. Redmond had tried to come to terms with the ramifications, but there was no escaping the fact that he'd never pursue his engineering dreams; he was destined to follow in Father's footsteps and become a newspaper proprietor. He heaved a sigh and shook away his morbid thoughts. Right now he wanted to hold on to the glow of the day.

Five minutes later he stood outside the offices. The lights still blazed downstairs in the basement. Sid would be preparing the Friday edition. He'd have a word, let him know about their trip, tell him how well Theodora and Clarrie had got on and that she was to call in to see Theodora tomorrow.

He dusted off his hands; all in all, an excellent day. "Hey, Sid. Are you there?"

"Down here, Mr. Kendall."

Redmond took the stairs two at a time, into the basement where the odor of printing ink permeated even the walls. As a child he'd hated the smell, inextricably mixed with Father's ire, but now, with his daily visits to the premises, his memories had mellowed. The heavy atmosphere and sense of misery had eased with the introduction of a few simple changes and all the print room boys were happier. Mostly because he'd upped their pay and tied it to the hours they worked.

Sid lifted his head from the tray of letters. "Just about finishing up. I'll have the proofs on your desk for the morning."

"No hurry, Sid; we're ahead of schedule for once. I've got some news—and I might have a story for you if you'd like to follow it up."

Sid's head came up with a snap and a look of anticipation lit his face. "You might?"

"Indeed. In fact, I'm full of news." He settled on the high stool in front of the upper- and lowercase trays. "Where do you want me to start? You or Clarrie?"

"Clarrie? Is there something wrong? Thought she was with you and Miss Theodora today."

"She was. We went out to Ash Island as planned. Theodora found what she was looking for. A swarm of butterflies. Didn't think I was much interested in butterflies, more of a ladylike pursuit, but this was incredible. Hundreds of them clustered in the branches of the trees. Almost as though they were hibernating, waiting for the spring. Seems it might be a new variety, flown all the way here from the Americas."

"You're kidding me."

"That's what Theodora says and she's had word from some bloke at the Australian Museum. Thought it might make an interesting story for the paper. Only problem is we don't want to encourage people to go there and disturb them. Maybe don't mention Ash Island, but no harm in getting the details. It would make an interesting piece. Have a word with Clarrie about it; she was pretty impressed, and Theodora wants her to call in tomorrow."

"Why would she want Clarrie to do that?"

"To pick her brain about what she remembers. They formed quite a bond. With any luck she might offer her a job. Just until the sisters get back. They're down a maid because Biddy's gone to Sydney, and Theodora's finding Wilcox a dour chaperone and Mrs. Starling is overloaded. Theodora and Clarrie really hit it off. And if Clarrie goes to work there, she'll have somewhere to stay and Mrs. Starling will have some help around the place and a bit more freedom."

Sid's mouth gaped. "Too good to be true."

"Don't get your hopes up. It depends on Theodora and whether Clarrie's prepared to take a job on without any security. I've no idea how long it will last. How long the sisters will be away. Thought you might like to go around and have a chat with Clarrie this evening. Make sure she calls in to-morrow morning and talks to Theodora. Around ten o'clock should suit. She's going to have to get Mrs. Starling on her side though."

Sid was on his feet pulling his cap on and buttoning his jacket before Redmond had finished speaking. He thrust out his hand. "I can't thank you enough, sir." He bounced to the door. "I'll go and talk to Clarrie right now."

"And make sure those proofs are on my desk for the morning."

"Yes, sir!"

Clarrie let herself into Maud's house. Not a single light was on and the house had a strange, hollow feeling. With her heart in her mouth and her hand flat against the wall, she crept down the hallway to the babies' room. No sound from any of them, all sleeping quietly, just gentle snuffles and the odd snatched breath. She bent over Charlie's drawer and ran her hand across his head. He gave a bit of a wriggle and waved his fingers in greeting—at least that's what it looked like.

According to Maud, he always slept peacefully when she was busy, as long as he got his feed. As much as it had pained her, she'd let Maud give him a bottle because she wanted him to get used to it, just so it wouldn't come as a shock if she got a job. She lifted him to her shoulder and wandered down the hallway into the kitchen. Maud was nowhere to be seen. She must be out doing her rounds; perhaps one of her ladies had a problem and she'd been called away unexpectedly.

Surely she wouldn't leave the babies alone unless it was a dire emergency. She hitched Charlie higher up and patted his back but he didn't stir; he'd fallen asleep again. She laid him down on the rag rug, lit the lamp, then topped up the stove and filled the kettle.

As the water came to the boil, a scratching on the window caught her attention and Sid's smiling face appeared. She scooped Charlie up and opened the back door. "What is it? I can't let you in. Maud's not here and I promised I wouldn't open the door to anyone while she was away."

Sid leaned forward and dropped a kiss on her cheek, then ran a hand over Charlie's head. "I won't come in, but I've got some news from Mr. Kendall I thought you'd want to hear."

"He's such a nice man. We had a lovely time. You should have seen the butterflies. They were so pretty." She handed Charlie over to Sid. "Here, have a cuddle."

He took the baby and tucked him comfortably in the crook of his arm. "I haven't got long. I've got to get some proofs done. Said they'd be on Mr. Kendall's desk by the morning. Can you get Maud to look after Charlie again tomorrow?"

"Why? I don't want to ask again, not after today."

Charlie stirred, blinked at Sid, found his thumb, and waved it around in front of his face. Clarrie tucked it into his mouth. "Maud expects me to be here; the woman who helps her is out of town and I have lots of jobs around the house. Have you any idea how many diapers half a dozen babies go through?"

"You need to be at The Landing by ten o'clock. Miss Breckenridge wants a word with you."

"She probably wants to know how much I can remember about the butterflies."

"Mr. Kendall reckons she might offer you a job trial. If you'd be interested."

Interested? She'd be more than interested after the wonderful day they'd had. Miss Breckenridge seemed more like a friend than a boss. She'd take any job she offered, no need to go and talk to her. "Just ask him to tell Miss Breckenridge yes. I'd like to take the job. Mr. Kendall gave me five shillings when I left. Five shillings for hunting butterflies. Sid, I really think Charlie has switched our luck around."

"I think he might have too, but you've got to go and convince the cook, Mrs. Starling, that you're happy to help out doing all sorts of odds and sods."

"'Course I am." She inhaled Charlie's warm milky baby smell. He'd settled in Sid's arms. "Maybe you could look after Charlie while I'm there."

Sid shook his head. "Can't. Got too much on and I don't want to upset the apple cart. Mr. Redmond's been so good to us. Mustn't let him down."

In that case she'd have to ask Maud. Surely she'd agree, especially if it meant she got her money quicker. "I'll sort it out. Do I just turn up?"

"Yep, ten o'clock, like I said. You've got to butter up Mrs. Starling, not just Miss Breckenridge. Here, he's dropped off." He handed Charlie back to her and brushed his lips against hers. "I've got to go. Let me know what happens on your way back tomorrow." Sid rammed his cap back on his head and left with a wave.

A few moments later the front door groaned open—Maud back from her rounds. Clarrie put Charlie down on the rag rug and poured the water into the teapot, then picked him up again to put him to bed. As she reached the hallway the front door banged closed and Maud stumbled toward her, mumbling.

"Tea's made. I'll just put Charlie to bed and then pour you a cup. All the others are fast asleep." She eased past Maud, who was propped against the wall. "Are you all right?"

"Gettin' me breath." Maud stumbled toward the kitchen.

Clarrie tucked Charlie in and shot back down to find Maud slumped at the table, her head in her hands and her shoulders shaking. Unsure what to do, Clarrie poured a cup of tea and added some sugar. "Here's a nice drink. It'll make you feel better."

"It's going to take more than tea to make me feel better." Maud lifted her ravaged face. "Rent's been upped. I can't offer no more charity. You'll have to start paying your way or you and Charlie are going to have to go."

Clarrie stuck her hand into her pocket. Her fingers closed over the five shillings Mr. Kendall had given her. So much for savings; still, if she got on the right side of this Mrs. Starling tomorrow, their problems might well be over. She pulled out the money and put it down on the table. "Will this help?"

Maud blinked owlishly at her. "Where did you get that?"

"Mr. Kendall gave it to me for today."

"Five shillings! You watch yourself."

Color flooded Clarrie's cheeks. "No, it wasn't like that. I was there to keep Miss Breckenridge company. We went to Ash Island, and I've got to go back and see her tomorrow morning."

"Fine for some." Maud sniffed. "And what're you going to do with Charlie while you're gone? You're supposed to be pulling your weight around here, not gallivanting off on boat trips and paying social calls."

"That's not what I'm doing; it's about a job." She slid the coins closer to Maud's fingers. "I'm hoping things will work out and then I can pay you to look after Charlie while I'm working. Will this help with the rent?"

Quick as a cut snake, Maud pocketed the money. "Free board and lodging stops at the end of the week."

CHAPTER 17

MORPETH, 1922

The irony of the situation didn't escape Verity as she sat at a table in the front room of the terrace that had been home to *The Morpeth Want* for almost eighty years. She'd set out to uncover the connection between Mrs. Treadwell and The Landing and now, because of her duplicity, she was following her own family story. By the time she'd bolted some breakfast at the Commercial and strolled down the road, Arlo was waiting, looking even more rumpled than yesterday, his sleeves rolled to the elbows and hands stained with ink, even a smudge on his cheek.

He'd opened the shutters and light flooded into the dusty front room where large shelves of bound books covered every available inch of wall space. One copy of every edition ever published, in chronological order, dating back to the 1830s when Arlo's grandfather had started the paper, or so he'd told her before he'd disappeared down the stairs.

"Where shall we start?" Arlo's voice from the doorway made her jump. "I didn't mean to startle you."

"I was thinking of Grandpa Sid and wondering when he'd

first started in the print room. Which editions he'd had a hand in printing."

"Do you know how old he was when he came here?"

Verity shook her head. "He always said old Mr. Kendall gave him his first opportunity as a copyboy, then he worked his way up and learned the trade, became a compositor."

"Back then the copyboys were young, maybe ten or twelve. I'm sure we can find out. The newspaper archives go back to the beginning. I've never looked at them. Never had the time, or the inclination."

As much as she'd loved Grandpa Sid, she really didn't want to spend time on his past, not right now. She wanted to see the name Treadwell tied to Morpeth, or more specifically, to The Landing. "I don't want to take up your time. If you could perhaps point me in the right direction, I can manage. You must have work to do."

"I have a few things to catch up with. The folders are in date order, starting next to the window. I'll leave you for a while, then come back and give you a hand. Shout out if you need anything." Shoving his inky hands deep in his pockets, he ambled off.

When the enormity of the task became apparent, Verity made a random choice and pulled down one of the large books and laid it on the table. Like *The Arrow*, the front page of each edition was dedicated to classifieds. Everything from shipping times to lost and stolen horses, wanted and public notices, and recommendations for medical tonics, pills, and ointments; even a dozen baskets of champagne and a sausage-chopping machine. Far more varied than the copy she'd spent her days on in Sydney. She skimmed the Family Notices and flicked half-heartedly through the remainder of the paper, but there was no mention of the name Treadwell.

She couldn't ask Arlo if there was a local family called Treadwell because he was convinced she was looking for information about Sid. And then her mistake dawned on her—if Mrs. Treadwell had spent time in Morpeth as a child, before her marriage, looking for the name Treadwell would be of no use.

There had to be an easier way. Churches had records of baptisms, marriages, and deaths, didn't they?

She replaced the oversize book, debated heading off for the nearest church, then thought again. The *Cawarra* sank in 1866. Why not start there? It was as good a place as any. Surely there would be a report, death notices, references to the Breckenridge family, and perhaps tributes from people associated with them. It was a long shot, but the ladies at the School of Arts had said Captain Breckenridge's steamship company was well known, so the whole story would have to be thoroughly covered. She pulled down three heavy volumes, releasing a musty waft of decay.

The thought that Grandpa Sid might well have taken on the laborious task of setting each letter in the little metal trays, forming the sentences that would then be printed onto the sheets, brought a wistful smile to her lips. Not only this edition but some of the earlier ones too. She couldn't imagine going to work at twelve; it seemed so young. But back then school wasn't compulsory, so someone, old Mr. Kendall perhaps, must have taught Sid the trade.

The next page contained lists of births, deaths, and marriages. She ran her finger down the page, but nothing jumped out at her until she turned to the next.

The Loss of the *Cawarra*: The following information has been obtained from Frederick Valliant Hedges, the only survivor of the ill-fated *Cawarra* . . .

She skimmed the paragraph as a rash of goose bumps stippled her skin.

The captain at once made for the port and rounded Nobby's shortly after two o'clock. In doing so, the heavy running sea struck the steamer several times with tremendous force and the rush of water on deck—some of which went below— was frightful. The vessel became unmanageable . . . they all perished in the surf close to the Oyster Bank.

"Would you like to sit down? Your face is the color of chalk." Arlo's warm hands clasped her shoulders and eased her down into the chair.

"Really, I'm perfectly well. I stumbled across the report of the *Cawarra*. Your poor mother and her sisters losing their parents and their brother in one fell swoop. How old were they?" She rummaged in her satchel for her notebook. More to give herself a moment to gather her wits than for any intention to take notes.

"Mother would have been close to twenty. The others—" He shrugged. "I don't know exactly."

How very peculiar. She couldn't imagine belonging to a large family and knowing nothing about them. So sad— that beautiful fairy-tale family shattered by such a dreadful accident.

Arlo perched on the side of the table, his long legs crossed at the ankles and his arms folded. "So dates . . . What would you like to know about Sid? I'm not sure I'll be able to answer all your questions, and I've asked the boys in the basement, but they don't know much more than I do." He opened the large wooden cover of the newspaper archive on the desk. "You said Sid moved to Sydney in the late 1860s?"

"Yes, I'm not sure exactly when. Mid to late 1868." Sid and Clarrie's certificate of marriage was issued in Sydney and dated October 1868.

"If he walked straight into a job as a stringer on *The Arrow,* he must have had some experience beforehand. Let's see if we can find any reference to him, a mention of his name or a piece he wrote."

She opened the cover and stared down at the first newspaper, January 1868, the front page covered with the usual classifieds. Her nose tickled and she reached into her pocket for a handkerchief. "What's the strange smell?"

"It's the paper. That's why the window shutters are usually closed. Newspapers aren't meant to be kept. The light makes the paper yellow and disintegrate and the ink fade. You keep going here and I'll look through the next one."

Arlo settled on the floor, legs bent up almost to his ears as he pored over another of the archive books, and Verity tried to concentrate on the pages of print—but every time one of the trams rattled past the whole building shook, making her already frayed nerves jangle.

"This is interesting. It's a wedding announcement." Arlo lifted the metal rod, released the newspaper, and brought it across to the table. "I didn't know my aunts had a double marriage."

Verity moved to his side and read the words aloud, "'On *25th September the marriage of Constance Isabella Breckenridge to John Huntington Smythe of Grosvenor Square London, and her younger sister, Viola Jenifer Breckenridge, to William Thomas Goodsire of Richmond, Surrey, at St. Andrews Cathedral, Sydney. No general invitations were extended.'"

Arlo scratched his head. "No general invitations extended.

What does that mean? I wonder whether Mother attended, and what about the other sister?"

A sense of disappointment laced his voice, making Verity want to console him. Perhaps the archives weren't such a good idea. "You knew they settled in England, didn't you?"

"I remember Mother saying one of her sisters was a sought-after cellist and gave recitals, but other than that, I don't have a particular memory of her talking about them. I wonder if they had children. That would mean I had English cousins."

A forlorn smile drifted across his face. One Verity had no difficulty in understanding.

"Would you like me to open the door?" he asked. "It's very stuffy in here. I can't open the window—the last thing we want are papers blowing everywhere. We need to keep them in date order. Where are you up to?"

"Just about to start the second half of 1868."

"Found anything you think might be Sid's? Are you sure you don't know the exact date he went to Sydney?"

She shook her head. "It was a bit of a guess. I don't think it was earlier because my father was born in Morpeth in May 1868, although his birth wasn't registered until they lived in Sydney."

"Fancy a glass of water? It's too hot for tea. Or I could pop next door and rustle up some lemonade."

"That would be lovely. I'd like to stay here, if that's all right, and keep looking."

"Of course. I'll only be a moment."

The minute he left, Verity picked up the next group of papers.

The Family Notices seemed to be particularly useful.

She worked through the papers, ignoring everything but the Family Notices, page after page of them. No mention of

Charlie, none of the Breckenridge family, and certainly nothing that mentioned the name Treadwell. It was a wild goose chase. What had she hoped to find? And now, because of her ridiculous deviousness, she couldn't even ask Arlo if the Treadwell name was familiar without giving herself away.

With a grunt of annoyance, Verity flicked to the last paper and gasped.

On 23rd September the marriage of Florence Jane Breckenridge to Mr. Edward Treadwell of Elizabeth Bay, Sydney. The marriage was held at St. Andrews Cathedral, Sydney.

Mrs. Treadwell was Florence Breckenridge, the daughter of Alexander and Julianna, Arlo's aunt, one of the four sisters. Verity let out an unrestrained whoop of excitement. "I was right."

"I'm sorry?" Arlo stood in the doorway, two uncapped bottles of lemonade in his hands.

"There is a connection. I knew I was right. The painting was a memento of Mrs. Treadwell's childhood, far more than a place she had once visited. She was born here, lived here until she married. She was your aunt." She clapped her hand over her mouth.

A curious expression knotted Arlo's brow into a frown as if facing a puzzle he couldn't solve. "I thought we were looking for information about your grandfather."

Not game to incriminate herself further, she nodded.

"What's going on, Verity?" He dumped the bottles of lemonade on the table and glowered at her.

It didn't seem right to continue without telling him the truth. She took a sip of the lemonade, hoping to douse the excruciating twist of embarrassment, then put the bottle back on the table and wiped the dewy water from her hands. "I haven't told you the truth."

Realization dawned with a massive gut punch. Arlo couldn't quite catch a breath. "You're not here to find out about your grandfather; it's not a pilgrimage as you said." She hadn't said a pilgrimage. He'd suggested it, but she'd agreed. "I think you better explain yourself."

His fingers tensed, the newspaper scrunched in his fist. No doubt about it, Verity knew what she was looking for and it had nothing to do with Sid Binks. Why hadn't she leveled with him? He gave a slow shake of his head and forced his fingers to relax. No point in destroying the archives. He smoothed the newspaper. She'd had no need to lie. She could have asked him outright; he'd spoken of his aunts. She'd had ample opportunity when they'd found Viola's and Constance's wedding announcement, if not before. He paced the room. What would he have said if she had told him the truth?

A surge of anger tightened his jaw and he clamped his teeth. Grinding to a halt in front of her, he stared into her eyes. "Why? Why lie and tell me you were looking for information about your grandfather?"

She squirmed in her seat, a traitorous flush of guilt tainting her cheeks. "I am, but I'm also looking for other information. For another piece I was asked to write."

"So not a Sid pilgrimage?"

"Not entirely," she stuttered and bit down on her lip.

Lips he'd wanted to kiss. He shook the thought away and peered out into the quiet street. Was his life really so narrow, so lonely, that he could be drawn in by the first young woman who caught his attention? "That's disappointing."

More than disappointing. Annoying, infuriating, and pathetic. She'd taken him for a fool.

He spun around. "I thought we'd established some sort of connection, and now you're telling me you lied to me."

"I didn't lie."

"By omission."

The atmosphere in the room burgeoned, no sound except the *click, click* of her pencil as she tapped it on the table. Why hadn't she told him right from the beginning what she was searching for? "Well?"

"I've been asked to write an article. About the Treadwell Foundation. They run a charity that helps women who find themselves in a difficult position."

"What sort of a difficult . . . I see. Unmarried mothers?" Was that why she hadn't told him? He cast a surreptitious look at her body, no sign of anything untoward. He couldn't ask—she probably wouldn't level with him anyway.

"Yes, that's it. The foundation received funding from the Sydney Artists' Ball and Mr. Treadwell wanted me to write the history to encourage further donations."

It all sounded ridiculous. Couldn't she come up with anything better?

She took another deep breath. "I was anonymously sent an invitation and costume to attend the ball, which is where I was introduced to Mr. Treadwell. He asked me to write about the foundation and I called on him at Treadwell House. While I was there, I saw the painting of The Landing, which I told you about. He thought it was painted by one of the Scott sisters, but I am now convinced it was your mother's work."

So she was trying to involve his family. Whatever was

the woman up to? He scanned her face, searching for a clue. "I'm certain you're incorrect. My mother didn't sell any of her paintings."

Her blue eyes widened and she studied his face. "Your aunt, Florence Treadwell, bought the painting at a gallery in Sydney. Her son told me she spent time at The Landing as a child and had fond memories of the place." Her voice grew steady, determined. "He brushed my questions aside and it made me wonder if there was more to the story. I thought it might be relevant to the history of the Treadwell Foundation. The costume I was sent was black and orange—a butterfly, the same as the one in the painting, and the same as those in your mother's sketchbook."

Arlo brought the palm of his hand down on the desktop with a slap that shot Verity to her feet.

"And the nonsense about your name? Verity Binks. Am I supposed to believe that?"

"Yes, my grandfather truly was Sid Binks and my father was Charles Binks, the war correspondent."

"And does your father know about this ridiculous nonsense?"

"No. He died in Palestine during the war."

Heat singed the top of his ears, a sure sign he was losing his temper—or perhaps it was embarrassment. He clenched his fist. "I'm sorry." And he was. He genuinely liked the girl. But she had no one to blame but herself for his reaction.

As though she could read his mind, she picked up her notebook and pencil and slipped them into her satchel, then reached across the desk to pick up the folder of newspapers, but it slipped from her fingers.

"Leave it alone. I'll do it."

"Arlo, I want—"

He grunted as he hefted a pile of the volumes back onto the shelf. He wanted her out of the place, out of his life. He exhaled slowly. "I'm sure you have discovered everything you need to know. I'll arrange a lift into Maitland for the train." He couldn't bear the thought of having her here a moment longer.

"Don't concern yourself. I have my bicycle." She ran her fingers through her hair, but didn't meet his eyes. "Thank you for your help."

CHAPTER 18

MORPETH, 1868

Clarrie tucked Charlie under the blanket and settled him into his drawer in the darkened room with the other babies. Maud said she had an overactive imagination, but she was certain Charlie's big blue eyes followed her every time she crossed the room to leave. She'd no idea where the blue had come from; not her or Sid—they both had brown eyes. Maud reckoned Charlie's eyes would change as he got older. Clarrie paused for a moment, waiting to see if he would settle. All the other babies seemed so dopey; they never took any notice of what was happening, but Charlie did. And eat. He could take so much. She only had two, maybe three hours before he'd be hungry again. And she'd so much rather feed him than let Maud give him a bottle. Still, he'd survived when she'd gone to Ash Island with Miss Breckenridge and Mr. Kendall.

Heart twisting, she closed the door, collected her hat and coat, and tiptoed down the hallway to the kitchen.

Maud sat, feet propped on a stool, with the inevitable cup of tea in front of her. "Where are you off to?"

"I'm going to The Landing. I told you last night. To talk to Miss Breckenridge and Mrs. Starling about a job."

"They've got staff. Wilcox and that maid of all work, Biddy. Right stuck-up piece of work she is."

"Biddy has gone to Sydney with Miss Breckenridge's sisters so she might have something for me until they get back."

Maud uttered some sort of a humph. "You'll have to be lucky. Mrs. Barnett does the hiring and firing, not the cook."

"She's in Sydney too."

"Is she now? That's not what I heard. Still, that's not your concern, and I suppose you're making the effort. When will you be back? Charlie will want feeding."

"I've just fed him. Could you give him a bottle and change him if he wakes up before I return, please?"

"Of course I will, but you're going to have to come up with the nine shillings a week. I'm sorry, love, but my rent's calculated on the number of babies I have here."

Which Clarrie hadn't known about. "I'll be as quick as I can." She offered her most docile smile and closed the door behind her.

The punt trip across the river and the walk to The Landing would take her a good hour, so she couldn't take the time to call in and see Sid. He knew what was going on. Maybe on the way back she'd have some good news to share. She picked up her pace and headed down toward the punt.

Miss Breckenridge's kindness had left her with a warm feeling. She'd treated her more like a friend than a maid, maybe because Miss Breckenridge had been beside herself with excitement. All over a bunch of butterflies. Pretty as they were, it didn't seem important in the real world, a pastime for a lady. Besides, Clarrie didn't believe a creature as frail as a butterfly could fly all the way from the Americas. Its wings would be worn out.

Luck was on her side, and the punt had a head of steam and was ready to make the crossing. A huge dray and two carthorses took up most of the space, but she tucked herself in the corner and dropped her penny in Thomas's tin.

In a matter of moments they'd reached the other side of the river and she ducked under the chain and took off up the track. The autumn sun had quite a bite to it. She unbuttoned her coat and folded it over her arm. She'd put it back on before she reached the house.

Set amid green gardens, the rooftop was just visible through the trees. She and Sid used to sit and look across the river at it when they had their picnics, but she'd never, not in her wildest dreams, imagined she'd be striding up the drive and through the gardens to see about a job. She stopped for a moment when she reached the two stone pillars topped with great round balls that marked the driveway. Groups of trees provided spots of shade and a stone wall surrounded a large, round garden. Butterflies, flower gardens, and painting—she couldn't imagine filling her days that way and having someone else do all the work. Still, she shouldn't complain. But for that she wouldn't have any chance for a job. She crossed her fingers for luck and cut across the grass toward the house.

A path ran through the center of the garden, so with a glimpse over her shoulder to make sure no one was watching, she slipped inside and hurried along. Piles of dead branches and rubbish littered the paving stones and close by a barrow with a rake and some shears. She skirted the barrow carefully, making sure she didn't trample anything important. Not that she knew what was or wasn't.

"Oi! Watch where you're going." Archer's head popped out from behind a clump of dead sticks.

"What're you doing here?"

He pulled off his cap and swiped his hand over his forehead. "Working. What's it look like?"

Her stomach sank. "Working. You work here?"

"Started a few weeks ago. Miss Breckenridge wants the garden sorted for spring. I guess you're here to see her 'bout that job."

Wretched boy. Was there anything he didn't know? "What's it to you?"

"Thought I might save you the hike up to the house. She's over there, in the folly, painting." He pointed to a wall that looked as though it would fall down in the next gust of wind. "Look through the window."

Clarrie squinted against the sun and stared through a strange arch. It was like looking at a picture. A stretch of the river and the quirky little shelter, unlike anything she'd ever seen before—a funny round dome atop pillars that belonged in a church, no walls or doors—but she picked out a figure sitting in front of an easel. Dazzling red hair caught the rays of the sun, shining almost as bright as the butterflies they'd seen. "I think I better go up to the house. It wouldn't be proper . . ."

"Nah. Miss Theodora's not like that. Not one to stand on ceremony. Thought you would have noticed that on your boat trip."

She had, but this was different. This was about a job. The boat ride had been more like friends going on a picnic.

"Go on. She won't bite your head off. Just make sure you call out. Doesn't like it if you make her jump. Says it spoils her concentrating."

Swallowing the churn of nerves in her belly, Clarrie took Archer's advice and followed his pointed finger through a gap in the garden wall. When she reached the little house—the folly, such a strange name; surely a folly was something foolish—she cleared her throat, hoping to announce her arrival.

Nothing happened. Miss Breckenridge sat head bent, a

paintbrush in one hand and a set of paints on the stone bench. Clarrie took a couple more steps up into the folly. "Excuse me, Miss Breckenridge."

Still she didn't move. Just dabbed the brush into the paint tray and made some more splodges on the paper.

Clarrie crept closer. The painting on the easel took her breath away. The butterfly so perfect it could at any moment spread its wings and take off. Just like the ones they'd seen at the island.

Miss Breckenridge's index finger hovered over the stone bench. She stepped closer to take a look. Skewered on a pile of thick paper was one of the poor butterflies, a pin plunged through its body and its wings spread. The beautiful patterns so clear to see. "Poor thing!" The words flew out of her mouth before she could swallow them and Miss Breckenridge spun around, dropping her paintbrush.

"I'm so sorry, miss. I didn't mean to—"

"It's perfectly all right, Clarrie. You made me jump, that's all. I hadn't realized the time." She picked up the paintbrush and swished it around in the water pot, wiped it on a cloth, then stood up, stretching her shoulders. "What do you think? Have I captured the likeness? The patterns are very complicated once you study them." She gestured to the poor creature on the bench beside her.

"Seems a shame to kill it just so you can paint it." What had ever made her say that? Lost the job for being smart-mouthed before it had even been offered. "I'm sorry, miss. I didn't mean to tell you your business."

"I used to think exactly the same, until Harriet and Helena explained to me that if we are to be scientific, we must be exact, and this is the only way to capture a true likeness. I wouldn't be able to do that if I hadn't pinned it."

"Are you certain it didn't hurt?"

"She wouldn't have felt a thing. I promise." She turned back to her painting. "I don't have long before the colors fade."

"Should I come back another day?"

"We can talk here. Then you can go up to the house to meet Mrs. Starling. She knows you're coming. Sit over there." Miss Breckenridge pointed to a large chest tucked next to the bench. "It makes a good seat. It's where we keep the ropes and lifelines in case anyone falls in the river."

Clarrie put down her hat and coat and sat. "Why wouldn't you just swim to the edge? There're even steps down there." It would be the perfect spot in the summer. She could imagine jumping in with Sid, hands clasped as they sank under the cool water.

"Not everyone can swim. My sisters can't. They don't think it's ladylike."

Foot in mouth again.

"But I can. Papa taught me, though we didn't tell Mama." Her lips tilted in a nostalgic smile. "He said I had to learn if I wanted to go sailing."

"I'm sorry for your loss." Everyone in Morpeth knew about the disaster of the *Cawarra,* but was it the right thing to say? The reverend always used those words, not that she ever thought he was truly sorry. He always seemed to enjoy funerals. An occasion to wear his good robes and offer an extra sermon. She shook the thought of the horrid man away.

"Thank you, Clarrie. Now let's chat about your experience and what you can do."

In no time at all, Clarrie was back on her feet, a huge smile cracking her face. She hadn't been given a real job, but just as

Mr. Kendall had told Sid, Miss Breckenridge had offered her a trial until her sisters returned from Sydney and then it would be up to Mrs. Barnett, the housekeeper. No matter what, she had her first step in the door. Now all she had to do was prove what a help she was and work as hard as she could.

"I'll come with you and introduce you to Mrs. Starling. As I said, you'll be doing all kinds of jobs; we're all helping out." Miss Breckenridge unpinned her painting from the easel and carefully put the butterfly inside the pill box and closed the lid. "Can you carry these up to the house? I'll bring my paints and sketchbook. Archer can bring the easel later. Come along. Don't forget your coat."

They ambled up to the house through the long grass dotted with prettily colored flowers until they reached the veranda. "Sit down here and I'll go and get Mrs. Starling."

Clarrie couldn't leave it any longer. She felt like a fraud not telling the whole story and she'd rather do it now, person to person. She straightened her shoulders. "Miss Breckenridge, there's one thing I have to tell you." Her voice wavered and she lifted her chin. She wasn't ashamed of Charlie and never would be. "Sid and I have a son. He won't interfere with my work. There's a woman in Swan Street, Maud the midwife; she's looking after him. If I get the job, I'd want to see him a couple of times a week. After all my work's done, of course."

Next thing she knew Miss Breckenridge was clasping her hand in both of hers. "Thank you for telling me. I was hoping you would. I know about Charlie. Redmond, Mr. Kendall, told me."

Clarrie's mouth gaped as she stared at Miss Breckenridge's retreating figure. She flopped down on the cushioned chair on the veranda. Miss Breckenridge had known about Charlie all along. And still she was going to give her a trial. Trying to control the smile that kept creeping across her face, she clenched her hands tightly in her lap. She couldn't wait to tell Sid.

In a matter of moments Miss Breckenridge was back, with a jug of lemonade and two glasses on a tray. "I expect you're thirsty." Without waiting for a response, she poured out the lemonade and handed her a glass.

As Clarrie sat sipping the drink, a small, round woman, white hair pulled back from her face and a floury apron straining against her ample bosom, stepped through the front door, wiping her hands. Clarrie jumped to her feet.

"Sit back down, love. We don't stand on ceremony when the others are away." She dropped down into the chair next to Clarrie with a sigh. "I hear you worked for the Reverend Lodestar."

Clarrie clamped her teeth together, willing the color to subside from her cheeks. She had no doubt the whole world knew every step she'd taken in the last weeks.

"If you managed him, there won't be much you can't handle here. Miss Breckenridge, would you like me to have a word around the town?"

"I don't think that will be necessary, Mrs. Starling. I've offered Clarrie a trial until the girls come back from Sydney and then we can hand the matter over to Mrs. Barnett. We've been down one maid for the last few months and I think we need another, don't you?"

"If Clarrie's prepared to muck in and do what's needed, then I'm happy."

"I can do anything you need," Clarrie spluttered. "I used to do the cooking for the reverend, serve his meals, do his laundry and the cleaning and shopping."

"No wonder he's having a hard time finding someone to replace you. Serves the cantankerous fool right."

Miss Breckenridge's lips twitched and she stood up. "I'll leave you to tell Clarrie what's required. I need to go and chase Archer; he hasn't brought up my easel. I think Clarrie could start tomorrow." And with that, Miss Breckenridge drifted off through the grass before Clarrie had time to thank her.

"Like to start tomorrow, love?"

"Yes, please." She itched to tell Sid. Everything, just everything, had worked out better than she'd ever dreamed. "What time should I be here?"

"Seven o'clock would be about right. But what about that baby of yours? You can't bring him here. Not if you want to keep the job permanently. Mrs. Barnett won't stand for it."

"That's not a problem. Charlie is with a woman in Swan Street, and she's happy to look after him." She licked her lips. In for a penny, what did she have to lose? "I don't have anywhere to stay once I leave Maud's though."

"Reckon we can see to that. There's two beds in Biddy's room. She won't be too happy, but you can share. You'll get twelve shillings a week and four hours off on Sundays. Reckon that'll suit?"

Twelve shillings. Twice what the reverend paid her. She wouldn't get to see Charlie as much as she'd hoped, but Sid could call in during the week. "That's wonderful, thank you."

"It's only a trial. Don't know when they'll be back from Sydney, but it'll give you a bit of time to settle in and get to know the place. I'll be happy to have the help."

"Thank you, thank you very much, Mrs. Starling. I'll do my best." Resisting the impulse to kiss the woman's rosy cheek, Clarrie leaped to her feet. "I'll be here tomorrow at seven sharp."

Clarrie bounded down the driveway, the great dome of sky bright and blue above her and the sun shining, her heart just about bursting. With twelve shillings a week she and Sid would even be able to put a bit away. She'd just take a moment to call in and tell him and then she'd be back in time to feed Charlie.

The front door of the newspaper offices stood open, but she didn't have the time to explain what she was doing to Mr. Kendall so she ducked around the back and rapped on the grimy window of the print room. A face peered back at her and a moment later the door opened.

"Sid!" She threw her arms around him.

The print room exploded into a riot of hoots and whistles. Sid unpeeled her arms with an embarrassed grin. "What are you so excited about?"

"I've been to see Miss Breckenridge and she's offered me a trial until the sisters come back from Sydney, then it's up to Mrs. Barnett."

With a grin at their audience, Sid picked her up and swirled her around. "There. I told you everything would work out."

"Not only that, she's paying me twelve shillings a week and board and lodging, but I only get four hours off on a Sunday to see Charlie. Can you visit him during the week?"

"'Course I can. Mr. Kendall will let me pop out now and again. Might not be the same time every day but I can work around it."

"I'd better get back to Maud's. I've got enough in my savings to give her the next two weeks for Charlie." Clarrie started to leave, then stopped. "I can't believe how well everything has worked out."

"Come here." Sid pulled her into a hug and dropped a smacking great kiss on her lips.

She grinned—her face had to be the color of a beetroot—and

slipped out of the door, leaving him to deal with the ruckus from the men in the basement.

With a skip in her step, Clarrie gamboled down the road to Maud's cottage, longing to tell Charlie her good news. The front door was ajar and not a sound came from the house, nor was there any sign of Maud. Charlie must be hungry. Once she'd fed him, she'd take him out the back and sit in the sun with him. Maybe even take some of the other babies too. A bit of sun had to be good for them. She pushed open the door to their room and waited for a moment for her eyes to adjust to the gloom.

All she could hear was the regular breathing and occasional snuffle. Every one of the babies lying wrapped tightly in the row of cots. Charlie lay on his back, fast asleep, his thumb resting on his cheek where it had fallen from his mouth. She brushed his hair back from his forehead and still he didn't stir.

Tiptoeing out of the room she closed the door behind her and went through to the kitchen in search of Maud.

She found her, as usual, sitting at the table with a cup of tea. "Back, are you?"

"I got the job." The words blurted out of Clarrie's mouth. "And it comes with a bed. I start tomorrow at seven. I'll have Sundays to see Charlie and Sid will come during the week."

"Well, that's all for the best." Maud rocked back in the chair and looked her up and down.

Clarrie licked her lips, Maud's tone and manner stripping her excitement. "I thought you'd be pleased. I've got the money for the first two weeks."

Maud put out her hand and lifted her eyebrows.

"It's in my room; I'll go and get it. Charlie's still asleep. Do you think I should wake him? He's due for a feed."

"I've done it, along with all the others; he'll be good until the evening. There's washing that needs doing though."

"I might wake Charlie, give him a bit of a cuddle, tell him my news, then I'll do the washing."

"I don't want any of them disturbed. Once one wakes they all do. And I don't like giving them too much of this, though everyone swears by it." Maud pointed to a bottle in the middle of the table.

Clarrie reached for the bottle. She'd seen it before, thought it was Maud's tipple, not for the babies. "What is it?"

"Mrs. Barnett's herbal tonic. She reckons it's good for them, makes sure they get enough sleep. She says it's much better than that Godfrey's rubbish you buy at the apothecary. I'll listen out for the babies; you go and get my money, then head for the scullery."

Clarrie made for the door, then stopped. "Do you think Charlie's sick? He didn't stir when I looked in." Her mouth dried, the mere thought bringing her out in a cold sweat.

"He's fine. Stop your worrying."

On her way down the hallway, Clarrie slipped into the babies' room again. Charlie lay just as she'd left him. She bent down to drop a kiss on his head, inhaling his usual milky scent and something else, something sweet—maybe it was the tonic Maud had given him.

"Hurry along. I haven't got all day." Maud's voice echoed down the hallway.

Clarrie needlessly neatened the blanket around Charlie and, with one last look at his pale face, left the room. He'd seemed so happy this morning, full of smiles, which Maud insisted were nothing more than wind, his little fingers warm against her skin as she'd fed him.

She closed the door to her room and untied her blanket

bundle, delving down into the corner for her clean chemise. She emptied the coins into her palm and counted them out. More than enough for Maud. Without a second thought she left only two pennies and a sixpence, then took the remainder back to the kitchen. Maud had been so good to her; it was only right she should pay back the favor and then Charlie's place would be secure.

"I had a bit more than I thought. With the five shillings I gave you yesterday this should cover Charlie for three weeks, and I'll be earning so there won't be a problem with the rest."

Maud shifted each coin across the table with her fingertip, then scooped them into her hand and slipped them into her pocket. "That should fix my rent and keep the landlady at bay."

CHAPTER 19

MORPETH, 1922

Verity wheeled her bicycle onto the platform and propped it against the wall of the waiting room. Sweat trickled down her back, and her blouse stuck in nasty damp patches under her arms and across her back; even the band of her hat was sodden.

Cycling might well have done more for women's independence than anything else but it had done little for her peace of mind. She'd dashed back to the Commercial, paid her bill, ignored Mrs. Peers's pointed questions, then slogged all the way into Maitland thinking she'd miss the train, only to find it hadn't even arrived. Standing on the packed platform, she wiped her hands down her skirt and flexed her fingers. Hopefully she'd be able to find a seat to herself because she couldn't imagine anyone wanting to sit near her. She flapped her hand in front of her face in a vain attempt to cool down and let out a disgruntled puff.

She only had herself to blame. She should have told Arlo the truth from the outset. He'd been so kind. An embarrassed flush rose to her cheeks—more than kind. From the first time they'd met she'd sensed a connection, a feeling of déjà vu, as

197

though they'd known each other in a past life and had instantly recognized one another, and she'd done nothing but abuse his hospitality.

Heaving another disgruntled humph, she patted her satchel and felt the outline of her notebook through the leather. There was little point in getting worked up. The trip to Newcastle and then on to Sydney would give her plenty of time to write up her notes, and when she got back she'd make an appointment to see Mrs. Treadwell and ask her outright about her childhood, the significance of her sister's painting, and if she was responsible for the invitation and costume.

The ground began to vibrate and a whiff of coal dust filled the air. She pushed to her feet and wheeled her bicycle down to the end of the platform. The train huffed and puffed its way into the station and came to a halt.

She stood waiting for the guard to open the door. Hopefully he'd give her a hand with her bicycle, and if he was as friendly as the man on the way up, she'd travel in the guard's van again.

Another station employee dressed in a green uniform pushed a cart laden with mailbags alongside her. "I'll give you a hand with that once I've loaded this lot."

She nodded her thanks, rammed her hat down over her soggy hair, moved back a few steps to give him a bit more room, and crashed right into the person standing behind her. She whipped around. "I'm so sorry."

The woman hobbled a few steps and rubbed the toe of her shoe on her calf. "I'm perfectly fine."

She must have wheeled her bicycle right over her foot. "I'm dreadfully sorry. I didn't see you behind me."

"Right you are, love. Let's get this into the van." The man in the green uniform heaved the front wheel up through the door. "Hold her steady." He jumped inside, grabbed the handlebars, and in a moment the bicycle was lodged against a pile of postal bags.

"Thank you." She clutched the handrail and put her foot up on the step.

"No passengers in the guard's van." He stood above her, blocking her way.

"But I . . . My carpetbag is strapped to the carrier."

"Won't come to any harm and there's plenty of room in the carriage next door. Name?"

"Binks. Verity Binks. I traveled up in the guard's van."

"Don't care what they do out of Sydney, but you're not getting in the guard's van at this station." He scrawled her name onto two labels, waved them in front of her nose, then made a show of tying one onto the handlebars and the other onto her bag before handing her the stubs. "Show them to the ticket master at Newcastle and he'll get your bicycle out for you."

Swallowing a mouthful of complaints, she made her way along the platform. The officious little man kept his eyes on her until she climbed inside the carriage, which thankfully was almost empty. She found a nice window seat facing forward, untangled her satchel, and slumped down, thrusting the two stubs into her pocket with her ticket. She was becoming a regular harridan. After the way she'd treated Arlo, ignored Mrs. Peers's well-meaning questions, and almost shouted at the poor stationmaster who was only doing his job, she was well on the way to becoming one of those dreadful spinsters who whined and complained over the slightest thing. Leaning back in the seat, she pulled out her notebook and pencil, made a pillow out of her satchel, and sat back, legs stretched out in front of her.

With a great deal of door-slamming, shouting, and

whistleblowing, the train eased its way along the platform and out of the station. The soothing *clickety-clack* of the wheels calmed her. Just a few moments to gather her thoughts and then she'd plan her interview with Mrs. Treadwell.

Once they'd left the outskirts of town, the train sped up, spewing buckets of black grimy smoke and thick steam. Verity's eyelids flickered; she leaned her head back and drifted off.

When the train slowed, she shook herself awake. The Newcastle station sign flashed past and the train came to a shuddering halt. She'd slept the whole way.

She bundled her belongings together and made for the door. Several people stood in front of her waiting to descend, including the woman she'd all but run over at Maitland station who, thankfully, swung down from the train and walked across the platform without any sign of injury.

By the time she reached the guard's van, the stationmaster was standing holding her bicycle, scanning the platform. She raised her hand and ran toward him. "Thank you." She reached out to take the handlebars.

"Ticket stubs." He pointed to the labels tied to her bike.

She rummaged in her pocket and handed them over, then followed the signs for Platform 3 where the Sydney train left. Unwilling to go through the entire argument about traveling in the guard's van, she went straight to the ticket office.

"I'm going to Sydney and would like to put my bicycle in the guard's van. I've got my ticket."

"Right. Fill in your name and address." The ticket officer pushed two labels toward her and she scrawled her details. "You can leave your bicycle and bag with me; pick them up from the guard's van when you get to Sydney. Train leaves in half an hour."

Much easier. She ran her tongue around her dry mouth.

What she wouldn't give for a cup of tea. "Is there a tearoom on the platform?"

"Yep. Down to your right."

She pushed open the door to the crowded restaurant and groaned. Just about every table was filled, and waitresses ran hither and thither with pots of tea and plates of sandwiches and cakes. Her stomach rumbled.

"There's room for one more at that table over there." The waitress pointed to a two-person table tucked into the shadows of the back corner of the room.

"I couldn't."

"I've already asked her if she minds sharing, and she's quite happy. You won't get served otherwise before the train arrives. What would you like? I'll add it to the table order."

"A pot of tea and a sandwich of some sort would be perfect. Maybe a bit of cake? Thank you."

Apologizing as she went, Verity squeezed her way through the room to the small table in the corner. "It's so kind of you, thank . . ." Her words dried. The woman she'd run over at Maitland station smiled. Verity swallowed her embarrassment. "I do hope your foot isn't too painful."

"No harm done." The woman waved a foot out from under the table, revealing a smart laced brogue. "Sensible footwear saved me. Stella Trey." She held out her hand.

"Verity Binks." Verity took the cool hand and gave it a quick shake and sat down. The woman looked older than she'd first thought, in her late thirties, maybe early forties; there was a streak of gray in the front of her dark hair.

"Well, Miss Binks, it seems we're both making the same journey."

"Actually, I've been in Morpeth for a few days."

"Visiting family?"

"Not really. My grandfather grew up in Morpeth, but he moved to Sydney to work years ago. I've been researching several pieces for newspaper publication." Whatever had made her say that?

"Congratulations! How delightful to see a woman making a mark in an area dominated by men."

Heat rose to Verity's cheeks. She hadn't intended to big note herself. She was still half asleep, and she certainly shouldn't be talking about Treadwell until he'd seen her article, which she hadn't even written yet. She searched for the waitress. "I think our order is coming now. I added to yours; I hope that's all right." She burrowed down into her satchel and brought out her purse.

"Pot of tea for two. Some sandwiches and two slices of fruitcake." The waitress unpacked the tray and hovered, holding a saucer with a crumpled piece of paper on it.

Before Verity could pick up the bill, Miss Trey placed a handful of coins on the saucer. "Keep the change."

The waitress offered a quick bob and grinned. "Thank you, ma'am."

No, that wasn't at all what Verity intended. She opened her purse. She should be paying, an apology for running the poor woman over. "Please, let me . . ."

"I insist. Next time." Miss Trey beamed, the dark lenses of her full-rimmed tortoiseshell glasses catching the light.

Next time? There wouldn't be a next time. Apart from anything else, she would take far more care when loading her bicycle.

"Here you are. I expect you're parched. I always like a cup of tea when I wake up."

Verity flashed a look at the woman, saw her mouth tilt in a smile.

"I was in the same carriage as you," she said by way of explanation. Verity sipped the tea while her companion nibbled on one of the sandwiches and then dabbed at her mouth with her handkerchief before picking up her cup. "Come along, eat up. The Sydney train leaves soon."

And just how did Miss Trey know she was traveling on to Sydney? Verity chewed thoughtfully on the sandwich, running through the uncanny set of events. Her shoulders sagged. For goodness' sake, she was being ridiculously suspicious. She was on the Sydney platform. Too much poking and prodding in Morpeth, trying to make sense of everything. "Do you live in Sydney?" She took a bite of the fruitcake and felt her body respond. Good heavens, she was starving.

Miss Trey put down her cup and dabbed at her mouth again and nodded. "We should be making a move. Have you finished?"

Verity swallowed the last mouthful.

"Then we'll go and find ourselves a seat. Here's the train now."

Right on cue, the room shuddered and the train wheezed its way alongside the platform. Chairs scraped back and as one, the crowd in the tearoom rose and made for the door. With a glance over her shoulder to ensure Verity followed, Miss Trey made a beeline for the carriage in front of the guard's van.

Two minutes later they were sitting side by side, watching as the remainder of the seats filled. "You simply can't hang around, otherwise you never get a seat." Miss Trey smiled and gave a little shimmy as she settled and tilted back her head.

A billow of smoke wafted in through the window, filling the carriage with swirls of wet steam, specks of dirt, and a horrible stench of coal and oil. Verity reached up and slammed the window closed, then delved into her satchel and took out her notebook and pencil. She had no time to waste; her snooze between Maitland and Newcastle had seen to that.

Page by page she read through her notes, starting with the story of the Breckenridge family coming to Australia, the dreadful tragedy of the sinking of the *Cawarra*, Viola's and Constance's marriages, and then finally Florence's marriage to Treadwell—but she still had no idea what had inspired Mrs. Treadwell to establish the charity.

She nibbled the end of her pencil, wrote down a couple of theories and a series of headings with the odd idea that supported her thoughts, then *Philanthropist honors mother's history* . . . Not bad. A bubble of excitement rose in her chest. Yes! That would make an excellent angle and one Treadwell would surely appreciate, as it threw him into a good light. A lot of men would have ignored a charity that only benefited women.

"Ah! Shorthand."

Verity lifted her head.

Miss Trey peered over her shoulder at her notebook. "How very clever."

Resisting the temptation to snap her notebook shut, Verity relaxed. Miss Trey probably wouldn't be able to read her scribbles.

"Not a skill I've ever mastered."

Verity's shoulders dropped. Reading anyone else's shorthand was always difficult. Over time her style had taken on its own idiosyncrasies. Why, even Grandpa Sid had had trouble reading hers, although she'd always suspected it was his eyesight rather than an inability to read her swirls, squiggles, dots, and dashes.

"So you're following in your father's footsteps?"

Verity's head came up with a snap. She hadn't mentioned Charlie, had she? "My father?"

"I presumed your father was Charles Binks, the war correspondent. Binks is an unusual name."

"Yes, yes, he was."

"I met him during the war, in Egypt; everyone knew
everyone. He was a charming man. A great loss."

Verity offered a conciliatory smile; she never knew what to
say when anyone spoke of Charlie. She ought to be used to it by
now. Miss Trey turned her attention to the passing landscape
and Verity buried her head in her notebook, but the words
simply refused to come. It was almost as though she'd decided
what she wanted to write before she'd arrived in Morpeth and
then once she'd got there she'd discovered she'd fabricated the
entire story—it was wishful thinking. Nothing sinister, nothing unusual. Florence Breckenridge married into the Treadwell
family. That was that. She tapped the pencil against her teeth,
then pushed it and her notebook back into her satchel with a
sigh.

"Are the words not flowing?" Miss Trey asked, a sympa-
thetic expression etched on her face.

"No, they're not."

"I'm sure they will. What do you believe is the best piece
you've ever written? Perhaps talking about that might help."

"I haven't had an awful lot published. I used to work on the
advertising desk, but I've recently lost my job."

"Returned servicemen?"

She nodded. "It's not that I begrudge them a job; in fact,
I believe they should be given every opportunity after their
service to their country, it's just . . ."

"That you'd rather it wasn't your job?"

"No, not even that. It's more about the security of a
weekly pay packet. I've always wanted to write. Losing my job
came as a shock, but at least I have an opportunity. Mr. Bailey,

the editor, said he'd take a look at anything I wrote, and he's already published two of my articles. The first was about bicycles and how they've revolutionized women's lives, and the second was a report of the Artists' Ball." She gave a derogatory laugh.

"Obviously writing from personal experience—the best way. Bicycles truly have changed lives."

"I don't know what I'd do without my bicycle. It's not only the easiest form of transport, it's the sense of freedom, the ability to go wherever I want, whenever I want. And it's excellent exercise. Before the war women rarely exercised; how could they? Trussed up and contorted in Gibson Girl corsets. Once they embraced bicycles, their style of dress had to change and, as a consequence, their health improved." Good heavens, she was preaching. "I'm sorry; it's a bit of a passion."

"And very rightly so. A woman after my own heart." Miss Trey nodded. "I'd like to discuss this further. I'm a working woman myself. I own a business in the Strand Arcade. We specialize in botanical prints and favor women artists. I'm there most afternoons. Perhaps you'd like to call and I could show you around, then maybe you'd like to stay for supper? We have a discussion group that meets at the gallery. You never know, ideas for stories. Rose Scott has been a great supporter of our little group, but lately she's been unwell and has retired from public life; however, I believe she might be interested in giving a newspaper interview. She's disillusioned about women's progress since we got the vote."

A thrill of excitement sparked her blood. "I would . . . I would like that very much." Imagine if she could interview Rose Scott! Her work was legendary. She'd been instrumental in securing women's right to vote in Australia, and Saturday-afternoon visits to her garden were highly sought after. And then she stilled. Rose Scott. "Is she related to the Scott sisters, the botanical artists?"

"Cousins, I believe. Though Helena and Harriet both died several years ago, before the war; neither of them left any descendants."

The door that Verity had envisaged opening slammed shut and she swallowed her groan of annoyance.

Miss Trey handed her a small card. "Here's the address of the gallery. And please call me Stella. Just turn up, after midday. I'm always there during the week."

The remainder of the trip passed in a flurry. A baby behind them began crying when he dropped his toy; an older boy, his brother more than like, crawled under the seat and managed to get stuck. They extricated him after a bit of trouble, a lot of laughter, and even more apologies from the boy's red-faced mother, and then the train pulled into the Central Station.

"It was lovely to meet you," Stella said as they exited the train. "I look forward to seeing you soon." With a wave of her hand, she merged into the crowd.

CHAPTER 20

MORPETH, 1868

Sit yourself down, love. You've been flat out since you arrived."

Clarrie slumped down at the kitchen table. "Thank you, Mrs. Starling." She'd arrived bang on the dot of seven, before the sun was fully up, and after a quick tour of the house, Mrs. Starling had set her to work.

She sipped the cup of tea. "I didn't have time for breakfast. Charlie must have sensed that I was leaving. He wouldn't settle."

"No breakfast? We can't be having that." Mrs. Starling bundled off into the pantry and emerged with a slice of pie. "Get that into you, egg and bacon. One of my specialties. And tomorrow you'll have a decent breakfast before you start. I'm sure young Charlie will settle with Maud. She has plenty of experience—her mother taught her well—and then before you know it it'll be your day off and you'll see him."

Clarrie demolished the slice of pie in about three mouthfuls, trying to stop worrying about Charlie. It wasn't because he wouldn't settle that she'd missed breakfast, more the gnawing feeling in the pit of her stomach and the fact she had hardly been able to see what she was doing because of the tears pouring down her face. She hadn't imagined it would be so difficult to leave Charlie. She knew there was no alternative—it was the best thing in the long run—however, she hadn't known it would hurt so much. She sniffed back her threatening tears and finished her cup of tea. When she lifted her head, Mrs. Starling's kindly stare met hers.

"He'll be fine and you'll get used to it. You've done a wonderful job, and if you keep going the way you have this morning, I'll have a word with Miss Theodora and see if we can't find the time for you to visit once in a while during the week, tie it in with a bit of shopping or the like. There's always errands to be run, odds and ends to be picked up in the town, and mail to be collected. Then you can call in for a quick cuddle."

"That would be wonderful." Clarrie's heart lifted. "What would you like me to do now? I've finished the fireplaces, changed the sheets and washed them, swept the floors."

"Let's find you a job that's a little less like hard work. The library needs dusting. I haven't had time to get to it since they left for Sydney. I'll be back in a moment."

Mrs. Starling returned two minutes later with a feather duster and cloths. "Rule number one: put everything back exactly where you find it. Number two: don't open any of the display cabinets, and if you need to take down any books, make sure they go back in the exact same place. And the furniture could do with a bit of a wipe with this." She handed Clarrie a tin of beeswax and another cloth. "No need to go to town, just use the cloth to wipe down what you can reach."

That didn't sound too difficult. She'd managed to keep the reverend's study clean despite the array of books littering every available space. With the feather duster tucked under her arm and the pail containing the cleaning cloths and beeswax, she made her way to the front of the house.

The door stood ajar so she stuck her head in. Miss Breckenridge sat, her back to the door, paints and sketchbook and the poor dead butterflies littering the surface of the desk. Clarrie gave a quick shudder. Surely animals had senses. She clasped her hand to her throat, remembering the way Miss Breckenridge had pinched the poor things and squeezed out their air. "Excuse me, miss."

Miss Breckenridge lifted her head and smiled, a smudge of orange paint slashed across one cheek and her fingers holding the brush were blackened.

"Mrs. Starling asked me to come and dust in here, but I can come back later if you're busy."

"That's all right, just leave the desk where I'm working. And why don't you call me Miss Theodora, like everyone else."

"I'm not sure . . ."

"Rubbish. *Miss Breckenridge* makes me feel like an old spinster, and since we're going to be living under the same roof we don't have to stand on ceremony."

"I don't think I could." In fact, she couldn't think of anyone who looked less like an old spinster with her wonderfully bright hair, piercing blue eyes, and the dusting of cinnamon freckles across her nose. Miss Breck—Miss Theodora, she corrected herself—looked more like the princess from a fairy-tale book she'd borrowed from the School of Arts. "You're far too pretty." Clarrie clamped her hand over her mouth. Much too familiar. It was just that Miss Theodora was so friendly.

"Thank you. I don't think there are many people who would agree with you, but it's a lovely compliment. How are you settling in?"

"Well, I think. Mrs. Starling said I'd done a wonderful

job." Clarrie picked up the feather duster and started on the bookshelves, her face burning. Whatever had made her say that? It sounded like bragging.

"I'm sure you have. You're very welcome to borrow any of the books you notice when you're dusting. Just make sure you put them back in the same place."

Miss Theodora picked up her paintbrush and was soon lost to her butterflies again.

Theodora put the final touches to the wash and rinsed her brush. "Come and tell me what you think, Clarrie." She pushed back the chair and stood, stretching her shoulders and flexing her fingers.

"Miss Theodora, it's just beautiful." Clarrie pushed back the hair that had escaped its pins and peered slightly myopically at the painting and then at the specimen. She lifted her head and frowned, her hand hovering over the butterfly. "I think you might have missed these two little black spots." Her finger indicated the hind wings.

Never one to take criticism well, Theodora bristled and drew her brows together in an answering frown. Clarrie must be mistaken; she'd sketched every spot before she'd started painting. "Why don't you start on the cabinets now. The books look just fine."

Theodora studied her painting and then the specimen until a cool calm settled. The girl was correct. She should be thanking her, not bristling like a hog hairbrush. A line from Harriet's letter slipped into her mind. She pulled open the top drawer of the desk and took out the note that had accompanied the letter, studying the cramped handwriting. *The male of the species has a small black spot on the surface of the hind wings . . .* How had she missed it?

"I think you're right. This isn't a female, as we imagined. It's most definitely a male. The notes said that the male has a small black spot on its hind wings."

She received no answer and assumed the silly girl was sulking. Not an endearing trait. How disappointing. She hadn't imagined Clarrie would behave that way.

When she glanced over her shoulder, she found Clarrie smiling at her. "I'm so pleased; Sid always says I have an eye for detail."

"You certainly have. Thank you." Theodora picked up a clean brush, the one she'd reserved for lamp black, not wanting to dull any other colors with residual pigment. "Would you like to paint it in?"

"Me? I couldn't do that."

"I think you should. After all, we were together when we found the cluster of butterflies. You should make your mark on the painting. Come here."

Clarrie shook her head. "Thank you, but no. It's your work. I wouldn't want to spoil it."

The poor girl's face rivaled vermillion paint. "Why do you think you'd spoil it? I wouldn't have asked you if I thought you would."

"It's your painting."

How very strange. Biddy would have jumped at the opportunity. Or would she? She wouldn't have noticed the discrepancy, and neither would Constance or Viola, for that matter. Florence, maybe. She had an eagle eye for detail, particularly if it related to money. "Is there anything else you remember about the butterflies that I might have forgotten?"

"What sort of thing?"

"The way they were clustered, any of the nearby plants, the sun, the shadows. You didn't see any caterpillars or eggs, did you?" Quite why she asked that question she had no idea because she was certain there wouldn't be any at this time of the year.

"I did notice the funny seedpods on the bushes around the back of the house when we came back to the boat. Same as the ones in the garden that Archer was pulling out. The ones that look like balls of fluff. I've never seen plants like that before."

"There was cotton bush in the Scotts' garden?"

"I don't know what it's called, but I can show you the ones I mean."

"Leave the duster here and come with me. I told Archer to cut down all the cotton bushes so they'd bloom early. He said he was going to have a fire. Quickly." If Clarrie was correct, then it might have been the cotton bush that had attracted the first butterfly.

"But Mrs. Starling said I should—"

"This is more important. Come along, quickly."

Theodora held out her hand and together she and Clarrie galloped toward the curl of smoke rising behind the garden wall.

They slithered to a halt in front of the fire. "Archer! Stop!"

"Sorry, bit late now." Archer stood leaning on the end of the rake, watching the dry cuttings flare.

Theodora bit back the string of expletives she'd learned from Jamie and Redmond. She had no one to blame but herself. She'd been so caught up with her painting she hadn't asked Clarrie what she'd seen at Ash Island as she intended.

"Miss."

Theodora whipped around. Clarrie was standing next to

the barrow holding one of the seed pods from the cotton bush in her hand.

"Be careful of the sap. It will give you a nasty rash."

"I don't think so; it's very dry." Clarrie twisted the stem in her fingers. "This is what I noticed. See how the pods burst and all the fluff pops out? They're really quite pretty."

"That's the seeds. The wind carries them enormous distances."

"Do they have flowers?"

"Yes. Lovely reddish-orange and pinkish-purple clusters, a little like dandelions. They flower right the way through spring and into autumn." And that would be where the butterflies would lay their eggs in the spring. Either at The Landing or on Ash Island. "Hold on to that; we'll take it up to the house."

"Can I burn the rest of the rubbish, then?" Archer scratched his head, his mouth drawn down at the corners. "You told me to clear that garden bed and wear gloves."

"It's fine, Archer; you haven't done anything wrong. I'd missed something very important. You've done a great job in the garden and the cotton bush will come back in spring, just as I hoped." She reached for Clarrie's hand. "Thank you, thank you so much."

"I'm not sure what I've done."

"I'll explain on the way. I have to check some facts." Theodora slipped her arm through Clarrie's as they walked back up to the house. "Do you understand the life cycle of a butterfly?"

"No, not really." Clarrie shrugged. "The butterfly lays its eggs and they hatch into new butterflies."

"Not quite. There are actually four stages—the egg, as you said, but then from the egg comes the larvae, a caterpillar that eats and eats until it spins itself a silken cocoon, and from that cocoon the butterfly emerges."

"And then that butterfly lays an egg and it all starts all over again. How very clever." Clarrie's face creased in a frown. "But how long does all of that take? It took me nine months to hatch Charlie." Color blossomed on her cheeks. "Sorry."

"That's what I don't really remember. Most butterflies spend winter as larvae or pupae, waiting to emerge as a butterfly in spring, but the butterflies we saw looked as though they might spend winter as adults. Every butterfly has its favorite plant; that's where it lays its eggs. If we can find that, then we'll know where to look for the eggs in the spring. I'm wondering if the cotton bush might attract them, since that's where I saw the first one, and you, you clever girl, noticed the same plant growing on Ash Island."

As they drew closer to the house, Clarrie became quieter. Mrs. Starling stood on the veranda, fisted hands on her hips and a ferocious scowl on her face. "And what do you think you're up to, missy? I've got jobs that need doing."

Before Clarrie could open her mouth and apologize, Theodora jumped in. "Clarrie's giving me a hand. I need her help in the library. She can finish her other tasks later."

A sound resembling a frustrated cow billowed out of Mrs. Starling's mouth and she swiveled on her heel and marched back into the house.

"Don't worry about her. Her bark's far worse than her bite. Come with me; I need to check Harriet's letter again."

So captivated by the butterfly, Theodora hadn't thought to clarify the host plant. What a foolish mistake. She cleared the desk and then carefully opened Harriet's letter and unfolded the small piece of paper.

"What's that, miss?"

"It's a description I received about the butterflies. It says their life span is about a month to six weeks in summer but longer over winter when they almost hibernate. We saw them in their dormant stage. And I'd forgotten . . . here it is . . . the larvae, caterpillars, are poisonous because of what they eat." *Asclepias.* "We have to look up *Asclepias.*"

"*Asclep*— I don't know what that is, and besides, animals as pretty as those butterflies couldn't be poisonous."

"Many poisonous insects are colorful. It's a warning to their predators—other animals that might eat them. Now, let me see if I can find Mama's botanical reference. Bring the library steps over here."

Theodora climbed to the top rung and stretched up on her tiptoes.

"You be careful; it's very high and those books look heavy."

Theodora ran her finger along the spines until she found what she was looking for. She pulled the slim volume from the top shelf and handed it to Clarrie before climbing down. What a blessing Redmond had introduced her to Clarrie. It was such a delight to have someone to share her interests again, and Clarrie seemed to be a keen learner. "Now let's have a look and see what we can find."

With Clarrie hanging over her shoulder, she opened the book to the first page. It wasn't a thick volume, but the wafer-thin pages and close-set type held a wealth of information.

"This belonged to my mother; it came with her from Cornwall, and she'd marked all her favorite plants and brought seeds and cuttings with her and planted out the walled garden. Many of them are used for herbal remedies. The book's very old." Theodora ran her finger over the title. "'*The Herball or Generall Historie of Plantes 1597.*' Now we'll look and see if we can find *Asclepias.*"

Theodora reached the end of the book and heaved a frustrated sigh. She'd been so certain she had the perfect solution.

"Isn't it there?" Clarrie's furrowed brow mirrored her own confusion.

"No, it's not and I don't understand why." She dropped the book onto the desk and slumped down in the chair.

"Maybe it's a new plant. That's a very old book." Clarrie tipped her head back, peering up at the wall of shelving.

"It doesn't make sense. It's in the garden; Mama must have planted it."

"Some plants come up on their own, and what about the ones in the bush? They won't be in that old book because Australia didn't exist in"—Clarrie lifted the cover of the book—"1597."

"It did exist, Clarrie; it's been here for millions of years. Europeans hadn't found it."

"I know about that. Captain Cook found Australia. He sailed everywhere with that man who collected plants . . ."

"Banks. Joseph Banks. He started a wonderful garden in England at a place called Kew. They investigate plants found in the colonies . . . Clarrie, you are so clever, so very, very clever. Bring the ladder over here." Theodora squinted up at the top shelves where a pile of pamphlets sat. They used to arrive four times a year and Mama always looked forward to them. "What would I do without you?"

"I'm not really sure what I've done." Clarrie held the bottom of the ladder steady and Theodora scooted up to the top.

"*Curtis's Botanical Magazine*. Here they are." She passed part of the pile to Clarrie, a nostalgic memory of sitting at Mama's feet copying an illustration of a passionflower tugging her heartstrings. "Put them down. I'll get the rest."

In no time they had a teetering stack sitting on the desk.

Clarrie stood scratching her head. "We'll never get through this lot."

"Yes, we will. What we're looking for is the index, or if we're very lucky, Mama may have marked the page. She was very conscientious about her garden. The index will look like one of the magazines, but it will say Index on the front."

"*Conscientious*," Clarrie mumbled. "*Conscientious* . . . *index* . . . *botanical* . . . I'm not sure I know what all those words mean."

She was such a dear. Theodora curbed a smile as they took one magazine at a time off the pile, scanned the cover, and placed it upside down alongside.

"Eureka! *General Indexes to the Plants Contained in the Botanical Magazine (1801–1860)*." Heart racing, Theodora ran her finger down the list. "Here it is. Page one hundred and forty-three." Her voice shook. "'*Asclepias* is a genus of herbaceous, perennial, flowering plants known as milkweeds, named for their milky latex. Most species are toxic to humans and many other species. Native to the Americas' . . ." It had to be the cotton bush that had made her hands so sore. "The thick white sap must be why it's known as milkweed. I think we have our answer. I wonder how the seeds made their way into Mama's garden?" She seized Clarrie's hands and squeezed. "I can't thank you enough."

"I didn't do much, miss."

"Yes, you did. But for your sharp eyes I might still be thinking I had dreamed my butterfly and that I would never see it again in the garden. Now, you'd better go and find Mrs. Starling. I've got work to do."

She shuffled through her paintings. She'd send Harriet a series that would scientifically represent the butterfly. None of the slapdash rubbish she'd sent before. Her cheeks burned.

How could she have done such a stupid thing? She had no idea, but then, if she hadn't, she wouldn't have thought to go to Ash Island, wouldn't have seen the clusters on the trees, and Clarrie wouldn't have spotted the cotton bush growing in the garden.

And then everything went still and quiet.

Redmond had said Hench padded his jacket with the seedpods from the cotton bush. Papa had employed Hench in Sydney; he'd come off a ship from the Americas and now he was working at Ash Island. Was that how the cotton bush had come to grow in both places? Was Hench, the man she disliked so very much, responsible for bringing the butterflies to the area?

Fired with fresh enthusiasm, she returned to the specimens she'd collected from Ash Island, working quickly lest the colors faded or the tiny hairs and scales flattened, or worse, dried and fell off; and making sure she had the palpi, antennae, legs, and wings in natural positions before they became stiff and unmanageable. She was buoyed by the knowledge their food source grew in Mama's garden—it meant the butterflies would undoubtedly return in the spring.

CHAPTER 21

SYDNEY, 1922

Despite her best efforts, Verity remained dissatisfied with her progress on the Treadwell article. She'd included all of the information she'd unearthed in Morpeth and the odd bit she'd found in the folder Mr. Treadwell had given her. Nothing particularly exciting—a copy of the original land grant made to Oliver Treadwell, although much of the land surrounding the house had been sold off, and the plans drawn up by none other than Francis Greenway, the government architect back in the day.

She had tried a hundred times to include Mrs. Treadwell's early life. A description of the house at The Landing and the story of the Breckenridge family, the dreadful loss of her parents and the marriages of her younger sisters and their removal to England, and then her own marriage, but it read simply as two entirely unconnected stories and neither of them answered the most important question: Why had Mrs. Treadwell dedicated her life, and the Treadwell family fortune, to establishing a charity to help young girls?

Verity's stomach churned at the prospect of explaining to Mr. Treadwell that the article would appeal to so many more people if it engaged readers' attention and sympathy, so they could identify with Mrs. Treadwell's commitment to the women the foundation helped.

She needed to speak to Mrs. Treadwell. The story was hers to tell, not her pompous son's. He seemed to want to take all the credit for his mother's endeavors. She would go down to the post office and ring Mr. Treadwell and confirm their appointment for tomorrow and ask to speak to Mrs. Treadwell at the same time. And if she was to succeed, she would need to look the part, efficient and competent, and that would require her most respectable blue skirt and striped blouse, polished boots, a serious attempt to tame her unruly hair, and no bicycle.

The next morning Verity raised her hand to the lion-head knocker and brought it down on the door with a no-nonsense rap. As before, she had to wait several minutes; however, this time she was prepared.

"Good morning, Mary. Mr. Treadwell is expecting me."

"He's not available."

And she wasn't going to be treated like a tradesman. "I telephoned and I have an appointment to see him, and Mrs. Treadwell, at eleven o'clock sharp."

"She's not available either."

"Would you go and make certain, Mary?"

"Ain't no point. They both left in the motor an hour ago."

Verity swallowed the string of words she'd very much like to have delivered and plastered a smile on her face. "When are you expecting them back?"

"Not until this evening."

Anger simmered. Treadwell had suggested the time when she rang, said he'd speak to his mother and ensure she would be at home. Verity took a step forward, wanting to peer inside and make sure Mary hadn't been sent to spin some yarn, but the girl had her measure. "Please tell Mr. Treadwell I called and that I will telephone him tomorrow morning to—"

The knocker clanged as the door shut in her face.

Ranting and raving, Verity stomped down the driveway and headed toward Darlinghurst Road to pick up the tram, then came to a halt. Exercise would do her good. She'd walk, clear her head, and perhaps improve her mood. Maybe she simply wasn't cut out to be a newspaperman—woman. That was the problem. No one took women seriously. She'd put money on the fact Treadwell would have kept his appointment if she'd been a man. He wouldn't have left Charlie—famous war correspondent—standing on the doorstep listening to some hoity-toity young girl who deserved a dressing down for her rudeness. Women might have the vote, but it had done nothing to improve the attitude of the general population. Fine, and valuable even, as wives and mothers, but not much else. It was time she joined one of the groups that fought for serious equality.

Verity pushed back a damp strand of hair from her face. Though still winter, the sun was warm and she'd covered the distance to Hyde Park almost as fast as the tram. Did they have women tram drivers? She'd never thought to wonder. She glanced around, lamenting the felling of the fig trees. The construction of St. James and Museum stations had meant the whole park had been dug up; hopefully the trees would be reinstated. A few remained outside the Australian Museum, so she stopped in the shade, pulled off her cloche, and unbuttoned her jacket. Was Stella serious when she'd said she might be able to organize a meeting with Rose Scott? It would be the perfect follow-up to the story of the Treadwell Foundation, but that had to come first. So very annoying that the Treadwells hadn't kept their appointment.

She needed to hear Mrs. Treadwell's story. If Mr. Treadwell was to be believed. What had he said? His mother had tried to reach out but her efforts were ignored. Something must have caused the family breakup. Unless it had to do with Arlo's mother's refusal to leave The Landing . . . The bustle of the streets faded as the other pictures she'd seen at The Landing filled her vision. Each one had contained the orange and black butterfly.

She bolted up the stairs and into the foyer of the museum, her breath rasping as she skidded to a halt at the desk. "Excuse me."

A young man lifted his head. "How can I help you?"

"Do you have a butterfly collection?"

He quirked a smile. "You could say that. Mr. Olliff's collection is held in very high regard and we also hold a copy of *Australian Lepidoptera and Their Transformations* by A. W. Scott. A remarkable book; of course, the credit should go to Scott's daughters. They were responsible for all the artwork. A comprehensive record of Australia's moths and butterflies."

"I'm looking for information about a specific butterfly; it's quite large, about"—she stretched her index finger and thumb apart—"about four- or five-inch wingspan, black and orange with white dots on its wings."

"Ah! Olliff's little Wanderer? A fascinating story." He squinted at the clock on the wall behind him. "I'm due for a break in ten minutes. I'd be happy to show you."

A fascinating story. A thrill of anticipation danced across her skin, making the fine hairs on her arms prickle.

"Why don't you have a seat over there? You look as though you're a little flustered."

She was a little flustered. More than a little. Why hadn't she thought to find out about the butterfly before? Thank heavens she'd stopped outside the museum.

The young man's promised ten minutes crawled into fifteen and then twenty while Verity sat fidgeting on the wooden bench. Finally, he ambled over, dangling a key. "Follow me." He led the way down the stairs past a series of closed doors and then came to a halt and unlocked a door marked *Lepidoptera*. "Butterfly archives," he said as he flicked a light switch, illuminating rows and rows of display cabinets with shallow glass-topped drawers, the butterflies pinned in neat columns and the smell of camphor thick in the air. "Over here. Such an interesting story. *Danaus plexippus*. Known as the Monarch butterfly in the Americas, although I prefer the name we use, 'the Wanderer.'" With a theatrical flourish, he lifted the lid of the display case.

Verity couldn't control her smile. No doubt about it. Although the colors were a little faded, the butterfly was identical to the drawings and samples she'd seen at The Landing, and identical to the costume she'd worn to the Artists' Ball.

"Common along the whole of the eastern coast of Australia today. It was first recorded in Queensland."

Exactly as Arlo had told her. Perhaps there was nothing more to learn.

"Olliff maintained there was a sighting in a remote locality north of Sydney before that, but it was never authenticated."

A remote locality. Verity's pulse picked up. "May I take some notes?" She rummaged in her satchel and brought out her pencil and notebook.

He rubbed his hands together, warming to his theme. "The most popular theory revolves around a series of cyclones during the summer of 1870–71. The generally accepted theory is that the butterflies were picked up in the wind system and deposited on the Queensland east coast."

Verity's pencil stopped. Theodora Breckenridge's paintings were dated 1868. Had Arlo's mother truly discovered that first cluster? Arlo would be thrilled. And then her stomach dropped. If he'd speak to her again.

"We'll never know about the earlier sighting because there is nothing in the records." He shrugged. "By 1873, Mr. Masters of the Entomological Society had recorded them as the most common butterfly along the whole eastern coast."

Verity jotted down the last name and date. She needed to do some thinking. "Thank you very much for your help."

"It's a pleasure. The Wanderer is one of my personal interests. May I ask what prompted your inquiry?"

Tricky. It wasn't her place to tell this man about Arlo's mother. "I saw a painting of the butterfly and was struck by its beauty. Curiosity more than anything else."

He led the way back to the foyer. "It was delightful to meet you, Miss . . ."

"Binks. Verity Binks."

"Arthur Bardwell." He held out his hand. "Don't hesitate to call in if I can be of any further assistance."

"Thank you."

Restraining a whoop of excitement, Verity toppled down the steps and collapsed onto a seat in the park. So many opportunities right under her nose for articles. She needed to make her peace with Arlo, and what better way to do that than confirm that his mother was probably the first person to report a sighting of the Wanderer butterfly in Australia? It might go some way toward apologizing for her ridiculous behavior and give her the opportunity to see him again.

She pulled on her hat and ambled across the remains of the

park. As much as she'd enjoyed her little sojourn at the museum, she still had to decide what she would do about Treadwell. If she kept Mr. Bailey waiting too long, he'd probably forget his promise to take the article; she needed to come up with something else.

She rounded the corner into Pitt Street and stopped in her tracks. The Strand Arcade. She delved into her bag for the card Stella had given her. Unless she was very much mistaken, she was only two minutes away.

Tucked between a milliner and a jeweler, the gallery was easy to find. Two easels sat in the bay window displaying beautiful ink drawings of banksias, every detail of the foliage and seed heads beautifully portrayed.

A small bell tinkled as Verity pushed open the door and the curtain at the back of the shop parted.

"Verity! How lovely to see you." Stella held out both hands. "I wasn't expecting a visit so soon."

"I was passing and—" Heat rose to her cheeks. "I wanted to talk to you about Rose Scott. You said that you might be able to arrange a meeting and I . . ." To her horror her voice wavered and tears prickled. Anger at the way Treadwell ignored their appointment or disappointment over her behavior toward Arlo? All at sixes and sevens, she scuffed her hand over her face.

"My dear, come and sit down. How can I help?"

"I'm perfectly fine. Just angry, with myself more than anyone else."

"Come with me and we'll have a cup of tea. I have a pot brewing out at the back. Have you had lunch?" Without waiting for a response, Stella led the way back behind the curtain to a small room, the walls lined with canvases and a large table covered with prints and framing materials. She made a small space at the corner of the table. "Sit down."

Verity perched on the edge of the chair. "Do you frame the pictures yourself?"

"Not all of them, but I enjoy doing it. I'm a dab hand with a saw and a glue pot." Stella picked up a small porcelain cup, which had neither a saucer nor handle, and put it on the table before pouring a stream of pale tea into it from a matching pot.

Verity inhaled the sweet floral fragrance.

"Jasmine tea. I hope you like it. I'm afraid I haven't any other."

"I've never tried it." She took a sip. "It's lovely. Very refreshing."

She took another taste and the rich warmth spread, easing the tightness.

"Now, would you like to tell me what's wrong?" Stella perched on the edge of the table, her legs crossed neatly at the ankles, revealing a smart pair of T-strap shoes made of what looked remarkably like crocodile skin.

Verity glanced down at her own functional but thoroughly boring laced boots, which showed serious signs of wear despite her efforts with the polish. "I'm being foolish. I had an appointment with someone today about a piece I'm writing and they weren't there. I think they'd forgotten."

"The article you were struggling with on the train?"

"Yes. I rang and made the appointment to speak to Mr. and Mrs. Treadwell yesterday, but when I arrived they'd gone out. I really can't complete the story until I have spoken to Mrs. Treadwell." She bit her lips. She done it again. Not only was she behaving like a spoiled child, tears threatening at the first hurdle, but she would never make a decent journalist if she talked about her stories. She huffed out a sigh.

"Mrs. Treadwell of Elizabeth Bay?"

Verity nodded. She cast a quick glance around the room

and through the door. *"A little gallery in the Strand Arcade."* Had Mrs. Treadwell bought the painting of The Landing from Stella?

"I think fate might have led you to my door because I am acquainted with Mrs. Treadwell. She is a patron of the arts. Women's art in particular, and she often frequents exhibitions we hold."

What a perfect opportunity. If Verity could see Mrs. Treadwell alone, without her son, she might be happy to talk of her past and her reasons for starting the charity. She sipped the last of the tea and dismissed the idea of asking Stella about the butterfly painting until she'd spoken to Mrs. Treadwell. She put the cup down carefully on the corner of the strewn table. "I don't suppose . . ."

"It would be my pleasure. There is a showing in the Queen Victoria Building. I would expect Mrs. Treadwell to attend. Would you like me to arrange an invitation?"

CHAPTER 22

MORPETH, 1868

Clarrie couldn't believe how quickly the days had passed. For the first time in her life, she felt as though she was a help. She wrapped the cloth around her hands and slid the orange cake out of the oven and onto the rack to cool. Miss Theodora liked cake and company with her afternoon tea, and that was another job she'd taken on—hardly a job, much more a pleasure. Even at this time of the year the sun struck the veranda and warmed the flagstones, making it a delightful spot. They often sat sipping tea and discussing their trip to Ash Island—going over and over every moment, making sure they hadn't missed anything. Clarrie would love to visit again, but she didn't know how to suggest it without looking as though she was poking her nose in.

Once she'd laid the tray, she made the tea and took everything outside. There was no sign of Miss Theodora, but that was nothing new; she was always late. Clarrie plumped the cushions and settled down into one of the lovely wicker chairs to admire the view over the river. Just two more days and she would see Charlie.

She missed him so much, but Sid visited and had sent messages with Archer telling her how Charlie was faring and little stories about him—blowing bubbles was his latest trick. She truly appreciated Sid's efforts, but she needed to see Charlie for herself, hold him tight. She let her eyelids fall and inhaled, hoping to conjure his sweet, milky scent.

"I'm late, I'm sorry." Theodora slithered to a halt in front of her, her blue eyes wide and concern written all over her face. "My goodness! What's the matter?" She crouched down in front of Clarrie. "Why are you crying?"

Clarrie scuffed her hand over her face, wiping away the tears she hadn't known were there. "I'm all right, perfectly all right. I was thinking about Charlie."

"And missing him. You poor dear." Theodora sat and poured out the tea and handed Clarrie a cup.

"You shouldn't be doing that."

"Rubbish. I'm quite capable of pouring tea and serving cake. In fact, when my sisters are home it's my job." She cut a huge slice of orange cake, slipped it onto the plate. "There you are. Cake fixes everything."

Clarrie nibbled at the slice, then sipped her tea. "I don't want to make a fuss. It's just . . ."

Miss Theodora waved her hand in the air until she finished her mouthful. "I've written a letter to the Scott sisters telling them about our trip to Ash Island. Perhaps you could take it to Morpeth and see if you can catch the evening steamer. I was going to ask Archer, but it occurred to me it might give you the opportunity to check on Charlie. You must be worrying about him."

Clarrie clasped her arms tightly at her waist to quell the urge to throw them around Miss Theodora. She'd tried so very hard to stop thinking about Charlie, but it was nigh impossible when her body kept reminding her it was time for his feed. "Could I? I wouldn't be very long, an hour, maybe a bit more— depends on the punt."

"I've got a better idea—we'll ask Archer to row you across. He's got to be back at the newspaper for his evening shift, and then you can get the punt back. How does that sound?"

"Just perfect, just perfect."

An hour later, Clarrie stood outside Maud's cottage bent double, her pulse thumping. She'd run all the way from Queens Wharf after delivering Miss Theodora's letter to the steamship office, but already the light was fading.

She rapped on the door, waited, tried again, cupped her hands, and peered through the window into the front room. No one. She tried Maud's bedroom window too, but the curtains were pulled. Swallowing a howl of frustration, she ducked back into the street and made her way around to the rear of the row of four terraces. Stone walls separated the yards, and a wooden gate led from the laneway to each house. Although she'd never used the gate, she'd hung more baby clothes in the backyard than she'd like to count.

She slipped under the washing lines and walked up the steps to the door, which opened with a groan. Maud sat at the kitchen table, head in hands. She looked up, her face red and blotched. "What are you doing here?" She sniffed.

"I'm here to see Charlie." Clarrie made for the hallway.

"Hang on a minute. I thought Sunday was your day off."

"It is. I had an errand to run so I thought I'd call in."

"Next time make sure you let me know."

Clarrie pulled open the kitchen door, heard a swish of a skirt, footsteps, and a clunk as the front door closed. Maud

must have had a visitor, perhaps a new client, and she'd interrupted. When she opened the door to the babies' room, the
reek hit her first. Soiled babies and the strange sweet and sticky
odor. She reached into Charlie's drawer. Her fingers found a
pile of wet, clammy bedding, but he didn't stir. She scooped
him up and took him into the kitchen, blood boiling. "He's
sodden and needs changing. I can't believe he hasn't woken.
Have you given him more of that tonic?" She flopped down on
the chair and laid him on her lap. His eyelids flickered, then
his lashes fell again.

"He's been fed, settled for the night. Change him if you
want. You'll have to do it out here. I don't want the others
to wake." Maud gestured to an unfolded pile of clothing and
blankets tossed into a basket in the corner of the room.

Holding Charlie close, Clarrie picked out a clean nightgown, undershirt, and cap, laid him back across her knees, and
took off his damp, smelly clothes. By the time she'd finished
he'd woken and Maud had vanished. Ignoring the ache in her
breasts and the temptation to feed him, she cuddled him close
while she heated a bottle of milk. He took some of it, his big
blue eyes glued to her face as though drinking in the sight of
her, and then his eyelids fluttered closed and he dropped off
again.

She held up the bottle, but he'd only drunk half of it. Still,
Maud said she'd fed him not long ago, so perhaps it made
sense. Snatching up some clean bedclothes, she tiptoed into
the babies' room, remade his drawer, tucked him in, and went
back to the kitchen where Maud stood folding the washing.

"Would you like some help changing the other babies?"

Maud sighed. "No. I'll do it when they wake for their next
feed. You'd better go else you won't get back before dark."

Clarrie glanced out into the twilight. She'd thought to see

Sid but didn't have a hope. "I'll be back the day after tomorrow. See you then."

Receiving nothing but a grunt, she pulled her cloak close and bolted back to the punt.

Redmond strolled down the road to the wharf with an energetic bounce. For the first time since he'd taken over from the old man, he'd put the paper to bed on time, and now all he wanted was a good meal and a soothing drink before a decent night's sleep. If the good lord ever saw fit to provide him with a son, he'd make damn certain he learned the newspaper trade and wasn't thrown in out of his depth. He'd never intended to take on the job; always thought Father would die at his desk, not be taken by a sudden apoplexy—a weak heart, according to Dr. Morson. Hopefully it wasn't hereditary. Within minutes he was heading downriver toward the punt.

With any luck Thomas would have called it quits and he wouldn't have to worry about getting tangled in the ferry's chains.

Two lights shone from the shore, marking the spot. He drifted to a halt. Thomas stood, hands on hips, arguing with a young woman dressed in a dark cloak with the hood pulled up, masking her face.

"Hey, Thomas. Finished up for the night?"

"Mr. Kendall! Thought I had but it looks as though I've got another fare." His exasperated voice wafted across the water.

Redmond cut the engine and let the boat drift into the shore. "What's the problem?"

"Lass here needs to get across to The Landing."

"Mr. Kendall." The woman threw back her hood, long

hair flowing around her face, and stepped closer to the edge of the jetty.

"Clarrie! What are you doing out here?"

"I had an errand to run for Miss Theodora and I called in to see Charlie." Her voice caught. "I didn't realize it was so late."

"I'll run you back. It's on my way." He edged the boat into the wharf. "I'll sort this out, Thomas; you pack up."

"Thanks. The missus will be at me if I'm late home."

Redmond held out his hand and helped Clarrie aboard.

"Thank you so much."

"Not a problem. How's young Charlie, then?"

Her sniff echoed in the stillness. "He's all right, but I miss him something rotten. Sid's been calling in . . ." She lifted her shoulders, tears beginning to well in her eyes.

"I'd better have a word with young Sid and make sure he lets you know how Charlie is more often. Better still, why don't we have a chat with Theodora? I'm sure she'll give you a bit more time off to see him."

"She's real good to me; it just took Archer longer than we thought to row across because of the current and then by the time I'd delivered Miss Theodora's letter to Queens Wharf for the Sydney steamer and run back to Maud's the time got away."

"I'll tell you what. I make this trip at least twice a day. Why don't I call in and see if you've got some free time when I'm passing?" Redmond pressed his lips together. Scheming so-and-so he was, the perfect excuse to see Theodora more often. "We're almost there. Can you handle the rope?"

With a flick of her wrist, Clarrie sent the rope curling over the bollard.

"Not bad after only one trip."

"I'm getting the hang of it." She hitched up her skirts and scrambled onto the wharf.

"I'll walk you up to the house. Say hello to Theodora."

"She'll like that."

CHAPTER 23

Verity unwrapped the dress she had bought on her way home from the gallery, although she could hardly afford it. Looking at Stella's lovely shoes and immaculate day dress had made her realize that if she was to mingle with the patrons at an art exhibition, she would have to look the part.

She shook out the magenta dress and held it against her shoulders. Worn underneath her black overcoat, with her black cloche, her single pair of good shoes, and stockings, she should be able to hold her head up.

True to her word, Stella had sent an invitation to the opening. A young boy had delivered it earlier, though Verity had no recollection of having given Stella her address. She'd spent several hours writing down a series of questions she wanted to ask Mrs. Treadwell and committing them to memory, and she had an hour to change and catch a tram to the Queen Victoria Building.

The afternoon opening meant that she would be home not long before dark, so she left a pot of soup on the stove and damped down the fire.

The tram took an eternity to clang and clatter its way along George Street, stopping at every stop, and when it finally approached the intersection with Market, she rang the bell and swung off.

Ahead of her the elaborate facade of the building towered, its copper domes reflecting the last rays of sunshine. The last time she'd set foot inside she'd been with Grandpa Sid. He loved to visit the City Library, housed in the impressive ballroom of yesteryear, and chat to the array of shop owners. She'd always had the suspicion that he picked up his leads from the palmists and clairvoyants, though she'd never seen him indulge in any reading. He seemed to know everyone. A habit she should cultivate if she intended to make a name for herself.

She found the gallery on the first floor and the showing underway. A round of applause greeted her as she slipped inside the door and a woman stepped from the podium. The crowd broke up and drifted toward the paintings that covered every available space on the walls.

"Hello. Can I help you?" A young woman with a very modern shingle haircut smiled at her.

"My name is Verity Binks. Miss Trey, Stella, arranged an invitation for me." She held out the small cream-colored card.

"Ah, Miss Binks, yes. Stella told me you'd be coming. Unfortunately, she won't be here this evening; however, we're looking forward to your visit. Any publicity for our gallery is always welcome. If you have any questions, please don't hesitate to ask. I believe you write for *The Sydney Arrow*?"

Verity swallowed. She lifted her chin. Surely she could write an article about the exhibition. Especially as all the artists were women—it would give it a nice twist. It seemed Stella might be the one to introduce her to many opportunities.

"Yes, I am a writer and I am interested in women's affairs most especially."

"You might like a copy of our catalogue." The young woman handed her a printed leaflet. "Let me know if there's anything I can do." She raised her hand to greet a couple standing at the door.

"Excuse me, just one moment, before you go. Could you point out Mrs. Treadwell? I believe she is a patron."

"Indeed. I saw her arrive." She surveyed the crowd, then nodded toward the far corner of the room. "She's over there. You can't miss her. She's dressed entirely in black. She's still mourning the death of her companion last year, poor dear. Such a dreadful situation. They were very, very close."

An upright older woman wearing a drop-waisted dress that set off her neat figure stood across the room perusing the catalogue.

"Thank you." Verity crossed the room, trying her very best not to gallop. She came to a halt a few paces away and studied the painting in front of her—a beautifully colored picture of red gum flowers—and then flicked through the catalogue, trying to find the name of the artist. Her mouth dried as she tried to frame the words to introduce herself. It was ridiculous. She'd had a thousand questions lined up, but suddenly they seemed to have flown.

Fortunately, fate seemed to be on her side. The catalogue slipped from Mrs. Treadwell's hand and fluttered to the ground. Verity bent to retrieve it, then straightened up and smiled into a pair of tawny eyes that were in no way dimmed by the apparent age of their owner. She held out the leaflet. "Your catalogue."

Mrs. Treadwell took it. "Thank you," she murmured and moved on to the next painting.

Now or never. "It's Mrs. Treadwell, isn't it?"

The woman ground to a halt and peered over her shoulder. "And who might you be?"

"Verity Binks . . ." She paused for a moment, hoping Mrs. Treadwell might recognize her name and thus confirm she knew of the invitation to the ball. No such luck. And obviously Mr. Treadwell hadn't mentioned her, which seemed strange since he'd agreed to her speaking with Mrs. Treadwell. Perhaps he'd changed his mind and still wanted the article to be a surprise—she hadn't thought of that. What a fool! "I write for *The Sydney Arrow* and I believe you are a keen supporter of women's art, yes?"

Mrs. Treadwell hovered, then faced Verity, her painted eyebrows raised.

"I would like to ask you a few questions. I'm writing a piece about the exhibition. It is so important women artists are recognized." Verity had no idea where the words came from.

The beginning of a smile tilted Mrs. Treadwell's mouth. "I concur; however, it is a private interest."

Tricky. "Surely you would like your good works to be recognized, not only in the arts. The Treadwell Foundation is such a worthwhile charity. You must have helped hundreds of young women over the years. Could I ask what inspired you to start the foundation?"

"A desire to assist others. Is that so unusual? Now, if you'll excuse me, I'm here for the exhibition." Without another word she crossed the floor, leaving Verity marooned in the middle of the room.

She sank onto a conveniently placed bench seat. Whatever had possessed her to charge in like that? She had the tact of a rhinoceros and slightly less intelligence. She wasn't cut out for this job. Not at all. Not one bit. She'd be better off writing fiction. There was a large possibility that Mrs. Treadwell had nothing to hide. So what if her son didn't know she was once Florence Breckenridge? Perhaps he did and knew she didn't want the past discussed. She rested her elbows on her knees and dropped her head into her hands.

"I thought you might like this." The young woman who had greeted her at the door held out a glass of water. "You look a bit despondent."

A good word. But not one she wanted to explore with this bright, shiny young thing.

"Don't let Mrs. Treadwell upset you too much. She's had a difficult year." The girl shook her head. "Her lifelong companion suffered quite horribly." She lowered her voice. "It was all most peculiar. Her body was found in the back lanes of Surry Hills. Her injuries suggested she had fallen beneath the wheels of a motor van."

Verity's jaw slackened. "How dreadful."

The girl sat beside her. "It wasn't reported in the newspapers." She glanced over her shoulder. "According to rumor"—she lowered her voice—"she didn't fall; it was a totally unprovoked attack by another woman. Another woman! Can you imagine?"

Good heavens! A wave of shame swept over Verity. She'd barged in and bailed up poor Mrs. Treadwell, not giving a thought to her situation, and then jumped to all sorts of horrible, conspiratorial conclusions. No wonder the woman had bought a painting that reminded her of her childhood, of happier times, a way of assuaging her sorrow. "I should have been more empathetic."

"I thought you might cheer her up. Give her something else to think about. She gives so much to others; it's time her kindness was repaid."

Verity sat gaping like a stranded fish, then took a sip of the water. "It seems I've made a fool of myself."

"I doubt that."

"I should apologize." Verity looked up in time to see Mrs. Treadwell leaving.

"It might be a bit late. A note, perhaps? I can give you her address."

"No, thank you. I have it. It's time I was going too."

"We'd be delighted if you wrote an article about the exhibition, and I'm sure our artists would be happy to talk to you."

The following day Verity made her way through the crowds into the Strand Arcade. She wanted to thank Stella for the invitation to the exhibition. Whether she'd admit to her failure with Mrs. Treadwell she hadn't quite decided, but she certainly wanted to let Stella know that it had led to the possibility of another article.

The sign on the gallery door read *Open* so she went in, but Stella was nowhere in sight. She parted the curtain and pushed through into the workroom at the back of the shop, made a quick circuit of the table. "Stella. Are you here?"

Receiving no response, she went back out into the gallery. Two women stood outside the window admiring the paintings on the easels; she smiled at them and stood behind the desk. Perhaps Stella had unexpectedly needed to go next door, or maybe a call of nature. She couldn't have gone far. She wandered around the small gallery admiring the artworks and ended up back at the desk. If Stella had popped out, the least she could do was make herself useful. The women outside might want to make a purchase.

She leaned on her elbows and studied the lovely line

drawing—another of the banksia ink sketches similar to the ones in the window.

A snagged gasp caught her attention and she peered over the desk.

Stella!

Tucked in the corner, her knees pulled up to her chest, Stella was crouched with her head buried in her hands.

Verity dashed around the desk and dropped down. "Are you hurt?"

Stella lifted her head, tears streaming down her bloated face.

"How can I help?"

Stella stared at her, her eyes sparkling like colored glass despite their red rims. She shook her head and scrubbed at her face with a handkerchief, releasing a pungent, exotic scent. "It's nothing; I'm so sorry."

"A little more than nothing." Verity reached out her hand, inhaled again, exotic hints of saffron, rose, and vanilla. "Up you get. Let me make you a cup of tea." She led the way through the curtain to the workroom, lit the small burner, and placed the kettle on the heat.

"I'll do it."

Verity turned, and her heart stopped. A memory floated, just out of reach, the recollection of a similar scrutiny—penetrating and bright, coupled with that distinctive fragrance. "We've met before."

Stella gave her face one last scrub with her handkerchief. "Of course we have." She gave a muffled laugh. "We met on the train to Sydney."

"No. Before that. I recognize your perfume." Verity inhaled the exotic scent again, incense-like in its intensity. It made her think of the mask. The white beak and black circles around eyes like Venetian glass. "At the Artists' Ball. You were one of the troubadours. Did you send me the invitation and the costume?"

The hint of a smile, overshadowed by a haunting sadness, crossed Stella's face. She tipped her head to one side and gave a frail smile. "I have a confession to make."

"A confession! Who are you?" Verity's words ended in a high-pitched squeak. Her entire existence had revolved around that initial meeting—before their first meeting, in fact. From the moment she'd come home and found the invitation and costume on her kitchen table.

"Sit down. I'll make the tea." Stella placed one of the two delicate cups in front of Verity.

"Let me do it." Verity relished the thought of the simple ritual, anything to give her time to gather her tumultuous thoughts.

"No, no. I'm perfectly fine; today's the anniversary of the death of someone I loved. I'm simply indulging in a little self-pity." She pulled her spectacles from her pocket and hooked them over her ears.

Verity sat dazed, her spiraling confusion making her dizzy. What was Stella going to tell her?

Stella poured the tea, then sipped it, scrutinizing Verity's face. "It's easier if I start at the beginning."

Verity opened her mouth, but before she could berate Stella, the woman took both of her hands and held them tight.

"It doesn't affect the story you are writing about the Treadwell Foundation, but it does fill in the background and I hope, when I've told you everything, you will still regard me in a kind light, that we can be friends and you will help me."

Verity pulled her hands free and picked up her teacup, slopped some over the side before lifting it to her mouth, her teeth hitting the porcelain. Now she knew how Arlo must have felt when he'd discovered she'd lied to him. No matter what else happened, she had to see him again and apologize for her foolish behavior.

"Go on," she murmured through gritted teeth.

"The scent I wear—few people notice it." Stella held her wrist up to her nose, her face taking on a rosy glow as she inhaled and smiled into the distance. "It was a gift . . . a gift from the man I loved."

A hush descended on the small room and Verity leaned forward, transported by the look of longing and loss on Stella's face. "I met him at the beginning of the war when I was nursing. We were to be married." Stella's color deepened. "He gave me the painting; we planned to settle in Morpeth when the war was over."

"The painting Mrs. Treadwell bought of The Landing?" How could Stella have parted with it? More to the point, how could she have sold it if it was a reminder of her lost love? There was no doubt Theodora had painted that picture. Verity had known it from the moment Arlo had taken her into the library and showed her his mother's work. Apart from the fact the style was identical, it carried the trademark butterfly, an absolute giveaway. "Hence the butterfly costume."

"A fit of whimsy," Stella admitted.

So it wasn't Mrs. Treadwell—another of her foolish leaps of fantasy. "Why would you sell the painting if it meant so much to you?"

"To find my daughter I'd give up my life."

"Your daughter?" Verity clapped her hand over her gaping mouth.

"As I said, I want you to know the whole story." Stella pushed back the hair from her face, her attention riveted on a spot on the wall where, perhaps, the painting had once hung.

"We met when I was nursing. I had to return to Australia. He was killed only a few weeks later."

Verity's heart clenched, the memory of the dreadful day Sid had received the telegram about Charlie uppermost in her thoughts. "I'm so sorry." She reached out and took Stella's cold hand and chafed it. They sat for a moment, entrenched in their own thoughts but united by grief.

Stella reclaimed her hand and dabbed her face with her handkerchief. "I didn't know I was carrying his child until after he'd died." She shook her head from side to side. "I told my parents. I thought they'd understand, that I could bring the child up in the safety and security of their house, my home. A lasting memory of the man I loved." She gave a strangled, choked sob. "I was wrong, so very wrong."

Verity stilled as an icy realization settled. "They sent you to Treadwell House to have the baby?"

Stella nodded. "I was sent to hide the disgrace of my condition." She shook her head as though she might clear the memories. "I don't remember very much of the birth—I was very weak. I lost a lot of blood. I remember the nurse placing her in my arms. I held her for a moment or two and then she was taken from me. The next day they told me she'd died, but I knew in my heart it couldn't be. They wouldn't give me any details or tell me where she was buried—my parents insisted it was better that way. Finally the nurse who'd attended to me told me the truth. She'd hoped to ease my pain. My baby had been taken for adoption, much the same as many of the children born at Treadwell House. My mother and father had allowed them to give her away."

"But surely . . . Was there nothing you could do?"

Stella's mouth formed a pale slash across her face, her expression cold, hard, and flinty. "Nothing."

"What about the birth certificate? Was her birth registered?"

Stella gave a harsh laugh. "It is perfectly legal for families, doctors, and places like the Treadwell Foundation to organize an adoption. There is no law to prevent it. However, in the case of Treadwell House, a significant amount of money changes hands and a bonny baby's birth is registered by the adoptive parents—the title 'mother' given to a woman who never carried the child, never felt her move and grow in her womb, never held the baby in their first moments of life."

A chill whisked across Verity's skin.

"Young women caught, for one reason or another, in a difficult situation. Midwives often offer solutions; they advertise to adopt babies or take weekly payments to care for them, claim they failed to thrive and died, and pocket the payment when they sell the baby to a childless couple. It's a practice as old as time itself. Wealthy women who cannot produce an heir, never mind a spare, falsify a pregnancy, pad their clothing, and when the time comes, the midwife arrives carrying in her bag a newborn baby that is often drugged to ensure silence and an afterbirth belonging to a sheep. The sheets are duly sullied, the newborn baby placed in the mother's arms, and an announcement of the joyful event made. More often than not even the husband wouldn't know of the deception. There are as many stories as there are broken hearts."

"But that's not what was happening at Treadwell House. The babies are unwanted; that's why they are adopted. Surely that's better if the mother can't care for them?"

"My child was not unwanted. The adoption was against my wishes and the registration of my child is false. What's the point in registering a child's birth if it is a lie? If the mother isn't acknowledged, isn't given the opportunity to decide the fate of her child?"

"Have you asked your parents? Surely they . . . their grandchild . . ."

"They will do nothing. Their standing in society is more important to them. Their only daughter giving birth to an illegitimate child? But it's not only the disgrace; they are well acquainted with Mr. Treadwell. To acknowledge my child would be to uncover the tale behind their charity." She gave a macabre laugh. "They are baby farmers, nothing more. No better than the hundreds of other women and men who have profited from others' misery. Case after case has come up before the courts, but more often than not the offenders escape with a reprimand. A doctor speaks in their favor, says the child had failed to thrive. Thousands of babies die every year, some from natural causes, others . . ." Stella shook her head, then lifted her tear-stained face. "I will find my daughter. I know she can never be mine, but I want to at least know that she is safe, well, and cared for. In the darkest part of the night, I have visions of her destitute, broken, or worse." Tears tumbled down her cheeks. "That's why I need your help. I cannot be the only woman to have had her child taken away, but I need proof. It is a travesty that they should hide behind a charitable façade when it is nothing more than a lucrative money-making scheme—children taken in for profit rather than welfare. And I need someone to help me."

"Of course." The words slipped unthinkingly from her lips and a second later the implication of her response settled. "You want me to write an article and expose the true nature of the Treadwell Foundation. You had this planned all along, from the moment you sent the invitation and the costume. That's why you introduced me to Mr. Treadwell. What made you think he'd agree to an article?"

Stella's lips quirked. "I appealed to his vanity, and his greed."

That didn't, however, explain how Stella knew she'd be traveling back to Sydney from Morpeth. It wasn't a coincidence; it couldn't be. "How did you know I'd be on the train?"

"I saw you board the Newcastle train, and I followed you to Morpeth and stayed at the Commercial Hotel. I left when you did and hired a sulky. I was so concerned I wouldn't get to the station in time."

A flash of anger took Verity by surprise. "What the hell are you playing at? Why me?"

"Because of the connection we have."

"A connection. What connection?"

"Charles Binks was my daughter's father."

CHAPTER 24

MORPETH, 1868

Clarrie woke at daybreak and whipped through her jobs at a rapid rate of knots; she cleaned and laid the fires, set the kettle to boil, left the dough proofing, peeled the vegetables for lunch, and prepared Miss Theodora's breakfast tray. By seven o'clock she sat twiddling her fingers, waiting for Mrs. Starling to give her permission to leave for the morning.

She'd arranged to meet Sid at the punt and they'd go straight to Maud's, pick up Charlie, and take him out for the morning. It might be a bit cold down by the river, but that was covered. She smoothed her hand over the beautiful blue blanket Miss Theodora had given her. She'd said it belonged to her brother when he was a baby. Clarrie still felt a bit embarrassed about taking it, but in the end she'd allowed herself to be talked around. She'd never seen anything so beautiful. It was soft as down and had a lovely shiny satin ribbon sewn around the edge.

"You've been busy. Looking forward to your day out with Sid and young Charlie?" Mrs. Starling's kindly smile bathed her in a warm glow. "Go on, off you go, and don't forget to get back here in time to clear up lunch."

"I've prepared the vegetables and stuffed the chicken." Clarrie gestured to the large bowl of water where the potatoes, sprouts, and carrots sat next to the trussed chicken covered by a cloth.

"Good girl. Mr. Kendall's coming for lunch so it'll be in the dining room."

Clarrie threw her cloak over her shoulders, tucked the blanket under her arm, and flew out of the door and down the drive to the punt. Luck was on her side and Thomas sat, face tilted to the sun, enjoying his pipe.

"Hello, Thomas."

He grinned at her. "Morning. Off to see young Charlie?"

She smiled back at him. "And Sid. I'm meeting him on the Morpeth side. We're going to take Charlie for a walk. I've got to be back to clear up lunch."

"I'll still be working then. Sunday's often one of my best days, 'specially when the sun's shining. On you come."

Once they were midstream, Clarrie picked Sid out, standing on the wharf atop one of the bollards waving his hands in the air. Her heart skipped a beat. She'd missed him almost as much as Charlie. There was no sneaking out for a quick meeting before bedtime as she'd done when she was working for the reverend, but she wouldn't swap her job at The Landing for anything. Miss Theodora was so kind; sometimes Clarrie had to remember that she was only the maid. Ever since the trip to Ash Island and the discovery of the butterflies, they'd had a sort of a bond.

The punt bumped against the bank and she ducked under the rope and threw herself into Sid's arms, laid her cheek against the rough wool of his jacket, and inhaled his comforting warmth. "I've missed you." She lifted her face to him.

Sid smiled down at her, his eyes bright as currants in a hot bun, the corners crinkling. "Let's get moving. I want as much time with you and Charlie as I can get. When have you got to be back?"

"In time to clear up lunch. Miss Theodora's entertaining Mr. Kendall."

"Is she, indeed? I hope she's got a chaperone."

"Sid!" She dug him in the ribs. "She's not like that, and besides, Mrs. Starling's there. She can be quite fierce sometimes, but most of the time she's real nice."

In no time they were standing outside Maud's cottage. "I hope Charlie's all right." Clarrie squeezed Sid's hand.

"Why wouldn't he be? He was fine when I saw him last night, bit sleepy but it was past his bedtime."

"He seemed dozy when I saw him. And Maud hadn't changed him. He was as wet as a dishrag. Do you think she's looking after him?"

"He's fine. Babies sleep a lot." He bunched his fist and rapped on the door.

"And how would you know how much babies sleep?" Clarrie gave him another dig in the ribs.

Before Sid could reply, the door swung open and Maud stood there, a baby tucked into the crook of her arm and a startled look on her face. "I forgot you'd be coming."

"We're going to take Charlie out for the morning." Clarrie stepped over the threshold.

"Hold on a minute." Maud blocked her path. "Charlie's asleep and I don't want the others disturbed."

"I'll just pick him up and bring him straight out. We're going to take him for a walk." Clarrie pushed past Maud and into the darkened room. She leaned over the drawer and ran her hand across Charlie's head.

Hot! Really hot. She scooped him up and held him close.

"Sid!" She peeled back the blanket and took Charlie to the doorway where the light was better. His flushed, feverish little face stared up at her. "Sid!" It took an age for Sid to come inside. "Charlie's sick."

"No, he's not, at least not very sick. Maud says it's just a touch of infant fever and he'll be right as rain tomorrow."

"We need to call a doctor."

"Clarrie, settle. Feel his cheeks. He's just a little bit hot. I'm not surprised, bundled up in all those blankets. Unwrap him." He tugged off the blanket.

Clarrie peered down at Charlie; all she could hear was her own snatched breaths and her thudding heartbeat. Charlie couldn't be sick. Sid had seen him yesterday and he'd been fine; she'd seen him the day before. "We've got to take him to the doctor."

"He doesn't need a doctor." Maud forced her way between her and Sid. "If he was sick, I wouldn't have him in there with the others, would I? Babies often get hot and cold, same as you do. It shows their bodies are working. Now give him here and I'll put him back down."

"No!" Clarrie ran her hand over Charlie's legs. He did seem a little cooler.

"Come on, Clarrie. Don't spoil everything. Why don't we stay here for a while and keep an eye on him? Then we'll give him his feed and put him down. Might not be a good idea to take him out. There's quite a wind coming off the river."

"Good job someone has some sense," Maud grumbled and wandered off.

Sid pulled Clarrie close, his forehead touching hers, Charlie safe between them. "Everything will be fine. I'll come back and check on him later this afternoon."

Clarrie left Sid cradling Charlie and went searching for

Maud. As she expected, she found her sitting at the kitchen table, feet resting on the stool, a cup of tea in front of her.

"Are you sure you haven't noticed anything amiss with Charlie? He still seems sleepy."

"He's fine. Quit your fussing. All babies need their sleep."

Perhaps Maud was right; she had a lot more experience with babies. It was just that Charlie was so precious . . . "Sid said he'd call in this afternoon and make sure he's no worse. I'll come back tomorrow."

Maud tipped her head to one side and scrutinized her. "I thought you were working."

"I am, but Miss Theodora will agree. There'll be errands to run." None she'd heard about, but with a bit of sidestepping she'd surely be able to find a reason.

"It's not convenient. I'm expecting a visitor."

Clarrie bit her lip. No point in arguing; she couldn't afford to get Maud offside, not now everything was working out.

When she got back to the babies' room, Sid had vanished and Charlie was tucked up in his drawer, fast asleep. She dropped a kiss onto his forehead and lay the blanket Miss Theodora had given her over his toes.

She found Sid out the front, leaning against the fence. "All set then?" He threw his arm around her shoulder and gave her a hug. "What say I get the punt back with you and we'll go up through the gardens to the house? Not enough time to do much else."

Clarrie tucked herself into his shoulder. A sense of dread hanging like a cloud. "Did you change Charlie's diaper?"

"Nope. He wasn't wet. Never seems to be—Maud must be keeping an eye on him, looking after him. Stop being such a worrywart. Come on; the punt's in." Sid took her hand and together they ran down the path.

Slithering and sliding on the muddy bank, they made it just in time and sat tucked out of the wind as Thomas puffed and wheezed in time with his engine until he had a head of steam.

Clarrie couldn't shake her feeling of despondency. She'd tossed and fidgeted all night, even got dressed at one stage, then realized she couldn't get across the river without the punt. Now every movement was an effort, and she'd sagged and drooped her way through her chores. She'd scalded her hand while she was stirring the copper, dropped a perfectly clean pillowcase into the dirt, and smashed a brand-new jar of jam on the flagstone floor. She surveyed the sticky mess and groaned.

"You're all fingers and thumbs this morning. Come and sit down for a minute."

"I can't, Mrs. Starling. I've got the laundry to finish yet." Clarrie jammed her burned hand under her arm.

"And what have you got there?"

"Nothing much. I burned my fingers on the copper." She pulled out her hand and wiggled her fingers.

"Ouch! That's no good. Bit of butter will fix it. Come with me." Mrs. Starling sat her down at the kitchen table. "Let's have a closer look." She took Clarrie's hand in hers, tutting and carrying on all the while, then smeared a great dob of butter over her hand. "You smooth it in. Won't hurt so much if you do it yourself. I'll put the kettle on and call Miss Theodora to have a look."

Clarrie's heart sank. "Please don't do that. I promise I'll be more careful."

"More careful of what?" Miss Theodora stood in the doorway.

"Clarrie's not having the best day." Mrs. Starling gestured to Clarrie's burned fingers and pursed her lips.

"You poor dear." Miss Theodora sat next to her. "Shall I help?"

"I can do it. I'm sorry, miss. I didn't mean to break the jam or drop the . . ." The words dried and she hiccupped a great sob.

"Clarrie, Clarrie. It's not that bad. Nothing that can't be fixed. Now what's truly bothering you?"

Clarrie jerked up her head. She gave a huge sniff, almost wiped her nose on the back of her greasy hand. "It's Charlie."

"What's wrong with Charlie? You saw him yesterday, didn't you?"

She nodded. "But I don't think he's well. He's hot one minute, cold the next, and sleepy. And he isn't drinking much, and his diaper wasn't wet."

Mrs. Starling flopped down opposite her. "And what else?" she asked with a frown.

Clarrie thought back. "Maud says he's fine, a touch of infant fever, but he's not right. It's like he doesn't notice I'm there."

"Mother knows best," Mrs. Starling murmured.

"In that case, you must take him to the doctor." Miss Theodora pushed back her chair. "Dr. Morson will see him."

Clarrie's thoughts darted to her chemise bunched in the bottom of her carpetbag. Sixpence and two pennies. Just two pennies, nothing more, and she was sure Sid wouldn't have enough. Doctors cost money, a lot of money. "I can't do that."

"Don't be silly, of course you can. We can manage if you take some time off; can't we, Mrs. Starling?" Whatever was the matter with the girl? If Charlie was sick, of course he had to see the doctor.

Mrs. Starling coughed and tipped her head toward the back door.

Whatever was going on? Theodora patted Clarrie on the shoulder. "Stay here, take some deep breaths, and calm down." She slipped outside to speak to Mrs. Starling. "What is it? Why are you frowning at me like that? If someone is sick, you call the doctor. If Clarrie has to take some time off, so be it. Her baby's welfare is far more important than a pot of jam."

"I doubt Clarrie would dispute that. Problem is, she can't afford the doctor."

"And how would you know that?"

"Stands to reason, doesn't it? She's giving Maud money to look after the baby. She and Sid have had to cough up for her lying-in costs, and she's only been here a week and I haven't paid her yet."

"In that case, advance her what she's owed."

"It ain't going to cover a trip to the doctor and whatever he might prescribe."

"I wasn't thinking. I'll pay for the doctor. Now come on; let's get back in there and sort the poor child out. We can't have her worried sick about her baby."

Theodora hung on to Clarrie's arm to prevent her from leaping out of the sulky before Wilcox drew to a halt outside Maud's house in Swan Street. They'd decided to collect Charlie and take him directly to Dr. Morson and hopefully save time; whether he'd be home or not was in the lap of the gods, but it seemed the most sensible plan.

The minute the sulky stopped, Clarrie tumbled out and

tore up the steps and straight inside. In no time she was back with Charlie in her arms, a very red-faced woman hot on her heels.

"Miss Breckenridge, it's lovely to see you. Please"—she held the door open—"come inside. I wasn't expecting visitors, but I'd be happy to—"

"This isn't a social call; we're here to take Charlie to the doctor. Clarrie tells me he's unwell."

"Nothing to worry about, just a bit of infant fever. I've given him a tonic to help him sleep."

"And what would that be?" Theodora snapped.

"Why, one of Mrs. Barnett's mixtures, similar to Godfrey's Tonic but more effective. The doctor will be familiar with it." The woman gave some sort of bob, a curtsy perhaps.

Theodora reached out her arms and took Charlie from Clarrie while she climbed up into the sulky. "Dr. Morson's, please, Wilcox."

Wilcox clicked his tongue and the horse headed toward High Street.

"Won't be long now, Clarrie." Theodora handed Charlie back, his body limp and his eyes glazed. There was no doubt he needed to see the doctor. She tried for an encouraging smile, but Clarrie's attention, not surprisingly, was focused entirely on her son.

They drew to a halt outside the doctor's house, a place Theodora had never visited. Dr. Morson always came to The Landing if anyone required his services, but time was of the essence. She jumped down from the sulky and marched up to the front door and rang the bell.

A smiling woman opened the door. "Miss Breckenridge, to what do we owe—" Her words faltered as she noticed Wilcox handing Clarrie and Charlie down from the carriage with infinite care. "Oh dear. Dr. Morson is in his study. I'll go and tell him you're here."

"Thank you." Theodora encouraged Clarrie through the front door. The poor girl's face was the color of a wet dishrag and tracks of tears marked her usually pink cheeks. "It'll be all right. The doctor will see him in a moment."

Clarrie sniffed and tucked Charlie's blanket closer. "He's hardly moved at all."

"Miss Breckenridge." Dr. Morson's gravelly tones took her back to her childhood.

"It's very good of you to see us, Dr. Morson. This is Clarrie and her son, Charlie. He doesn't seem to be very well. Maud, the midwife, has been looking after him while Clarrie is working. She says he's had some of Mrs. Barnett's tonic to settle him."

Dr. Morson gave a harrumph. "Follow me, Clarrie, and bring young Charlie. You wait here, Miss Breckenridge." He opened the door to a cozy parlor at the front of the house, then escorted Clarrie down the hallway.

Theodora perched on the edge of the sofa. Quite why she hadn't insisted on going with Clarrie, she didn't know; some childhood habit. The doctor knew best. She swallowed a sigh and tried to still the fidgeting in her leg.

The waiting was worse than any diagnosis, but she knew nothing about babies. Some vague memories of Viola and Constance as squalling red-faced bundles clasped in Mama's embrace, her face radiant, but nothing else. Nothing that would help. The obvious solution would be for Clarrie to bring Charlie to The Landing, but Mrs. Barnett and the girls would be home before too long and Clarrie would never keep her job with a baby in tow.

After an eternity, a door opened and footsteps sounded in the hallway, heralding a smiling Clarrie and Dr. Morson.

"Nothing that can't be fixed. A touch of infant fever. The lethargy is due to the tonic he's had and he's a little underweight, not thriving. My suggestion is a new product that has recently become available. It's a combination of malt, cows' milk, sugar, and flour. You simply dilute with some water. It's sold as Nestlé's Infant Food. I've suggested to Clarrie that she pop down to Campbells. I happen to know they had a delivery recently. A lot more goodness in that than the arrowroot and sago mix I suspect Maud has been feeding him. Then some fresh air and sunshine should see him right. I'll look at him in a few days if you're still worried. And tell Maud to hold back on Mrs. Barnett's tonic. It might keep him quiet but it'll steal his appetite."

"Thank you, Dr. Morson. Thank you so much." Unshed tears glittered in Clarrie's eyes.

Theodora reached for her hand. What a relief! "Should we make another appointment to see you?"

"No, just call in if the situation changes."

CHAPTER 25

The world stilled. Charlie was the father of Stella's child. She, Verity Binks, had a sister, a blood relation. A bubble of joy blossomed in her chest. She had a sister. She reached out and squeezed Stella's hand. "You cannot imagine how happy that makes me. I can't wait to meet her."

The look of anguish on Stella's face ripped a trail to her heart. What a foolish thing to say. Stella didn't know where her daughter was, who had adopted her. Didn't know if she was alive or dead, loved or cared for. In that moment Stella's pain became her own. She blinked away her tears as her path became clear. "I will help you. Whatever it takes. We will find her."

"Charlotte. Her name is Charlotte." Stella smiled, her relief at having shared her secret written all over her face. "I do have a plan. The piece about the foundation—if we can get it published throughout New South Wales, Australia even, it would uncover the Treadwells' heartless venture, bring them to justice and many more like them. There has been a spate of stories in the papers about baby farming and dubious adoptions.

We might even get the law changed so no other women need to suffer."

Such fine words, such indignation, but how could she prove Stella's story? "I'm not sure where to start," Verity admitted.

"I've had longer to think and plan than you. Let me explain. The reason I couldn't come with you to the exhibition was because I was concerned Mrs. Treadwell would recognize me. While I was staying at Treadwell House, I made a nuisance of myself. Once I'd learned that Charlotte hadn't died, I was determined to find out where she'd gone. I hoped I could claim her back, refuse to allow the adoption, but of course that wasn't possible because, technically, she hadn't been adopted. There was nothing to prove that I had given birth to her."

Verity's heart clenched. "Surely there must have been some way. What about the nurse who'd told you about what had happened to her?"

"That was my first mistake. I confronted Mrs. Treadwell and demanded to see the registration of Charlotte's birth, her death certificate, and to know her burial place. When that failed, I searched high and low for the nurse who'd told me about Charlotte's adoption, but she'd vanished. I've spent almost six years exploring every avenue, even employed a private investigator, but it is an impossible task. I only had the nurse's first name—Jane. I suspect a handsome sum enticed her to move on and keep her mouth closed."

"Surely your parents want to help you."

"I've already explained the last thing they want is for my indiscretion to become public knowledge. The weeks after I gave birth are little more than a blur. I believe I was drugged; my stay was much longer than anticipated. To the world I was suffering from hysteria brought about by the death of my fiancé."

"I'm so sorry. I really don't understand how they can get away with it. What about the other women whose children were taken?"

"The majority of them accept their fate; their life resumes with their problem solved. That is the nature of the place and the nature of society's attitude to women who stumble."

"And they provide children to couples for a fee?"

"Yes, a very large fee. In the Treadwells' case it is a very sophisticated operation and almost guaranteed to remain undiscovered. The receiving parents have broken the law by illegally registering the birth of a child who is not their own, so they are unlikely to draw attention to themselves, and the children grow up none the wiser."

"Who would be evil enough to construct such a plan? Surely not Mr. Treadwell? Why would he draw attention to the scam by asking me to write the article?"

"It can't be Mr. Treadwell. The charity has been operating since the late 1800s; he would only have been a boy. The private investigator I hired also looked into the family history. It seems the death of Mrs. Treadwell's husband coincided with the depression in the 1890s. He'd made a series of bad investments. There are rumors that he took his own life."

And Mrs. Treadwell started the charity after her husband's death. But that made no sense. If her husband took his life because his investments failed during the depression, Mrs. Treadwell could well have had financial problems. The upkeep of a property the size of Treadwell House would cost a fortune. "Are you suggesting Mrs. Treadwell is responsible for the business and not Mr. Treadwell?"

"It seems to be the obvious answer. But I need proof."

"What sort of proof?"

"The night before I left Treadwell House I went searching. Mr. Treadwell has a study, and at that time I didn't think Mrs. Treadwell had very much to do with the running of the business, that as she'd aged she'd become more of a figurehead, but there had to be records."

Verity's thoughts slipped back to her interview with Treadwell. "The records wouldn't be in his study; they'd be in the library. Mr. Treadwell said his mother was responsible for the day-to-day running of the charity. He gave me some papers describing the history of Treadwell House. He took them out of the center drawer of the desk in the library, along with a red book that he said were the accounts."

Stella's face lit up. "A ledger, a record of the business—that's what I need."

"I don't have it."

Stella dropped her head into her hands. "We have to get it."

"And what do you imagine doing? Waltzing in and asking Mrs. Treadwell if you can see the business records? You've already said she'd recognize you." Verity let out an irritated groan. "And how did you manage to sell her the painting of The Landing? Surely she would have remembered you." Stella was mad. Was her story true?

"I didn't sell her the painting of The Landing. I had finished reframing it and it was on an easel in the gallery. Mrs. Treadwell came into the shop. I immediately ducked out the back, hoping she hadn't seen me. She appeared to be drawn to the painting, mesmerized—she stood for ages staring at it, tears silently falling down her cheeks. She picked it up from the easel and brought it to the desk. I have a girl, Beth, who helps me in the gallery. She explained the painting was not for sale, but Mrs. Treadwell was most emphatic that she wanted to buy it. It occurred to me, because of her reaction, it may be a connection to her past that my private investigator had failed to uncover. Beth came and asked me what I wanted to do. I told her to sell it to Mrs. Treadwell." Stella's bright eyes pinned her. "Don't you believe me?"

Verity swallowed. She did believe her. She had to. She couldn't turn her back on Charlotte, Charlie's daughter, her only living blood relation. "I believe you. I want to help you."

"You already have. You've made my job much easier. I now know what I'm looking for. I need that ledger, and once I have it, I need you to write the truth about the foundation, expose their filthy business."

A spiderlike crawl inched its way up Verity's spine as reality dawned. "You're going to break into Treadwell House and steal the ledger." Her flat statement hung in the air as she and Stella stared at each other.

Finally Stella let out an exasperated sigh. "I'm not expecting you to come with me."

It took Verity barely a moment to respond. "This is my story too. You won't be alone."

Verity paced the hallway, from the front door down to the kitchen and back again, her heels clicking on the floorboards. Stella's revelation had stirred up such a range of emotions: shock, disbelief, bittersweet pleasure.

She could imagine Charlie and Stella together, heads bent over a book, holding hands, laughing, exploring the Great Pyramid of Giza, taking a leisurely trip down the Nile. Was she jealous? No, not jealous of their relationship, but perhaps disappointed that Charlie hadn't shared his newfound happiness. Had Grandpa Sid known about Stella? Would he have helped find his grandchild? She didn't need to ask that question. She knew the answer. He wouldn't have rested until he had Charlotte home safe and sound where she belonged.

Verity peered out of the front window; Stella had said she'd come to the house once darkness fell. She glanced next door. No sign of any lights and not a sound except for the usual nightly noises of The Rocks, settling in for the night. The last thing she wanted was a visit from Mrs. Carr and her incurable nosiness.

The knock, when it finally came, sent her heart into her mouth.

Verity inched open the front door, finger to lips.

Stella threw a furtive glance over her shoulder, then slipped inside. "I'm sorry I'm so late. It took me longer than I expected to collect everything we need." She hoisted a waxed canvas bag onto the table and undid the buckles. "Many of the costumes for the Artists' Ball came from the wardrobe room at the technical college theater. As one of the organizers I still had access so I borrowed a few bits and pieces."

She unbuttoned her coat to reveal a pair of black men's trousers and a black long-sleeved blouse. "The troubadours costumes are most useful. I have one for you too. We need to make sure we have no flesh showing and hide our hair." She produced two close-fitting caps and pulled one over her head, leaving only her eyes and mouth free.

Verity shuddered; it gave Stella the look of a corpse.

"It's a balaclava. They're often worn under masks and wigs. It will hide your hair. And here are some gloves." She passed a pile of clothing to Verity. "Go and get changed, then I'll tell you my plan."

Five minutes later Verity closed her bedroom door and tiptoed down to the kitchen, unsure whether she should have agreed to help Stella without first hearing the details. "What's the plan?" she asked.

"I have it on good authority that Mr. and Mrs. Treadwell are out tonight; there's an event at Government House. Treadwell House is empty. They haven't taken guests since Mrs. Treadwell's companion died so there will be no one there. The kitchen door is never locked. The maid and the cook leave after serving the evening meal and don't start until six in the morning. The place runs like clockwork. You couldn't even get a cup of tea unless it was planned." Stella pushed up her sleeve and glanced at her wristwatch. "It's nine thirty. If we pick up a tram on the corner of George Street and change at Park, we can be there in less than an hour."

Madness. The conductors knew Verity too well and besides, at this time of night the trams rarely ran to schedule. "I've got a better idea. Why don't we cycle?"

Stella frowned at her. "Take bicycles? I don't have one and we must go tonight. I have no idea when the next opportunity might present."

"Grandpa Sid's bicycle is in the shed. I know it's in working order because my neighbor, Mr. Carr, borrows it on occasion. You can ride a bicycle, can't you?"

"I've ridden one in the past, a long time ago, but . . ."

"You never forget, not once you've learned. It'll make it much easier. We'll cut through the Botanic Gardens and then take the track from Finger Wharf along the cliff top. There are only two hills to contend with. If worse comes to worst we can walk."

Everything went according to plan; no one took any notice of two black-clad figures on bicycles, and once they were away from the main tram route, the streets were deserted. In a matter of minutes they entered the Botanic Gardens. When Verity's calves began to burn, she glanced over her shoulder. Stella had her head down, pumping the pedals as if her life depended on it, but she was having trouble keeping up; Verity would have to stop to allow her to rest. She coasted to a halt at the end of Wylde Street and waited.

"I think I'm going to have to get a bicycle," Stella puffed. "I had no idea I was so unfit. I do like the freedom it offers. It can't be much farther; I can hear the halyards on the sailing boats moored in the bay."

"We have to find somewhere to leave the bicycles."

"There's a tall hedge down one side of the property. They'll be out of sight. It's easy to access the back of the house from there. Come on." Stella pushed off and wobbled a little before gathering speed and heading toward the bay.

Light splayed across the front porch, but the windows on either side of the house were dark.

"I can get through here." Looking from left to right to make sure the coast was clear, Stella slipped sideways through the hedge. "I need to be in and out as quickly as possible. You wait here." She took off across the expanse of manicured lawn.

Ignoring Stella's ludicrous suggestion, Verity bolted after her. By the time she'd made it to the door, Stella had slipped inside, nothing more than a shadow. Verity followed. Light from the hallway spewed faded shadows across the floor.

"I told you to wait," Stella hissed. "Hurry up. I'm not leaving you alone."

Stella crouched low and made a beeline for the library. Verity followed, right on her heels. The library door opened without a sound. They slipped inside and flattened themselves against the wall.

Once Verity's pupils adjusted to the darkness, the room

revealed itself, much as she remembered. Stella dropped to her hands and knees and crawled toward the desk. Beside the lamp an inkwell and fountain pen stood next to the telephone. She opened the file drawer and slipped her hand inside and brought out a few odds and ends: envelopes, the skein of embroidery silk, and packet of needles. With a disgruntled sigh, she pushed the contents back inside and rocked back on her heels. "Now what?" Her whisper, laced with disappointment, cut Verity to the core. To have come this far and to be thwarted.

"Maybe Treadwell's study?" Verity took one last look around the room. The desk under the window, the two wing-back chairs in front of the marble fireplace, and the empty occasional table between them. The walls lined with books . . . "Just a moment."

She edged along the bookshelves, her fingers running over the embossed spines releasing the familiar hint of leather and beeswax polish. And then she stopped. With a smile, she hooked her finger over *Great Expectations*. She'd imagined a secret door when she'd discovered the faux books while she'd waited for Treadwell in the very same spot. This might prove their use. She tilted the books and they slanted toward her. Standing on tiptoe she felt behind the spines.

Stella's breath rasped in her ear as she peered over her shoulder. "These volumes are faux, nothing more than a sham, but a perfect hiding place." With a grim smile, Verity plucked out the ledger and handed it to Stella.

Stella fanned the pages. "This is it. It goes back years." She snapped the ledger closed.

The sound of a motor car broke the silence.

With a panicked glance, Stella tiptoed to the window and peered around the curtain. "They're back. Come on."

A car door banged and the front door opened. Mr. Treadwell's voice echoed in the cavernous hallway. "A nightcap for me. Can I get you anything?"

"No, thank you." Mrs. Treadwell's heels clipped as she crossed the floor and mounted the stairs.

Verity shot a panicked look at Stella. Where else would Treadwell take a nightcap but the library? She glanced at the occasional table. No sign of any decanter or glasses.

Stella covered her lips with her fingers and crept to the half-opened door.

Footsteps again. Treadwell. Another door opened, then closed.

Stella crooked her finger and slipped into the hallway. Heart racing, Verity followed.

Less than an hour later, Verity and Stella threw their bicycles down in the lean-to and stumbled through the yard and into the kitchen at Tara Terrace.

"I cannot believe we got away with that." Stella pulled the ledger from her waistband.

Verity leaned over her shoulder, Stella's familiar, heady perfume filling the space between them. "Is it what we want?"

"I don't rightly know. I'm certain it holds the key." Stella laid it on the table and opened it to the first page. Her hand shook as she pulled it closer, flipping through the pages and running her finger down the dates, murmuring an indecipherable string of words.

Verity tried to read the copperplate, but Stella flicked through the pages so fast nothing made any sense. Pages, divided into columns, each crammed with handwriting. The first two columns contained the year and the date, the second headed *Narration* had several lines of writing, and the final column was an amount, followed by two, sometimes three additional notes.

Stella continued to scan the pages, then, with a muffled cry, she flattened the spine with the palm of her hand and sank down at the table.

On the left-hand page, headed *Narration*, was a description, age, coloring, and sex of a child, costs and expenses incurred, and on the right-hand page headed *Disposed* were names, dates, and monies received, expenses deducted, and the net profit neatly recorded.

Verity clamped her hand over her mouth, swallowing her horror. A record of payments received—a trading ledger—and a list of children sold.

"I've found her." Stella's cry shattered the uncanny silence and the candle flickered.

The horror of it made Verity's eyes smart and her vision dim. Charlotte had indeed been bought and sold at the behest of Stella's parents. The privilege of registration would have fallen to the people who'd paid for the acquisition of a child. She squinted at the open page on the table in front of Stella. Against the amount, the name *Greene* and a suburb—Hunters Hill. If nothing else, Stella would have the answer to the puzzle that had plagued her for so long. But what could they do about it? If the child was registered to Mr. and Mrs. Greene, there was no proof that Stella had given birth to Charlotte. No proof either that Charlie was Charlotte's father, that Charlotte was her half sister.

Stella lifted her head, wiping away her tears with an impatient hand. "I knew what I would find. I wanted proof. I hadn't thought it would hurt this much—not after so many years. See here. September 23, 1916." Her shaking finger traced the words. "'Healthy female, fair hair, blue eyes.'" Her finger stopped, hovered as realization dawned. "Cost. What does that mean? I thought Mother and Father paid a donation to the foundation."

Her bottom lip trembled as she scanned the right-hand page of the ledger. "'Adoption—£500.' They sold my baby," she wailed and dropped her head to her hands, filling the little kitchen with great wracking sobs.

Verity wrapped her arm around Stella's shoulders and pulled her close. There was nothing she could say that would ease her pain, nothing that could ease her own. The candle guttered, the last wax pooling on the tabletop while Verity gathered Stella close, her heart aching.

Eventually Stella calmed and mopped her tears, then with a frail smile she stood. "I'm going to go home."

"Let me make you a cup of tea, and there's a spare bed; you shouldn't be alone." Not at a time like this. Heaven only knew what Stella might do, and Verity wasn't sure she wanted to be alone either. The prospect of throwing the ledger in Treadwell's face and writing the truth about his mother's filthy business sent a rush of heat through her.

"Thank you, but no. I want to be by myself. I'm not going to do anything foolish. I'll leave the ledger here and come back tomorrow afternoon and we can decide what we are going to do next. Is that suitable?"

How on earth could Stella think of going to work? "That's perfectly fine, but why don't I walk you home? I can't leave you at a time like this."

Stella patted her hand. "You're a dear, sweet girl, but I need to be alone with my thoughts to come to terms with this and plan my next move." She shrugged into her coat. "I'll leave this bag here, if that's all right. I don't have to take the costumes back until next week."

Next week. By next week Verity could have the article written. And if there was a god, the Treadwells' unprincipled rort would be exposed.

CHAPTER 26

Clarrie couldn't believe the difference in Charlie. Despite Maud's flapping and fussing, he'd taken to the Nestlé milk like a miner to a strike and the new rubber teat Miss Theodora had bought made everything so much easier. Sid called in every evening to give him his bottle, and each time Mrs. Starling wanted an errand run she'd asked Clarrie to go so she could pop in and see Charlie.

Nevertheless, Clarrie couldn't wait to spend some time with her little family. She rushed through her Sunday morning jobs and by eight o'clock was ready to leave.

"I'll be off now, Mrs. Starling. Everything's done."

"Before you go . . ."

With a muffled groan, Clarrie halted in her tracks, unable to mask the look of annoyance on her face.

"Miss Theodora wondered if you could take this down to the wharf." Mrs. Starling fastened the lid on the hamper sitting on the kitchen table.

It was the last thing Clarrie wanted to do. If she had to

tramp all that way before she went to the punt it would make her about half an hour late. Sid would be worried sick. "What is it?"

Mrs. Starling shrugged. "Not my business. Not yours either. Off you go."

Clarrie trudged down the path, not game to take a short-cut because of the wet grass—the last thing she wanted was a sopping skirt flapping around her ankles all day. She shifted the hamper; the farther she walked, the heavier it became. Sticking her nose against the lid, she sniffed. Not a whiff of paint. Nothing to do with Miss Theodora's art kit and, anyway, she always looked after that herself, said she didn't like people touching, so Mrs. Starling wouldn't have come near it. She inhaled again. A definite undertone of baking—scones, unless she was mistaken. Clarrie plonked the hamper down on the ground and unstrapped it.

"All right for some," she muttered as the contents became clear. Red-and-white checked cloths wrapped around freshly baked scones, some cream and jam, chicken and ham, and a jar of pickles . . . She straightened up with a groan. A picnic. Miss Theodora must be expecting Mr. Redmond. She refastened the buckles and continued on, gritting her teeth. Her only free time . . . Not strictly true. In fact, not fair. She'd been into Morpeth four times in the last week to see Charlie.

She thumped the hamper down on the wharf and straightened up.

"Surprise!"

Clarrie gaped.

Miss Theodora and Mr. Redmond stood in the boat off the end of the wharf waving their hands, their faces beaming. "Your private ferry awaits."

"Oh, miss." Clarrie cupped her burning cheeks. All

those bad thoughts and here they were ready to take her into Morpeth. But what about Sid? "I've said I'll meet Sid at the punt."

"Let me get that hamper. We can't go without our lunch." Redmond bounded up onto the wharf. "Sid's waiting for us. It's all organized."

"Come on, Clarrie," Miss Theodora encouraged. "We'll pick up Sid and Charlie and then go for a ride down the river and find a spot for a picnic. The weather is perfect."

Clarrie jumped down onto the deck, her heart bursting. She couldn't think of a better way to spend her day off.

In no time at all they'd crossed the river and moored at the punt. She clutched Sid's hand and together they galloped up the road to fetch Charlie.

"I can't believe Miss Theodora did this." Clarrie's breath came in short, sharp puffs as she tried to keep up with Sid.

"Mr. Redmond too. I expect he wanted a chaperone." Sid smothered a snort. "He likes spending time with Miss Theodora, likes it a lot." He swung the gate open and rapped on the door.

It took an age for Maud to answer. Clarrie stood on the step, fidgeting. She could hardly stand still. Eventually the door opened a crack and Maud peered out.

"We've come to pick up Charlie. We're going to take him for a boat ride."

Maud ran her hand through her mussed hair and a red bloom covered her cheeks. "You can't."

Clarrie's heart took a dive right down to her boots. "Why not?" Nothing could be wrong with Charlie. He'd been bright and happy only a day ago, blowing bubbles and blinking his huge blue eyes, smiling and burbling and kicking his little legs.

"He's not here."

Clarrie shoved her way past Maud and into the hallway. "What do you mean, 'not here'?"

In the background, Sid gave a loud cough. A warning. She didn't care. "Where's my baby?"

"I'm sorry." Maud sniffed. "He's not here."

It was as though someone had emptied a bucket of freezing water over her head.

"Where is he?" Sid growled, stepping alongside her.

Clarrie leaned against him. She was cold, so very, very cold. Nothing could have happened to Charlie. He wasn't sick anymore.

"He's out."

"Out!" Clarrie screeched. "Out where?"

Sid ran his hand up and down her arm. "Shh, that won't help."

Maud wiped her nose with the back of her hand. "Out. Out taking the air. You told me the doctor said fresh air and sunshine. He's getting some of that."

"Who's taken him?" Clarrie wiped her clammy hands down her skirt.

Maud peered up and down the street. "A friend of mine. The woman who comes and gives me a hand now and again, when I have to do my rounds. You know . . ."

Clarrie reached for Sid's hand, her fingers shaking. She'd heard about this woman who came and helped but she'd never met her. "Where's she taken him?" Her words came out in a strangled squawk.

"For a walk." Maud shrugged. "Down by the river to watch the boats. He's wrapped up tight in his blanket. He'll be fine."

"Come on." Sid's fingers tightened around her hand and squeezed. He towed her down the street.

"We'll go down to the punt and walk along the bank until

we get to Queens Wharf." Even Sid's voice sounded strained and his face had become a nasty chalky color.

Clarrie ground to a halt. "We should have checked that Charlie wasn't there. He might be sick, he might be . . ." She swallowed a mouthful of bile.

"No, he's not. Don't even think that. Maud would've let us see him if he was." Sid's pinched face belied his words. "She's got to be telling the truth." He didn't sound too confident.

"How can you tell?"

"I just know. Come on; we haven't got any time to waste."

"We don't even know who we're looking for."

"A woman with a baby wrapped in a blue blanket. Can't be that difficult. Not on a Sunday morning in Morpeth. Most people will be in church. Let's go and tell Mr. Redmond; he'll help. Down here."

Clarrie reefed away from him and veered off in the opposite direction, arms swinging at her sides and a spike of fear, sharp as a blade, tearing her insides. They hadn't a moment to waste, not until they found Charlie.

But for an old man with a dog, sitting on the bank, a fishing rod lying on the grass beside him, there wasn't a person in sight. "Excuse me. I'm looking for a . . . friend . . . She's out walking, with a baby . . ." Her words snatched and she swallowed down a rush of fear. "Have you seen them?"

He peered up at her. His rheumy eyes, buried deep in wrinkled skin, held a look of concern. "Haven't seen much of anyone. It's always quiet on a Sunday morning. Few people down at Queens Wharf—the Newcastle ferry's about to leave."

Clarrie flew down the path. Fresh air and sunshine. The idea of taking Charlie on Mr. Redmond's boat had taken her fancy, but an outing with a stranger wasn't anything she'd imagined.

The number of people increased as she approached Queens Wharf—the usual bustle and noise. So much for everyone being in church. The steamer towered over the wharf and the usual raggle-taggle bunch of boys swarmed, eager to earn a penny or two playing porter.

Families in their Sunday best taking a trip on the river or visiting family pushed forward, but no sign of anyone with a babe in arms; no sign of Charlie. No sign of Sid either. Where was he when she needed him?

The crowd surged up the gangplank. She scanned every person as they stepped up onto the deck, but no one carrying a baby. Finally, the steamer let out a great whistle and two men pulled the gangplank aboard and released the ropes. The ship edged out into the river and, with a deal of grinding and swirling, swung around until its head pointed downstream, ready for the return journey to Newcastle.

Clarrie slumped on the grass, head in hands. Now what? A wave of dizziness swamped her. Gritting her teeth, she glanced up and down the wharf, deserted except for a small figure perching on one of the bollards like a hungry kookaburra. As she approached, the sound of some long-forgotten lullaby stirred Clarrie's memory.

"Hello." The girl trilled the last bar and jumped down. "Have you been here all morning?"

"Been here since before the steamer came in. What's it to you?" She pushed her scraggy hair back from her face, revealing a flaming red mark on her cheek.

"I'm looking for someone. I wondered if you could help me."

The girl scuffed her bare feet and lifted her shoulders. "P'raps."

"I can't find my friend. She took my son out for some air. He's just a little baby and I'm worried. I'm supposed to meet her here. He's wrapped in a blue blanket; maybe you noticed them?"

The girl folded her arms and glared. "She got on the steamer and she didn't give me the penny she promised."

Clarrie's heart picked up a beat and she curbed the temptation to run and find Sid. She needed to know more. Ramming her hands into her pocket, her fingers closed around her last remaining penny—the change from Charlie's milk. She pinched it between her thumb and forefinger and held it up.

The girl's hand shot out, but Clarrie trapped the penny in her fist. "It's yours as soon as you tell me what happened." Her heart thumped so fast her hand shook. "What's your name?"

The girl chewed on her lip and hung her head. "Maggie."

The penny glinted in the sun as Clarrie waved it to and fro in front of her face. "Right, Maggie. Let's have it."

"She asked me to look after her bag. She had to go and get her ticket."

Clarrie gritted her teeth, waiting for more, then snapped, "And she had a baby with her?"

"Nope. Leastways, I didn't think she did. Said she'd give me a penny if I looked after her bag." Maggie scuffed her feet and stared out across the river, willing it to swallow her more than like. "I opened the bag," she murmured.

"You opened the bag?"

"Yeah. It was wriggling. Thought she'd got an animal in there."

A chill worked its way over Clarrie's skin. "And it was a baby?"

Maggie nodded. "I just wanted to touch the blanket; it looked real soft—blue with a shiny ribbon all around the edge. Miserable cow slapped me across the face." Her hand cradled the red mark on her cheek. "Snatched her bag and bolted onto the steamer. She didn't give me my penny."

"What did this woman look like? Old or young? What was she wearing?"

Maggie lifted her shoulders. "Dunno. Not young but not real old. She's got a black dress on, with a white lace collar. And the bag was old and frayed like a piece of dirty carpet."

Clarrie thrust the penny into Maggie's hand, lifted her skirts, and took off. She had to find Sid. Her feet pounded on the tow path and she snatched in ragged gasps of damp air. As she rounded the bend in the river, the *Petrel* came into view, chugging along in midstream. She ground to a halt, raised her hands above her head, and waved frantically.

Sid spotted her, his mouth opened and closed, but his words drifted off in the breeze as the nose of the boat swung around. She slithered down the bank to Analbys Wharf, cupped her hands around her mouth, and yelled, "She's taken Charlie on the Newcastle steamer!"

Redmond nudged the bow into the wharf and let the clinker swing around. Sid jumped ashore, more interested in reaching Clarrie than securing the rope—fair go. If their positions were reversed and Theodora stood sobbing and wringing her hands on the bank, he'd probably forget the rope too.

Quick off the mark as always, Theodora jumped ashore and pulled the stern around.

Why would anyone take a baby on the Newcastle steamer? That was taking the fresh air and sunshine Sid had mentioned a bit far. What he really wanted was the full story, but he'd have to wait. A moment later Sid yelled, "Follow the steamer," as he helped Clarrie, face blotched and damp with tears, aboard.

"Cast off, Theodora!" He shouted the instructions knowing she could manage. Jamie had insisted on it. If she wanted to play with the boys, she had to behave like one. No shirking just because she was a girl. A smile curled his lips. She hadn't forgotten. Shame the mood wasn't like the carefree day they'd spent chasing butterflies on Ash Island.

The boat chugged into midstream and he swung the tiller and headed downriver. Clarrie, Sid, and Theodora sat in a huddle, but their words were lost in the flurry of wind.

"Is anyone going to tell me what's going on?"

Theodora slid along the seat next to him. Her familiar fragrance—lavender and a touch of turpentine—teased his nostrils, reminding him of the day he'd planned when he suggested the trip.

"Do you think we can catch the steamer?"

"Depends. If it stops at one of the private wharves, there's a fair chance. What's going on?"

She edged closer and spoke in a low voice. "Clarrie seems to think Charlie's been snatched."

"Snatched? That's a bit rich. What do you mean? Kidnapped? Why would anyone kidnap Charlie?" It all sounded ridiculously far-fetched. "It's not as though Sid and Clarrie can afford to pay a ransom. Didn't Sid say a friend of Maud's had taken him out?"

"Clarrie spoke to a young girl at Queens Wharf. She said a woman went aboard with a baby in a carpetbag. She described Jamie's blanket."

Jamie's blanket? He frowned at her. "Are you all right?"

"Of course I am. I gave Clarrie Jamie's baby blanket for Charlie and the girl described it. He was wrapped in it inside the carpetbag."

"Theodora, do you think perhaps . . . What was so special about this blanket? How can you be sure it was the one you gave Clarrie?"

"Because she described it—said the baby was wrapped in a blue blanket with a shiny ribbon around it and that it was very soft. Jamie's blanket was cashmere edged with a blue satin ribbon, expensive, and I'm not jumping to conclusions. Why would anyone put a baby in a carpetbag? I'll start at the beginning."

By the time Theodora recounted Clarrie's story in its entirety, he could see her point. It all sounded most peculiar. "But why?"

Theodora flapped her hands and shook her head. "I have no idea."

"We'll worry about that later. We can catch the steamer when she stops. Fingers crossed it'll call in at some of the private wharves, otherwise it'll be Raymond Terrace or beyond. Take the tiller; I'll see if I can get any more out of her."

He bent to the engine, squeezing every skerrick of power from its pipes. Sid and Clarrie sat hunched together, murmuring quietly while Theodora kept her attention on the river ahead and her hand on the tiller.

The blue sky of the morning had become slate gray, the clouds glowered, dank and clammy, and the river was nothing more than a ribbon of steel, dark and sinuous when it narrowed, the rotten egg stink from the mangroves adding to the sinister malaise.

Once the river widened again Theodora swung the tiller

and took them out into midstream. The *Petrel* didn't let them down; her speed picked up a good six or seven knots, but no sign of the steamer. It'd be Raymond Terrace before they caught sight of it.

CHAPTER 27

MORPETH, 1922

The last of the print room boys left. Arlo pulled down the blinds and locked the back door. He hadn't had time to scratch himself since Verity's departure, although he couldn't get her out of his mind. The look of abject misery on her face when he'd jumped down her throat was engraved on his soul. Quite why her admission had gutted him so badly, he couldn't fathom.

The newspaper archives still covered the table, the one carrying Florence's marriage announcement folded open. His mother's three sisters all married within a year. Was it more than a coincidence? Did the agony of losing their parents and beloved brother fracture the family? Surely it would have brought them together. So many unanswered questions. He pulled the pencil from behind his ear and aimlessly flicked through the next pages. Verity might well be looking for information about his family, but there was a story of her own that she might not have recognized. Strange to think that her grandfather had set the print for all these pages. What had made him leave Morpeth? And how did a compositor manage to snag a job as a stringer with one of the biggest newspapers in Sydney? No one, no matter how good they were in a print room, fell into a job as a stringer. They needed a knowledge of the city, a web of contacts and references, and . . . He ran his fingers through his hair. What business was it of his?

Ignoring the mess in the archive room, he slammed the door, locked up, and left.

A fierce wind whipped up from the river as he made his way to Queens Wharf. On evenings like this he occasionally questioned the sense of relying on the *Petrel* to get him home. Now the bridge was built he could just as easily bring the trap into town. Perhaps he should invest in a bicycle. Verity seemed to enjoy the independence it offered. His mouth quirked as a picture of her, hair the color of sunshine streaming behind her and legs pumping the pedals as she'd taken off to catch the train, tossing aside his offer—albeit a tight-lipped and infuriated one—of a ride to Maitland.

He loosened the rope around the bollard and stepped across onto the deck. The tide was high, but there was no sign of the nine o'clock steamer; perhaps it was later than he thought. Definitely later; most of the lights in the town were doused. One still shimmered above the Commercial Hotel. The lure of an ale and one of Molly's pies dangled, but he tossed the thought aside and cast off. He'd be home in fifteen or so minutes and there'd be a meal left for him in the kitchen; Mrs. Brown knew the strange hours he kept. His stomach rumbled in anticipation.

The house seemed hollow, empty. He took off his glasses and rubbed his eyes. Two years since Father passed, a dreadful year that had begun with his apoplexy and only weeks later resulted in his death. In retrospect it had been a thankful reprieve. Always an energetic man, he wouldn't have tolerated the inability to live the life he loved. His passing might have provided him with a release, but it had signed Mother's death warrant. Years of disappointment waiting for her butterflies to return and her fruitless quest to have her discovery of the Wanderer butterfly recognized, followed by the loss of her closest friend and lover, she withered. But even during that dreadful year he'd never felt so alone as he did right now.

Armed with a plate of bread, cheese, and pickle, he wandered through the house switching on the lights as he went. So many rooms, so empty. The constant cost of repairs and the upkeep drained the small profit the paper made. Was it all worth it? Possibly not, but he couldn't leave the river and the wildlife; his very blood ran with its moods and colors. The Landing was his home, though a lonely one.

Arlo pushed open the door to his father's study, lit the lamp, and threw off the dust sheet covering the desk and chair. As a child he'd sneak into the room and sit in this very spot, a newspaper spread in front of him and a pencil tucked behind his ear, holding imaginary conversations with a stream of copyboys, pretending to edit a blank piece of paper with one of the big, blunt, red pencils Father kept especially for the task. It had never occurred to him that he might not be up for the job, that the paper would fail, that sales would dwindle to such a small number. But too many people depended on him; he couldn't bring himself to lay off the delivery boys and the men in the print room.

Chewing his way through the heel of the bread, he pulled open the top drawer of the desk, pushing aside the rubble— erasers; pencils; nibs; a bottle of ink, long dried; and the knife Father had used to sharpen his pencils. He turned to the second drawer and then the third, where he found a cardboard box full of the thick red pencils. He tipped one out and opened the bottom drawer, searching for a piece of paper. His fingers closed around a notebook, the tattered cover faded and discolored, hanging loosely by a series of tangled threads, the marbled end papers blotched by damp, and a folded piece of paper trapped between the pages. He pulled it out and, just as he'd done as a child, practiced Father's initials, the sweeping strokes—*RK*—and the bold slash he used to cross out anything he didn't see fit for publication.

With a cynical laugh he flicked the paper over; tightly packed scrawls covered the other side of the sheet and a great red slash ran from corner to corner. Father's initials splayed across the page, rendering the faded pencil words nonsensical. Arlo squinted, angled the lamp, and held the sheet to the light.

LOCAL NEWS

Case of Kidnapping at Morpeth—A singular case of kidnapping of an infant occurred at Morpeth on Sunday last. Assistance is sought in discovering the whereabouts of a MISSING WOMAN, Mrs. Barnett, housekeeper at The Landing, Morpeth, last seen boarding the Newcastle steamer at Queens Wharf. The woman can be described as in her late twenties or early thirties.

Dark-eyed, she wears her hair in a tight bun at the nape of her neck. Since the demise of Alexander Breckenridge and his wife, Julianna, in the wreck of the *Cawarra*, she has favored mourning attire, the austerity of her dress relieved only by a small white lace collar.

Exhaustive inquiries suggest Mrs. Barnett is the primary organizer of a baby farming enterprise operating in Morpeth, Maitland, and possibly Newcastle. She is the owner of several workers' cottages that she rents to midwives who offer child-care and a lying-in service for young unmarried women and their offspring.

Underlying this apparent charitable service lies a more sinister enterprise. It was Mrs. Barnett's habit to advertise on behalf of her tenants for children to adopt, promising a "good home under the kind treatment of Christian people."

Children were then taken into "care," left in squalor and filth, given improper and insufficient food, neglected and silenced by an herbal tonic created and supplied by none other than Mrs. Barnett herself. When their poor bodies could tolerate no more, Mrs. Barnett would dispose of them.

A familiar sight on the Morpeth to Newcastle steamers, it is believed Mrs. Barnett boarded the steamer on Sunday last carrying a carpetbag containing a baby she intended to deliver to an adopting family unbeknownst to the parents.

Employed by the Breckenridge family as their house-keeper, Mrs. Barnett was a familiar figure in Morpeth. The story of the Breckenridge family is well known and often revered as the perfect fairy tale. However, the discovery of a ledger dating back to that time, kept by none other than the Breckenridges' trusted housekeeper herself, details differently.

Arlo's mouth dried and he reached for the notebook. He flicked through the pages from back to front. An impeccable record of transactions, including expenses and income—a business ledger. A rushing sound filled his ears as he returned to the article.

Not only was Mrs. Barnett the instigator of an insidious baby farming enterprise, she had also expanded her operation. She procured and provided babies to wealthy families who would pay a high premium to ensure their dynasty. While the writer fully endorses the placement of unwanted children with adopting families with the agreement of the natural parents, this unfortunately is not always the case.

We shall never entirely rid society of the scourge of these baby farmers as long as there are no regulations and we allow parents, without restriction, to make private bargains with casual and unknown strangers for the nurture and maintenance of their children. It is imperative that this pernicious woman, this culprit, Mrs. Barnett, who profits from others' misery, be brought to justice.

The veracity of these statements can be confirmed by the writer, whose son suffered at the hands of this despicable woman. Any information should be delivered to Sid Binks c/o *The Morpeth Want*.

Arlo rocked back in the chair, letting a long, slow breath whistle out between his lips—*whose son suffered at the hands of this despicable woman*—Sid's son. Verity's father or an earlier child? Stuffing the paper back between the pages of the book, he leaped to his feet. Verity might well have been searching for a connection to the Treadwell family, but this was far more significant. She deserved to know the story.

Mrs. Carr's insistent hammering on the back door woke Verity and she shot upright. The Treadwell Foundation ledger still lay open on the kitchen table and the fire had died. She wrapped her arms around her body, her fingers grasping the soft cotton of the troubadour's shirt. Mrs. Carr couldn't see her like this, or see the ledger. She scuffed about pushing the chairs around and banging the kettle, then called out, "I don't seem to be able to find the key." She crossed her fingers against the lie, blessing the moment last night when she'd left it inside on the table instead of under the rock outside the back door as usual.

"I'll use the spare."

Verity pressed her face against the window as Mrs. Carr bent down and lifted the rock.

"It's not here."

"I must have brought it in and put it somewhere. Don't worry, I'll find it soon."

"Let me know when you do. I've got some nice scones in the oven. Thought we could have a natter. I haven't seen much of you lately."

"That would be lovely. I'll be over before long." Which was the very last thing Verity wanted to do. The ledger was far more intriguing than scones and she wanted to cross-check some entries before Stella came back as promised.

She snatched the canvas hold-all and clattered up the stairs, changed into the skirt and blouse she'd worn the day before, and stuffed the troubadour costume inside the bag and stopped. Charlotte! She still couldn't quite believe that she had a sister, a blood relative.

Of course she had to go through the ledger, but the entries portrayed stories of such sadness. After her initial outburst, Stella had seemed almost resigned to the information she'd uncovered. Knowing had to be better than imagining, but would she want to try to find Charlotte? Stella had said she'd do anything for the sake of her child, and now that she had a name and a suburb, her search could truly begin.

What about Treadwell and the story she was supposed to produce? She couldn't write the sort of article he wanted, not now. She simply had to make sense of the information she had and write the truth. However, she needed to make her peace with Mrs. Carr first.

By the time she'd cleared the kitchen table, Mrs. Carr was back, armed with a plate covered in a red-and-white tea towel. Verity opened the door.

"So you found the key."

She failed to control the flush in her cheeks. "I found it on the floor. I must have dropped it when I locked the door. Come in. I'll put the kettle on."

"Can't see it boiling for a while—the stove's out. I'll leave these here for you." Mrs. Carr peered into her face. "You look tired. Shouldn't be. Your light was out early."

Wretched busybody. Verity brushed her hair back from her face. "I'm fine." She tried for a smile. "A bit caught up with work."

"I heard tell you hadn't got a job no more." She folded her arms across her ample chest.

Could nothing remain private? "I'm doing some work for Mr. Bailey. Writing a couple of articles." No lie in that. "My job in advertising went to someone else."

"That's no good. What would Sid say?"

"I expect he'd say it was right and proper. We have to make way for the boys who've come home and need work."

"S'pose so. I'll be getting on. Light the stove, make yourself a cuppa, and have a bite to eat." She started to leave, then stopped. "You might want to do your blouse up proper. The buttons are all out of line. Must have had a sleepless night." She gave a sniff before banging the door behind her.

Verity fiddled with the buttons on her blouse. Unless she was very much mistaken, Mrs. Carr suspected her of entertaining an overnight visitor. She must have seen Stella leaving through the front door. Dressed all in black she'd easily be mistaken for a man. After all, Verity had fallen into that trap herself at the Artists' Ball.

Once she'd lit the stove and put on the kettle to boil, she opened the ledger again.

Identical handwriting throughout. She ran her finger down a random selection of pages. Turning to the fly leaf, she made note of the date, 1894—no end date—and beneath it *Accounts The Treadwell Foundation* and an indecipherable, scrawled signature.

She fanned the pages of tightly packed script. So many entries, so many children taken from their mothers. Surely Stella couldn't be the only one who wondered about the fate of their child? She ran her finger down a random page . . . *Jane Smith: Total costs £20/5/6d*. Twenty pounds, five shillings, and sixpence. Was that all a life was worth?

Despondent, she lifted the kettle and filled the teapot, inhaling the comforting steam. No, that wasn't what a child was worth; that was what it cost the Treadwell Foundation to provide a lying-in service.

The right-hand page told the rest of the story—*Total income: £200/12/3d*. Studying page after page, she confirmed her suspicions. Mrs. Treadwell charged far, far more—£200, £250, £300, and in one case, £500—for the provision of a child. This was no charity; it was a highly lucrative business. An obscene trade that should be condemned, not rewarded by donations. She chafed her cold hands. To hell with Mrs. Treadwell and her charity and good works. She deserved to be behind bars.

A sense of determination flooded Verity's veins. She was the person to bring it to light. Mr. Bailey would jump at the opportunity to publish this story. She poured herself a cup of tea and sniffed one of Mrs. Carr's scones. She couldn't remember the last time she'd eaten. Crumbs scattered across the tabletop as she pulled her notebook and pencil toward her.

"You there, Verity?"

Mrs. Carr's voice broke her concentration; she lifted her aching head.

"Your visitor's back. Standing out the front hammering and screaming like a banshee."

Verity shot to her feet, lifted her hand in acknowledgment, and rushed to the front door.

A heady fragrance filled the air. Stella stood on the footpath, her face hidden behind a huge bunch of freesias. She peered around them and smiled. "Can you spare me a moment?"

A moment? More than anything else, Verity wanted to drag Stella over the threshold and discuss all she had discovered. "Come on, come in. Are you feeling better?"

Stella pushed the bunch of flowers into her hands. "These are to say thank you."

"Whatever for?" She closed the door and gestured to the kitchen. "They're beautiful." She inhaled. "They're delicious. Like your perfume."

"For coming with me last night. I'm sorry I ran off."

She couldn't imagine the anguish Stella was suffering. "Please, don't apologize. I understand." She didn't, couldn't. In a perverse way the knowledge that she had a sister, albeit a half sister, filled her with an enormous sense of joy. She'd believed herself to be alone in the world. Since Grandma Clarrie's and Grandpa Sid's deaths, she'd had no one who shared her blood; now that had all changed.

She glanced around the kitchen, looking for a jam jar. She'd never received flowers before. Grandpa Sid always bought

Grandma Clarrie a bunch to celebrate her birthdate. "Excuse me a minute." She bolted up the stairs to the front bedroom. She opened the door; she had to make the time to sort out the room, but she couldn't bring herself to do it. "Soon." she promised. "Soon."

Glancing around she searched for Grandma Clarrie's green vase that had always sat on the dressing table. No sign of it. She pulled open the wardrobe. A waft of Grandpa Sid's tobacco drifted from his clothes as she pushed aside his two jackets. Sitting on the small shelf above the set of drawers stood Grandma Clarrie's vase balanced on Grandpa Sid's tin. She lifted it up and smiled. The place he kept all his treasures. Soon she'd find the strength to go through it; she had a reason now. She placed it on the dressing table next to Grandma Clarrie's glass tray.

"Verity?" Stella's voice floated up the stairs.

"I won't be a moment. I'm coming." She clattered down the stairs, the vase cradled in both hands. "I knew there was one somewhere." She filled it up with water and arranged the flowers. "There!" She placed it in the middle of the table.

"Perhaps we should put the flowers somewhere else. I'd hate to spill water on the ledger. We went to such trouble to get it." Stella picked up the vase. "On the mantelpiece, perhaps?" She carried it across the room and came to a halt, gave a strangled cry, and placed the vase on the corner. "Charlie."

Verity lifted her head from the notebook. "Yes. It was taken before he left for Cairo."

"What a handsome man he was." Stella ran her finger over the photograph, adjusted the vase, and offered a frail smile. "You have his coloring."

Verity blinked back a tear and changed the subject. "Have a look at this." She pointed to the last entry in the ledger.

"There are no entries since December last year. Don't you think it's odd?"

Stella dragged her attention from the photograph. "Why odd?"

"If this is a record of births at Treadwell House, which we know it is because of . . ."

Stella dropped her head into her hands. "Charlotte. That's her name. Charlotte. That's the name I picked out for her."

Verity swallowed. Every time she opened her mouth she was terrified she'd upset Stella. She sighed. "I'm sorry. It must be so very hard."

"Actually, this has come as a relief. I now know I'm not going mad. I believe the entries stopped because Mrs. Treadwell's companion died. I think she was responsible for the record keeping. I'm on my way to see Mr. Millar, the private investigator I've used in the past. He was the one who told me Treadwell House had stopped taking guests. I'm going to ask him to see if he can track down the Greenes."

Verity clamped her mouth closed. She needed time. Time to put the facts together and time to write her article.

"That's wonderful, but don't you think we should keep this"—she slapped her palm down on top of the ledger—"quiet until we've decided what to do? It seems to me that we've discovered a rort that has been going on for years. The Treadwells have made a fortune out of others' misery."

"I have the utmost faith in Mr. Millar, and I will give him no indication of the source of my information."

Verity snatched a quick breath. She had one more hurdle. "I still want to write the article."

"And so you should. That's why I am here. I thought you might come with me to see Mr. Millar."

Chapter 28

MORPETH, 1868

Theodora sat, fingers clenched around the tiller. Clarrie's and Sid's ashen faces and clutched hands made her heart bleed. A chill traced her skin. She couldn't ignore the description of the woman: the black dress with a white lace collar and the old, frayed carpetbag. The description fit Mrs. Barnett perfectly. More times than she could count she'd seen her leaving The Landing carrying a similar bag. Dilapidated and worn, it always accompanied her when she traveled on the steamer. She'd presumed it carried Mrs. Barnett's lotions and potions that she delivered to Maitland and Newcastle.

The river ahead was smooth and still, no waves lapping the shore. Redmond had squeezed every ounce of power from the engine and it clanked and chattered and miraculously didn't miss a beat, but there was no sign of the steamer as they rounded the bend.

Raymond Terrace loomed ahead, hardly a person on the wharf. Perhaps the steamer hadn't even stopped. Ash Island was next, but why would it stop there? On a weekday, maybe. It used to call in regularly when the Scott family lived there, delivering supplies and taking crates of oranges to the Sydney markets, but today was Sunday, and the Scotts long gone.

Theodora took a deep, pained gulp of air. If only she'd told Clarrie she could bring Charlie to live at The Landing, this would never have happened; if only she'd paid more attention to the doctor's concern over Mrs. Barnett's tonic and Charlie's failure to thrive; if only . . .

The clinker spluttered and Redmond grabbed the tiller from her. She dragged her attention back to the moment as they edged between two small islands, the stink of the mud-flats and mangroves tainting the air. "Redmond." She lowered her voice. "I think it's Mrs. Barnett who has taken Charlie."

"Don't be ridiculous. She's in Sydney with your sisters. Why would you think that?"

"Clarrie's description of the woman and the bag. Mrs. Barnett always carries a carpetbag when she goes on the steamer, and she's worn a black dress with a white lace collar since the *Cawarra* went down."

Redmond threw her a disbelieving look. "You're jumping to conclusions."

She wasn't; she knew she wasn't. All the times she'd seen Mrs. Barnett with her carpetbag; she never went anywhere without it.

All her trips to Maitland and Newcastle . . .

"She's not jumping to conclusions." Clarrie's face was paper white, her lips a sickly gray.

"Clarrie?"

She made no move, no sign she'd heard her name. Her eyes had a glazed look as though someone had slapped her hard. Theodora reached for Clarrie's hand.

"It's her. The baby snatcher." Two vermillion smudges stained Clarrie's pale cheeks, her eyes now wide with horror.

"The baby snatcher?"

"That's what people say. Sid's been doing some poking around for the paper. It started when he was checking out Maud, before I had Charlie. There's lots of women who advertise and take children in, and then when the mothers don't want them no more, the lady in black takes them, gets rid of them. I didn't believe it, but then I remembered the time I went to Sydney to see my mother. I saw the woman in black, and I saw her do it." Her tongue flicked over her dry lips. "I saw her throw a parcel overboard from the steamer."

"Surely not." Theodora squeezed her cold hand.

Clarrie raised her chin. "That's what I saw," she said, her voice stubborn. "And she's got my Charlie on that steamer."

"Ash Island ahead." Redmond's voice boomed.

Sid gave a cry and jumped to his feet as the *Petrel* glided between the thick green of the riverbanks and rounded the corner. "There it is."

Ahead, the steamer's paddle churned as it eased away from the wharf and headed downstream.

"We've missed it. It's too late." Clarrie's voice broke and she buried her head in Sid's shoulder.

"No. Look." Theodora pointed to the two Norfolk pines marking the Scotts' wharf where a dark-clad figure carrying a bag scurried along the rickety jetty.

The engine shuddered and Redmond nosed into the wharf. Theodora shot to her feet and grasped the rope, waiting for the opportunity to leap ashore. "Come on, Redmond. Hurry!"

The *Petrel* bumped against the timbers; Theodora braced herself, ready to jump from the gunwale onto the jetty.

"Oi! Private property. No trespassing. Told you that last time."

Theodora toppled back onto the deck. "Hench." His name

298

whistled between her lips. "We need to come ashore. Who got off the steamer?"

He hunched his shoulders and folded his arms across his chest, his lips pulled back in a snarl, revealing his revolting mouthful of blackened teeth. "Stay where you are."

Redmond stepped beside her. "What's the problem, Hench? Mr. Scott wouldn't mind. He'd allow Theodora to go ashore. She just wants a word—"

The clinker lurched as Hench landed with a thud on the deck. "What're you doing here?" He lowered his bullet head, wiped his bloody hands down his apron, releasing a putrid stench of rotten fish, then lunged. Redmond fell back, his head cracking against the seat.

Outraged, Theodora wrenched Hench's hair and reefed him away from Redmond. He spun around snarling, spittle flying, and shoved. With a horrible crunch her own head hit the deck. Stars filled her vision. She struggled upright, wiped a hand across her mouth, and tried to force her thoughts into line. Before she had time, a second blow sent her to her knees.

The stench of fish guts, blood, and mangroves filled her nostrils. Hench's arm wrapped around her throat, cutting off her airways, and he tossed her aside.

A blinding pain bloomed in her head again and the world exploded into a million fragments of brilliant color.

Clarrie couldn't control her scream. She dropped to her knees, cradling Theodora's head in her lap. Her lashes rested like half-moons on her pale cheeks and she lay horribly still.

A thud rocked the deck and Mr. Kendall lunged at Hench. He threw him back against the gunwale and dangled Hench out over the water. "Tell me where the baby is or you're in the drink."

Hench's face, all grimy and sweaty, grimaced. "Leave me be. I can't swim."

"Where's my baby? Where's Charlie?" Clarrie yelled, torn between leaving Theodora and scratching out Hench's bulging eyes.

Mr. Kendall tipped Hench farther out over the water, so his head almost went under. "Where is he?" he growled.

"Dunno." Hench tried for a shrug. "How would I know? Let me go."

The air left Clarrie's chest in a rush as Mr. Kendall slackened his grip, then pushed hard against Hench's chest. He wavered for a moment, feet losing purchase, legs flailing. Serve the sod right if he did go overboard.

"Who got off the steamer?" Mr. Kendall growled, sounding nothing like his usual mild-mannered self.

Hench shook himself like a beggar's cur, and with a mighty heave threw Mr. Kendall aside and struggled to his feet.

The fist came from nowhere, the punch hard and fast. Hench's head snapped back against the engine housing, releasing a billow of steam from the overheated boiler.

Sid stood, mouth gaping, rubbing his knuckles. "Bastard," he muttered.

The gentle rise and fall of Theodora's chest drove away Clarrie's worst fears. "She's got a nasty lump on the back of her head." She leaned forward, lifted her skirt, and tore off a chunk of her petticoat. "Wet it." She waved the material at Mr. Kendall and managed a frail smile. She should have known Sid could handle himself. What a hero.

Mr. Kendall leaned over the side and dangled the cloth into the river and wrung it out. "Is Theodora all right?" He dropped on his knees beside them and smoothed Theodora's hair back from her bone-white face. "Theodora. Stay with me. Stay awake. Speak to me." His voice cracked.

Clarrie's heart wrenched. Mr. Kendall's anguished face told its own story. Nobody looked at a friend like that. He was in love with Miss Theodora.

"Theodora," Mr. Kendall moaned.

Her eyes fluttered open. "I'm fine." She wiped her hand across her face. "Go and find Charlie. Where's Hench?"

"Bugger Hench, out cold—worse, with any luck. Cracked his head on the engine casing when Sid clobbered him. He isn't going anywhere."

"Where's Sid?" Clarrie shot to her feet, heart in her mouth. A curl of smoke rose from the cottage chimney, the curtains billowing in the breeze. "Hench knew she was coming. She's got to be here somewhere." Forcing back her fear, Clarrie threw herself onto the wharf, lifted her skirts, and bolted.

"Clarrie, wait!" Mr. Kendall's voice sounded behind her but she didn't stop.

No sign of the woman, no sign of any movement at the house, no sign of the carpetbag, and worse, no sign of Charlie or Sid.

The wharf juddered beneath her feet.

Two arms reached around her waist and brought her to a grinding halt. Fist raised, she wrenched free.

Sid!

He clutched her tight for a moment, then rushed to the end of the wharf. She charged after him. If Mrs. Barnett was in the house with the doors open, she would have heard their voices, might even be watching from one of the windows. They hadn't a moment to lose.

She snatched at Sid's hand and dragged him across the

flower bed in front of the house. Eyes closed, she tried to recall the layout. Sitting room on one side of the hallway, Mr. Scott's study opposite. Lifting her finger to her lips, she silenced Sid and pointed down the veranda.

The solid flagstones absorbed all sound as they tiptoed along and peered in through the French doors. The door swung open. Papers lay strewn across the desk and littered the floor, nothing like the neat room Theodora had shown her on their first visit.

"Someone's been here."

"Could be Hench." Sid glanced around, taking in the mess.

"He lives in the boathouse. I can't imagine him poking around in here. He'd risk losing his job."

A thump sounded from the back of the house. Heart hammering, Clarrie looked to Sid and threw up her hands, her mind nothing but a blank pit of fear. Think. She had to think.

"Is the kitchen out the back?" Sid's voice had dropped to an urgent whisper.

Clarrie nodded. "There's a covered walkway from the back of the house."

Sid pulled himself up to his full height. "You will stay here. Do you understand me? If I haven't come back by the time the sun dips behind the hills, you will leave. Go back to the boat and tell Redmond to dump Hench and take you and Theodora home."

He'd never spoken to her like that. Never. She stamped her foot. "I will do no such thing."

He grasped her hand, dark eyes drilling into her. "You will do as I say." Then he gave her hand a final squeeze and took off down the hallway.

Not a chance. Charlie was her baby; he needed her, not just his father.

The kitchen door hung wide and she stuck her head inside. No sign of Sid, no sign of anyone. She opened her mouth to call him, then snapped it closed. In the corner, by the chimney breast, Sid stood peering down a flight of stairs, hardly more than a ladder, leading down into the darkness of the unlit basement. "What are we going to do?"

"You're going to stay here. I'm going down there." With a very un-Sid-like smile, he dropped a kiss on her forehead, then eased his way down the ladder into the darkness.

Clarrie's heart stuttered and the fine hairs on her arms rose. Inhaling deeply, she followed. It didn't smell as she imagined, no odor of vermin; instead, a thick, cloying sense of sadness. An unyielding darkness. Sid had vanished.

Gradually the world realigned. Loath to move, Theodora lay cradled against Redmond's chest, the safest she'd felt in a long time. Her head still throbbed, and probably would do for a day or two. She lifted her fingers to her hair and felt for a lump.

"How are you feeling?"

"Aside from a splitting headache? My vision is blurry and the world keeps tilting. Where are Sid and Clarrie?"

"Gone up to the house."

"Then why are we sitting here? They need help." She struggled against him. "Why didn't you go with them?"

"And leave you lying here out for the count with only Hench for company?"

She glanced across the deck where Hench's body lay sprawled in an ugly mess against the engine housing. "Leave me here. I'll be fine. Hench isn't going anywhere. Sid's punch saw to that. I didn't think he had it in him." She crawled across the deck and peered into Hench's face.

Like a striking red-belly snake, Hench twisted to his feet and from the back of his waistband whipped out a knife, long-bladed and honed to a razor's edge. His face tightened, his nostrils flared, and his breath blew hot in her face, swamping her with a lifetime of sweat, fish guts, and rotten teeth. Her stomach heaved.

With a string of curses, he lunged.

Theodora froze. Hench raised the knife to strike downward, the tip mere inches from her chest. Her teeth snapped together on her tongue and she tasted blood.

The knife hovered above her.

Redmond's fingers wrapped around Hench's wrist but he bore down, his lips pulled back in a snarl as the tip sank closer. Grunting, Redmond tightened his grip and twisted Hench's arm up and back until the knife clattered to the deck.

With a cry, Theodora leaped away. The most stupid thing she could have done. Redmond reached for her.

Hench yanked his arm free and leaped from the boat into the shallows, a maniacal gleam in his eyes, and disappeared into the stinking mangroves.

CHAPTER 29

SYDNEY, 1922

Verity jumped off the tram at the end of Argyle Street. She'd expected to be home long before, but unfortunately Mr. Millar hadn't been in the office when she and Stella had arrived. While they waited for his return they'd consumed numerous cups of tea, eaten some particularly delicious cakes, and discussed again the implication of the ledger—most particularly the vast amount of money and the length of time the Treadwell Foundation had been in business.

The interview, when they found the obsequious Mr. Millar, was an eye-opener. Verity had had no idea such people existed. The writing on the glass door of his office proclaimed him to be the owner of A. H. Millar Private Detective Agency, which sounded much more impressive than was the dingy office up two flights of smelly stairs in a building in Market Street. He apparently prided himself on his reliable and discreet work and specialized in divorce inquiries and tracing lost friends, all for the sum of one guinea, which Stella dutifully handed over. Hopefully his inquiries, with the additional information, would be more successful this time.

The entire situation made Verity's flesh crawl, but Stella

seemed buoyed by the visit. When they parted at the tram stop, she'd thanked her profusely for her help and told her to call if she needed any information for her story before she delivered it to Mr. Bailey.

Verity slipped into the alleyway behind Tara Terrace, opened the back gate, and stopped in her tracks.

A light blazed from the house, illuminating the back door steps where a body sat, hands clasped around a steaming cup. She paused for a moment, then ran up the path. The long, lanky body unwound.

Arlo!

She slowed, took the last few steps, her heart thrumming. He was the last person she'd expected to see. "Hello." Her voice trembled. She'd tried to push all thoughts of their last meeting away, not willing to dwell further on her own behavior and the look of misery on Arlo's face when she'd admitted her duplicity.

"There you are." Mrs. Carr stepped through the gap in the fence. "I found him hammering on your front door, brought him round the back. Didn't think it would look too good after last night—another strange man at your door."

A blush rose, making her uncomfortably warm. "This is Mr. Kendall—Arlo." Whatever would he think? She covered her embarrassment by flashing him a smile and his lips twitched in response.

"He told me that." Mrs. Carr folded her arms and glowered.

"He owns the newspaper in Morpeth that Grandpa Sid worked for before he and Clarrie came to Sydney."

Mrs. Carr's eyes opened wide. "Kendall? You said. Kendalls of Morpeth?"

"The very same." Arlo spoke for the first time.

"Well, why didn't you say? Clarrie told me all about Mr. Kendall. He'd be your father?" She didn't pause for an answer. "A real gentleman, Clarrie said. Saved her and young Charlie from the gutter. It was thanks to your father that she and Sid got their start in Sydney." Mrs. Carr beamed. "You still haven't told me what you're here for, nor where you intend to spend the night."

"I have some important information for Verity." He shot a pleading look at her, then pinned Mrs. Carr with a steely gaze. "I've got a room booked at the Australian."

He had? The skin on her arms prickled. She couldn't wait to tell him about Charlotte. "Come inside." Verity pushed open the back door and ushered Arlo in, Mrs. Carr hot on his heels. She inserted herself between the two of them. "Thanks very much, Mrs. Carr, I'll see you tomorrow." A little harsh, but she didn't want Mrs. Carr sticking her nose in. Besides, she had no idea what information Arlo could have.

The woman gave a disgruntled shrug. "Very well then. I'll take my cup." She as good as peeled it from Arlo's fingers, tossed the remains of his tea under the fig tree, and stomped off.

Verity closed the door and gestured to the table. "Sit down. I've got soup. Would you like some?" All of a sudden she was at sixes and sevens. Arlo's great, lanky frame filled the kitchen and it seemed wrong, just wrong. He didn't belong in her little terrace; he swamped the cozy kitchen. He belonged in the sweeping hallway and high-ceilinged rooms of The Landing.

"Come and sit down. Let me tell you my news." He reached out his hand across the table.

She sank into the chair. He sounded a little frail; there was no sign of the terse, angry man she'd last seen in Morpeth, but she couldn't take his hand, not yet. She swallowed and steepled her fingers. "I have to apologize to you for not telling you the truth about the reason for my visit to Morpeth. I thought there might be some connection between Mrs. Treadwell and

Morpeth. I was digging for a story. And I have something else to tell you."

Arlo held up his hand to stall her. "You were right, but it seems the story might be a bit more complex than you anticipated." He delved into his inside pocket and brought out a crumpled piece of paper covered in red scribbles. "Apology accepted." He unfolded the scrappy sheet. "I couldn't stop thinking about the past after you left. I know so little of my family." He gave an embarrassed cough. "It made me a bit maudlin."

Raking back his hair, he grimaced. "I found this in my father's desk." The words tumbled out of his mouth in a rush as he smoothed the piece of paper. "I thought you'd want to see it. I know you were looking for information about the Treadwells, but this seemed important."

Verity squinted at the tightly packed writing. *MISSING WOMAN . . . housekeeper at The Landing.* She glanced down the page. *A baby farming enterprise in Morpeth, Maitland, and Newcastle.* Stella's heartrending description echoed . . . a lying-in service for young unmarried women. The housekeeper at The Landing, Arlo's family home, sold children for adoption.

The parallel with the Treadwell Foundation scrambled her thoughts. She lifted her head. Arlo sat with his hands tightly clasped, his attention fixed on her face. She bent to the paper again: *The veracity of these statements can be confirmed by the writer, whose son suffered at the hands of this despicable woman. Any information should be delivered to Sid Binks c/o The Morpeth Want.*

"Sid's son? My father? Charlie?" She glanced at the photograph on the mantelpiece. What did it mean? "Why has it got a red line through it?" She couldn't control the quaver in her voice.

"I presume because it was never published."

She offered a brief, baffled shrug.

Arlo took the flimsy piece of paper from her. "A red line usually indicates that it is not for publication." He pointed to a scrawl at the bottom of the page and the date: 28/6/1868. "Those are my father's initials: RK—Redmond Kendall."

Verity's mouth dried. The man who had given Grandpa Sid his start in Sydney, his job with *The Arrow*. Why hadn't she put two and two together before? Why hadn't Sid's article been published? "What happened to Charlie?"

Arlo shook his head. "I don't know. I had a look through the archives for the rest of 1868, but I didn't see any other mention."

"The registration of Charlie's birth is upstairs. He was obviously found; otherwise, I wouldn't be here," Verity concluded. And neither would Charlotte. She opened her mouth to tell Arlo of Stella's revelation and stopped. It wasn't her story to tell—not yet, not without Stella. "Why didn't your father print the article?"

"I don't know. Perhaps he didn't think it was true."

"Rubbish." Verity's skin prickled. "Grandpa Sid wouldn't have written this if it wasn't true. And who was this Mrs. Barnett woman?" She stabbed her finger at the paper. "You're telling me your family's housekeeper ran a baby farming racket?" She shook her head. It was beyond comprehension. "It says the Barnett woman boarded the ferry with a carpetbag containing a baby. How would Sid know that?"

"He must have made it his job to find out. Because it was Charlie, his son. That's obvious. When did your grandparents marry?"

"Not until they'd left Morpeth."

"Do you know the exact date they came to Sydney?"

Verity scrunched up her face and swallowed. "I'm not sure, but I might be able to work it out. Their marriage certificate is upstairs, along with the registration of Charlie's birth." She rushed up the stairs and into Sid and Clarrie's bedroom, pulled Sid's tin from the wardrobe, and shot back downstairs.

She prized off the lid and lifted the small pile of treasures out and laid them on the table. Arlo picked up the telegram and raised an eyebrow.

"Notification of Charlie's death."

"I'm sorry."

Verity didn't respond. Instead, she unfolded the registration of Charlie's birth. "I've always thought this was odd. The date is October 1868, but we celebrated his birthday at the end of May. They weren't married when Charlie was born; I presumed that was why. But Sid and Clarrie are listed as his parents . . ." And then her blood went cold as Stella's words came back to haunt her: *"The adopting parents register the child's birth."* Surely not. Sid wouldn't do a thing like that. Family was far too important to him. Charlie had to be their natural son.

"What's this?" Arlo's words broke into her thoughts. He had a letter in his fingers, twisting it this way and that. Then he held it up to his nose and inhaled.

"What on earth are you doing?"

He handed it to her. "Have you read this?"

Verity shook her head. "I've tried to go through the tin so many times but it makes me miserable."

Arlo reached out and took hold of her hand. His warm fingers encouraged her, gave her strength. She unfolded the thick piece of cartridge paper, releasing a very faint but familiar scent.

"It's camphor." Arlo inhaled again. "My mother used it to preserve the butterflies she pinned. You commented on the smell when I showed you her painting room. Remember?"

Her thoughts darted back to her visit to The Landing, the cabinet of butterflies against the wall, and she nodded. "Are you saying this is from your mother?"

He studied the address. "It's her handwriting, perfect copperplate, and the purple ink she favored. What does it say?"

Verity scanned the sheet of paper. "It's a thank-you letter of some sort, dated July 1868. Why does everything come back to 1868?"

"Because we're getting closer to answering the question about why Sid left Morpeth and possibly why my mother was estranged from her sisters."

The air in the kitchen closed around them. Verity swallowed. "And you think it might relate to Sid's article?" She didn't wait for a reply; instead, she let out a breath, forcing the tightness in her belly to ease as Arlo's words sank in.

She rubbed her temples, trying to chase away the threatening pain.

Dear Sid and Clarrie,

Just a few lines to express my deep gratitude to you both. I hardly know where to begin.

Sid, I know Redmond's rejection of your article must have come as a dreadful disappointment and I understand how much you wish to bring Mrs. Barnett to justice.

No one has seen her since the day on Ash Island, if that was indeed her we glimpsed. The police have interviewed Maud but as yet have found nothing untoward, as Doctor Morson spoke in her favor and had never signed death certificates for any babies in her care. She maintains

Mrs. Barnett took Charlie out for a walk and that she had no idea she had arranged an adoption. I ask you to understand our reasons for not publishing the article—the implications of the ledger would destroy the Breckenridge family.

I cannot thank you enough for your understanding and I trust that you, Clarrie, and Charlie will be happy in your new life in Sydney.

"Charlie came to Sydney with Clarrie and Sid." The air whistled out between her lips and her pounding heart slowed. Receiving no answer, she lifted her head from the letter. Arlo sat staring into space, an agonized look on his face. "Are you all right?"

"No. Not really." He reached into his pocket and brought out a teal-blue ledger, identical, except in color, to the one lying in her satchel from Treadwell House.

"Where did you get that?"

"From my father's desk. Sid's article was inside."

She took it from him and flicked to the fly leaf, deckle-edged and in places foxed with pale brown spots: *1842* and beneath it *Accounts Morpeth*—the same handwriting and scrawl as the ledger she and Stella had taken from Treadwell House. It served only to intensify her raging headache. "It's very similar to this one." She reached into her satchel, took out the Treadwell ledger, and pushed it across the table.

He fanned the pages. "No doubt about that. Where did you get it?"

Heat rose to her face. "I stole it from Treadwell House."

His mouth dropped open and behind his spectacles his eyes widened. "You did what?"

While Verity recounted the details of the trip to Treadwell House, Arlo sat contemplating her face with what might possibly be the beginning of a smile.

"And who was your accomplice?" he asked when she'd finished.

"Her name's Stella Trey. It's a very long story, but she gave birth to a daughter at Treadwell House and has been trying to trace her child for six years. The child was adopted without Stella's permission." Verity opened the ledger to the page and pointed out the name Greene.

"So it seems my family weren't the only ones to be taken in."

"Your family?" Verity paused, unable to find the words to describe the litany of misery contained between the pages of the two ledgers.

"It's all in here." Arlo tapped the cover of the Morpeth ledger.

No wonder the poor man looked shell-shocked when she'd arrived, and he'd managed to keep quiet while he'd told her about Sid. Not knowing what to say, she reached for his hand. His fingers threaded through hers and he swallowed loudly. "I didn't realize what it contained. Sid's article was inside, so I left it in there to protect it. Once I was on the train, I started leafing through it to pass the time." He unlaced his fingers, flicked through several pages, then slid it across the table.

Apr 21st 1846 Female, chestnut hair . . . Total expenses £3/0/0

Her finger traced to the right-hand page.

Breckenridge, Morpeth . . . Received £200 adoption fee

313

The next entry:

Sept 9th 1847 Female, Titian . . . Total expenses £4/20/6d
Breckenridge, Morpeth . . . Received £200 adoption fee
    Dec 20th 1848 Female, fair/strawberry . . . Total
expenses £2/20/6d Breckenridge, Morpeth . . . Received
£250 adoption fee
    Oct 19th 1849 Female, copper . . . Total expenses £5/6/6d
Breckenridge, Morpeth . . . Received £250 adoption fee

Her cup clattered to the floor and shattered. Breckenridge!
Four girls. Arlo's mother, Theodora, and her sisters were
adopted. The picture-perfect Breckenridge family was nothing
more than a charade.

She bent and retrieved the shards, mopped up the tea with
the dishcloth, then slumped down at the table. Randomly she
flicked through the pages, scanning the copperplate and the
neat accounting. The same person who had kept the Treadwell
ledger. Who? Mrs. Treadwell? No. It couldn't be Florence
Treadwell. She was one of the adopted Breckenridge girls.
The marriage notice in the newspaper archives proved that. It
also ruled out Mr. Treadwell; he wasn't even born when the
whole sorry business began. Someone had made a fortune. She
flipped to the next page, and the next.

No wonder Sid's story was buried.

"There's no reference to Mother's brother, Jamie, their son
and heir." Arlo's voice broke her thought pattern. "So I can
only presume he was their natural child and Mother and her
three sisters were not."

"I wonder how they managed to source so many redheaded
girls." My god, it sounded as though she were discussing a
cattle auction.

"The trademark Breckenridge Celtic coloring." He raked his fingers through the lock of hair falling over his forehead. "I didn't inherit it." He gave a dry laugh.

"Who would do a thing like that?" Once the words were out of her mouth the stupidity of her question struck her.

"I may have an answer." He flipped to the fly leaf of the teal ledger, then the red one and traced his finger across the scrawled signatures. "I think both say Mrs. Barnett."

"Barnett." She reached for Sid's article. "Mrs. Barnett, housekeeper at The Landing, Morpeth, is also the person responsible for the running of the Treadwell Foundation."

"One and the same."

CHAPTER 30

SYDNEY, 1922

Arlo's thoughts circled. Reading the entries in the ledger he'd found in Father's desk had thrown him into the past. He'd glossed over his childhood when Verity had asked him.

Mother had spoken of the past and so had Father—halcyon days when they were growing up, before the wreck of the *Cawarra*—but Mother rarely mentioned her sisters. He'd always presumed the tragedy had fractured the family, but reading the entries in the ledger painted a very different picture. Sid's article was dated 1868. Had Sid found Mrs. Barnett's ledger and discovered the picture-perfect Breckenridge family was a lie? The events of that year were the ones that had finally shattered the family, not only the sinking of the *Cawarra*.

The sound of Verity clattering down the stairs brought him back to the present. She thumped a dilapidated Remington down on the kitchen table, wound a piece of paper onto the roller, and began hammering the keys like a woman possessed. "I'm going to write this article once and for all. There is enough evidence in these two ledgers to prove a baby farming racket had been running for over fifty years and there are two consistent figures—your aunt, Florence Treadwell, and this Barnett person, who we know, thanks to Grandpa Sid's article, was the housekeeper at The Landing. And it seems your mother and father were complicit in the cover-up. I'm sorry to be so blunt, but the facts speak for themselves."

She was right, as much as he was unwilling to admit it. And to add insult to injury, he was fairly certain, having read his mother's letter, that Sid's move to Sydney was as a result of Redmond's high-handedness.

"In hindsight, I'm thrilled I didn't see Mr. Treadwell, because now I can take the true story directly to Mr. Bailey, the editor of *The Sydney Arrow*."

"Is that a good idea?"

"Whyever not? It's a much more significant story. Stella has tried for ages to uncover the facts. This might be the 'why.' The reason Florence Treadwell decided to set up the charity after her husband died. It was a money-making scheme, and Mrs. Barnett, whom she'd known since childhood, helped her."

"You've got no real proof . . ."

"Don't be ridiculous. Apart from anything else, the handwriting and layout in both ledgers are the same. Do you know anything about this Mrs. Barnett?"

He'd spent time on the train thinking about Mrs. Barnett—he couldn't remember one instance of Mother mentioning her. She spoke of a nursemaid and a governess and a housekeeper, but never any names. Maybe that was deliberate. He groaned. The last thing he'd imagined when Verity came through the doors of *The Morpeth Want* was that he would become personally embroiled. He stood up and looked over Verity's shoulder at the rapidly increasing lines of type. "Do you think you should confirm your beliefs? Talk to the Treadwells again?"

"I'm not going to show the article to Treadwell and give

him the opportunity to come up with a series of lies and cover-ups. Besides, there's little point. I'm convinced Mrs. Treadwell's companion who recently died was Mrs. Barnett." Her finger tapped the signature in the ledger.

"What do you plan to do with the ledgers?"

"I'll show them to Mr. Bailey. They're proof, along with Sid's article, of the fraudulent practices of the Treadwell Foundation; proof, in fact, of how long it has been going on."

"Proof also that you and Stella broke into Treadwell House and stole private property."

She tipped her head back and studied the outline of the fig tree beyond the window. "I hadn't thought of that."

"Your Mr. Bailey, if he's worth his salt, isn't going to accept the article for publication if you've come by the evidence illegally."

Verity slapped her hand down on the table. "What am I going to do? Sid's article and your ledger prove the link between Morpeth and the Treadwell Foundation."

He had to stop her jumping in. She needed to take stock, think through the possible ramifications. He agreed the story should be told and the Treadwells' business exposed—except that he wasn't sure that they were doing anything illegal. Immoral, without a doubt, but illegal? "Unless I'm mistaken, families, doctors, and the church—a range of people—organize fostering and adoptions. It's happened for years."

"Perhaps, but I'm sure it's illegal for the adopting parents to register the child as their own. That's what happens at Treadwell House—Stella has confirmed that. And look at the amount of money they are charging for providing these families with babies." She jabbed her finger at the ledgers. "You can't trade in people; it's called slavery. It's illegal and has been for years and years."

She was right about that, but he couldn't see her throw away all her plans for the future, jeopardize a career that was only just beginning. "I've got an idea."

She tipped her head to one side, the corners of her mouth twitching in a smile.

He curbed the desire to pull her into his arms. "I think you should write the piece and show it to Treadwell; if he incriminates himself, you'll be on much firmer ground."

"No!" She leaped to her feet, chest heaving with indignation. "I've told you I am not going to pander to him. Apart from anything else, they don't deserve the money raised by the Artists' Ball. They should be called out. It could be better spent going to others who truly need it. They've made a fortune out of this adoption business; they don't need public funds. There are people far more deserving."

"Settle down and listen to me." He waited while she fidgeted from foot to foot and finally subsided onto the chair. "If we take some notes, names and places and amounts, then go to Treadwell House and replace the ledger, you can write the article exposing the foundation. Simply don't reveal your source."

"How are we going to do that? Stroll up to the front door and hand it over?"

"Pretty much. Yes. We'll see when we get there. Think about it until tomorrow. It's time I left before I lose the room I've booked at the Australian Hotel."

Verity doubted Arlo's sanity, and her own. Whatever had possessed her to go along with his ridiculous plan? She smoothed down her jacket and raised her hand to the lion-head knocker.

After the inevitable wait, the door opened and the same pretentious maid in her lacy cap stood in front of them.

Verity gave what she hoped was a winning smile. "I wondered if Mr. Treadwell was available."

"No. He's not." Miss Mary Hoity-Toity folded her arms and smirked.

Now what? She'd known all along this was a futile exercise. She'd like to give the girl a good talking-to.

"But Mrs. Treadwell is."

Verity snapped her mouth closed. Maybe luck was on their side.

"Who's the gent?"

Before Verity could respond, Arlo stepped forward. "Miss Binks and Mr. Kendall."

"Wait here." The door closed, leaving Verity and Arlo studying the black paintwork.

"Are you insane?" Verity hissed. "Have you forgotten who Mrs. Treadwell is? Your aunt. Your mother's sister. She'll recognize your name."

"I hope so." Arlo grinned at her and brushed his hair off his face. "Slip this into your satchel." He pulled the Treadwell ledger from his inside pocket. "You'll have a better chance of getting it back onto the shelves. With any luck, Mrs. Treadwell won't be able to take her eyes off me when I introduce myself." He laughed. "That makes me sound a bit arrogant, doesn't it?"

Verity swallowed a snarky response and fumbled with the buckle on her satchel, managing to slip the notebook inside as the door reopened.

"Mrs. Treadwell will see you now. Follow me."

Arlo's elbow nudged Verity forward and together they made their way across the checkerboard floor to the library.

Mary threw open the door and announced, "Mr. Kendall and Miss Binks."

They stepped over the threshold.

Mrs. Treadwell sat in one of the two chairs in front of the fire. She pinned Verity with a questioning stare. "Miss Binks. The name is familiar. Have we met before?"

Verity smiled, trying to cover her sense of panic. "At a gallery opening, in the Queen Victoria Building—botanical art."

A frown flitted across Mrs. Treadwell's brow. "An excellent showing. I'm not sure I recollect our meeting. How can I help you?"

What a godsend. She hadn't remembered her. "Thank you for seeing us. This is Mr. Kendall."

Mrs. Treadwell studied Arlo. Visibly uncomfortable with her scrutiny, he pushed the lock of hair back from his forehead. The movement must have sparked her memory, because she stilled. "The Kendalls of Hinton. The spitting image of your father."

A spot of color bloomed on Arlo's cheeks. "Many people say that. Sadly, he passed away two years ago."

"And your mother?" Mrs. Treadwell gestured to the seat opposite her, ignoring Verity.

Arlo sat down. Hands resting on his knees, he stared blatantly into her face. "Your sister, Theodora?" He paused for a moment, then reached forward and took Mrs. Treadwell's hand. Much to Verity's amazement, she didn't pull away. "I'm sorry to say she passed last year, not long after my father. I wanted to come personally and give you the sad news. It has taken me longer than I anticipated to find you."

Verity stood forgotten as if watching a stage play from the wings. Her pulse slowed as she waited, and waited, while Arlo spoke of his mother's final days. Not the way she'd expected the scene to play out.

The sound of Arlo clearing his throat broke the spell. What was the matter with her? This was her opportunity. She took two steps until she stood alongside the shelves, tugged gently, and the faux books tilted silently. Now to get the notebook from her satchel without Mrs. Treadwell noticing the movement. She glanced up.

Mrs. Treadwell's back was to her and her attention firmly fixed on Arlo's face as she listened to him describe his mother's resting place in the walled garden she'd loved so much.

Verity eased her satchel over her hip, felt for the ledger, lifted it out, and slid it between the faux cover of one of the books. Too easy. She stepped aside.

Mrs. Treadwell dabbed her eyes with a small scrap of white lace. Was she truly upset? She hadn't seen her sister for more than fifty years, apparently had no communication. Poor Arlo. How must he be feeling?

As though he could read her thoughts, he raised an eyebrow in question.

She dropped her lashes in answer.

"I am writing a family history and Miss Binks is assisting me. Perhaps you remember, my family owns a newspaper, *The Morpeth Want*. I'd very much like to discover more about the past, write a tribute to the Breckenridge family, who played such an important part in the development of Morpeth. There are so many questions I wish I had asked my mother. I wondered if you would help me."

How could he sit there and say such a thing? He'd concocted it on the spur of the moment. It was an out-and-out lie.

Arlo wasn't entirely sure where the words had come from. He'd had no specific plan other than to distract Mrs. Treadwell and enable Verity to replace the notebook, which she'd accomplished with an impressive amount of stealth.

When Mrs. Treadwell had recognized him, he'd almost fallen over, but then again, he'd been told many times he and Father were alike, had been from the moment he was born, if Mother was to be believed—not that it had ever impressed him. He rather wanted to be his own person, not a replica. What had Mrs. Treadwell said? He had to concentrate. "I beg your pardon?"

"I asked you why you thought I might be able to help. I left The Landing when I married and never returned. Surely your mother spoke of her childhood."

"Very infrequently. She was committed to her research and painting."

"And do you have brothers and sisters?"

"I am an only child. Some would say I had a lonely life, but it never felt that way. I had a tutor for a time, but largely my education fell to my father."

"And you didn't go to war, to fight for your country?"

"No, I didn't."

Verity shot him a piercing glance, probably wondering whether he should be given a white feather. She wouldn't be alone in thinking that way. A shame he'd had to live with. In 1916, he'd fronted for his medical examination along with thousands of others, healthy, fit, just shy of six feet tall, a mouthful of his own teeth, confident he wouldn't be rejected, only to be told he was unfit for service because he wore glasses. Had done from the moment Dr. Morson picked it when he couldn't tie a fisherman's knot. Acute myopia of the right eye. "Medically unfit." Instead, he'd started at the bottom of the ladder as a copyboy on the newspaper with no choice but to follow in Father's footsteps.

Mrs. Treadwell pursed her lips. "I see."

Did she? He doubted it, if the pinched look on her face was any indication. He took off his spectacles and rubbed the bridge of his nose.

"And how did you find me?"

"I stumbled across an announcement of your marriage in the newspaper archives. It gave me your surname. I'd heard of the Treadwell Foundation and—" He clamped his lips closed. If he wasn't careful, he'd drop himself in it, mention the ledgers, ask about Mrs. Barnett. "If now is not a good moment, perhaps we could arrange a suitable time—that is, if you are prepared to assist me."

A shadow crossed the woman's face. He couldn't work her out. Had no idea if she was telling the truth or toying with him. She couldn't know that he had seen the ledger, that he knew of the financial dealings of the foundation.

"I'm not sure there's very much I can tell you. No doubt you're aware of the sinking of the *Cawarra*. I lost my mother and father and my brother."

How strange that she didn't say "we." But then again, Mother rarely acknowledged her sisters. She often spoke of her brother, Jamie, and her father, but not her sisters. "A terrible tragedy."

"It destroyed the family. After a suitable mourning period, Viola, Constance, and I came to Sydney. Viola and Constance both met their husbands that season and traveled to England immediately after they married. They haven't visited Australia since. We corresponded for a while and then gradually the letters became more and more infrequent. We were never a close family. I haven't heard from them for many years."

Which all tallied with Mother's comments. Perhaps Verity's enthusiasm and conviction had led him astray. Maybe there was no story to tell. He needed more background and he didn't have the time to pore over old newspapers. He glanced across the room at Verity. She stood studying the bookshelves with a fierce concentration, as though she wasn't aware of their conversation. He coughed in a vain attempt to attract her attention and failed.

"Mr. Kendall. I'm going to have to ask you to leave. We'll meet another time. Good afternoon." And with that, Mrs. Treadwell drifted through the door in a rustle of silk and a cloud of expensive perfume.

"Verity. It's time to go."

Ashen faced, she allowed him to lead her into the hallway where they were escorted out by Mary, the maid.

It wasn't until they reached the end of the driveway that he stopped. "Verity, what is it? You look terrified."

She offered him a frail smile. "I was. Still am. Let's go. I want you to meet Stella. She owns a gallery in the city. She sold your mother's painting to Mrs. Treadwell."

CHAPTER 31

SYDNEY, 1922

The familiar comforting bustle of the city soothed Verity. By the time they'd reached the intersection of Park and Market streets she'd stopped shaking. Why couldn't Arlo have given her some warning of his intentions? It had completely blindsided her, and the thought that Mrs. Treadwell might have guessed about the ledger brought her out in a cold sweat. She wanted to tell Arlo about Charlotte, but she couldn't do that without Stella's permission and she had to tell her they'd returned the ledger. She stopped and took a deep breath.

Arlo turned to her. "Your color's come back. Feeling better?"

"Let's get off here and I'll take you to meet Stella." She hit the bell and swung down, Arlo behind her. "It's just around the corner."

"Will the gallery be open?" Arlo thrust his hands deep into the pockets of his trench coat and hunched his shoulders.

She hadn't thought about that; however, luck was on her side and they found Stella unlocking the front door.

"This is a nice surprise. I don't usually open until after lunch, but I had some tidying up to do."

"This is Arlo Kendall. He runs the newspaper in Morpeth. I found him on my doorstep when I got home yesterday. Can we come in?"

"Of course, of course. How do you do, Mr. Kendall?" Stella held out her gloved hand.

"My pleasure. Verity has mentioned you."

"All good, I hope." Stella ushered them inside.

Arlo didn't answer. He made for the display of paintings, searching perhaps for another of his mother's.

Stella rested her hand on Verity's arm. "I wasn't expecting to see you so soon. Have you been working on your piece?"

Before she had time to respond, Arlo interrupted. "Verity, if you're recovered, I might leave you two ladies. I have some unfinished business to attend to before I go back to Morpeth. Delighted to meet you." He nodded to Stella, pushed his hands down into his pockets, and left.

"What was that all about?"

"I have no idea." She'd hoped Arlo would stay a little longer so she and Stella could tell him about Charlotte. "I've had the strangest time since I last saw you. Can we sit down?"

"Of course. Come out the back. I'm not expecting any customers this early."

"I haven't very much time. I thought Arlo might like to know about the painting you sold Mrs. Treadwell. I'm certain his mother painted it, but I can't imagine how it came into Charlie's hands." She paused for a moment. "I don't quite know where to start. Arlo arrived with a copy of an article Grandpa Sid had written—Charlie was stolen, kidnapped."

"Kidnapped?"

"Sid's article proves the plan was foiled. Arlo found Sid's

article between the pages of another ledger dating back to the 1840s. The records and the handwriting were very similar to the one we took from Treadwell House."

"The contents?" Stella almost spat the words.

"Similar, but more extensive. Not only adoptions but other entries—children who didn't survive, midwives' fees, burial costs, and payments for death certificates. From Morpeth to Newcastle, and . . ." Verity's words petered out. She wiped her hand across her face. "It painted a dreadful picture."

"I'm so sorry."

"It's worse. There was a reference to Arlo's mother and her sisters. They were adopted. And this is the most awful thing . . . the signature on the frontispiece. It was the Breckenridge family housekeeper, Mrs. Barnett."

"Edith Barnett?" Stella's hand covered her mouth and she stared at Verity. "Am I understanding you correctly? You're saying that his family employed Mrs. Treadwell's companion, the woman who kept the records? Where is this Morpeth ledger?"

"Arlo has it."

"What about the Treadwell ledger?"

"He convinced me to take it back. We've just come from there."

"You returned it?" Stella choked back a strangled cry. "It's the only evidence of my claim."

"He convinced me it was the right thing to do, that Mr. Bailey wouldn't be interested in my piece if he knew it was based on stolen information. He introduced himself to Mrs. Treadwell. She recognized him! I slipped the ledger back onto the bookshelf. Now I am not so sure I should have done that."

"Do you think Arlo might be involved?"

Verity dropped her head into her hands. That was exactly her problem—the very thought that had almost brought her to her knees while they were at Treadwell House. "Why would he show me the ledger and Sid's article if he was involved? It makes no sense."

Except it did. A possibility she didn't want to entertain, that Arlo had duped her, intended all along to act as his father had done and suppress any reference to the Breckenridge family. "I am determined to finish the Treadwell piece and I am going to take it directly to Mr. Bailey. I need make no mention of your name, but people should know, people should be aware of what has happened."

"And you will have my every support. It's what I wanted from the outset. I can't rewrite my own history, but we can make certain their immoral profiting from other people's misery doesn't continue."

"If only Mrs. Barnett were still alive. Did you meet her when you were at Treadwell House?"

"I did. I remember her quite well. She was a little older than Mrs. Treadwell, but hale and hearty, somewhat intimidating. One of those people who always appears from behind doors or around corners when you least expect it, but I can understand why Mrs. Treadwell would miss her. It's obvious she kept all the records, controlled the finances, and was responsible for organizing the adoptions, which ties in very nicely with Mr. Millar's statement that the foundation was no longer taking clients. That stopped when Mrs. Barnett died."

A cloud of smoke enveloped Arlo as he pushed open the door to the Glebe Hotel. It hadn't occurred to him until he'd spent a few hours pounding the footpaths trying to get his head straight that there was an alternative to old newspapers—old newspapermen. He'd first visited the hotel with Father, hardly dry behind the ears; they'd spent a week at the Australian Hotel and Father had taken him to visit several of the Sydney papers, an attempt to lead him away from his passion for ornithology.

Men of all shapes and sizes crammed the bar, the six o'clock swill in full swing. He edged his way through the crowded drinkers and smoke haze to the back corner of the bar where an old bloke sat propped on a stool, head buried in a newspaper. Arlo recognized him immediately.

Arlo pulled up a stool.

The bloke knocked back the last of his beer and put down his glass. "Kendall. Well, I'll be damned."

"Junior." Arlo grinned and rested his elbow on the bar.

"Not anymore by the looks of you. How's your old man? Enjoying the quiet life?"

Not a conversation he wanted to get into. "Lost him a couple of years back."

"Sorry to hear that. So you're behind the desk now?"

Arlo gave a noncommittal grunt. He didn't want to explain the way *The Morpeth Want* had dwindled into almost obscurity under his watch. "How's things with you, Bob?"

"Can't complain. Threw it in once the boys started coming home. Still miss it though. Like to keep a few of the old habits." He folded his newspaper and peered into his empty glass, his message clear.

"What can I get you?"

"Resch's. Make it two. They'll be calling time before long." He waved his glass at the barman, who slid two beers down the bar before being asked.

Bob took a long swig and eyed him over the top of the glass. "I'm guessing you didn't come in here just to buy me a beer, son."

Arlo laughed. "No. I want to pick your brain, test your memory."

"Let's have it."

"What do you know about baby farming?"

Bob put down his glass and rocked back on the stool. "Strange topic for a lad like you." He pursed his lips and shook his head. "Pretty much come to an end now. The authorities got wise to it after the Makin case."

"The Makin case?"

"Come on. Morpeth isn't that much of a backwater; surely you read about it?"

Arlo's mouth dried. "When?"

"Let me think. Be about the time of the run on the Sydney banks during the depression." He scratched at the sprinkling of hairs covering his domed head. "I reckon around 1893. Dragged on for about six months."

"Not the kind of thing I knew anything about back then." But just after Treadwell House opened its doors, according to the ledger.

"Nah. I guess you're right. Your father would've remembered it. Husband and wife, John and Sarah Makin. Charged with murdering a child in their care. Then it came out that they'd been burying babies in the backyards of the places they'd rented, twelve in all. They were both sentenced to death by hanging. Her sentence was commuted after an appeal— blamed her husband, said she hadn't got any option but to do as he said. She spent eighteen years in jail for her sins. He wasn't so lucky. Nasty business."

"And the Makin case was an end to it?"

"Nah. Plenty of other cases over the years." Bob scratched at his head. "Now you're testing me. There was a change in the legislation—took a while for it to filter through all the states though." Bob swung around on his stool. "Hey, Larry, got a minute?"

A wizened gnome of a man picked up his empty glass and ambled over.

"This is Kendall, *Morpeth Want*."

"Arlo Kendall." Arlo held out his hand.

"Larry, Larry Walsh." He grasped Arlo's hand and pumped it up and down with an unexpected amount of vigor. "*Sydney Morning Herald*."

"Not anymore, you old coot."

"Once a newspaperman, always a newspaperman. What can I do for you?"

Bob held up three fingers and another set of beers slid down the bar. "He's picking me brain and we ain't getting far. Do you know anything about baby farming?"

"Cheers." Larry chugged down a good half of the beer and wiped his mouth on the back of his hand. "Happened all over the country. They hung the Makin bloke, and some woman in Perth earned the title of Australia's most tenacious murderer."

"What else have you got?"

"There were three cases in Sydney. That one in Richmond, two women committed for manslaughter in 1875; one in Woollahra; and another one on the outskirts of the city, sometime later, on the Lane Cove River. Remember that?"

Bob's face broke into a gruesome grin. "I do. A woman running a lying-in and baby farming establishment. If I remember rightly, they thought the same person was behind all three. Never caught up with them."

Arlo's head pounded as he tried to commit the facts to

memory. Shame he hadn't asked Verity to come with him. He could have used her shorthand skills. Not that she would have been allowed into the bar, nor would the information have flown as freely.

"Bailey's sitting over there; he might remember a bit more. He's chief editor at *The Arrow* now."

Bailey. The bloke Verity was supposed to give her Treadwell article to. Bailey sat alone, shrouded in a cloud of cigarette smoke, a half-empty glass in front of him.

"Oi! Bailey." Bob's voice carried over the noise and Bailey lifted his head. "Over here." He beckoned.

Bailey pushed back his chair and ambled over. "What's your problem, Bob . . . Larry?"

Arlo resisted the temptation to squirm as Bailey studied him. "This is Arlo Kendall, *Morpeth Want*. He's got a few questions. Thought you might be able to help."

Bailey lit another cigarette from the stub of the last and inhaled. "*Morpeth Want*. Sorry to hear about your father. What can I do for you?"

Before Arlo could get a word in, Bob launched into a recap of their earlier conversation. Arlo shoved his hands deep into his pockets and braced himself, wondering how much Verity had told Bailey about Treadwell.

"That's going back a bit, a long way. Victoria was the first to pass the Infant Life Protection Act, and New South Wales followed a couple of years later, then, at the end of the war, we got the Maintenance of Children Act, giving an allowance to mothers without any other means of support." Bailey gestured to the barman, who refilled his empty glass. "That pretty much put the lid on it. They never did find out who was behind the Sydney rackets."

Arlo let his breath whistle out between his lips as the six

o'clock call rang out. "If you can't drink it, leave it and if you can't leave it, drink it."

Larry and Bob downed the remainder of their beers and stood. "That's us for the night. Nice to catch up with you, young man, and thanks for the beer." Bob neatly sidestepped the crush of bodies and left through the front doors.

"Thanks, Mr. Bailey. That's my questions answered." Arlo stuck out his hand, but Bailey had his fist wrapped around his refilled glass so he resorted to a nod, dumped the money for the beers on the bar, and left.

After grabbing a steaming bowl of noodle soup on the way back to the Australian, Arlo hunkered down with a notebook and tried to remember everything Larry, Bob, and Bailey had told him, cursing his ridiculous idea of replacing the Treadwell ledger. There was no doubt about the adoptions, but had it included baby farming? He couldn't get over the coincidence of the timing and Bailey's suggestion that the same person was behind all three Sydney cases at the very time they couldn't account for Mrs. Barnett's whereabouts. The dates tied together perfectly. The Morpeth ledger ended in 1868, then nothing until Mrs. Barnett popped up at Treadwell House in 1894. He'd put money on her being behind the Woollahra, Richmond, and Lane Cove rackets.

It was well after ten when a knock on the door made him raise his head.

"You there, Mr. Kendall?"

He pulled off his glasses, puffed on them, gave them a quick wipe on his shirt, and opened up to find the doorman wringing his hands.

"What's up, Jack?"

334

"Just had a telephone call. They've got a problem with the printing press and want you back."

Bugger. That'd put pay to his idea of telling Verity about his theory over breakfast. "Right you are. Thanks for that. Any idea when the last train for Newcastle leaves?"

"Too late now. Milk train's your best bet. That'll get you into Newcastle in time for breakfast."

CHAPTER 32

SYDNEY, 1922

Verity spent the remainder of the day with the door locked to keep Mrs. Carr at bay and her attention focused solely on the facts, determined to finish the story before she had to explain her decision to Arlo.

Dusk softened the outlines of the roofs and chimney pots before she hit the final full stop and leaned back. "That's it." The paper made a satisfying noise when she pulled it from the roller and separated the carbon paper. She made two neat piles, tapped them into alignment, then took one copy upstairs and slipped it under her pillow before making her way down from her attic bedroom to collect her bicycle.

The city hummed, people making their way home, the last of the street vendors packing up their carts and the six o'clock swill depositing crowds of beer-soaked drinkers onto the footpath. Mr. Bailey would have left. He frequented the Glebe Hotel, as much a part of his daily routine as the coffee he drank for breakfast, but she knew only too well that newspaper offices never closed. She intended to leave the story on Mr. Bailey's desk for him to find in the morning and then await his summons. He would probably want some changes and facts clarified as he had with her bicycle story, but he'd be keen to publish it; it would be an exclusive.

The next day passed at a funereal pace. Verity cleaned the house from top to bottom, used half of her remaining savings to restock the pantry, washed just about everything she could lay her hands on, but not a word from Mr. Bailey. She couldn't wait a moment longer. Whatever had possessed her to leave her article on his desk? Anyone could have gone into his office and read it, or worse: taken it, rewritten it, and claimed it as their own.

"Mrs. Carr, are you there?" Verity called from the back door.

"Yes, lovey."

She was back in favor again. "I'm going out. I have some errands to run. Is there anything you want?"

"Nothing for me, but you could do with some fresh air."

Verity wheeled her bicycle out of the shed and set off down the road. When she reached the corner of Gloucester and Cumberland streets, she coasted to a halt. Ahead of her stood the Australian Hotel. She had no idea whether Arlo was still in Sydney or, more importantly, his plans. She had a nagging concern that she should have shown him the article before she delivered it to Mr. Bailey—after all, it risked bringing his family into the limelight. She propped her bicycle against the wall and entered through the side door.

A man sat inside a small cubbyhole, his newspaper open at the form guide.

"I wonder if you could help me. I'm looking for Arlo Kendall. I believe he's staying here."

He looked her up and down and raised his eyebrows. "And who'd be asking?"

"Verity Binks. I'm a friend of his."

His face broke into a smile. "Well, why didn't you say so? Didn't recognize you. How are you doing, love? Still missing Sid, I'll be bound."

"Yes, and Clarrie." She raised her shoulders. What else could she say?

"So you're after young Mr. Kendall. Sorry to say he's left. Went back to Morpeth early this morning, got the milk train."

Less than a mile away and he hadn't bothered to call in and say goodbye. More than likely he didn't dare face her after his performance at Treadwell House. Well, it was too late.

"Said he'd got some problem with the printing press. They rang here so they've got the telephone on. Why don't you give him a call?"

"I might do that, thank you."

"Sorry I couldn't be of more help," he called after her as she left.

Pumping the pedals madly, she flew along Sussex Street toward the newspaper offices on Broadway. Arlo must know that she would write the article; if he didn't want it published, then why hadn't he told her outright? Surely he didn't believe she'd back down. Or maybe he'd trusted her not to mention his family. But if Mr. Bailey wanted more information and had questions, she wouldn't shy away. Although Arlo had taken Sid's article and the Morpeth ledger, the combination of her memory and the notes she'd made had given her more than enough factual information.

A pair of young boys called to her and waved their cloth caps before leaping off the road as she sped past, anticipation and a grin she couldn't control fueling her pace. This was going to be her big start—not a fluffy piece for women readers but a serious investigative article with political and social ramifications. No one else was going to take the credit for it. The more she'd thought about it, the more she'd concluded that the law about adoption needed to be changed. Stella would agree, and if she could organize a meeting with Rose Scott, she might be able to get her thoughts on the matter of adoption, which would add weight to the argument.

Verity padlocked her bicycle to the railing behind the building and bounded up the stairwell. Despite the gloom, her feet followed the familiar route and in a matter of moments she stood outside Mr. Bailey's office.

Through the textured glass she could see the outline of his head shrouded in a wreath of cigarette smoke. She knocked on the door, opened it, and stuck her head around the corner.

"Verity." He stubbed out his cigarette. "Come in. Sit down."

"I wondered if you'd read my piece on the Treadwell Foundation." She pressed her fingernails into the palms of her hands; it hadn't occurred to her she'd be so nervous. She'd known Mr. Bailey since she'd worn a school uniform.

He tapped a cigarette from the packet and spent an eternity trying to get the Zippo lighter to catch, then inhaled deeply. "I have, Verity. I have." He blew out a cloud of smoke. "Bottom line—can't publish it."

"Can't publish it? Why not? It's outrageous. The Treadwell Foundation is receiving a large amount from the Red Cross, part of the money raised at the Artists' Ball. You said you'd publish it. People deserve to know—"

"Verity, wait . . ."

An unpleasant queasiness swamped her. What was he talking about? There couldn't be anything wrong with the writing; she'd gone over it a hundred times before the final copy. There might be a few changes, sentences he didn't like . . .

"There's nothing wrong with it; in fact, I'd say it's your best work yet. But I simply can't publish a story that defames a reputable citizen who is held in high regard by people in positions of significant importance in the city. Our editorial policies are based upon candor, honesty, and honor. Both your father and grandfather understood. We have no wish to mislead or defame."

Verity dropped her head into her hands. "But it's true," she mumbled.

He held out the bundle of paper she'd left on his desk, the red slash through the first page as bright as a beacon. "I spoke to Treadwell. I thought he should have the opportunity to comment. He pointed out, in great detail, that he was doing nothing illegal."

A prickle of apprehension traced her skin. "Of course he'd deny it." She let out a moan of indignation.

"It's perfectly legal for doctors or community organizations to facilitate fostering or adoption arrangements."

"But not for births to be registered to people who are not the parents."

"You have no proof of that."

"But I have. I . . ." Verity let the remainder of the sentence evaporate. She couldn't quote Stella as an example without her permission after she'd promised not to mention her name, and thanks to Arlo, she had no other proof because she'd allowed him to convince her to return the ledger. It was almost as though Arlo and Mr. Bailey were in cahoots.

"Take it." Mr. Bailey brushed a trail of cigarette ash from the pages. "You'll thank me for this one day, Verity. Now, off you go, and write me another of those lovely pieces about bicycles or social events. The David Jones Christmas catalogue's due out soon. It'll have some interesting new fashions."

He had to be joking. She snatched the sheaf of paper from his hand, stuffed it into her satchel, and left, not daring to utter another word.

It was a ridiculous diversion, but the sun was shining and Verity needed to clear her head. Without thinking where she was going—head down, legs pumping, the waves of indignation clogging her chest—she cycled on and on. Gradually her angst abated and the air cleared.

The clattering of halyards filled her ears and the salty breeze blowing in across the harbor teased her nostrils. Where was she? Cruising to a halt, she stared out across the sweep of the bay to the North Shore. With a jolt she swung around. The gates of Treadwell House loomed ahead.

Two large vans and a dray stood in the driveway; men scuttling like disturbed ants ferried furniture from the house and down the steps. She threw her bicycle against the hedge and strode up the driveway. What did she have to lose? If Treadwell was there, so be it. He couldn't do much to her in front of a crowd of workmen.

On second thought, maybe her reception from Mrs. Treadwell might be better.

"Excuse me. I'm looking for Mrs. Treadwell."

A large bloke with a florid face wiped his hands down his leather apron. "She ain't here and he's not neither. Ask the girl. She's organizing everything." He pointed to the front door.

Slumped against the column, arms folded and a scowl on her face, stood Mary, the maid. Apron dirty, no sign of her lace cap, and her hair in disarray. Verity crossed the driveway and mounted the steps.

"If you'd shown up an hour later wouldn't be no one here. We're packing up. Let me guess . . . you're owed money?"

Verity shook her head. "I wanted to have a word with Mrs. Treadwell."

"They ain't here. Just me and Cook left to sort out this shambles." Her hand sketched a wide arc. "And we won't get paid neither. Them's the bailiffs." She flicked her thumb at the men gathered around one of the vans.

"But what about the girls booked to stay?" Mr. Millar had told Stella there had been no visitors since Mrs. Barnett died, but there was no harm in getting confirmation.

"Girls? What girls? We haven't had no guests, not since Mrs. Barnett copped it. Nigh on six months ago. None of the shops will deliver no more. There's no food in the house. Cook and I ain't been paid for months. I reckon they've done a runner. Hang on a tick." She heaved upright and slipped back into the house.

Verity jumped to one side as two men mumbling a string of curses wrangled a heavy piece of furniture down the steps. They as good as dropped their cargo at the back of the closest van and wandered away.

So the Treadwells had left, done a runner, but when? Had Mr. Bailey's visit caused them to leave? It could only have been this morning. In fact, he might not even have come here. They could have met in the city. Mary had said they hadn't been paid and there was no food in the house. It couldn't have been a decision made on the spur of the moment. And the bailiffs—surely they didn't turn up out of the blue. A dray and two vans . . . Her breath caught. The desk—the one from the library—sat in the middle of the driveway. Was there a possibility that the ledger could be in the desk drawer? Unlikely but worth a try.

Throwing a quick glance over her shoulder, she shot down the steps. The two men were lolling against the side of the van, stealing a quick cigarette. Mary was nowhere to be seen. The dray driver looked as though he was catching some shut-eye. She crept to the back of the van and eased open the desk drawer.

Nothing. Not even a pencil stub. Could it still be on the library shelves where she'd left it?

She marched back up the steps, head held high, no point in looking guilty. Mary hadn't returned. With a quick glance over her shoulder, she entered the house and scuttled into the library.

Without the furniture the room seemed cavernous, but the bookshelves remained. Maybe faux books didn't have much value. She tipped the covers and reached behind them. Her fingers closed around the ledger. She tucked it into her waistband and pulled down her jacket, then left the room. Once she stood in the middle of the hallway she called, "Mary, are you there, Mary?"

Two minutes later Mary wandered out from the back of the house. "You still here?"

"I just wanted to let you know I was leaving. If you hear from Mr. or Mrs. Treadwell, would you let them know I called please?"

"Unlikely." Mary raised her eyebrows to the heavens. "I've got things to do."

With a smile, Verity left the house and made her way down the driveway toward her bicycle, trying to restrain the spring in her step and the need to keep checking over her shoulder to make certain no one had followed her.

Heart beating nineteen to the dozen, she swung onto the saddle and pedaled off. Stealing again. She was making quite a habit of it, but there might be other women, like Stella, who wanted to find their children, know if they were safe and happy. And there was a strong likelihood Mr. Bailey might think differently if he learned about the Treadwells' hurried departure. But before she could go and see Mr. Bailey again, she needed to speak to Arlo. She couldn't get out of her mind the possibility that he was behind Mr. Bailey's refusal to publish the article.

CHAPTER 33

MORPETH, 1922

With a sense of determination, Verity stuffed a change of clothes into her satchel. She couldn't let the story die— her own flesh and blood, the sister she'd always wanted. She could hardly rewrite the Treadwell piece and tell the full story without including the information in Mrs. Barnett's Morpeth notebook, which Arlo had taken with him, nor could she fail to mention the Breckenridge family. Arlo had said the relationship between Mrs. Barnett and his family was longstanding, and if time was any indication, a close one. Surely Arlo would see the importance of uncovering the full truth about Mrs. Barnett.

Well before midday she was sitting on a train heading for Newcastle, the Treadwell Foundation ledger open on her lap and her notebook at hand. Since she was intent on revealing the truth, the least she could do was ensure she understood the evidence.

Once they'd left the outskirts of Sydney, the train picked up speed, clunking and clattering, spewing buckets of black grimy smoke and thick steam. Verity latched the window and sank into a tale of heartache and misery dating back thirty years.

Entry after entry showed the birth of healthy babies and

the names of adopting parents, a shopping list of requirements: male or female; fair, dark, or red hair; even eye color. Grandma Clarrie said most babies' eye color changed in their first year of life, though Charlie's hadn't. He'd had piercing blue eyes right from the moment he was born. But then Clarrie had always thought Charlie was pretty special.

Pushing back the memories, she returned to the ledger. Far worse than the shopping list was the number of babies who failed to thrive, receipts for the cost of funeral expenses and death certificates. Rubbing her hands up and down her arms, she shrank farther into her coat, trying to quell the creeping sense of anguish and distress.

By the time she reached Newcastle her notebook was full of examples she could add to the article, her penciled shorthand smudged by her tears and her determination further entrenched. She would not allow Arlo or Mr. Bailey to stand in the way of the truth.

The train for Maitland was waiting at the platform, and since she didn't have her bicycle to contend with, she jumped aboard. Through the window the passing scenery flickered, brick buildings giving way to farmland and barns, glimpses of the Hunter River and green fields before the lace-encrusted buildings of Maitland came into view and the train slowed.

Without her bicycle she would simply have to rely on the Morpeth tram. Sitting in the offices of *The Morpeth Want* with Arlo, she'd heard the trams rattling by, shaking the building.

Verity spotted Arlo through the window, sitting in the archive room, poring over an array of handwritten notes and newspapers. She rapped on the glass and watched with a certain amount of pleasure as he jumped and spun around, his expression one of bewilderment.

He left the desk and greeted her at the door. "What a surprise." No sign of the usual smile, but then he'd have to be a fool to think she was paying a social call. Arlo was a lot of things, but she couldn't accuse him of that.

"I want to talk to you. I thought I'd have the opportunity before you left Sydney, but when I called into the Australian Hotel I discovered you'd gone."

A touch of color highlighted his cheeks. "I had to get back." He gestured down the hall to the print room. "Problems with the press. Would you like to come in?"

Finally. "Thank you."

She swept past him into the archive room, determined not to be swayed by the flutter in her heart. Her foot caught in the rug and he reached out his hand to steady her. Her stomach lurched.

She spun around to face him, the force of her anger taking her breath. "Mr. Bailey rejected my piece. What right have either of you to act as censor? Just because your family is involved doesn't mean this appalling miscarriage of justice should be covered up. You're no better than the Treadwells."

An infuriating grin tilted the corner of his lips. She threw her satchel down on the desk, pulled out her notebook, and stared at the pages covered with her blurred shorthand. "Hundreds of girls, their babies taken from them. My own sister will never know her mother; worse, she may have died."

His eyes widened. "Verity, sit down. Please." He pulled a chair up to the desk and held it for her. "Come on, sit down."

With a groan of pure exasperation, she slumped down. "I am determined to piece together the full story. I will not be silenced. I want the Morpeth ledger."

He moved around to the other side of the desk and pulled open the drawer. "Here's the ledger." He pushed it toward her.

Hand shaking, she covered it with her palm.

"Now tell me about your sister."

"You'd know if you hadn't stormed off and disappeared. That's why I took you to Stella's gallery. I wanted us to tell you together." She choked back a sob.

Arlo's warm hands came down on her shoulders. "Tell me now." Verity drew in a steadying breath and squeezed her eyes closed. Would Stella forgive her? If it meant finding Charlotte, she would. She'd said she'd do anything to find her.

She snapped her eyes open, saw the depth of compassion in Arlo's eyes. "Stella's daughter, Charlotte, who was taken from her against her will, is my half sister. Charlie's daughter. She was born at Treadwell House."

"Your sister?" Arlo scrubbed his hand over his chin. "I did see Mr. Bailey when I was in Sydney, but we didn't discuss you or what you had written. We didn't discuss Treadwell House, neither did I tell him of our relationship."

"Keeping more secrets," she snapped.

"Will you let me finish?" He shook his head and threw himself down in the chair. "After I left Stella's, I went to the Glebe Hotel. I spent the time at the bar, asking questions, which is where I came across Bailey."

Not what she had expected at all.

"And that evening I wrote up my findings before they rang about the press. I got the milk train back to Morpeth yesterday morning."

"Findings?" she squeaked. "What findings?"

"The Treadwell ledger covered a period of time from the early 1890s to the present day. Correct?"

"Not entirely, no. It ended six months ago." She reached into her satchel, pulled out the Treadwell ledger.

Arlo scratched his head and leaned toward her. "Where did you get that?"

"Let's say I retrieved it from the bailiffs."

"Bailiffs?"

"The ones who were stripping Treadwell House."

"Treadwell House?"

He was beginning to sound like a parrot. She couldn't wait for him to weave his excuses. "Did you ask Mr. Bailey not to publish my piece about Treadwell House?"

He shook his head. "I've told you. We didn't discuss you or Treadwell House. I'm not even sure Bailey knows of our association. I thought it better that way."

Then what had they discussed? She shook her head in a vain attempt to make sense of his words. "Mr. Bailey spoke to Treadwell about my story. He said a man of Treadwell's standing in the community should have the right of reply." Verity ignored another frustrated sigh from Arlo and plowed on. "Needless to say, Treadwell refuted it. So Bailey refused to publish. I was angry. It reminded me of your father—the way he'd silenced Grandpa Sid. I took off on my bicycle and found myself outside Treadwell House. Mary, the maid, told me the Treadwells had left before the bailiffs arrived, that the place hadn't operated since Mrs. Barnett passed away and that they were all owed money. I sneaked into the library and retrieved the ledger. Mary was right; there are no entries for the last six months, no income, no outgoings. Mary said none of them had been paid and there'd been no 'clients.'" She couldn't restrain her sarcasm.

Arlo threaded his fingers and propped his chin on his hands, his river-green eyes pinning her. "And your conclusion?"

"Obviously that Mrs. Barnett was running the business. Your aunt, Mrs. Treadwell, must have known about it. I suspect her son's bid for the donations from the Artists' Ball was through necessity, to shore up the family's failing finances. And I think Mrs. Barnett, *your* family's one-time housekeeper"— she couldn't help but slip that dig in—"was responsible for the somewhat upmarket version of the baby farming exercise she'd operated in Morpeth and Maitland. The only thing I don't understand is what she was doing between Grandpa Sid uncovering her dealings and the early 1890s, when the Treadwell Foundation opened." There, she'd said it. Laid everything out on the table.

A heavy silence burgeoned, like thunderclouds before a storm. Verity squirmed, opened her mouth several times to add more, but managed to refrain and hold Arlo's piercing scrutiny.

Finally, he rocked back in his chair. "That's what I was trying to tell you. I have a theory about the intervening years, although I don't have any proof. The Glebe Hotel is where all the newspapermen, old and young, congregate. The perfect place to get answers—they've all got memories that would put an elephant to shame. It seems there were baby farming enterprises all over the country at that time. It was the ones in Sydney that interested me particularly: one in Richmond, another sometime later on the Lane Cove River, and one in Woollahra." He swung his hand in an arc over the desk. "We don't have a ledger covering those years, but I would put money on Mrs. Barnett being behind them. The operations were all similar to the one detailed in the Morpeth ledger. The two old codgers I spoke to remembered the cases, and they maintained the same person was behind all three; that person was never found or brought to trial."

With a clunk, the pieces of the puzzle fell into place. "And you think Mrs. Barnett was responsible?"

"I think when Florence Treadwell's husband died, she was left with a huge property, a standing in society, a young son, and no way of supporting their lifestyle."

"But the Treadwells were rich." They must have been. "They owned that huge house in one of the smartest suburbs in Sydney and led a lavish lifestyle."

"Originally, yes. The depression in the 1890s brought many an old family down. So here's my theory. I think my aunt found herself in financial difficulties when her husband, old Mr. Treadwell, died. She had no one to turn to: she was estranged from her sisters; The Landing no longer belonged to the Breckenridge family; she'd received her dowry and it was all she was entitled to. Mother was bordering on destitute when she and Father married; she'd paid out her sisters' dowries. All Florence had was Treadwell House, the building, and no means of supporting herself or her son. Viola and Constance were in England; perhaps Florence reached out to them, perhaps not.

"Somehow she and Mrs. Barnett reconnected; maybe they had never lost touch. Mrs. Barnett came to her rescue, and the one-time family mansion became the Treadwell Foundation and it flourished. Sufficiently to see young Treadwell through school and university and into a reputable position in Sydney society."

Arlo was still trying to justify his family's involvement, still trying to throw a golden light on the situation. "All funded by the immoral and ill-gotten gains of baby farming," Verity spat. "There are entries showing babies who died, the receipts for the cost of funeral expenses and death certificates."

"Not all babies survive; the deaths might be legitimate.

You said death certificates, so a doctor would have to have been involved. Mrs. Barnett refined the operation—adoption paid well, particularly if you had access to the higher echelons of society. It was foolproof. The babies were registered by the adopting families. Families guaranteed to keep the Treadwell Foundation's secret."

A cold shudder traced Verity's spine. "I didn't really believe Stella when she told me about it initially. I thought she was talking about the last century. She said wealthy women who couldn't produce an heir would falsify a pregnancy, and at times even their husbands were hoodwinked." Heat swarmed up to her face as she realized what she'd said—what the Morpeth notebook detailed, the very first entries. Arlo's mother and her three sisters. "I'm sorry," she murmured.

"Don't be. I don't see the shame in it. If my mother and her sisters were adopted, saved from a life of penury and poverty, is it such a bad thing? An extremely well-run business that developed and expanded over time and ultimately broke no laws. It is not illegal to arrange an adoption, nor to adopt a child."

"Well, it damn well should be if the mother doesn't give her consent! The law needs changing. And it doesn't answer the question of why your father refused to publish Sid's story. Hundreds of babies' lives might have been saved; hundreds of women like Stella would know the fate of their child. I would know my sister." She leaped to her feet, anger heating her blood. "What right had your father to cover up Mrs. Barnett's activities?" And more to the point, why had Grandpa Sid accepted it? "Much of this"—her hand swept the two ledgers—"never would have happened if Grandpa Sid's article had been published and Mrs. Barnett brought to justice."

"I agree."

Arlo's words brought Verity's tirade to a standstill. She threw up her hands. "Then why?"

"Because of this." Arlo picked up the Morpeth ledger and tapped the Breckenridge entries. "It's obvious. The reason my father suppressed Sid's article was to protect the Breckenridge name."

And it was why Sid and Clarrie had left Morpeth and moved to Sydney. Sid had been given an introduction to the job of his dreams to keep the Breckenridges' secret. The job he'd always coveted. Theodora's "thank-you" letter spoke for itself. Sid was as much to blame as the Breckenridge family.

CHAPTER 34

MORPETH, 1922

Mrs. Peers had greeted Verity like a long-lost friend and insisted "her" room was ready and waiting, fed her an enormous meal of battered flathead, and packed her off, telling her she looked tired and drawn and needed a decent night's sleep. Which was all remarkably comforting and had the desired effect because Verity woke invigorated, with a clear plan.

She had to unearth the full story—not the story of the Treadwell Foundation, not Stella's story, not Sid's story, or even that of the Breckenridge family, but the story of Mrs. Barnett. Who was she and where had she come from?

Verity clattered downstairs. She needed local information—truth be told, she needed gossip—but sadly there was no sign of Mrs. Peers. The dining room was set for breakfast, three silver domes on the sideboard. She lifted the first—deviled kidneys—and quickly replaced it. The second harbored scrambled eggs that may well have been delicious an hour or so ago but now sat marooned in a sea of seeping liquid, and, under the third dome, a pile of toast. She took two pieces, poured a cup of lukewarm tea, grabbed a copy of the newspaper, then made her way to a table overlooking the sleepy street.

While she munched her way through the cold toast, she studied the pictures on the walls, the ones she'd seen the first time she'd entered the dining room—the overcrowded quay, the ladies in their fine clothes, carriages and drays. Before Sid's time; before Mrs. Barnett's time too. If she was Mrs. Treadwell's companion, surely they'd have been of a similar age, late seventies? She let out a huff of annoyance. Which meant she would have been in her twenties when Sid and Clarrie came across her. How could she have organized the adoption of the Breckenridge girls? There was so much that didn't tie up. She glanced down at the copy of the *Want* lying next to her plate. If only there was some way she could search the archives without having to wade through every edition, some miraculous means of searching for Mrs. Barnett's name. She flicked through the pages of the newspaper. Not even a photograph, despite the fact they'd been used in the Sydney papers since before the war. Time really had stood still in Morpeth.

As she closed the paper, she spotted a small boxed notice:

The Ladies Reading Circle meets every Wednesday at The Morpeth School of Arts at 10 a.m. We wish to invite new members. An opportunity not only to read and discuss the latest novels but also a meeting place for friends and visitors alike.

Of course! How could she have forgotten? The perfect place to explore the local scuttlebutt. She glanced at the top of the paper, beneath the banner—Wednesday, 20th September, 1922.

On the dot of ten o'clock, Verity pushed open the door to the School of Arts. As before, the hum of chattering voices and a cacophony of laughter greeted her arrival. She made her way to the book-lined room at the back of the building and stuck her head around the door.

"Well, hello there. Miss Binks, isn't it? Back in Morpeth and here to join us. How very delightful."

Verity smiled down at the diminutive white-haired woman she remembered from her first visit. "Yes, that's right. Please call me Verity."

"Come along then, dear, and sit next to me. My name's Mrs. Kelly." She patted the seat next to her with a liver-spotted hand.

Verity unhooked her satchel and hung it on the back of her chair.

"Have you brought the book back?"

"I beg your pardon?"

"*My Brilliant Career.* You borrowed a copy last time you were here."

For goodness' sake. What had she done with it? She must have taken it back to Sydney and, in the rush of the last week, forgotten all about it. "I'm so sorry. I've left it in Sydney."

"Why don't you post it when you get home? We like to keep sufficient copies for the group. We've been advertising for new members. Are you here for a longer stay this time?"

She hadn't thought her plans through, just acted on impulse again. "I'm searching for some information about my father. He was born in Morpeth." And that was the truth, not like her foolish Sid pilgrimage. Charlie had suffered at Mrs. Barnett's hands, if Sid's article was to be believed.

"Binks—that'd be Charlie, Sid and Clarrie's son."

Verity's mouth dropped open. "You knew Sid and Clarrie?"

"Ladies, ladies. Please. We'd like to begin."

Mrs. Kelly smiled reassuringly. "We'll talk later."

The meeting dragged on, slower than the Darlinghurst tram. Try as she might, Verity couldn't concentrate on the conversation around the table. Every minute or two she'd sneak a glance at Mrs. Kelly, trying to guess her age, looking at her hands, the nails buffed and the skin—though spotted with age—smooth, her patterned cotton dress bright, hair neatly pulled back in a tight bun.

A couple of times Verity pushed back her chair, the temptation to leave almost overpowering, but on both occasions Mrs. Kelly reached out and patted her hand as much as to say "patience."

Finally, someone passed a book across to her. She glanced down at the title: *Norah of Billabong* by Mary Grant Bruce. Not an author she'd heard of, but a woman, at least. A woman who, if the first pages were anything to go by, was making quite a career out of writing—author of *A Little Bush Maid*, *Mates at Billabong*, *Glen Eyre*, *Timothy in Bushland*, and many more.

"Now we can leave." Mrs. Kelly placed her hands flat on the table and rose with a groan. She reached for her walking stick. "Would you like to come out into the garden? There's a lovely bench seat under the apple tree."

"Don't forget your books, ladies. We'll meet again next week." A nameless woman tapped the table with her index finger.

Verity picked up her copy of *Norah*, and Mrs. Kelly's,

smiled her thanks, and followed Mrs. Kelly out of the room to the back of the building, a strange fluttering in her chest.

"There we are. It's a lovely spot." Mrs. Kelly lowered herself onto the seat with a wheeze and hung her stick on the armrest. "The scourge of age. Although I shouldn't complain. I lost dear Mr. Kelly some ten years ago, but life goes on. Now, where were we?"

"You said you knew Sid and Clarrie, my grandparents. And my father, Charlie?"

"Indeed I did. In fact, I can rightly claim that I brought young Charlie into the world in my cottage in Swan Street, down near the river."

Speechless, Verity stared at the woman, racking her brain for anything Clarrie or Sid may have said that she'd failed to remember. Why hadn't she asked more questions when she'd had the opportunity?

"He'd be a fine man by now. Such a bonny blue-eyed boy with a shock of corn-colored hair, much like your own."

Verity swallowed, licked her dry lips. "He died in Palestine, during the war."

"We lost so many brave men. And Sid and Clarrie?"

"They've gone too." Tears sprang unbidden to her eyes.

"Sid had a heart of gold. If Clarrie hadn't caught his eye I wouldn't have thought twice." Mrs. Kelly reached for her hand again. "And you're all alone in this world?"

She lowered her head, the beginning of a nod, not trusting herself to speak, and stopped. "No. No I'm not. I have a half sister, Charlotte." That was why she was here and why she had to grasp this opportunity before it slipped through her fingers. "I wondered if you knew a Mrs. Barnett."

Mrs. Kelly removed her hand and shifted slightly on the bench seat. Verity followed suit until they were face-to-face.

"Yes, I did. A very long time ago. It's time her story was told."

Arlo paced the footpath outside the Commercial. He'd imagined the information he'd uncovered would have in some way appeased Verity, but she'd left last afternoon without giving him the benefit of her opinion. After her revelation about Charlotte, he understood her determination that the story should be published, but he also understood why his father had suppressed Sid's article to protect the woman he loved. But the Breckenridge family had done no wrong, of that he was certain. The culprit in all of this was Mrs. Barnett.

"How much longer are you going to stand out there wearing out the footpath?"

Mrs. Peers stood on the doorstep, hands on hips and a knowing grin on her face. "She's not here. Ate breakfast and took off without a word."

"And you've no idea where she's gone?"

"Nope. Better come in and I'll pour you an ale. Fancy a bite of lunch?"

He followed her through the door into the cool. "Fred, Joe. How're you doing?" He nodded to the bargemen propping up one end of the bar and slid onto a stool.

Mrs. Peers dumped a foaming glass in front of him, rested her elbows on the bar, and propped her chin in her cupped hands. "You look as though you've lost a quid and found sixpence."

"More like found a quid and lost it in one fell swoop."

"Ah! Girl trouble."

"Girl trouble? Nah!" The cool ale worked its magic. "I've found out my father, Redmond, did something I'm not overproud of, and to add insult to injury, my aunt Florence, whom I hadn't met until a few days ago, was more than likely embroiled in a rather unpleasant business venture."

Rubbing a tea towel around the rim of a glass, Mrs. Peers eyed him. It made him want to squirm. Probably should have kept his mouth shut. "Better out than in. Let's have it."

"What do you remember of Mrs. Barnett, housekeeper at The Landing?"

"That was a while ago. Before my time."

He raised an eyebrow.

"Well, I'd have been just a slip of a girl when she died."

"Died?" His heartbeat picked up, almost loud enough to drum out her words.

"Went down with the *Cawarra*, along with your grandparents and their son."

"I don't believe she did. Mrs. Barnett served the Breckenridge family for many years, until the girls married."

"Edith Barnett did, sure enough, but it was her mother who went down on the *Cawarra*. Edith stepped right into her shoes. She was born at The Landing, grew up there. Knew more about the running of the place than anyone else. Not only that, she'd inherited her mother's skills with herbs and as a midwife."

Arlo's thoughts slipped to the Morpeth ledger. He took off his spectacles, rubbed the bridge of his nose, and tried to visualize the early entries, the neat copperplate handwriting— *female, chestnut hair*; *female, Titian*; *female, strawberry*; *female, copper*—Florence, Theodora, Viola, and Constance.

"Arlo! If you're not interested in what I've got to say, there's better ways for me to spend my time."

He snapped back. "Redmond and Jamie. Father used to talk about the times they had with Mother, trips up the river, Ash Island, and the Scott family . . ." Nothing about Mrs. Barnett. "They can't both be Mrs. Barnett. Surely her daughter would be *Miss* Barnett?"

"Tut, tut. You young things. No idea what life was like back then. It's just a courtesy title. All housekeepers are titled Mrs.—married or not. Not even sure the first Mrs. Barnett was married. Rumor had it some American sailor was young Edith's father. She would have been born about the same time as Jamie, brought up with the daughters." She screwed up her nose and shook her head. "I've got work to do, and unless I'm very much mistaken, that girl of yours is coming down the road."

He threw back the remains of his ale, rummaged in his pocket for some coins. His hand came up empty. "I'll have to owe you for that one."

"Go on, off you go. And don't forget your spectacles."

Arlo hooked the wire over his ears. That was the problem with spending his entire life in one place; it was as though he'd never grown up.

"Verity." His call rolled down the street and just about everyone, except Verity, lifted their head. He caught up with her as she reached the accommodation door around the corner. "I've been waiting for you."

She peered up at him, a vacant look on her face. She was miles away.

"Verity?"

"Hello, Arlo."

"Where have you been?"

"Talking. Talking to Mrs. Kelly at the reading circle. I need to take another look at the Morpeth ledger. Have you got it in the office?"

"I took it home with me last night. I was about to head that way. I want to check the ledger too. I've got news." Actually, he wanted to blurt it all out right there and then. Two women, mother and daughter. It threw a completely different light on the story.

CHAPTER 35

MORPETH, 1922

The wind snatched at Verity's hair, fraying her thoughts as the *Petrel* cut through the current. She hadn't taken a single note as she'd sat listening to Mrs. Kelly, and now she was worried she'd forget some significant point. Most importantly, she wanted to check the ledger and see if there was a record of Charlie's birth. A trickle of excitement pricked her skull.

"Here, take this." Arlo threw the end of the rope to her as the boat bumped against the wharf. "You know the way it works. No dozing on the job."

"I wasn't dozing," she snapped back, balancing on the gunwale, ready to leap ashore as soon as the gap narrowed.

"My mistake."

She twisted around and caught the grin on his face. She had to stop being so unpleasant.

Once she'd fastened the rope, she waited while Arlo did whatever it was he did to the engine. To her right stood a lovely little building, a folly that she hadn't paid very much attention to on her first visit. It was perfectly placed overlooking the river, and beyond it stood the remains of a wall with a small arched window. "Was that the original house?" she asked as Arlo reached her side.

"Just another bit of whimsy. My grandfather had them built, part of the gardens. That's where my mother and father are buried." He gestured to a low brick wall surrounding a rambling garden. "An old monastery once stood on the site of my grandmother's family home in Cornwall. This is a replica of the remains. Would you like to have a look?"

More of the Breckenridge fairy-tale romance. She'd love to look at the garden, but first she had to unravel the not-so-pleasant side of the story, and she had no intention of sharing Mrs. Kelly's information until she'd checked the Morpeth ledger and knew she was dealing with fact and not tittle-tattle. "Maybe later. Another day? I really need to look at the ledger."

"Right you are. Business before pleasure." He smiled down at her, threaded his arm through hers, and led her along the path.

"My father's study." Arlo drew back the heavy brocade curtains, revealing a large cedar desk and a leather swivel chair. Bunched up on the floor beside it lay a crumpled white dust sheet. "This is where I found Sid's article and the Morpeth ledger." He pulled open the bottom drawer and took out the ledger. "Come and sit down." He stood behind the swivel chair and gave it a spin. "It's the newspaper proprietor's desk; been handed down through the family. Not that I ever use it. I feel as though I'm wearing my father's old clothes."

Verity dropped her satchel on the floor and sat in the chair, swinging first one way and then the other.

"It suits you."

"Bit above my station."

"You never know. Now what is it you want to find in the ledger?" He leaned over the desk and switched on a green-shaded lamp.

Verity didn't intend to keep Mrs. Kelly's story quiet; it was more that she wanted to prove it before she made a fool of herself and offered some half-baked theory. She reached for the ledger and fanned the pages.

Arlo parked himself on the corner of the desk, legs stretched out, watching her every move.

"I'm looking for Charlie's birthdate. May 5th, 1868."

"I doubt that'll be recorded in there. I've been through it from cover to cover. Full of expenses interspersed with . . . It doesn't paint a pretty picture." He shook his head. "Baby farming, without a doubt. Houses here, in Maitland and Newcastle. I can't understand why she wasn't caught."

"Do you remember Sid's article where it said his son had suffered at the hands of this despicable woman?"

"I do, because Sid and Clarrie registered Charlie's birth in Sydney, you said later in the year after they'd married. I rather presumed it was a scare."

His words washed over her as she tracked the dates. Toward the end of the ledger her finger came to rest on the final entries—May 1868. "Here it is."

Arlo leaned forward, pressed his nose almost to the pages of the book. "Read it to me; the light's not good enough." He rubbed his hand over his face and blinked like a disturbed koala.

"May 5th, 1868. Male, fair hair, blue eyes. Swan Street. Lying-in costs."

Her finger traced to the right-hand page.

"Clarrie, Morpeth . . . Received 12/6 lying-in. May 10th,

1868 . . . Received 9/Two weeks care. May 12th Oswald, Sydney, Adoption fee £100 to be paid on delivery."

Verity's voice caught on a sob and she clamped her hand over her mouth, a sense of utter helplessness swamping her.

Silence filled the room.

Arlo took the ledger and closed it with a snap. "There's something you're not telling me."

She brushed the tears from her cheeks. "Mrs. Kelly was telling the truth. She's the midwife who delivered Charlie and looked after him."

"Why is it that I feel as though I've missed the point? I think you'd better explain."

Verity sucked in a lungful of dusty air. "There's one other thing I need to clarify first." She took out the Treadwell ledger and lay the two books next to each other. "The Morpeth ledger began in 1845 and Charlie's adoption in 1868 was the final entry; the Treadwell ledger began in 1894 and ended six months ago, when Mrs. Barnett died. It doesn't make sense. Mrs. Barnett would have had to be over a hundred if she was responsible for the entries in both ledgers."

"Ah!" Arlo bent his head and ran his finger across the dates. "I can answer that question. The Morpeth ledger was started by Mrs. Barnett and continued after her death by her daughter—also Mrs. Barnett. Edith Barnett."

A streak of anger rushed through Verity. "Why didn't you tell me?"

"Because I didn't know until . . ." He twisted his wrist and pushed up his cuff, checking his watch. "About an hour ago."

"An hour ago! Who? How?"

"Mrs. Peers."

"Why didn't she tell me?"

"I don't expect she thought you'd be interested. I had a chat with her while I was waiting for you. Mrs. Barnett senior, the original housekeeper, died on the *Cawarra* with my grand-parents and their son, Jamie. Her daughter, Edith Barnett, who'd grown up here, picked up the reins and stepped into the role of housekeeper and, it would seem, took over her mother's business." He wrinkled his nose in distaste.

"How could they both be Mrs. Barnett?"

"According to Mrs. Peers, all housekeepers are given the title Mrs., whether they're married or not."

Such a simple answer. Why hadn't she known that? "But the handwriting, the penmanship. It's almost identical." She traced her finger over the perfectly formed copperplate script.

"My mother's writing is the same; my father's not so much."

Verity unfolded Sid's article. "Sid's penmanship wasn't the best, hardly legible."

"I doubt he had a formal education. Now, are you going to tell me about this Mrs. Kelly?"

Verity pushed out of the chair. The atmosphere of the room was as depressing as the story she had to tell. "Can we open the window, or go outside, perhaps?"

"Of course." He led the way out of the house and through the overlong grass to the walled garden.

Verity inhaled the fresh breeze blowing in from the river laced with the scent of the herbs and flowers coming into bloom and settled on the ruined wall, Arlo next to her.

"I went back to the reading circle. That was where I first heard the story of your grandparents." A flush of heat warmed her cheeks. "I thought I might hear some more tid-bits that would fill in the blanks. I wanted to see if anyone remembered Mrs. Barnett. I spoke to an older woman; she remembered me from the first time I'd visited. Looking back,

I think she'd recognized my name—I'm sure she had. When we started talking, she asked after Charlie, Sid, and Clarrie. She told me she was the local midwife and she'd delivered Charlie and looked after him when he was a baby. She lived in one of the cottages in Swan Street, which she rented from Mrs. Barnett."

Behind his pebble spectacles, Arlo blinked furiously. "She was a baby farmer? Why would she admit to that?"

"She didn't, and she seemed very upset that she'd been involved. Her mother was also a midwife and taught her the trade, and when she died, Mrs. Kelly, Maud, carried on. But she was young and inexperienced and couldn't cope. She fell behind with the rent, and Mrs. Barnett suggested that she advertise for babies to adopt or care for and in that way she'd be able to pay the arrears. That was when the baby farming began; it was Edith Barnett's idea. It hadn't occurred to me that there were two Mrs. Barnetts. It wasn't until I was having breakfast that I started wondering about Mrs. Barnett's age."

"And what about Charlie?"

"Mrs. Kelly told me the whole story."

Arlo leaped up. "Well, come on! What happened?"

"Sid and Clarrie were paying her to look after Charlie. It's recorded in the ledger. I think she'd taken a shine to Sid and Clarrie, said they were a lovely young couple, and when Clarrie got herself a job here, Mrs. Kelly cared for Charlie. Unknown to her, Edith Barnett had found a family in Sydney who wanted to adopt Charlie; that's in the ledger too. '*May 12th Oswald, Sydney, Adoption fee £100 to be paid on delivery.*'" Her voice wavered.

Arlo leaned closer, reached for her hand, and squeezed her fingers. His encouragement gave her strength. Mrs. Kelly's story made her blood run cold, not only because of Charlie's near miss but also the horror of those poor babies who'd been disposed of like unwanted kittens. She beat back the thought. "Edith Barnett arrived at Mrs. Kelly's house unexpectedly and took Charlie. Mrs. Kelly tried to stop her, to tell her Sid and Clarrie were coming to visit Charlie, but she threatened her, said she'd dob her in to the authorities if she mentioned a word."

"But that's ridiculous. She should have stuck up for herself, told the truth."

"Arlo, she was scared. Edith Barnett had standing in the community; everyone knew her, she worked for the Breckenridge family, and she even had a reputation as a healer. She made all sorts of herbal tonics, lotions, salves, and potions, which she sold from here to Newcastle." Verity huffed out her displeasure and pulled her hand away. Why couldn't he understand the position Mrs. Kelly was in? A young woman having to fend for herself. "Do you want to hear the rest or not?"

"I'm sorry. Yes, tell me."

"When Sid and Clarrie got to Mrs. Kelly's, she told them a friend had taken Charlie out for some fresh air, for a walk down by the river to watch the boats, hoping they'd give chase. She didn't find out what had happened until Sid came back to see her."

Arlo flinched and gave a small yelp. "Sid took Charlie back to her?"

"Of course he didn't. Your mother invited Clarrie to bring Charlie here, to The Landing."

"Go on." Arlo reached for her hand again, and this time she didn't pull away. His warm grasp gave her strength. "How did they find Charlie?"

Arlo's eyes never left Verity's face as she recounted the story Mrs. Kelly had told her.

"Edith Barnett was at Ash Island?"

"That's what Mrs. Kelly said. Clarrie and Sid found Charlie in the basement of the Scotts' old house. Mrs. Barnett had hidden him in her carpetbag. The bag she used to deliver babies to adopting parents and"—Verity couldn't control the wobble in her voice—"the way she disposed of the babies that didn't thrive. She threw their poor little bodies into the river from the steamer."

Arlo wrinkled his nose. "And how on earth did Mrs. Kelly find out?" The tone of skepticism lacing his voice made Verity's hackles rise. "Are you sure this isn't just local gossip?"

"I'm positive. A man called Hench was caretaking the place, an American sailor who'd worked for the Breckenridge family."

"An American?" Arlo raked his hair back, practically knocking his glasses off in the process. "Mrs. Peers mentioned an American sailor," he murmured. "Go on."

"Hench tried to stop them. He knocked your mother out and Edith Barnett and Hench vanished. Sid and Clarrie found Charlie in the bag, and underneath his blanket they found the ledger."

"For goodness' sake. It's ridiculously far-fetched."

"How do you think your father got hold of the Morpeth ledger? That, and the information from Mrs. Kelly, formed the basis for Sid's article. The one your father scuppered."

Arlo dropped his head into his hands, scratched at his hair, took off his spectacles, and blinked at her. "Why would Mrs. Kelly tell you all this?"

"She said she'd kept quiet for too long and the story needed to be told. She hadn't understood the full extent of

Mrs. Barnett's business until Sid showed her the ledger. As soon as she could she left Swan Street and married Mr. Kelly not long afterward. I told you, she was terrified she'd be accused of baby farming."

"I'm not surprised. There's more than enough evidence in that ledger to send anyone to the gallows."

"But nothing that incriminates Mrs. Kelly. I believe her. None of the children in her care died, and she had no idea that Mrs. Barnett had sold Charlie to the people in Sydney. She was lucky that Sid and Clarrie got there in time and saved Charlie."

"Shame Mrs. Barnett didn't have to pay, wasn't brought to justice."

"I think fate played a hand. By all accounts she died a horrible death." Verity sighed. "It's too late now."

"But not too late for us." The timbre of Arlo's voice deepened and he reached out and brushed her hand with his fingers. "Look what you've achieved. You've uncovered an extortion racket spanning seventy years. One that has caused untold misery, anguish, and suffering."

"I didn't do it by myself. We worked together, and now we have the opportunity to make a difference, make sure the law is changed."

His eyes blazed in response, and something more, something that made her heartbeat quicken.

She raised her palm to her face, unsure whether the look on Arlo's face or the excitement of their achievement had caused her flurry of emotions. Captivated by the intensity in his river-green eyes, she asked, "What are we going to do?"

"Do what my father should have done in the first place. In the immortal words of Wellington, publish and be damned."

EPILOGUE

Verity handed the copy of *The Morpeth Want* to Stella. "I thought you might like to keep this."

"I'm going to frame it. That's all I wanted." Stella's voice wavered as she read the words aloud from the new Child Welfare Act: "'That the parents of the child or such one of them as is living consent or consents to the adoption or if the child is illegitimate that the mother consents to the adoption.' But for you, this clause might not have been included."

"There's a lot more that needs to be done. It's not the end, you know. Wouldn't it be wonderful if children could be allowed to contact their birth mother? Did Mr. Millar have any success?"

"He did." A beautiful smile lit Stella's face. "The Greenes were delightful. Perhaps not at first—I think my letter worried them enormously—but Mrs. Greene agreed to meet with me. She brought some photographs with her. Charlotte is gorgeous . . ." Tears welled. "She has Charlie's smile and his big blue eyes."

Verity's heart twisted as she contemplated her friend, the

mother of her half sister. She reached out and took Stella's hand. "Will you meet her?"

"One day I hope we both will. I promised Mrs. Greene I would leave the decision to her, when they thought Charlotte was old enough to understand. But what about you?" She raised her head, her attention drifting to the wharf, a smile tipping her lips.

Verity tried and failed to control the fluttery sensation in her breast. Arlo, stripped to the waist, was tinkering with the sails on the *Petrel*. He'd decided to remove the engine and reinstall the original sails. She wasn't so sure it was the best idea, but he seemed determined, although he had difficulty explaining his motives. He'd said he wanted to make his own mark and didn't want to live in the shadow of his father. Which was all a little strange, because since she'd moved to Morpeth, the newspaper had gone from strength to strength. It had started with the publication of her article about the Treadwell Foundation, which then appeared in newspapers around Australia—even *The Sydney Arrow*, which had afforded her an enormous amount of satisfaction. As a result, *The Morpeth Want* was now back to a three-day-a-week publishing schedule.

However, despite her every effort, she'd failed to track down the Treadwells. Even Mr. Millar had drawn a blank, though he had managed to unearth the story of Edith Barnett's demise. It wasn't pleasant, but it did explain what she had been doing in Surry Hills.

Edith had established a lucrative sideline selling a "Ladies Tonic" that claimed to be a sure and prompt cure of all complaints incidental to the female system. Put simply, it was an herbal abortifacient—it claimed to terminate unwanted pregnancies. After exhaustive inquiries, Mr. Millar had come to the conclusion that Edith Barnett's fall beneath the wheels of the motor van had been no accident. The gossip was correct. She was pushed. There had been many dissatisfied customers, but no one would talk.

"Come for a walk, Verity." Stella rose and strolled across the garden, her hand trailing, each touch releasing the pungent scent of the vast array of herbs.

"I'll be there in a moment." How she wished she could talk to Grandpa Sid and ask his advice. In the past year she'd spent more time in Morpeth than she had in Sydney, and the house in The Rocks had sat vacant. She'd been so busy. Arlo had moved his father's desk back to the newspaper office, along with the swivel chair, and as he'd predicted, the position did suit her. He'd handed over the running of the paper to her while he had meticulously collated all his mother's research and spent many hours down at the Australian Museum talking to the entomologist, Arthur Bardwell, who had confirmed Theodora had in fact recorded the first sighting of the Wanderer butterfly—the earlier sighting Mr. Olliff's notes referred to—and Arlo had donated her sketchbook and some of her specimens to the museum.

The satisfactory result had given him the time to do what he loved most, and with the aid of a new Eastman Kodak camera, he'd begun recording the waterbirds on the Hunter. He hadn't said anything, but she'd noticed what looked suspiciously like the beginnings of a book.

Verity forced her contemplation from the wharf and concentrated on the garden and all the plants she'd tended under the watchful eye of the old man, Archer, who still pottered around. She mentally ticked the plants off as the sweet, spicy perfume with a hint of honey wafted toward her, her attention lighting on the hedge of cotton bush following the curve of the wall, the carefully prepared beds, the flowers budding, the brilliant white creating a stunning display among the orange and red blooms.

Over the past year she'd spent every moment that she wasn't behind the desk at *The Morpeth Want* in the garden. Archer swore she'd given him a new lease on life as together they'd restored the beds, drawing on Theodora's paintings when Archer's memory failed.

And now, with the arrival of spring and Stella's news, the air sang with hope.

A shadow caught the edge of her vision and she stood squinting into the sun. A light graze brushed her fingertips. A butterfly hovered, wings drawing in and out, lifting and falling. Not any butterfly—striking orange with black and white markings.

Slowly releasing her breath, she reached out tentative fingers, her hand shaking. The butterfly's wings grazed her skin as it flew away, then came to rest on the cotton bush blooms.

Not daring to utter a sound, she wound her way to the back of the garden where the brightly colored hedge hid the old wall. A streaming cascade of fluttering wings hovered, translucent against the sunlight, liberated in a single gust. A cloud of orange and black and, with the sound of hundreds of wings beating in synchronized harmony, the butterflies took flight.

Lifting her skirt, Verity gave chase across the spongy tufted grass to the open meadow where each butterfly hovered and danced above the sea of flowers, their first taste of nectar giving them strength for the moment they'd ensure their species survival.

Her pulse pounded, an awed gasp burning deep inside her lungs. She sank onto the low stone wall where the meadow gave way to the tended beds of the walled garden, crossed the fingers on both hands, and waited for the butterflies to settle again and lay their eggs. It was enough to know that Theodora's dream had come true. How she wished Theodora could have witnessed the spectacle.

Arlo's arm wrapped around her shoulder and he pulled her close, the warmth of his regard brighter than the sunshine on her skin. For the first time in longer than she could remember, she felt truly alive.

She'd never believed she'd fall in love, that it would change the color of her world, turning it to a startling hue of brightness, purpose, and joy. The Wanderers, a symbol of love, a memorial to all those who had gone before, had brought that, and she'd made her decision, one she hoped Grandpa Sid would approve. She belonged here at The Landing with Arlo, and one day, in the not-too-distant future, maybe Stella and Charlotte would join them.

HISTORICAL NOTE

*A*s with my other books, *The Butterfly Collector* is a mixture of fact and fiction, the fictional story woven around a selection of historical facts.

Mr. Olliff was the entomologist at the Australian Museum from 1885 to 1889 and was aware of the arrival of the Monarch butterfly on Australian shores. One report states, "All available literature, with one exception, suggests that the Monarch butterfly was not known in Australia until the spring/summer of 1870/71. The exception is an unconfirmed report by Olliff, who states that the butterfly had been seen earlier by a third person near Sydney." (In 1856, in fact. I moved the date for the sake of the fictional timeline.)

Monarch butterflies are now a common sight along the east coast of Australia from Queensland to South Australia, and in Southwestern Australia. During the day, the butterflies fly, but as the temperature drops, they settle for the night in clusters. The butterflies return to the same trees every year and stay until September. Then they mate and fly off in search of food plants, where they lay their eggs. This has been reported in the Sydney Basin and Hunter Valley, as well as the Mt. Lofty Ranges, near Adelaide.

Harriet and Helena Scott donated their collection, acquired

during the writing of their book, *Australian Lepidoptera and Their Transformations*, to the Australian Museum in the late 1860s. Several of the anecdotes in the story are taken from their letters; artists like Conrad Martens, scientists and collectors such as John and Elizabeth Gould, and the explorer Ludwig Leichhardt all visited Ash Island. Leichhardt wrote in 1842 that the island "is a remarkably fine place, not only to enjoy the beauty of nature, a broad shining river, a luxuriant vegetation, a tasteful comfortable cottage with a plantation of orange trees . . . It's a romantic place, which I like well enough to think that—perhaps—I'd be content to live and die there."

The Scotts' family house stood for many years, but sadly all that remains now is the well and a few timbers from the wharf. In 1866, A. W. Scott was declared bankrupt and forced to sell the property. The island was subdivided, cleared, and drained for agriculture and dairy farms. Following a massive flood in 1955, the area fell under State control, and in the 1960s, large-scale industrial development took over and the island was renamed Kooragang Island. The name "Ash Island" now only refers to the land at the western end of this larger island.

In 1983, the Kooragang Nature Reserve was formed, and in 1993, the Kooragang Wetland Rehabilitation Project launched to restore and rehabilitate Ash Island and create new habitat for the diverse wildlife of the estuary. Fortunately, the previous occupants, Helena and Harriet Scott, had been passionate in recording and illustrating the island's botany. These records survived and are being used by KWRP as a management tool to help reestablish areas.

The descriptions of Morpeth in both timelines are, I hope, accurate. The history of the town is well documented, and I recommend a visit to the local museum. The School of Arts, the Commercial Hotel, Campbells Warehouse, the wharves, the ferry, the bridge, the trains, and, believe it or not, *The Morpeth Want* (and the lovely quote about the reason for its name—the paper provided everything anyone could want) are all factual, although *The Morpeth Want* was only published between 1899 and 1904. There was also a newspaper published in Sydney called *The Arrow*, but like the *Want*, I've stolen only its name. The town of Maitland and the railway stations have, over the years, moved and changed names. For the sake of consistency in both timelines I have referred only to "Maitland" and dropped the "East" and "West."

The SS *Cawarra* was wrecked off the oyster banks at the mouth of Port Hunter (Newcastle) in 1866, and there was only one survivor. There is a painting of the accident hanging in the Morpeth Museum. The facts used in the story are taken from the survivor's report published in the local newspapers.

The Sydney Artists' Masquerade Ball was held at Sydney Town Hall on August 23, 1922, and many of the descriptions are taken from newspaper reports of the event; however, there are no references to anyone wearing a butterfly costume.

Tara Terrace exists in The Rocks, although it has now been renamed, and the terraces were rented, then sold, advertised as being "suitable for small capitalists." The Cut still exists and is quite creepy on a dark night.

And finally, baby farming. Sadly, it was a lucrative and flourishing business in the late nineteenth and early twentieth century, generally in the larger cities. I highly recommend the book *The Baby Farmers* written by Annie Cossins, should you wish to delve further. Cases in Sydney, Melbourne, and Perth are well-documented, and those mentioned by the old newspapermen in the Glebe are factual. I have no idea whether baby farming existed in Morpeth, Maitland, and Newcastle, but I believe it is fair to assume that it would have happened. The first changes to the laws regarding adoption were introduced in the early twentieth century.

And now to the fiction:

The main characters, and most of the minor characters, are fictional, as is The Landing, Treadwell House and the foundation, the Breckenridge Steamship Company, and the *Petrel*—although the clinker is based on a Tasmanian boat shown at the Wooden Boat Festival some years ago. I can find no reference to the Scott sisters seeing or painting a Monarch butterfly, certainly not receiving a letter from Theodora about one being spotted in Morpeth.

ACKNOWLEDGMENTS

First, I would like to pay my respects to the Elders, past, present, and emerging, of the Awabakal and Worimi people, and acknowledge them as the traditional custodians of the beautiful lands and waters where this story is set.

As always there are so many people I wish to thank for their help in bringing this story to fruition:

Chief Researcher, Plot Wrangler, and ever-patient sounding board, I couldn't do it without you. Critique partners Sarah Barrie and Paula J. Beavan, who somehow managed to make sense of my early drafts and offer bucketloads of advice, support, and encouragement. Also to Annie Cossins, my next-door neighbor and author of *The Baby Farmers*, who patiently listened to my initial mad idea and then read, and corrected, my references to baby farming—I take full responsibility for any errors! And this year, a new addition to my staunch supporters: Beethoven, whose marvelous interpretative dance movements keep the mice, and the loneliness, at bay while I am at my desk. (Thank you, Sarah, for finding him!)

Massive thanks are due to the Australian Museum for tracking down a copy of *Transformations* by Vanessa Finney, the most beautiful book, no longer available (I may possibly have the last copy), about the lives of Harriet and Helena Scott, and for sourcing the article from their archives, which contains the line on which this story is based: "An unconfirmed report by '*Olliff, who states that the butterfly had been seen earlier (by a third person) near Sydney.*'"

Chief Researcher and I made several visits to Ash Island and Morpeth in between lockdowns. We received an immense amount of assistance, from both the Morpeth Museum and the School House at Kooragang Nature Reserve. My heartfelt thanks to those volunteers who keep our history alive and find answers to my incessant questions.

Last, but in no way least, the amazing team at HQ/HarperCollins: my wonderful publisher, Jo Mackay, thank you for your constant encouragement and patience, and to Annabel Blay, managing editor, who manages somehow to organize the team who turns my manuscript into a book; special thanks to Abigail Nathan and Kylie Mason for your eagle-eyed editing; Darren Holt of HarperCollins Design Studio, who once again has come up with the perfect cover; and, of course, Natika Palka and the HarperCollins sales team, who take my stories into the world.

And, finally, to my readers: without you I wouldn't get to do what I love—let my imagination roam free.

Discussion Questions

1. Do you have a hobby or passion that when engaged in it you lose all track of time, like Theodora and her painting?
2. Clarrie (and later on, Verity) was upset by the "stunning" and pinning of the butterflies for preservation. Did this also bother you? Why or why not?
3. The Kendalls (Redmond and then Arlo) both had other passions but felt obligated to continue running *The Morpeth Want*. Have you ever had a passion that you felt compelled to put to the side for family or other obligations?
4. Imagine yourself as Clarrie. How might you have handled all that she went through?
5. The author is deft at weaving into the narrative the obstacles women faced in the time period she writes about. What were some of the obstacles for women discussed in the book? In what ways have the issues discussed in the book improved (or not)?
6. In what ways are the differences in class, the privileges and hardships, exemplified by Clarrie and Theodora?

7. Clarrie described the large swarm of monarchs as "all those beating wings, like a great big heart, pumping with life." Have you ever seen the monarchs as they migrate, or some similar insect or animal encounter that took your breath away?

8. Theodora was never credited during her lifetime with first discovering the monarch butterfly in Australia, and this contributed to her reclusiveness. How might such a lack of acknowledgment have affected you if you were Theodora?

9. What do you think of the decision not to publish Sid's article detailing the baby farming back in 1868 in order to protect the Breckenridge name? In your opinion, was it ethical to withhold the information detailed in the article? Why or why not? Do you think reporters face the question even today whether to publish certain information? Can you think of any examples?

10. How do you feel about the character Maud (Mrs. Kelly)? Do you agree with Verity that she didn't deserve punishment for her part in Mrs. Barnett's actions?

11. The extent of Mrs. Barnett's baby farming enterprise, and its impact on many of the characters, is revealed by the end of the book. Which revelation/connection affected you the most? Why? Did you know anything about this practice in Australia or was this all-new information to you?

12. The book ends on a hopeful note. What did you think about the epilogue and what do you think the future might have held for Verity, Arlo, and Stella?

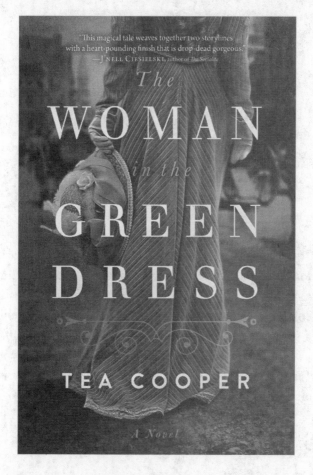

ABOUT THE AUTHOR

Copyright © Katy Clymo

Tea Cooper is an established Australian author of historical fiction. In a past life she was a teacher, a journalist, and a farmer. These days she haunts museums and indulges her passion for storytelling. She is the internationally bestselling author of several novels, including *The Naturalist's Daughter*; the *USA TODAY* bestselling *The Woman in the Green Dress*; *The Girl in the Painting*; *The Cartographer's Secret*, winner of the prestigious Daphne du Maurier Award; and *The Fossil Hunter*.

teacooperauthor.com
Instagram: @tea_cooper
Twitter: @TeaCooper1
Facebook: @TeaCooper
Pinterest: @teacooperauthor